IN THE WAKE OF THE WAR OF SOULS...

The power of the Dark Knights in
northern Ansalon is broken.

The Solamnic order is in disarray.

And in a shrouded mountain valley,
an army of evil gathers.

Against them stand a mysterious
outlawed warrior, a dwarf, and a
beautiful enchantress. With the aid
of two fugitive gnomes, they will
hold the banner of Good against
the forces of darkness. And from the
ashes of war, a new Solamnia will rise.

THE RISE OF SOLAMNIA

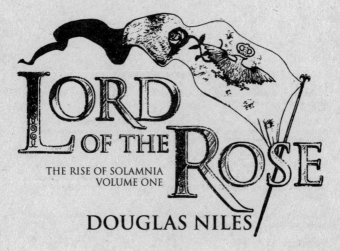

LORD OF THE ROSE

THE RISE OF SOLAMNIA
VOLUME ONE

DOUGLAS NILES

LORD OF THE ROSE

©2005 Wizards of the Coast, Inc.

Cover art by J.P. Targete
Map by Dennis Kauth
First Printing: March 2005
Library of Congress Catalog Card Number: 2004114591

9 8 7 6 5

ISBN: 978-0-7869-3146-0
620-96475-001-EN

U.S., CANADA, ASIA, PACIFIC, & LATIN AMERICA Wizards of the Coast, Inc. P.O. Box 707 Renton, WA 98057-0707 +1-800-324-6496	EUROPEAN HEADQUARTERS Hasbro UK Ltd. Caswell Way Newport, Gwent NP9 0YH GREAT BRITAIN Save this address for your records.

Visit our web site at www.wizards.com

TO MARGARET WEIS

For your leadership, inspiration, and friendship through all the ages of Krynn.

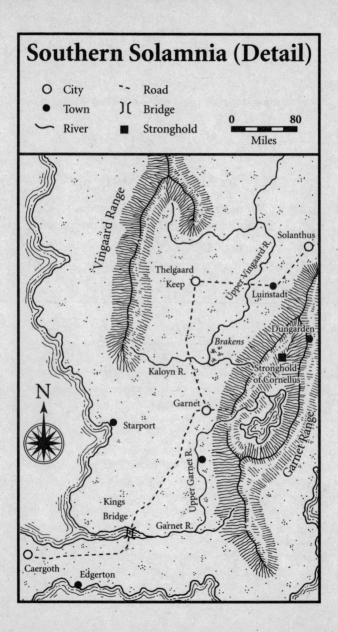

Southern Solamnia (Detail)

○	City	⌐ ⌐	Road
●	Town	)(	Bridge
∿	River	■	Stronghold

0 ___ 80
Miles

Vingaard Range

Solanthus

Thelgaard Keep

Upper Vingaard R.

Luinstadt

Brakens

Dungarden

Kaloyn R.

Stronghold of Cornellus

N

Garnet

Starport

Garnet Range

Upper Garnet R.

Kings Bridge

Garnet R.

Caergoth

Edgerton

PROLOGUE

39 SC

The War of Souls is over. . . .

The "One God," revealed as treacherous Takhisis, was slain by the misdirected fury of the elf heir, Silvanoshei—thanks to the great sacrifice of Paladine, patriarch of the gods. Giving up his own immortality so the Dark Queen could be destroyed, Paladine now wanders the world in mortal flesh, destined to live and die as any mundane creature.

The prophet of Takhisis was Mina. After vengefully killing Silvanoshei, she vanished, and it is said that she has removed herself to self-imposed exile. Even the whisper of her name can still bring a shiver of fear to the spine of a brave man.

With their god slain and their commander departed, the order of Dark Knights has struggled against disarray. Bereft of both leadership and faith, individual officers and companies have formed bands of brigands, or become mercenaries following the highest bidder.

In Solamnia, former Dark Knight comrades vied for control of the Palanthian docks, the rich Solanthian treasury, the grain exchange in Caergoth, and the wool markets in Garnet.

Even without Mina to guide them, the Dark Knights were able to preserve pockets of power. Only in Solanthus were they quickly expelled, overthrown by a popular rebellion of

1

the city's merchants. In Thelgaard, Garnet, and Caergoth, the knightly brigades served brutal warlords. The cities became private fiefdoms, the strong lording over the weak. The ancient Solmanic Code and Measure, the notion of Est Sularus oth Mithas—"My honor is my life"—seemed to most a quaint saying from ancient history.

But the Knights of Solamnia, moving swiftly to follow up their victory in the War of Souls, began to establish new bases of power. The city of Sanction, site of a legendary siege and the setting for the eventual defeat of the Dark Queen, became a bastion of the knighthood. Lord Tasgall, Chairman of the Whitestone Council, maintained his headquarters there, and the three orders—Crown, Rose, and Sword—began to accept squires and apprentices, schooling them in the traditions of the Solamnic Code.

The knights worshiped Kiri-Jolith the Just as their patron god. Mishakal the Merciful was also honored, and—in a signal of the evolving nature of Solamnic power—the merchant god Shinare was feted in many new temples and market rituals. In Sanction, business boomed.

But the traditional heartlands of the knighthood lay far from that city. In the aftermath of war, chaos and disorder still prevailed in many places. Historic Solamnia included the fortress-cities of Caergoth, Thelgaard, and Solanthus, as well as the great port of Palanthas. None of these yet came under the control of the knighthood.

The most strategically important of these city-states was Palanthas. Located to the north of the vast plains, secure on the shore of its deep bay behind the mountain barrier of the Vingaard Range, Palanthas had always been a beacon of culture and civilization. Even after decades of war, after conquest by the Dark Knights and subjugation by the mighty dragon overlord Khellendros, the city not only survived but thrived. During the course of one long night and bloody day in the autumn of 37 SC, Solamnic knights moved to arrest or kill the warlords and all remnants of the Dark Knight dynasty. The guilds, the docks, the garrisons and the gates were quickly seized, opposition quickly, ruthlessly suppressed.

In this swift reclamation, the knights were aided by a powerful wizard, a young woman named Coryn the White. She had come only recently to Palanthas, and was believed to be a protégé of Jenna, Mistress of the Red Robe. Coryn's spells duped the Dark Knights into slumber before the coordinated attacks, opened the gates to sealed towers, and brightened the path for the Knights of Solamnia's midnight forays. Only reluctantly did the white robed mage shed the blood of those who resisted, but she was resolute, and her efforts facilitated success with a minimum of destruction and violence.

In a gesture of true wisdom, Lord Tasgall did not choose a war leader to govern Palanthas after the knighthood regained control. Instead, he appointed a merchant prince. Lord Regent Bakkard du Chagne became, by decree of Lord Tasgall and the New Whitestone Council, the Ruling Mayor and Lord Regent of Palanthas. It was du Chagne who had organized and ordered the swift coup that reclaimed the city, and Tasgall recognized the new knighthood, at this point, needed not so much steel swords as steel coins.

Bakkard du Chagne was a man who knew steel coins, understood how to wield them. Aided by a loyal cadre of enforcers, du Chagne taxed the resurgent commerce at unprecedented levels, amassing a huge personal fortune, which he kept as gold bars locked atop the loftiest tower of his palace. The merchants didn't complain—much—because du Chagne dealt forcibly with all pirates and brigands. Trade thrived, and it seemed as though everyone in Palanthas was making money again.

The knighthood itself, meanwhile, grappled with a crisis of leadership. Many of the highest ranking nobles were tainted by alliances or outright collaboration with the Dark Knights and were thus deemed unacceptable to the new order. Most knights fervently wished to see a return to the days when the Oath and the Measure provided the norm for governance.

The first order of business was the securing of the vital

sea lanes between Sanction, Palanthas, and Sancrist. Key to this area was the great port and fortress of Caergoth, which the knights assaulted with a great army commanded by Lord Hubert, a Captain of the Rose. Lord Hubert expelled the warlords in a winter campaign, and by spring of 39 SC that mighty fortress was once again a bastion of the Knights of Solamnia. Hubert perished amidst his victory, but Crawford, his son, was appointed Duke of Caergoth, even though some whispered he was not cut from the same cloth.

Duke Crawford spearheaded subsequent campaigns, which removed the Dark Lords from power in Garnet, Thelgaard, and their other remaining centers. Even the merchant cabal in Solanthus was replaced by a duke appointed by the Lord Regent. By the autumn of 40 SC, Bakkard du Chagne had secured his realm. To the acclaim of the general public, the Solamnic Order—and the justice of the Code and the Measure—was restored.

For a brief time, the people allowed themselves to hope for a restoration of the ancient empire, even for a king who would once again unite the lands. The favorite of the people was a noble lord, Lorimar—he bore a mighty flaming sword, an ancient artifact of the knighthood. Lorimar's daughter, prophecies claimed, would be the new queen.

Instead, trouble disrupted the new prosperity. Growing numbers of goblins roamed the wilderness of the Garnet Range and the lands of Lemish. Lord Lorimar and his daughter were murdered by a mysterious killer, and the lord's great manor was burned in the attack. Lorimar's ancient sword, Giantsmiter, went missing—no one doubted that it had been stolen by the assassin.

And the people of the land could only dream of the future that was lost.

CHAPTER ONE

TWO RIDERS

42 SC, The Age of Mortals

There's a couple of 'em in the bushes, off to the right."

The dwarf announced his observation with no visible movement of his lips, the sound resembling a harsh cough hacking from the tangle of his gray-black beard. Lurching in the saddle even at the easy gait of his walking mare, he cursed and shifted, working the kinks out of his back. Riding made him even more irascible than usual. He glared at the cover to either side of the road ascending from the forested valley toward the crest of a rounded ridge.

"Knowin' Cornellus," he muttered, "I expect there's at least a half dozen others hiding somewheres we haven't spotted yet."

The dwarf's companion, a lanky human with a coarse bristle of unshaven whiskers, leaned over and spat ostentatiously, using the moment to conceal a glance to the left. A fringe of the pine forest extended close to the trail, providing perfect concealment. The man's eyes narrowed as if squinting against the afternoon sunlight as he studied the underbrush.

With an air of casual unconcern the two riders moved slowly past the bit of woods. A scaly claw touched a bristling green pine branch in that thicket, pulling it back to permit yellow slitted eyes a better view of the road. The man and dwarf both ignored the rustle of foliage, allowing their horses to amble along as each took note of the taloned hand.

"They've spotted us," the dwarf declared, after another two dozen steps. "No turning back from here." He twitched in his saddle again but resisted the urge to glance again over his shoulder. Instead, he whirled first one arm, then the other, through a series of loose, limbering circles.

"My gut is a bundle of knots!" he barked in disgust, very loudly. "Must have been that stanky bacon last night."

They looked like they had come a long way, these two. Tanned faces and untrimmed whiskers were grimy with dust. Despite their clear racial differences—the man was long and lean, while the dwarf's frame was a stocky square, slightly broader at the shoulders than at his keg-sized waist—they had the look of comfortable old companions.

A woolen cape as dirty and travel-stained as his face concealed the man's torso, covering his legs to his knees and even his arms except for the one gloved hand that emerged to grasp the reins. A leather cap covered his head, a stiff brim dropping down to protect his nape, forehead, and ears. His boots were plain and worn, the heels nearly scuffed away. A face that might have been handsome was rendered rough, even threatening, by the scruff of bristling whiskers. His eyes were narrowed, always moving. He sat straight in his saddle, the hilt of a tall sword jutting over his left shoulder and extending upward through the neck of his cape.

The dwarf was clad in a brown bearskin, a cloak with a stiff collar higher than his ears forming a cowl encircling his head. A stout battle-axe was strapped to his left side, and several scabbards suggested daggers of differing types hung from the right side of his belt, though the hilts of the weapons were concealed by his heavy cloak. He glowered and huffed as he made a show of looking from side to side.

Before the two riders the crest of the Garnet Range rose into the sky, a snowy palisade across the horizon beyond the ridge. That vista of glaciers and peaks gleamed now in the late afternoon sun. The near horizon was formed by the ridge, which was no more than a long bowshot away now, much closer than the high summits.

"Over this next hill," the dwarf whispered, concealing the movement of his lips with the back of his hands. "Then we'll be in sight of the place."

"As long as we have a clear road out of here," the human replied softly. His head remained immobile, as his eyes flicked back and forth from one side of the rutted road to the other. He leaned on the front of his saddle, seeming the very picture of trail-weary fatigue.

"I'll get the ball rolling," the dwarf muttered. "You take care of the loose ends."

"Yeah," said the human in a low voice. "Same as ever."

The man reined in as his stocky companion angrily pulled his own horse to a stop. "I'll be right back. I'm in desperate need of a little privacy!" he snorted, once again speaking more loudly than was necessary. "I can't ride another step with my insides all riled up. Wait for me here."

The human shrugged, resting easily astride his gelding while the dwarf dismounted and stomped off into the brush beside the road. He was muttering and cursing loudly, mingling remarks about foul bacon and saddles designed by torture-masters as he pushed through the underbrush, his voice growing fainter and fainter, until the noise faded all together.

After several minutes of waiting with his arms crossed on the pommel of his own saddle, the man grimaced and shook his head, sliding down from the saddle, twisting this way and that as if he, too, needed to work the kinks out of his back. Uncorking a battered canteen, he tilted back his head for a deep drink, watching the woods from the corner of his eye. He saw the pine branch rustle again, pulled back by the same clawed hand. Strapping the canteen to his saddle, he turned so that his back was toward the hidden observer. Both of his hands were concealed under his flowing cape.

The breeze died away completely, as if the woods, the whole

mountain range, held its breath. The sun slipped behind a cloud, and suddenly the mountain air felt much colder.

The stillness was broken by an ear-splitting scream, a cry of terrible anguish that immediately faded into a bubbling gurgle. The sound came from the far side of the road, near where the dwarf had disappeared. Shouts followed, intermingled with the unmistakable clash of steel blades ringing together.

The man spun, turning his back to the commotion, his narrowed eyes studying the woods where he had seen the hand of the concealed watcher. At that very moment three figures burst from that grove and charged toward him with short swords drawn. Two were humans, while the third was a kapak draconian. The latter, sword clenched in its teeth, had dropped to all fours and was sprinting like a cat, two flapping wings adding speed to its charge. Its reptilian body was slick, and wiry with taut sinew.

The dwarf's companion grimaced, as if faintly disappointed by this development. Both of his hands emerged from beneath the cape, each holding a small, cocked crossbow. He raised both weapons but first sighted carefully along the bolt in his right hand. When he pulled the trigger, the missile was released with a powerful, snapping *clank*. The deceptively small dart flew truly, the razor-sharp steel head lodging in the throat of one of the human attackers. Even as that fellow sprawled onto his face the man loosed the other crossbow, dropping the second human with a dart that punctured the leather tunic over his chest.

The draconian roared, rising to its rear legs and snatching up its sword with a taloned forepaw. Down the road, the dwarf emerged from the woods, retreating from attackers, swinging his bloodstained axe, the haft clutched in both hands. Two brown draconions—baaz—flanked him, hissing and snapping furiously, held at bay by the skillfully wielded axe.

The black draconian, spotting the dwarf, hesitated, casting a glance at the two dead men slain by the crossbows, next at the pair of baaz engaged in fierce battle with dwarf, and finally at the crest of the ridge, where the road vanished against the skyline some two hundred yards away. After only a moment's pause, the kapak made up its mind, turning from the battle, once again dropping to all fours, and racing up the road toward the crest.

The human rider saw that the dwarf was hard-pressed, for now a third brown draconian joined his attackers. But the dwarf could take care of himself. One stride took the human to his gelding, which had been standing nearby, shivering and wide-eyed during the fight. He threw himself into the saddle with an easy spring, kicked the horse's flanks, and snatched up the reins.

The horse sprang forward, head low, exploding into an almost instantaneous gallop. The twin crossbows were gone from view, tucked beneath his cape again, though the man made no move to draw the great sword that he wore strapped to his back. Instead, he pulled a shorter blade, single-edged and curved, from beneath his cape. The black kapak was in a full sprint, only a hundred yards from the crest of the ridge . . . eighty . . . sixty. The creature's black wings were flapping, adding speed, while the sinuous tail stretched out straight behind it.

The man's horse was fast. The kapak was still forty yards away from the summit when the steed drew up, ignoring the leathery wing that swatted the gelding's lathered shoulder. Wielding the cutlass in his left hand, the rider brought the weapon down in a single, speedy sweep, a blow that sliced the draconian's head cleanly from its shoulders. Even as he followed through with the blow, the man pulled the horse to the side, away from the spatter of acid that immediately erupted from the decapitated corpse. The kapak, in the way of its kind, immediately dissolved.

Turning sharply, the rider steered the animal through a tight semicircle and back down the road toward his companion. By the time he drew up at the side of the road, the three baaz were dead, their bodies lying grotesquely rigid—in their cursed fashion—in the poses they held when they died.

The dwarf was cleaning his axe on a dirty fringe of his tunic. He eyed the crest of the ridge. "I think that's all of 'em . . . so far. Help me pull these bastards into the brush," he said.

The man nodded, dismounting. Together they rolled, tumbled, and pulled the three petrified corpses off the road, dumping them in the underbrush. They did the same with the two humans the warrior had shot with his small crossbows. Up the road, the kapak had fully dissolved. The remains left a smoking scar of acid on the side of the road, but there was nothing they could do about that.

Swiftly reloading his two crossbows, the rider pulled himself back into his saddle and looked questioningly at the dwarf.

"Can't stop and rest now," grunted that stocky fighter. "Too bad. My backside could use a break from that saddle."

The human waited silently as the dwarf clomped over to his horse, shaking his head irritably. He grabbed the pommel, kicked a foot into the stirrup, and with surprising grace pulled himself up and astride the animal.

"Let's go make a call on Cornellus," he said as, once again, as the two of them continued side by side up the trail.

CHAPTER TWO

THE STRONGHOLD OF CORNELLUS

Two riders mounted a low and rounded ridgetop and came again into view of the great crest of the Garnet Range. A mile away, they saw the fortress sprawling across the slope. They halted and made sure they were observed by the guards.

This was the stronghold, known throughout the Garnet Range, of the bandit lord Cornellus the Large. The walled compound aspired to be a fortress but looked more like a series of mountainside shacks that had gradually expanded over the course of the centuries. An irregular wall surrounded the place, but because of the ascending slope beyond the outer barrier the two could see a maze of buildings within that crenellated battlement.

"That's the place," the dwarf noted laconically. "Looks just like it did fifty years ago when the old toad spent most of his time robbing from the mountain dwarves. Of course, maybe Cornel has mellowed in his old age," he added, before spitting contemptuously.

The human rider, his eyes narrowed, made no reply as he studied the crude fortress. A stout main gate blocked passage to the inner courtyard, and several smaller gates were set in the walls before corrals and other yards to either side. The steep slope rising beyond the stronghold served as a rear barrier. That ground was impassable for a horse, dangerous for a man, and eventually merged into the face of a cliff that formed one of the ramparts of the Garnet Range. There was no chance for attack or stealthy approach from that quarter.

Hooded figures were visible atop each of the two towers flanking the front gate. Others, bristling with speartips, patrolled the ramparts. By now most of the guards were staring at the two riders, and when one turned to speak to his companions, his profile revealed the outline of a long snout.

"Yep, ol' Cornellus has got plenty of draconians for his guards, now," the dwarf said in disgust. He chuckled. "Minus a few of 'em that he thinks are guarding his road."

The horses, as if glad to be done with the long climb, moved forward eagerly, the gelding even trotting a couple of paces until the warrior reined it in. At a steady walk they approached the gate, finally coming to a halt a stone's throw from the barrier.

"We seek entry to the Stronghold of Cornellus," the dwarf declared loudly. "Open the gate!"

A bozak draconian appeared above them, standing on a platform on the other side of the wall. He wore a bronze helmet and leather armor with no insignia. His forked tongue flicked in and out of his reptilian jaws.

"Entry is not granted for free," he called down. "What payment do you have to offer?"

"We offer our custom at the tavern and the inn," the dwarf replied. "Our coins are steel."

The draconian on the gate withdrew from sight. The two riders heard muffled voices followed by the clunk of a heavy latch. With a shudder and a creak, the wooden gate rolled inward, swaying precariously.

"That would collapse with the first touch of a battering ram," the dwarf observed, letting the noisy gate mask his voice.

The horses' ears pricked upward in alarm as the opened gate revealed a pair of draconians, each carrying a massive spear. These guards stepped forward aggressively and crossed the hafts of their weapons, blocking passage into the muddy courtyard.

The two were brutish baaz, crooked fangs bared in leering grins. With deceptively lazy eyes, yellow and hooded, they observed the riders, while chortling contemptuously. The bozak atop the gate stepped off the high platform, wings spread wide, and glided to the ground in front of the two horses. Rearing back with a nervous whinny, the mare fidgeted while the gelding froze, eyes trained on the reptilian creature.

"One steel apiece is today's entry fee," the big draconian declared, holding out a talon-studded paw. He wore gold chains around his neck, fat rings of the same metal on his fingers. With a shrug, the dwarf tossed a pair of shiny coins into the leathery palm. The draconian inspected them for a moment, finally nodding to his spear carriers, who shuffled out of the way.

"All right. You can go in," he hissed, "but behave yourselves, or you'll forfeit more than your steel."

If anything, the man looked bored as he nudged the chestnut gelding toward the large building directly opposite the gate. He didn't seem to be looking around, yet he saw and noted everything in the walled courtyard. There was a stable to the left, where a couple of men with ringed metal collars shoveled dung out of the stalls. A few horses watched the riders listlessly from a small corral, and a few more mounts were lashed to a railing. Just beyond, a swinging gate opened as a small, filthy gully dwarf pulled on a rope, releasing a small flock of sheep that went bleating out to the pasture beside the fortress.

A pair of large catapults stood in the courtyard. Each was cocked and loaded with a basket full of jagged, skull-sized boulders. A glance was enough to determine that the weapons were sighted in the general direction of the road the two riders had just traversed.

To the right was a sprawling structure like a barracks or series of sleeping rooms fronted with long porches. The ground floor had a wall of multicolored stones, clearly laid by indifferent masons, while the wooden walls of the upper floor displayed a patchwork of planking, some vertical, some horizontal. Dark windows broke the walls in varying size and irregular placement.

The inn itself was a huge structure. The riders pulled up and dismounted, approaching the railing where two dozen mounts were already tethered. A pair of large warhorses tacked with magnificent saddles snorted, but eventually shifted to make room for the new arrivals. The man lashed the bridles of both their horses to the railing with a quick loop.

The front door of the inn opened, and a young woman dressed in a filmy gown stumbled out, looking around wildly as she was trailed by a burst of raucous laughter. She appeared to be crying but stopped when she saw the dwarf and human. Quickly she turned her face away and started along the front porch toward the barracks. More laughter, roaring peals, came from the great room as a huge brute of a warrior came bursting through the door.

"Where'd she go?" he demanded, as the dwarf started toward the doors.

He was a monstrous fellow, perhaps six and a half feet tall, solid as a bear with arms that dangled well below his waist. His lower jaw jutted in an ugly sneer, a visage that looked to be shaped by more than a fraction of ogre blood.

"Who?" asked the dwarf innocently.

By then, the big fellow had glanced around and spotted the woman, who had been jolted into action by the sight of him and was fleeing. "Hold, there, wench!" he roared, chasing after her with a startling burst of speed.

It was no contest—after two dozen strides he wrapped a big paw around her waist, then snatched her up and, with a bellowed guffaw, tossed her over his shoulder. He swaggered back to the tavern doors, grinning broadly at the dwarf and the human.

"Loosen th' leash a bit and they run right off on ya!" he noted, before pushing through the doors, bearing his squirming prisoner into the room. He was greeted with whistles, whoops, and heavy stomping. The revelry overwhelmed the uneven notes of a flute, tones that wavered between sharp and flat.

"Just a second," said the human rider to his dwarf companion. He looked around the corral, his eyes alighting on the gully dwarf.

The dwarf scowled but stood still and waited while the man crossed the courtyard toward the scruffy fellow, who, after opening the gate for the sheep, had promptly sat down in the mud and apparently gone to sleep.

"Hey, you," the rider said, kicking the pudgy, rounded figure, slumped next to a clean-picked turkey carcass. The gully dwarf was already snoring loudly. "Wake up."

"Huh?" The gully dwarf, of indeterminate gender and age, glared up at the man. "You not Highbulp, order me around! Me sleep!" the creature declared.

"How'd you like a job?" asked the stranger. He withdrew two steel coins from his pocket, handing one to the suddenly slack-jawed Aghar.

"Sure, a job!" declared the gully dwarf, chomping on the coin and promptly breaking a tooth, then scowling suspiciously. "What I gotta do?"

"It's simple, little guy. I know this gate opens when that rope gets pulled. When my friend and I come out of the tavern and get on our horses, open the gate for us. I'll give you the other coin on our way out."

"Sure!" beamed the Aghar, before another dramatic mood swing brought a glower to his rounded, grimy face. "How I know you pay me?"

"If I don't pay you," the man said, patting the creature on the shoulder before turning back to the tavern, "I will owe you double next time I see you."

The Aghar grinned, a grin that turned to a frown, as he scratched his head and watched the human ambling back to his companion. With a contented sigh, he returned to his nap.

The two travelers pushed open the front doors of the tavern. The setting sun spilled in behind them, brightening the cavernous chamber and turning the room's collective attention to the new arrivals. The warrior walked as if he was alone and at his ease, barely glancing at anything, but the dwarf studied the room carefully. He glared at a quartet of baaz draconians leering from the table nearest the door, puffed out his chest and strutted as he

15

passed a table of scowling hill dwarves, met the steady, appraising gaze of a pair of Solamnic Knights who stood at the bar, and finally stared down a drunken half-ogre who stumbled into his path. After that, there was a general shifting around, and space cleared for them at the bar.

"Dwarf spirits, a double shot!" the dwarf barked at the harried old barmaid.

"I hear you, don't have to shout!" she snapped back. She finished drawing ale into a couple of mugs and set them down in front of the two knights, both of whom wore the emblem of the Rose. A miserable-looking goblin, his mouth gagged with a filthy rag while his wrists and ankles were shackled with stout metal manacles, huddled at the feet of one of the Solamnics. The creature was hunched over, holding something small in its clawed hands.

"All right, dwarf spirits—and you?" She looked at the warrior impatiently.

"Do you have any of that red ale from Coastlund?"

She snorted. "I got mead from Thelgaard and yellow ale from Solanthus."

"Well then, give me dwarf spirits, too. A double shot."

She slammed down two small, clay glasses and hoisted a jug from behind the bar. It was clearly heavy, but she held it steadily as she trickled each glass full. When they were topped off, she set down the jug, pushed the glasses across the bar and left to wait on a raucous draconian at the other end of the bar.

"Lively place," the dwarf remarked. He tossed back half of his glass and smacked his lips.

"Yep," the warrior replied. He took a sip from his own glass and winced as the fire ran across his tongue and down his gullet. "Cornellus always has a wild bunch around."

They leaned back and watched the musical entertainment for a few minutes. The minstrel was an elf, dressed in patched leather leggings and a threadbare cloak. He alternated between his flute and a mandolin, but whenever his tune verged on melodious the hill dwarves would jeer him into making a mistake, and then the whole room would erupt in laughter.

"I don't think I've seen you here before." The speaker was the nearer Knight of Solamnia. He had finished his mug and was pulling on his riding gloves as he stonily addressed the warrior. "This is a long way from any place."

"Easy enough to find," the warrior replied.

"You look familiar, though. Ever been through Sanction?" asked the knight, scrutinizing the whiskered, weather-beaten face.

The rider shook his head.

"What about Caergoth? I spend lots of time there, in the Ducal Guard. You one of Duke Crawford's men?"

"Nope." The stranger took a sip of his spirits.

"Cleaning out the riff-raff?" the dwarf asked the knight, nudging the shackled goblin with his foot. The wretched creature looked up apathetically then lowered his head. In his shackled hands he held a chip of stone, a greenish quartz, clutching the shard to his breast like it was great treasure.

"A rabble-rouser," said the second knight from behind the first. "Preaching about Hiddukel to all the gobs in the hills. We're taking him in for a talk with the duke." He laughed mirthlessly.

The first knight stared at the human warrior until his companion, also gloved, tapped him on the shoulder. Each of them took hold of the hobgoblin's wrist cuffs and pulled the creature roughly to his feet. Side by side, one watching to the right and the other left, they walked to the door, yanking the hobgoblin behind them.

"Some nerve, their kind coming up here," snapped the hag of a barmaid, returning to meet their eyes. She unleashed a tooth-less grin at the warrior. "Act like they own the place! Still, that Reynaud was looking you over, all right. Like he reckanized you from somewheres . . ."

The man shrugged.

"Bah, frightened of shadows, them knights," said the dwarf, extending his glass for a refill.

The crone poured. "Cornel don't have no use for them knights either, but he tolerates their business. To keep the peace, you know. Still, that hob was a good enough customer. Never bothered no one. Just sat there and rubbed his green stone— sometimes he'd rub it so hard it glowed!"

"Yeah, Cornellus. Now that you mention it, we need to see him," the warrior said softly.

She blinked and cocked her head as if she hadn't heard right. Her eyes narrowed, and she leaned over the bar. "Be careful what you ask for. You just might see up him up close and personal."

"That's our idea exactly. Can you tell him that we're here?"

"Who's here?" she demanded, shaking her head skeptically.

"Dram Feldspar," said the dwarf, standing and reaching across the bar to shake her hand. "Originally from Kayolin. Tell Cornellus that we've brought a bounty he'll be interested in. He'll want to see us right quick."

"It's your own funeral," the old woman muttered. "That'll be two steel," she said. "I think you better settle up now."

"Two steel for three drinks?" sputtered the dwarf.

"One steel for the drinks," she replied, glaring at him. "Another for making me go back there and face Cornellus."

CHAPTER THREE

A BANDIT LORD

The hag had been gone for about five minutes, her absence arousing an increasingly restive thirst along the length of the bar, when a door slammed somewhere in the back of the room. A sudden hush fell over the chamber as a hulking bozak draconian emerged from the shadows, swaggering and sneering. He held his muscular wings half-spread as he advanced, an arrogant gesture that forced customers to back out of his way or get whipped by one of the stiff, leathery pinions.

This draconian was even bigger than the gatekeeper. A least a dozen heavy chains draped his neck, jangling as he walked. A belt of the yellow metal encircled his lean waist, and golden cuffs gleamed from his ankles and wrists. He halted before the dwarf and the warrior, looming over them. Massive, taloned fists rested on his hips, and his forked tongue flickered out insolently, almost brushing the man's nose. The warrior didn't flinch, though his eyes narrowed slightly.

"You got the bounty? You show me the bounty," growled the bozak.

The human glanced sideways at his companion, and the dwarf raised his right hand to show a strand of cord that pierced a number of leathery flaps, like some crude, gigantic necklace.

"A score of goblin ears!" declared Dram Feldspar, tossing the grisly strand toward the draconian—who made a flailing swipe to try and catch it but had to bend over, muttering, to pick it up off the sawdust-covered floor. A growl rumbled within that massive chest, as he squinted at the first ear.

"Huh, real goblin." He nodded in apparent satisfaction, and starting sliding the dried ears past his fingers on the leathery strand. "Four . . . eight, ten . . .twelve, fourteen, sixteen, eighteen. Yep, two more makes a score."

He looked at the pair with somewhat more interest, filmy lids half-closing over the vertical slit pupils of his snake's eyes. "Come this way. Cornellus will see you. If he likes you, you might even come back out alive." The draconian threw back his head and roared with laughter that was echoed by appreciative chuckles from the dozen or so other draconians in the rooms.

The hobgoblins, close relatives of the goblin race, were not laughing. Instead, they glared murderously at the bounty hunters. One burly chieftain put his hand around the hilt of his knife, but—at a sharp glance from the bozak—made no move to draw the weapon.

Still chuckling, the gold-bedecked messenger raised a paw, the sharp talon of his forefinger extended like a stiletto toward the door at the back of the inn. The bozak stood back to let the visitors pass in front of him. The man led the way while Dram Feldspar stepped right behind, with a glance at the draconian who followed at a respectful distance.

Two baaz draconians armed with short swords flanked the sturdy, iron-strapped door. At a nod from the bozak, one of them pulled it open and the other drew his weapon, warily studying the dwarf and the human. The two sauntered inside.

Cornellus the Large was seated upon a stout wooden throne, a chair that would have held two normal sized men with room to spare. The bandit lord not only covered the seat, his body seemed to bulge outward over either arm of the massive platform. His half-ogre lineage was clear in the small, round eyes that glared from the folds in his fleshy face and in the twin tusks that jutted upward from his lower jaw. Those tusks were gold plated, an ostentatious display of the bandit lord's wealth.

Beams hewn from solid pine trunks supported a ceiling dozens of feet overhead. That space was cloaked in shadow, for no windows broke the solid stone walls of the chamber. A massive blaze roared in a cavernous fireplace, shedding light if not much heat. The flaring illumination revealed several other doors leading deeper into the mountain.

A plump human woman stood behind Cornellus, holding a fan. She gaped stupidly at the man and the dwarf as they approached until the bandit lord reached back and cuffed her. Quickly she began waving the huge feathered device.

Not that it was hot in here; it was frigid as a root cellar, half-buried in the bedrock of the mountain. The fire was so far from the throne that it had no effect on the chilly temperature. Still, Cornellus was sweating like a slave laboring in the hot sun. By the time the visitors reached him, another female slave had stepped forward with a towel. Gingerly she mopped the perspiration from his forehead, cheeks, and jowls.

"So, you claim to be brave goblin-slayers? Is this true?" His voice rumbled as though it came from a deep well, gurgling on the last words.

"As a matter of fact, Your Lordship, that is true," said Dram, stepping forward. He grinned, bowing with a flourish. "We are only too happy to—"

"I was asking *you*, warrior." The bandit lord raised a massive paw, pointed a wrinkled finger the size of a large sausage at the human. "You like to kill goblins?"

"I kill my share." His voice was quiet, matter of fact. "We work as a team."

"A score is many goblins. Where did you find them?"

"In the foothills of the Garnet range. South of the city the Solamnics call Solanthus."

"Ah, yes." Cornellus allowed himself a rumble of amusement. The sound was like a massive cauldron full of boiling water. "A realm of the knights. But the goblins breed like maggots down there, fill the valleys, spill through my woods. They are a plague upon my humble business."

It was well known that the bandit lord's humble business was the import of smuggled elf slaves and other contraband from the lands south of the Newsea. Goblin raids ate into his profits.

"We have heard of the bounty you offer for those enemies of your humble business!" said the dwarf. "That is what brings us here."

"Ah, the bounty. No one kills goblins just for the sport of it anymore—always, there has to be a reward." The half-ogre sounded rueful and contemplative. "Snaggart, have you inspected the ears?"

"Aye, Lord Cornellus," replied the bozak draconian, who had followed the visitors into the room. He still clutched the dried flaps and their leather thong. "Indeed they have a pretty score."

"Well, ahem, I regret to inform you that the bounty has changed," said the bandit lord tersely. "I pay only one steel for one ear, now."

"One steel?" sputtered the dwarf. "For years the bounty has been five!"

Cornellus shrugged, a massive rippling of his flesh. "You are out of touch. I offer one now. Take it, or do not take it. The gobs are no longer such enemies. Maybe soon they collect bounty for human and dwarf ears!" The bandit lord guffawed momentarily at that thought then scowled and added, sniffing, "Either way, you bore me. It is time for you to go. Maybe I tell gobs where to find you."

"One steel might be all right," said the warrior, his voice still calm and quiet, "but we also need a little information from you, just a few words."

"Eh? What words would these be?"

The man stepped forward, pulling a flat object from beneath his cape, and, not incidentally, revealing one of the small cross-bows, cocked and ready, that he wore at his waist. At the gesture, more draconians stepped forward from the shadows to either side, but Cornellus held up his hand and the guards halted. The half-ogre squinted his tiny eyes as the man unwrapped a piece of white stone about the size of a small dinner plate.

"This is a piece of marble, part of a tablet we found at a place near here. It bears a name." The man extended the shard upward for the bandit lord to take it with his sausage-sized fingers. The bandit lord looked at it, blinked once, and shook his head.

"I have never seen this name before. 'Brilliss.' What does that mean? It is nothing but a name!"

"Think. Hard. I have reason to believe that it was an important name known to some in the Garnet Range. Everyone knows that Cornellus is the best informed lord in all these hills and valleys."

"I tell you, I do not know this name. Where did you find this? Exactly where, tell me!" His beady eyes glittered, and the tip of his fat tongue showed between the grotesque flaps of his lips.

The man took the fragment back. "I may tell you if you tell me what I want to know first."

"I tell you, I know nothing of this gnome! Now, go!"

For several seconds the warrior's gaze held the bandit's broad face. Cornellus licked his lips, making a visible and ultimately unsuccessful effort not to glance down at the shard of tablet held so casually in the human's hand.

"I said nothing about a gnome," the stranger noted.

"That is obviously what it is. A foolish gnome's name."

"So he is a foolish gnome now," said the human warrior. With the wrist of his left arm he held his cape back, allowing easy access to the small crossbow.

"You dare to challenge me?" The half-ogre's eyes bulged from his meaty face, as more sweat beaded on his forehead. "You *dare?*"

In response the human snatched up the crossbow, spun, and fired the bolt straight into the chest of the nearest draconian—a baaz. That reptilian guard uttered a strangled growl and fell dead, already rigid.

The curved cutlass was in the warrior's hand even before the draconian died. The two slave women screamed and ran for the rear of the chamber as the man lunged at the throne, chopping a bloody gouge into the bandit lord's knee, drawing an ear-shattering bellow of pain.

The axe was whirling in the dwarf's hands as he rushed to the side, driving back the pair of draconians that had tried to close in from the right. With slashing swipes of that heavy blade he held them at bay, while the warrior pulled his sword from the bloody cut, raising it toward the bandit lord's face. Cornellus, his eyes wide, blubbered unintelligibly.

"Left side!" called Dram urgently.

"Durafus—bizzeerr—kar—" The gold-ornamented bozak had both hands raised, snaky eyes flashing as he started to spit out the words to a spell.

Without lowering his sword, the man whipped his second crossbow up with his left hand and shot the bolt. It took the bozak right in the gut, and the end of the spell became a bloody gurgle. With a bubbling cry the big draconian doubled forward and dropped to the floor.

"Kill them! Stop them!" shrieked Cornellus, using the momentary distraction to shift his massive bulk in his tall throne, tumbling the chair backward onto the floor. His great foot kicked out, knocking the cutlass away.

The bozak continued to thrash, screams growing weaker as it convulsed in its death throes. Knowing what was coming, the warrior and the dwarf were already moving, darting to the sides and ducking low.

The bandit lord cowered behind his overturned throne, eyes flashing from the two attackers to the dying bozak. The draconian expired and, in the next instant, exploded. The blast rocked the chamber, knocking dust from the massive beams below the ceiling and slamming the dwarf against the far wall. The man tumbled through a roll and bounced into a crouch, cutlass at the ready. The bandit lord, his face blackened by the effects of the blast, lumbered to his feet, turning his great head this way and that.

Baaz draconians, hissing with lust for blood, sprang forward from various alcoves. Spears raised, they spread out, a trio of them converging on the man, while another joined the pair of guards challenging the dwarf. Even as they attacked, Cornellus shoved past his bodyguards, ducked through an archway, and vanished into the shadows at the rear of the room.

The dwarf's battle-axe whirled, snapping off the tip of one draconian's spear and holding the other two at bay. Throwing down the nub of the spear, the first baaz sprang at Dram, pulsing its leathery wings, adding weight to the attack. Both hands, studded with wicked claws, slashed toward the dwarf's bearded face—then those hands, with forearms attached, tumbled to the floor, severed by a lightning slash of the dwarf's axe blade.

The baaz howled and staggered away, mangled arms clutched to its chest. The others stabbed and stabbed, but neither spear could get past the dwarf's dazzling, dancing axe. A cold grin split the thicket of beard, and Dram Feldspar began to advance, challenging first one, then the other draconian. He spun through an abrupt circle, bringing the axe into the flank of one baaz, tearing open its sinewy gut. The creature groaned a plaintive death cry, slumping, falling forward into a spreading pool of gore. The other bobbed and weaved, cautiously retreating as its comrade stiffened in the final posture of death.

Across the room, the warrior had retreated into a corner where he was using his cape like a shield, sweeping it past his chest and out again to hold spears at bay. He wielded his curve-bladed cutlass in his right hand, the weapon weaving like a living organism. A thrust here, then a parry, and with a lunge he stabbed one of the baaz right through the throat, at the same time knocking away another's spear tip with his deceptively sturdy cloak.

Gagging, the throat-pierced baaz fell back, as stiff and rigid as a statue by the time it struck the floor, breaking off one wing before it finally came to rest. The other two draconians pressed in, hissing, snapping fanged, jutting jaws. The warrior stabbed hard at one of them, hitting the lizard-like attacker in the open mouth. The blade penetrated the draconian's palate and sliced through its brain—and in that instant the creature turned to stone, pinning the weapon in its petrified flesh.

With a curse the man let go of his sword and spun away from his last attacker. The baaz's speartip thrust again and again, deflected each time by the warrior's sweeping cape as the pair bobbed across the stone floor. Abruptly, the last draconian gasped and toppled forward. Dram pulled his axe from the back of the creature's neck a split second before it solidified.

"Where did Cornellus go?" the dwarf asked.

"In here somewhere," the warrior replied, starting toward the dark alcove. He stopped, looked back at his trapped cutlass, and grimaced. Shaking his head, he reached both hands over his shoulder to pull out the heavy sword he wore strapped to his back. Holding the great pommel in both hands, he held the blade angled slightly upward and squinted into the shadows. "I'm ready now."

Nodding grimly, the dwarf held his axe ready and advanced at his companion's side. They paused at the archway. No look, no sound, no signal was needed—each knew what the other would do. Together they burst through the opening and spun around, back to back. They stabbed deep into the shadows—and the dwarf struck scaly flesh, his axe carving into the chest of a big, black draconian. The creature, a kapak, had been lurking in ambush with a large cudgel. Now it flung away the weapon and started to stumble off. It didn't get very far, before the sinewy draconian collapsed to the floor, thrashing and gurgling as its black body dissolved into a bubbling, steaming, toxic puddle. The dwarf skipped back an instant before the liquid spread to his boots.

The man twisted the hilt of his great sword as he slashed the long blade through the air. Flames burst, hot and blue, along its metal edge, light spilling through the shadows, revealing a door before him. The man struck one side of the wall, then the other, with the fiery blade. Flames surged eagerly into the dried logs, licking upward, spreading.

Dram stepped to his side, waving away the thickening smoke

with the broad blade of his axe. He pointed at the fire-framed doorway. "Well, it looks like he got away. He musta gone through there."

Tongues of flame still flickered along the long, broad sword blade. Raising it over his shoulder, turning his other side toward the door, the man gave a shout of frustration and brought his weapon around in a long swing. Flames and sparks trailed from the blade, lingering in the air. The sword struck the door and sliced through the stout, metal-banded boards as though they were a tapestry. With a grunt, followed by a sharp backswing and vertical slash, the man used the sword to carve his way through the locked door.

The bandit lord Cornellus stared at them through the hole, wild-eyed, deep within another cavernous room, this one a hall with many stout timbers, whole tree-trunks, supporting a lofty roof. The huge, blubbery half-ogre backed away from them as they kicked their way through the door. With a sudden move he lunged for a piece of lumber and lifted it like a club.

"Stay back!" he warned.

"Or what?" sneered Dram Feldspar, swaggering forward.

The man edged closer, waving his burning sword, then turned and chopped into one of the support pillars. Flames immediately took hold there, crackling eagerly, licking up the length of dry wood into the dry roof.

"You're crazy, the both of you," spat the bandit lord, watching the growing fire. "Let me out of here, or my retainers will take their vengeance. Even now, dozens of them are flocking outside, ready to kill you."

"Why ain't I scared?" the dwarf asked. He lunged, and Cornellus stumbled backward in his haste to elude the dwarf's deadly axe.

The warrior followed close behind. His sword no longer blazed, though the blade still flickered and pulsed as if the fires lingered below the hard surface of the metal. He held the hilt in both hands.

"Tell us what you know about that shard," the human said

27

coldly. "You recognized it—I saw the spark in your greedy little eyes. You knew that Brilliss was the name of a gnome. If you tell us what you know, I might yet decide to let you live."

"No! Yes! That is, perhaps there was a glimmer there, something I had heard rumored long ago," stammered the half-ogre. He looked to either side of them, seeing no means of escape, no rescuers on their way, then back at his two tormentors. "The name . . . what was it again?"

"The part I can read is 'Brilliss,' but it looks like that's only part of the word. What is the rest? Tell me!" The tip of the man's mighty sword was raised and pointed at the bandit's hammering heart.

"I—I can't be sure. There was a band of gnomes that lived in these mountains one time, south of here. Every so often they would come here to trade. I believe they had a master named Brillissander Firesplasher or something like that. The first part of his name, anyway, I remember—it was something like Brilliss. You know how gnomes are with their names."

"Aye," the dwarf said, his axe poised. "Your memory is getting better. What about this Brillissander? Where is he nowadays?"

"Dead as far as I know, I swear it! The whole town— Dungarden they called it—was destroyed three years ago. It was underground, like a dwarf cavern—but full of gnomes. They were always working on foolish things. Dangerous, too! The whole heart of the place was ripped out, I think one of the dragon overlords went in there and devoured it."

"Dead?" The dwarf scowled. "All of 'em? Not a single survivor?"

"Please—the whole town was destroyed! Firesplasher was killed! It wasn't my fault."

"Tell us about it," the human pressed. "Even destruction such as you describe would not have claimed the lives of all who lived there. Where did the survivors go?"

"I don't kn—!"

The advancing tip of the sword now pressed against

Cornellus's leather vest, sinking an inch into the soft flesh.

"Wait! Please!"

He held up his two fat hands, pleading. "There might have been a few who lived—gnomes are hardy souls, after all!"

"Where would these few survivors be?"

"I don't—wait, there is one place perhaps. Yes, it's the only one that makes sense. Caergoth!"

"Caergoth?" Dram spat contemptuously. "Why would they have gone to Caergoth?"

The human eased back on his sword, squinting at the blubbering bandit lord.

"The ghetto—they call it the 'Gnome Ghetto.' It's a filthy place along the waterfront. No decent person would go there, but the gnomes are living there, teeming like rats! All gnomes are welcome there!"

"What makes you so certain?" the warrior rasped. "You *are* certain, aren't you?"

"Because—all right, I admit it, because some of them came through here! I sold them two wagons and four oxen—there were twenty or thirty of the little wretches. All that was left of Dungarden. They needed wagons large and sturdy enough to get to Caergoth."

"Are you telling us the truth finally?" demanded the dwarf, brandishing the axe and baring his teeth.

"I think he's lying," the man said, holding the blade steady.

"No, it's the truth, I swear!" squawked the lord. "You said that you'd leave here, leave me alive if I told you the truth."

"I did? No, uh-uh, sorry. I don't recall saying that." The warrior swung his sword back, and flames exploded along the whole of the metallic edge. Cornellus cried out and hurled himself backward, tumbling across the floor. The human raised his blazing weapon high, took a swing at the hulking bandit lord—and missed, distracted by his companion's shout.

"To your right!" cried the dwarf, springing at the first of two or three draconians who crashed through part of the fire-weakened wall behind Cornellus. The winged creatures swarmed at them

29

out of the dark, as the bandit lord shouted orders and curses and scrambled away.

With one axe blow, the dwarf dispatched the first draconian, who petrified instantly. The second one pounced atop the dwarf and bore him to the floor, snapping wildly with his huge jaws. The third kicked and stomped, but the human warrior materialized from behind, swinging his blazing sword, killing first the one atop Dram, then his gaping fellow. He kicked away the bodies as they began to petrify.

"Where's Cornellus?" asked Dram, springing to his feet, axe still in hand.

The warrior peered ahead, realizing that the draconians had entered through a hidden storeroom. "There's a door back there—he went out that way." He started in that direction, his fiery sword raised over his head.

Above, flames roared through the ceiling, consuming the straw thatching overhead, sending cinders and ash spilling down into the warren of rooms. Smoke grew thicker, radiating heat. Burning straw and pieces of the ceiling fell, crackling and blazing, cascading sparks across the floor.

"Damn." The man frowned then turned and hacked the blazing sword into one wooden support pillar, then another. Fire ran up the dried poles, crackling hungrily, adding to the rapidly growing conflagration.

The dwarf laid a firm hand on his elbow. "Wait!" Dram said urgently

"For what?" demanded the human.

They heard shouts, the stamping of running feet, cries of warning and fury. The man grimaced and shook his head as the dwarf looked into his face and spoke. "Time to get out of here."

"Damn!" the warrior repeated. Again he chopped that blazing sword into a wooden pillar. More fire crackled up and out.

"To the horses!" Dram bolted out, his human companion sprinting right behind.

They crossed the large, empty chamber and burst into the crowded bar—where, to judge from the music and continued ribaldry, the nearby melee and growing fire had remained largely unnoticed. The dwarf knocked a hobgoblin to the floor, and they both sprang over the furious—but quite drunken—brute. Smoke billowed through the door, a choking cloud rolled into the tavern, and there were shouts of alarm, screams. The two raced straight out the front door.

They leaped down the steps. A quick flip of the warrior's hand freed the reins from the railing. In another second each had mounted, wheeling their stamping horses. The sheep gate opened with a rattle. The little gully dwarf stared at them, eyes big and mouth wide open, pulling on the rope as the two riders galloped toward him.

A draconian ran out to block their path, wings flapping, waving a spear menacingly. When the two showed no signs of slowing down he wisely darted out of the way.

"My coin! Give coin!" cried the gully dwarf. Instead, the man picked him up by the scruff of his neck and threw him across the pony's withers.

"First I'll save your life!" muttered the human warrior, following the dwarf and his steed through the gate. Side by side, they pounded into the night. Moments later, some draconian thought to trigger the two catapults poised on the courtyard. Tons of rock smashed and splintered on the roadway, hitting only the cloud of dust left by their thunderous flight.

CHAPTER FOUR

LORDS AND LADIES

Lord Regent Bakkard du Chagne, the Ruling Mayor of Palanthas and Vice Chairman of the New Whitestone Council, walked alone through the marbled hall of his palace. It was ever thus; whether here on the mountainside overlooking his splendid city, or within the streets of the city, he was alone. Oh, there were always other people around, crowding and clamoring for his attention, but the crushing weight of his station, the burden that was his solitary load, bore down on him with unmerciful force. Even in the midst of a teeming, adoring crowd, he felt alone.

It had been a long, hard climb into this palace. He had begun to plan his ascent while the Dark Knights still controlled the city, and after their power was broken by the fall of the One God and the disappearance of Mina, he had been ready to step into the vacuum. Facilitating commerce, hiring former knights to deal with brigands, encouraging the restoration of trade throughout all the lands of Solamnia, he had quickly established himself as the only irreplaceable power in the city. Rumors had spread quickly, blaming Mina for abandoning her followers, for turning her back on those who had devoted their lives to her. If some of these rumors had been started by the Lord Regent's own agents, no one voiced that accusation too loudly.

When the Knights of Solamnia had regained control of the city, they realized that they required a lord to guide them. Bakkard du Chagne—though not a warrior—had been nominated by Lord Tasgall in distant Sanction. In Palanthas that appointment met with nearly unanimous approval. Once again, those few who might have disagreed had possessed the good sense to keep their mouths shut.

Du Chagne climbed higher up the mountain, relishing the cool breeze blowing off the sea. He was high above the city now, and from this pinnacle—this tower called the Golden Spire—he could look across his domain from an almost godlike perspective. Despite the long climb, he experienced no fatigue as he approached the top. Instead, he felt energized.

He stood before a round, glass-walled room at the peak of the highest tower. He took the key—the only one in all Krynn—from his pocket, and opened the door. When he stepped inside, the sight, and even the smell, of his gold enfolded him in a welcoming embrace. The bars of the precious metal were stacked everywhere, in great piles that reached higher than his head. The sunlight streamed in through the many windows, reflecting off the shiny ingots, casting brilliant yellow ripples across the lord regent's transfixed face.

The room was hot, but it was a comforting heat that warmed du Chagne's heart. He tried, as he always did, to sense the magic here, the arcane protections the wizard Coryn had placed strategically around his treasure. He could not sense them—though he knew they were there—but the knowledge of their existence comforted him as much as the sight of his treasure.

How splendid the gold was! And what a great hoard! He knew, at the latest count, that there were twelve thousand four hundred and sixty eight bars of gold in here. And they all belonged to him!

There were those who claimed that steel, not gold, was the most precious metal. Others, like Duke Rathskell of Solanthus, preferred to keep their wealth in the form of precious gems, like those Stones of Garnet the duke was always boasting about. But to Bakkard du Chagne, there was nothing like the solidity of gold. It was good for his soul to come here, now and then—as often as possible, if truth be told—to bask in the sight of this vast fortune.

He stayed for more than an hour, occasionally touching one of the smooth bars, letting the essence of that treasure wash over him. Sweat slicked his head, ran down his face, but it was a cleansing perspiration and only invigorated him. Finally, he felt healed, complete, and ready again to face the world.

Emerging from the lofty tower-top room, he carefully locked the door and started down the long, winding staircase. It took a long time for him to descend to the great hall of his palace. The trip down was harder, and every step away from his gold seemed to add weight to his shoulders, to bring further burdens to his soul. By the time he reached the bottom, he felt fully mortal again, glum and moody about the challenges awaiting him.

Frowning, he crossed the vast courtyard and leaned against a chiseled column as he stared at the vast, blue expanse of the bay. Ships dotted that azure highway, two dozen sails that appeared as tiny dots from the regent's lofty vantage—each one representing another brick in the great house of trade that was once again bringing his cherished city into the forefront of world commerce. Sailors were sailing, merchants selling, craftsmen manufacturing, and vast sums of money were changing hands. Each transaction brought a percentage of profit to him, and every transaction made him richer. He was already rich beyond the imaginings of most.

Everyone had a task, a part to play, a job to do in the grand scheme of du Chagne's operations. His main work was to oversee, to organize. He had many to help him, and he paid his assistants, even his common workers, very well. Why, then, did it seem that the lord had to do all the really important things by himself?

With a sigh, Bakkard turned back to the high, arched doorway of his splendid domicile. He looked up one last time at the turrets, gleaming white against the sky. Tall windows, precious glass imported from Ergoth, gleamed like mirrors in the stone wall, reflecting the dazzling sweep of sea. Inside was the gold.

Well, didn't he deserve his rewards? After all, Palanthas had not been prosperous, clean, and productive for long. It was only three short years ago that Bakkard's knights had finally evicted the Dark Knights from the city and raised the Solamnic banner here for the first time since the before the Chaos War. Signs of devastation, of the thirty-nine years of scourge that had followed that shattering conflict still darkened whole swaths of the city. There were blocks, entire neighborhoods of shantytowns, where teeming thousands lived under tents, crate-planking, or thinly thatched roofs. Other places were still black ruin—catacombs and mazes of charred timber and blasted stone, domains only of rats and of things that preyed upon rats.

Yet so much of the city had sprung back to life under his leadership! All around was evidence of his success. Sometimes, though, he felt it was all too much. Too many things needed his attention, nothing worked properly without his direct involvement.

A guard in gleaming golden armor and scarlet tunic pulled open the door and mutely, probably even unconsciously, invited the prince back to his responsibilities. The regent held his head high as he stalked past the man into the lofty room.

The great chamber managed to be ornate and sterile at the same time. Sunlight poured through the windows, illuminating the relief works etched onto the two dozen columns, reflecting from the bronzed engravings lining the interior walls. Even so, he immediately felt as if he had entered a realm of shadow. The air was cool here, and now for some reason he shivered, though it was early summer and the day was balmy even at this morning hour.

"I have the maps displayed in the planning room, Excellency," noted Baron Dekage, his aide de camp. "Together with the dispatches that arrived overnight."

"Dispatches? More than one? What is it now?"

"I am afraid the squabble between the realms on the western shore continues to escalate. Word arrived by pigeon last night, after you had retired, sir, regarding Coastlund's claim that the fishing fleets of the south and Vinlund are encroaching upon Costian waters. This morning, shortly after dawn, a ship arrived at the docks, bearing word from a captain of the Southlund fishers. He says his comrades were attacked by Costian galleys. Boats have been burned and crews left to roast or drown."

"By Joli—how dare they play around with war! Do they know that the Princess Selinda was just sailing through those very waters?" snapped the regent. "By all the gods, if they so much as fired an arrow in my daughter's direction, I'll hang them all from the topmasts without so much as a by-your-leave!"

He went to a sideboard, poured a glass of cold water, and drank it. It was no good—the acid churning in his stomach continued unabated. "Who is my admiral in Caergoth, again?" he demanded crossly.

"That would be Lord Marrett," Dekage replied. "He took command this spring."

"Oh, yes, Marrett." The regent didn't recall much about the man—it was a routine promotion that had been necessary to appease the Duke of Caergoth—something involving in-laws of the recently married duke—but Lord Marrett would have to be ordered to sea. That would require a series of authorizations, issuances, and provisionings that would take half a day just to organize. Damn it! He was expecting quarterly reports tomorrow night and had been counting on these last two days to steel himself for the strain. There were always problems with the books, missing inventories from the iron mines and coal shipments, details that would inevitably cost time and money to resolve.

Now, he had extra work to do.

"Er, my lord . . . there is another thing," Dekage said hesitantly.

"What? Spit it out, man!"

"Patriarch Hower begs an audience. He is waiting outside."

"Very well then, send him in—and leave us alone."

Seconds later the aged priest, master of the temple of Shinare in Palanthas, came in and bowed humbly before the Lord Regent. He was a rotund bald man, clad in a robe of shimmering gold.

He mopped his pate nervously as du Chagne fixed him with a glare.

"What is it, old fellow? I have a lot to do today."

"Begging my lord's pardon—I must speak with you about the temple in Caergoth. It is the matter of the young patriarch, Issel. I fear, my lord, that he has offended some of the elders. I have received no less that four complaints during the last week. I know that young Issel was your personal selection for the post, and the man suggests great potential, but perhaps it is too soon for—"

"Have the collections suffered?" interrupted the lord regent curtly.

"No, my lord. If anything, the donations have increased slightly since Issel's arrival two months ago."

"Then tell these complaining priests that I am satisfied with the new patriarch. Furthermore, tell them that, if they continue to complain, I shall require you to share their names with me."

"My lord!" gasped the priest. "That would confound the sanctity of our order's sacred bond!"

"Nevertheless, do as I say. Tell them."

"Very well, my lord," replied the chubby patriarch, deflated in his gilded robe. He withdrew swiftly and silently, while the aide de camp returned to introduce more business.

"It is regarding the duke's conference to be convened in Caergoth next week. Princess Selinda is due to arrive in the next few days, depending on the vagaries of wind and tide, of course—"

"Yes, I know, I know. I fret for her, but she insisted upon going. The matter was out of my hands, and of course, there are a thousand—no, a million—things I need to attend to here! Matters of commerce, of taxation—of income and debt! Besides, my daughter will serve well as my representative at the conference."

"Er, I understand that, lord. I am certain the Lady Selinda will do a more than creditable job in your stead. No, my lord, the problem is the other two dukes. Both Thelgaard and Solanthus have sent missives in the last few hours, begging your lordship's pardon and pleading that they have been detained. Each will be several days late in arriving for the conference."

"By the gods!" The lord mayor's face flushed, his voice cracked. "This is an insult to my station, my very self! How dare they?"

"Begging my lord's pardon, since you sent your daughter to the conference to represent you, the insult—a potent one, to be sure—is directed at your delegated representative and is therefore *not*, technically, a wrong directed at your own august personage."

"Bah," he said, stroking his beardless double chin, blinking. "Are they acting in concert, conspiring against me?"

"No, rather I suspect that neither of them cares to arrive first, but both are equally concerned about arriving second. The second would have to honor the first by being present at the moment of his arrival," the baron suggested. "The Duke of Thelgaard claims that his wife is ill and will not be ready to travel for several days. You recall her, lord . . . she is rather elderly, and in poor health."

"That sick cow!" snapped du Chagne loudly. He felt a little better after the outburst. "Why doesn't he come without her? What about Solanthus? Sure he's not complaining of a sick wife! Why, if that slut were any healthier, Rathskell wouldn't be able to walk!"

"Er, yes, lord, and no." The aide de camp couldn't help but blush—the wedding of the Duke of Solanthus to a much younger woman had been a scandal in Solamnia just the year before. "No, he claims that he cannot afford to leave his holdings, just now. A matter of revenues uncollected, I believe. I suspect it is his attempt to influence trade in Garnet."

"Failures of revenue?" The lord mayor was outraged. "Why, he's a rich as any three gods! He has the Stones of Garnet in his treasury, by Shinare's sake! Well, never mind. I know how to hit him where it hurts!"

Du Chagne paced back and forth before his great windows, his heart pounding, his face flushed from his agitation.

"So the whole conference is delayed, for days, perhaps a fortnight, because of these stuffed up gamecocks?" he fumed. "I know just the thing to take them down a few pegs! Thwart my conference, will they? Dekage, take a letter."

"Aye, my lord." The baron hastened to the writing desk, drew out scrolls, quills, an inkwell and blotter. "I am ready, my lord."

"Address two sheets, identical letters. The first: To His Excellency, Duke Jarrod of Thelgaard, Lord of the Crown, Keeper of the Great Plain, Heir to the Throne of the White Swan, etcetera, etcetera. Good, got that? The other copy should be addressed to His Excellency, Duke Rathskell of Solanthus, Lord of the Sword, Master of the Garnet Spur, Inheritor of the Silver Blade, Guardian of the Solamnic Code, etcetera, etcetera."

"Yes, my lord."

"Write this: 'Regarding the disposition of the disputed city-state, Garnet, recently liberated from the Dark Knights by forces under my overall command. Each of you claims it by historical precedent. Let it be known that it is my sincere wish that the place shall remain independent of any sovereign lord, as pledged in the Compact of Freedom.' Yes." He chuckled. "A free-market center to compete with each of those greedy bastards!" The lord mayor waved away the baron's intention to copy these last words into the letter. "A little competition, taxes going to Palanthas of course, ought to make them sit up and take notice of their lord!"

"Quite, my lord," the baron answered. "However—most unfortunately—I must remind you that the Compact of Freedom is currently . . . uh, missing. It was, you recall, in Lord Lorimar's safe keeping at the time of his death. If it were the case that you could rule the plains from Palanthas by decree, Solamnia would surely be a greater realm, a place of loftier ideals and nobler accomplishments. Alas, this is a matter that can only be resolved by the council."

"Blast their eyes—and damn that old charter! Bah, you're right, I know. Very well, let us recast the letter."

With a shrug, Baron Dekage crumbled the first letters and painstakingly set out fresh pages. The lord mayor paced and

muttered as he tried to figure out what to say, while his aide surreptitiously—and anxiously—glanced across the table.

He was relieved to see he had brought plenty of blank paper.

⊱⊶⊷⊶⊷⊶❦⊷⊶⊷⊶⊷⊰

The Duke of Caergoth stood at a table, glaring irritably.
The surface before him was large and layered in green velvet.
A stripe of blue silk twisted through the middle of the table
like a river, and several heaps of cloth looked like miniature
hills. Across the table were spread hundreds of tiny figures
carved to look like knights, footmen, dwarven infantry, goblin
hordes—all of them commanded by a few gloriously decorated
lords mounted on horseback. The most resplendent of these, in
silver armor and mounted upon a rearing black stallion, held
the banner of Caergoth, a red rose on a field of blue, aloft on a
standard.

Duke Crawford examined the position of the Evil Ones—his
name for the enemy he faced on this make-believe battlefield.
Today his army was challenged by a powerful but undisciplined
horde. He had arranged an elaborate feint to draw the heavy
infantry, a brigade of ogres, into range of his catapults, and he
was preparing to unleash a devastating barrage. His own knights,
armored and mounted on powerful chargers, waited behind a
hill, ready for a smashing counterattack.

Only then did he feel the humming vibration in his stomach—the magical summons of his lord. He stepped to a small
door in the side of his game room, pulled it open, and saw the
outline of a pale glow by a small drape on the wall of the alcove.
He hastened over and pulled the curtain aside to reveal an ornate
crystal mirror—a mirror that was growing bright with magical
illumination.

"My Lord Regent!" Crawford said. "I hope I didn't keep you
waiting."

Bakkard du Chagne's dour image confronted him from the
depths of the mirror. "Never mind that," snapped the lord in
Palanthas, his voice transported across the miles through the

40

medium of magical mirrors in both places. "I have learned that both Solanthus and Thelgaard will be delayed in arriving for the conference."

Crawford blinked. He—or rather, his staff—had been preparing for the conference for months on end, and he had not been expecting problems. "But . . . why?" he asked, finally.

"Pride, no doubt. Even arrogance," snapped du Chagne. "Petty political maneuvering. The important thing is that we do not reward their posturing."

"Um, yes," Crawford agreed. "What do you want me to do?"

"My daughter is traveling there by royal galleon—she will be arriving in Caergoth within a matter of days. She will be hosting the conference, so you are to fete her as you would me—and let the tardy lords know when they arrive, that they have missed these signal honors."

"Certainly, my lord." The duke was dismayed to hear that the princess would be arriving so soon. He was within a week of having the Evil Ones utterly destroyed—and now the gods only knew how long it would be before he got back to his gaming table.

As if to further mock him, someone knocked firmly on the door.

"Go away! I'm busy with my general staff!" Duke Crawford barked.

"Beg pardon, my lord, but it's urgent." It was the stern voice of the duke's veteran captain, Sir Marckus.

Crawford looked back to the mirror, as the lord regent gestured impatiently. "Go—but remember what I have said."

"Of course, my Lord," replied the duke, bowing, then pulling the drapery back across the mirror. He stepped out of the alcove and closed the door. "Very well—come in!" he snapped to his officer outside the room.

Marckus, with his impressive flowing mustache and impeccable uniform, opened the door and stood back so a messenger could enter. The man, smelling of wet horse, dashed into the room with his hat in his hand and bowed, ready to apologize to the gathered nobles and officers but blinking in surprise as he raised his head and saw only the duke.

"Speak, man!" demanded the lord, as the messenger stared in astonishment at the war game arranged on the table.

"Begging your Excellency's pardon, but the harbor lookouts report that a convoy from Palanthas is approaching the port, ten stout galleons. They fly the flag of the princess—it must be the Lord Mayor's daughter and her entourage."

"By Joli, they're not expected until the day after tomorrow!" The duke glanced at his tabletop in disappointment. "I had the Evil Ones outmaneuvered—would have annihilated the whole force by tomorrow morning! Now it will be weeks before I get back to such fun!" The duke sniffed, then called out, "Sir Marckus!"

"Yes, Excellency!" The knight captain stepped into the game room, snapping to attention.

"See to an honor guard immediately—to be in attendance on the docks as the Lady of Palanthas disembarks. Get the street sweepers busy—I want the whole avenue between here and the waterfront spotless. Have people turn out in a proper welcome—you know, lining all the walkways, balconies, that sort of thing."

"Of course, Excellency. May I inquire as to the available time before her arrival?"

"Something less than an hour, so hop to it."

"As you wish, my lord. If you will excuse me?" Somehow, the knight—a veteran officer of many battle campaigns—maintained his dignity as he marched away.

The ten ships of the Lord Regent's fleet were lined at the docks of Caergoth, sails furled, gangplanks lowered. The captain of the Palanthian Guards, Sir Powell, led the procession of knights, a score of whom had been transported, with horses, on each vessel. All two hundred of the detachment were formed up, in neat ranks.

Lady Selinda Du Chagne debarked to enthusiastic cheers from the adoring populace of Caergoth. At eighteen, she was a stunningly beautiful young woman, with high cheekbones and hair the color of fine-spun gold. She smiled as she came down the gangplank, waving as she climbed into the waiting carriage.

For the first time in years, the "Princess of Palanthas" had been allowed to leave her native city. Caergoth was, she saw at a glance, a quite different place: solid and down to earth, compared to the elegant but rigid and stifling city to the north.

For eighteen years, Palanthas had stifled Lady Selinda very much indeed.

She was met on the dock by Sir Marckus Haum, captain of the ducal guard. He bowed to her and saluted Captain Powell, the dour but capable knight in charge of Selinda's escort. Moments later she was ensconced in an open carriage, rolling through the streets while the people lined three or four deep along the entire road from the waterfront to the castle. There was a naive enthusiasm in their uncritical shouts and cheers. Most of them had never heard of her a couple of hours earlier. At home Selinda was lucky if the jaded citizens of Palanthas took the trouble to move out of the way when her noble carriage traversed the streets.

Furthermore, she found the stone, square houses and shops of Caergoth comforting, reassuring. The place had a look of permanence about it, with broad walls sectioning off the neighborhoods of the city, ensuring that any attacker would have to fight his way through many gates before reaching the castle proper.

That vaulted edifice sat upon a commanding bluff overlooking the sheltered harbor. The steepness of the hill climbing away from the waterfront forced Lady Selinda to keep one hand firmly clenched around a support bar in her lurching carriage.

She observed the gleaming ranks of men-at-arms arrayed in compact formations in the broad square before the castle itself. There must be a thousand of them, she guessed, organized by arms: squares of pikemen, their tall weapons held high, straight ranks of archers with crossbows clutched at the ready, burly swordsmen in gleaming plate mail breastplates rigidly clasping their crimson shields over their hearts. A line of massive, steel-strapped catapults loomed behind the soldiers, an impressive array of artillery that looked capable of reducing a small castle to rubble with a single barrage.

Castle Caergoth loomed over her, more dominant, forbidding, and warlike than any structure in all of glorious Palanthas. Selinda couldn't help but gawk at the tall turrets, arched bridges, immense palisades, and studded ramparts. Gray and scuffed across its vast faces, it looked more a product of nature than man.

Sir Marckus broke into a gallop and raced across the drawbridge. At the dock he had introduced himself as the duke's representative and led the caravan of carriages and mounted knights through the city. The captain of her own escort, Sir Powell, rode along just behind Sir Marckus. It was impossible to imagine two more perfect symbols of the knighthood—the Code and the Measure practically oozed from their bodies like perspiration.

Now, within the gate, the two captains dismounted, stood aside, and saluted as Selinda's driver lashed his horses and urged the carriage over the broad drawbridge and into the huge courtyard. Gray walls rose to all sides, but the effect was more exhilarating than confining. At least a thousand men at arms lined the parapets, and they all saluted together, clapping their clenched fists onto shields emblazoned with the crimson sign of the Rose.

More people cheered from lower balconies as the carriage came to a stop before a wide veranda. These were nobles and courtiers, Selinda reckoned, noticing silken tunics of many colors, lush fur cloaks on some of the ladies, and here and there, the glint of gold, silver, and other ornaments. She recognized one man in the golden robes of a Patriarch of Shinare, as he hurried forward to her coach.

"Bishop Issel—excuse me, *Patriarch,*" said the princess as the carriage door opened and she rose to step down. "I had heard of your promotion—the youngest temple master in all Solamnia! Congratulations!"

"I pray to the Winged Master that your father's faith in me shall prove justified," said the cleric, bowing humbly. He was a handsome man with a dazzling smile, and she extended her hand to him. "May much profit attend your councils here."

"Thank you, Patriarch," she said, hoping the goddess was listening.

One pair of nobles stood alone before the open doors of the great keep. Selinda recognized the duke and duchess, whom she had met when they visited Palanthas. Now they came forward.

"My lady!" gushed the Duchess of Caergoth. "I'm Lady Martha, if you recall. It is *such* an honor to have you visit!" The duchess was only a few years older than Selinda but giggled like a ninny as she curtsied. The princess recalled that Martha had married Duke Crawford only one year previously.

"Thank you, my lady," replied Selinda graciously, as she had been taught. "It is an honor to enjoy your hospitality."

"Princess," said the duke, charming her with a dazzling smile as he offered his arm. "All Caergoth is delighted to welcome you— we will show you that here the Order of the Rose blooms like never before! But first, let us to show you to your apartments. Tonight there will be a welcome banquet in the great hall of the keep."

"That sounds wonderful," Selinda acknowledged, taking the nobleman's elbow.

She was surprised when the duchess took her other arm and leaned close with another giggle. "I just *know* we'll have a lot to talk about!"

❦❦❦❦❦❦❦❦

The great house in Palanthas was shrouded in darkness. What illumination existed here glowed deep within the walls, shielded from any prying eyes. Shadows yawned in every window, in every chamber except for one central room. Here, Coryn the White worked her magic, and those enchantments cast a pearly illumination through the gloom.

This was the great manor that had long belonged to Lady Jenna, Mistress of the Order of the Red Robes. Now Jenna was Head of the Conclave, the most powerful and influential wizard on all Krynn. She had held that rank for several years, and it was a station that required her almost constant presence in the Tower of High Sorcery in Wayreth Forest. As a result, she had granted her white-robed counterpart the use not just of her domicile but of the exceedingly well-furnished wizard's laboratory located there.

Coryn sat at a table on which she had arranged a series of small objects. Each was about the size of a sewing thimble and had been skillfully molded in solid gold. There was a miniature rose, a crown and sword, and a small model of a man-at-arms wielding a great sword. A tiny figurine of a hand mirror—in gold, not glass—sat to one side, and at the far end was a little set of balancing scales. In the very center of the table sat a shallow bowl filled with sparkling white wine. The bony white ceramic of the bowl was the source of the glow, an unnatural but pleasing light.

The wizard stared into the clear bubbling liquid and took up the tiny rose in her slender, delicate fingers. She concentrated, and moments later the image of the Duke of Caergoth appeared on the shimmering surface of the wine. He could be observed barking instructions to his wife, who bustled about in a petticoat while he wrestled with a formal black cape emblazoned with the symbol of the Rose. His wife, Duchess Martha, held up a red dress. He made a face, and she put it down to display a yellow gown. When this one was also rejected by the lord, the young duchess seemed to be on the verge of tears. Coryn didn't need to hear what they were saying, so she put down the rose and allowed the image in the bowl to fade.

Next she took up the tiny mirror, holding it between her fingers as she again studied the liquid in the creamy white bowl. She saw the Lord Regent du Chagne in his private chamber. The lord stalked back and forth, beside a table blanketed with papers, notes, and an open ledger. The image in the bowl was not magnified enough for Coryn to read any of those pages, but she had no interest in his epistles in any event. She knew that the lord regent was the richest man in Ansalon, and she felt a certain sense of sadness as she regarded his scowling visage.

He would not hold his lordly station if she had not helped him to drive the Dark Knights from Palanthas, for which, despite her melancholy, she bore no regrets. There was so much more to be done in the way of progress, and she didn't know if du Chagne was ever going to move beyond his increasingly petty concerns. When Coryn envisioned a return to Solamnic Rule, she thought of the great history of the Knighthood, of chivalry and a code of honor that protected the weak, advanced the cause of good against evil. She imagined pageantry and glamour, a state of civility in public affairs that worked toward the benefit of all. The Lord Regent, she had come to realize, thought merely in terms of profit and loss—his own, and that of his closest associates. She watched as he checked the door to his chambers, ensuring that it was locked, then moved to his secret mirror in the alcove. No doubt he needed to harp about profit margins to one of his lords.

Coryn also set that talisman aside. Holding the small crown, she now produced the image of the burly Duke of Thelgaard— Jarrod Yorgan. The big man sat beside a bed in which a sickly looking woman resided. The big man touched the woman's forehead with a cloth, then stiffened. A glow began to emanate from the mirror on the wall beside the bed, and it was then the wizard realized who du Chagne intended to harangue.

Next she moved to pick up the tiny sword. She watched for a moment with a wry smile as Duke Rathskell of Solanthus, a slender and fit man of more than fifty years, was slowly undressed by his much younger wife. When the sultry woman knelt to unbuckle her lord's boots, Cory quickly set down the tiny sword talisman.

For a long time she looked at the miniature of the swordsman. She felt a twinge of guilt when she used that spy, a reluctance that never bothered her with the others. The focus of this particular talisman was special, in so many ways . . . she remembered his strong arms, the fire she felt in her belly when he held her . . . . and the anger, the unquenched—possibly unquenchable—thirst for revenge that still burned inside of him. He craved . . . what? Justice, certainly, but justice on his own terms. Coryn, of course, wanted justice for all of Solamnia.

He was not a bad man. He was in such terrible danger, and he had suffered so much. He needed her, she knew, while the others merely feared her.

Her reluctance overcome, she took up the miniature of the warrior, and allowed another picture to swirl within the bowl.

CHAPTER FIVE

THE FREE CITY

The two horses raced through the night, the struggling gully dwarf's complaints notwithstanding. Galloping over the rutted mountain track, the dwarf and human riders urged their mounts to nearly reckless speed, relying on the light of the white moon, Solinari, to illuminate their path. When that moon set a few hours before dawn, they were many miles from the stronghold of Cornellus. Finally the warrior reined in his gelding, Dram Feldspar doing the same with his mare.

The little gully dwarf had fallen asleep some time earlier, belly down over the withers of the swordsman's steed, but now he awakened and pushed himself up, looking around in confusion.

"Lemme go!" he insisted, started to squirm. "I gotta go home!"

This time the rider pulled his horse to a halt, lowering the little fellow to the ground by the scruff of his neck.

"Are you sure you want to go back to Cornellus?" asked the man. "He might not welcome the Aghar that opened the gate for us."

"Hmmph!" snorted the gully dwarf. "Big Fat Guy not know one gully dwarf from one!"

"Suit yourself," Dram said, "but we could take you to a city. We're going to Garnet. Nicer place than that mountain fort,

49

that's for sure. You'll find some other Aghar living there, as I recall."

"You gives me one steel, and I go back to Big Fat Guy house!" insisted the gully dwarf.

With a shrug, the man flipped him the shiny coin, which the grimy Aghar caught and quickly stuffed down into his pants. Sniffing dismissively at the humans, he stomped back up the trail.

"He's headed the wrong way," Dram whispered, as the Aghar tromped determinedly along a fork in the track they had just passed. It connected to a side road leading into the south Garnet Range.

The rider shrugged. "Yes, I took that into consideration. He'll get lost up here, and it'll be days or weeks—if ever—before he finds his way back to the Big Fat Guy."

Dram Feldspar nodded, impressed with his companion's thinking. As the sun paled the eastern horizon, they set their own more leisurely pace before eventually stopping for a mid-morning camp. For three more days they made their way through the foothills and green valleys of the Garnet Mountains. Finally they emerged on the western slope of the range, descending on a good, straight road to the flat Vingaard plains. Within sight, though still eight or ten miles away, loomed the walls and towers, the temples and taverns, of a gleaming, prosperous city.

⊰⊹⊱⊰⊹⊱⊰⊹⊰❀⊱⊰⊹⊱⊰⊹⊱⊰⊹⊱

"Welcome to the Free City of Garnet!" proclaimed a herald as the two riders passed under the wide open gate. "Bring your goods here to sell—or come here to buy! You want to work, we've got a job—you want to hire, we've got skilled hands and strong backs looking for work!"

"Sounds like a perfect world," Dram muttered as they passed through the gate and joined a throng of travelers on the crowded main street. "I'll believe it when I see it."

His companion shrugged. "Garnet's better'n a lot of places

across these plains. No Solamnic dukes in charge here, at least."

"Maybe we can shop out our services, then," the dwarf said. "Make a few coins. Since we never got the bounty from Cornellus, we're down to about three steel pieces. If we picked up some extra, we could while away the nights in one of these fancy-lookin' drinking houses," he concluded hopefully, gesturing at a whole street of decorated taverns and inns. Colorful signs advertised the Dragon's Flagon, the Knight and Maiden, the Kaolyn Hole, and other inviting establishments.

"Why, look there—the Kaolyn Hole—makes me think of my own home, under the mountain. Ah, how I miss it."

"You miss the dwarf spirits, that's f'sure," the man said. "But you'd go crazy in a fortnight if you tried to live underground again."

Dram sniffed with the air of one who'd been greatly insulted then sighed, squinting at the sun as it slid downward through the late afternoon sky. "Never did think a mountain dwarf could grow so fond of that ol' ball of fire," he admitted, "but yer right—I get a kinda creepy feeling if I'm stuck in the dark too long, these days. That's what hanging around with humans too long'll do to a fellow!"

They rode along in companionable silence, enjoying the friendly bustle of the city after their long ride. It was the end of the business day, and merchants were folding up tents and awnings across several great marketplaces as people drifted away from the centers of commerce. A few vendors hawked the last of their fish, while others carted away wagonloads of woolen garments, kegs of beer, and casks of wheat to be saved for the next day of selling.

The taverns and inns sprang to life as the sky grew dark. The riders passed one called Granny's Garter, where a number of scantily clad women danced on the upper balcony. Music, in the forms of drums, lutes, pipes, and mandolins, echoed in every street.

"This city was kind of a scum-hole when the Dark Knights

ran the place," Dram said approvingly. "I thought it was the Solamnics who'd got the place back on its feet again—you say it ain't so?"

"Hardly," replied his companion. "You heard what the crier said. This is a Free City. Pledged by compact to none of the orders of knights. Rose, Crown, Sword—they all buy and sell here, but they don't get to tax the commerce."

"There are some knights now," the dwarf observed. He gestured toward the front of a gilded building on a side street, nestled between an inn and a dance hall. "Recognize them horses?"

The man peered in the direction of the dwarf's pointing finger, seeing two large war-horses and a scruffy mule lashed to a hitching rail.

"Yep," said the warrior, reining in and dismounting. He lashed the gelding's reins to a handy railing while he studied the huge horses.

The two steeds were easily distinguishable as knightly mounts, but it was the scrollwork on the saddles that marked them as the same two horses that had been tethered outside of Cornellus's tavern high up in the mountains. The two companions settled themselves on a bench outside an inn on a porch that allowed them to keep an eye on the pair of warhorses.

"Say, what kind of place is that?" Dram had been scrutinizing the gilded structure, which reflected the setting sun off a myriad of gold leaves and scrollwork along the building's upper façade.

"It's a temple. To Shinare. They call her Winged Victory nowadays, but I think of her as a set of moneyhandler's scales. She's the goddess of merchants and other thieves," the warrior said.

"Hmph!" snorted the dwarf. "In Thorbardin they call her the Silver Mistress. I keep my faith in Reorx, thank you very much."

The human shrugged. "Each to his own. I put my faith in my brains and some keen steel."

He leaned back on the bench and pulled his cap down low over his eyes, keeping his eye on the war-horses and the temple of Shinare. They were outside an inn called the Roseflower, and a cheerful barmaid spotted them and brought them several mugs of ale—the place had the Coastlund Red that they both favored. Meanwhile the sky grew dark and the streets, lit by oil lamps, seemed to grow even brighter than they had been during the day.

"It's two drinks for the price of one, today," the barmaid mentioned casually on their second round.

"What's the occasion?" asked Dram.

"Well, it's in honor of Dara Lorimar's birthday. She would have been twenty-two, today. My master was a loyal follower of her father's, so he pays tribute to her memory—it's a year and a half since she died."

"This city owes a lot to Lorimar?" asked the warrior with an air of disinterest.

"To both of them," the barmaid said proudly. "He freed us from the Dark Knights, and she was the Princess of the Plains, you know."

"Huh?" the dwarf asked. "Royalty?"

"You know, from the prophecy," the woman said. "A Princess of the Plains shall wed a Lord of No Sign—and Solamania will have a king, again." She shook her head sadly. "Of course, it's all just stories now, but it's nice to remember."

"Yes, worth remembering," Dram replied, as the warrior ignored the exchange. After the maid left, the dwarf poked his companion in the arm. "Ain't feeling too social, eh?" he asked.

The human shook his head. "People don't know what they're talking about," he said bitterly. The two sat in silence for another hour until the barmaid brought them another set of foaming mugs.

"That was our last coin," the dwarf remarked, after paying for their third round.

His companion simply nodded.

Finally the man stiffened and turned his head to the side. He watched surreptitiously as the two knights they had encountered in the stronghold finally emerged from the temple. They were still dragging the hapless goblin, thoroughly shackled. They hoisted the creature onto the mule, mounted their horses, and started off at a trot toward the city's western gate.

"Where do you think they're headed?" asked Dram.

"Caergoth," replied the man with certainty. "That's where the Order of the Rose is, these days."

"You know them two?"

The swordsman shook his head. "No, but the barmaid at Cornel's called that one Reynaud. I've heard of Captain Reynaud. He's a knight commander in Duke Crawford's army."

Dram whistled. "A damn good army, that one. I've seen it on the march—covers the whole horizon."

"It's a big one all right," his companion allowed with a shrug.

They waited a good half hour after the knights had left. Night had fallen by the time they rose, led their horses down the side street, and tethered them outside the temple. Dram followed as the man approached the front door and tried the latch. It was unlocked, so they strolled inside.

They found themselves standing in a small, stone-walled chamber. There was a large gold merchant's scale set up on a platform in the center of the room, with several rings of benches surrounding it. A huge pair of feathered wings, possibly a trophy claimed from a slain griffon, were prominently displayed on the far wall of the sanctuary.

A cleric dressed in white robes trimmed in gold emerged from a back room, bowing humbly before the two travelers.

"Greetings, Wayfarers," he said. "Do you come to make an offering to Shinare of the Scales?"

"Not exactly," said the human. "I wanted to ask you some questions about the Knights of the Rose. You work for them, don't you?"

The cleric, a young man with cherubic cheeks and a rotund waistline, drew himself up stiffly. "I should say not! We may have common cause, as we try to bring order to this accursed place, but I do my god's work, while they are in the service of their duke! The knighthood has no official power here in Garnet!"

The swordsman seemed to ignore the priest, walking slowly around the chamber, his hands concealed beneath his cape. On the far side of the large scale one arm emerged as he pointed to a strongbox on the floor. "Is this where you take donations? From the knights?"

"No! How dare you imply—" The chubby cleric shrieked as the warrior, moving with sudden speed, snatched the sword from his back-scabbard, whipped it over his head, and brought it down. Blue flames were already crackling along the blade as the keen steel edge smashed into the chest, slicing through the planks of the strongbox as though they were stale pieces of bread.

A cascade of coins and gems spilled out.

The priest staggered backward, gaping in horror as the man reached down and grabbed one glittering item. It was a golden medallion in the shape of a rose attached to a slender gold chain.

"I see that that someone pays you well," he drawled.

"Outrageous! Go at once! Know that that is a simple donation from a faithful follower!"

"Well, then, you can keep the simple stuff," said the swordsman, tossing it toward the cleric, who caught it clumsily in both hands, fingers clutching at the fine chain. "We can find plenty that is more elegant among the rest of this."

He held his weapon, no longer flaming, in one hand, as the cleric glared at him. Dram knelt and scooped fistful after fistful of coins and jewels into a leather sack. The dwarf paused for a second now and then to admire a particularly fetching gem but quickly filled the sack.

"That's about all it'll hold," the dwarf said, hefting the bulging sack. He was visibly disappointed, for there was still a considerable fortune strewn around the stone floor.

"It'll have to do," said his companion.

"Yeah, I suppose," said Dram regretfully.

"How dare you?" demanded the priest angrily. "When the duke hears of this—"

"The duke has no power here. Garnet is a free city. Remember?" the warrior chided.

"Your insolence will cost you dearly," warned the priest. With a sudden gesture he spun away, seized a tassle hanging from the ceiling, and pulled hard on the line. A gong sounded.

"Tch-tch. You shouldn't have done that," Dram said, shaking his head. The swordsman was already moving, stepping close to the priest. He reversed the heavy blade and brought the hilt down, hard, on the cleric's head, sending the priest sprawling to the floor, unconscious.

"Halt!" A strong voice boomed through the round chamber, even as the pair were racing for the door.

Both the dwarf and his human companion stopped, as if their feet were frozen to the floor.

Another priest, this one wearing a gown of pure gold, stalked into the room. He was older than the first, with a fringe of gray hair and a massive belly that swelled his garment. He stared at them with an air of command—clearly, he was the high priest of this temple.

"So even a temple is not safe from such villains and scoundrels. You will pay for your insolence on the rack! Duke Crawford himself will enjoy the spilling of your blood."

"Magic! I'm stuck to the floor!" Dram snarled in rage, snatched his axe from its belt strap, but he couldn't decide whether to hurl it—the high priest was too far away to be sure that he could strike him. "Damn your greedy god anyway!" he spat.

The human warrior, on the other hand, drew a deep breath and collected himself before calmly turning around, his feet gliding smoothly over the floor. "Duke Crawford has no power in Garnet," he said.

The patriarch glared indignantly. "You blaspheme the Balance of the Scales! He will, soon enough. Though you'll have breathed your last before then!"

The intruder calmly sheathed his great sword and drew out one of the small crossbows that he wore at his belt, concealed beneath his cape. With a measured crank of his hand, he cocked the weapon.

"Cease!" cried the high priest, his fingers splayed in a gesture of command. "Drop your weapon."

The warrior raised the crossbow, siting the weapon on the massive round target of the golden billowing robe. "Release my friend," he said calmly.

"I command you both to remain!" shouted the cleric. "My power rules here!"

The *clunk* of the crossbow's firing mechanism was the last sound he was fated to hear. The high priest groped at the dart that pierced his chest, looking in disbelief at the crimson rose—dyed in blood—that spread across his sacred garment. He collapsed with a groan.

The power of his spell was broken in that instant, and Dram stumbled free. "How did you get away from his magic?" he demanded of his companion.

The warrior pulled off his left glove, revealing a golden ring that glowed on the middle finger of his left hand. "A gift—from a lady who knows a thing or two about magic."

The dwarf nodded knowingly as the warrior was already hurrying toward the door.

"Time to go," the swordsman said. "This town is getting too religious for me."

Chapter Six

LORD OF THE GOBS

In the years of the Dragon Overlords Khellendros and Beryl, the savage tribes dwelling in the Garnet Mountains were hard pressed to find sustenance. The hobgoblins disbanded their great clanholds to scatter into the heights. Eating grubs and roots, they considered themselves lucky to discover such provender. They survived primarily through raiding, inflicting terror on many of the human settlements skirting the fringe of the range, pillaging from the hill dwarves with the aid of their teeming goblin lackeys. These raids inevitably led to reprisals from the Solamnic Knights, whose patrols drove the raiders higher and higher into the mountains.

One such band of hobs was captained by a former veteran of Lord Ariakan's, a surly brute by the name of Bonechisel Hobgoblin. Despite the ferocity of his warrior followers, Bonechisel had not found easy pickings during the overlord years.

Bonechisel's mate was named Laka. She had once been a comely wench—for a hobgoblin. In fact, it was her beauty that had drawn the chief's attentions. She had been mated previously to a young warrior, but Bonechisel secured a divorce for her by the simple expedient of bashing his rival's head until the poor fellows brains had run out and pooled upon the ground. The chief had stepped over the mess, taken Laka by the wrist, and informed her that now she was the chief's woman.

After several years of rudimentary efforts on Bonechisel's part, Laka had given birth to a son. Born at the very onset of winter, the infant was sickly and small, though the hob female attended to her tiny charge with all the diligence and care that one could hope for from a member of her brutish, savage race. Whether from malnutrition or simply the early onset of winter's dampness and chill, the suffering little hob perished in the second week of its short life.

Bonechisel took no note of the fact, and Laka sadly laid the little corpse to rest in a mossy alcove beside a flowing stream, the only place where deep snow didn't cover the ground. Not far away in the snowy wilds, the chief shivered, gloomy at the prospect of another long, cold season of hunt and roam.

He caught a tantalizing scent on a waft of wind, which bore a promise of warmth, comfort, and shelter, for it smelled of a fire of pine wood. Emerging from the forest, Bonechisel found the scent of smoke even stronger. The vapors emerged from the chimney of a small cabin, wafting upward, bearing hot red sparks on the winter wind. In those glowing embers Boneshisel saw doom for whomever skulked within the cabin and fed that alluring fire.

Bonechisel lifted his axe, which, though crude in the extreme, boasted a heavy chunk of sharp-edged granite for its blade, mounted securely atop a cudgel that was as thick around as a strong man's arm. He flexed and swung, crashing the stone head into the boards. Two blows were enough to make a crack, and three more swings shattered the door into two halves. One half, attached to leather hinges, still clung in place, while the other piece toppled inward to crash on the dry stone floor.

Bonechisel growled as he stepped through the entrance. Laka followed close behind him, pressed by other warriors, three or four more hobs and goblins each brandishing a heavy club of their own.

The first thing the hob-wench noticed was the warmth, a splendid blanket of moist, slightly cloudy air that surrounded her. The taint of smoke in the shelter was a welcome scent, and the low light cast by the embers fading in the fireplace was a pleasant welcome after the unmitigated gray-white of winter's first storm.

The second thing to draw Laka's attention was the small cradle, lined with furs, resting over on one side of the single chamber. She took no note of the huge creature seated at the table, the giant who still cradled his head in his hands, so lost in despair that he hadn't yet noticed the intruders. Carefully, the hob-wench sidled toward the cradle, drawn by an instinct deeper than her race. She heard the plaintive cry, and her breasts began to leak their milk.

Bonechisel, for his part, was fully aware of the giant seated at the table in the middle of the room. He had been prepared to rush in and attack the denizens of this shelter. Deep in his heart he had hoped they would be humans, preferably defenseless women and children, but he had steeled himself to fight goblins, hobgoblins, a knight or two, had even considered the dread thought that he might have to face an ogre. It was a measure of how cold, how frightened he was, that he was even willing to chance the latter possibility.

This! This was such an extraordinary *giant!*

He gave serious thought to running away. His cunning mind considered the throng of hobs and gobs behind him, and he figured that he could easily pull several of them into the house, knocking them to the floor even as he made his escape. By the time the giant was through smashing those hapless offerings, Bonechisel could be safely back in the woods . . .

On second thought, this did not seem like an ideal course of action. He well knew how cold those woods were, how snowy and barren. The tribe might survive another night out there. (Actually, Bonechisel himself would probably survive the night; the welfare of the tribe as whole could not be said to be much of a consideration.) But after another night with no food and no shelter, the upcoming days inevitably looked bleak, while the warmth of this stone-walled house was undeniably attractive.

In an instant the hobgoblin's eyes took in the mountain of

firewood stacked against the back wall. In a dark alcove near the back he could see haunches of dried meat, many of them. There was a great bed in the corner, a bed fit for an exalted chieftain such as Bonechisel Hob.

The issue was decided by the apathetic nature of this giant himself. The fellow had only now raised his head to blink stupidly at the strangers who had just spent several minutes smashing in his front door. Clearly, this giant was not blessed with lightning-quick reactions. The expression on his face bespoke an utter lack of intelligence and imagination. Perhaps it would not be madness to battle him for the prize of this shelter. Indeed, Bonechisel thought, a sudden, swarming attack might be the best option.

"Go!" cried Bonechisel, clapping one of his lackeys on the shoulder. "Kill giant!"

The goblin yelped as his chieftain pushed him forward. Two other warriors, equally slow and witless, lurched after, propelled by strong kicks to their posteriors.

"Attack!" cried Bonechisel, raising his club and advancing behind the screen of the three milling goblins.

The giant shook his head and blinked. His eyes went to something at the edge of the room—a bed for an infant, the hobgoblin perceived in a quick glance—and the giant's muscles tensed as he was suddenly galvanized by fear. At the same time, the three goblins in front of Bonechisel hesitated.

Disgusted, the hobgoblin charged between his cohorts in a bull rush. His axe, already raised above his head, whistled downward in a wild swing just as the giant sprang to his feet. The jagged edge of granite struck the fellow right in the middle of his forehead, the blow knocking him back into his seat then sending the chair toppling over backward, spilling the giant onto the floor where he lay motionless.

With a wild whoop of triumph, Bonechisel brought the axe down again, and again. The three other goblins, inspired by their chieftain's example, joined in the fun, rushing forward with their own stone clubs to batter and bash the helpless giant, until his body had been reduced to a shapeless pulp.

Bonechisel danced around the corpse of his slain foe in an ecstasy of triumph. "I am Giant-Slayer!" he crowed. He clubbed one of his lackeys. "Call me Giant-Slayer!" he ordered.

"Hail Bonechisel Giant-Slayer!" the goblin, no fool, shouted.

The hobgoblin danced to the back of the room then yelped when he realized that the great bed was occupied—by the mate of the giant. He bashed his club against the female and was startled by her utter lack of reaction. Leaning in, he sniffed. The scent of death filled his nostrils. Pulling back the quilt, he saw this was an ogress, not a giantess. A shrewder brain that Bonechisel's might have deduced that this oddly matched couple were outcasts from both giant and ogre tribes.

The chieftain remembered the third denizen of this stone house. He looked toward the infant bed and saw that Laka was peering over the lip of the cradle. Caught up in the blood-frenzy, Bonechisel raised his club and howled aloud, starting toward the last of his enemies.

To his surprise, Laka reached into the cradle, snatched up the infant, then turned and snarled at the chieftain with a startling display of big teeth. Her eyes blazed, and the import of her actions was clear and defiant.

"Give me babe!" demanded the hobgoblin. "I kill! I am Bonechisel Giant-Slayer!"

"This babe mine!" she declared. "Go kill someplace else!"

The infant was squalling and fussing, and the hobgoblin would have liked nothing better than to smash its little brains out on the floor, but he noted the glare of determination, of pure courage, in his mate's eye. He decided that killing this baby was not worth subjecting himself to the female wrath and recrimination that would follow.

Even as he stared in disbelief, his pig-eyes squinting, Laka slumped down to the floor, opened her tunic, and gave the baby one of her breasts for suckling. The baby half-breed's annoying wails faded to a surprised squawk, then a soft slurping as he fastened himself to the teat and began to nurse.

Laka called her babe Ankhar, and she cared for the half-giant infant with as much love and attention as if he had been born of her own flesh. From the first greedy suckle, Ankhar clung to his new mother with desperation, forming an inseparable bond.

Generally the adopted hobgoblin spent his time avoiding the mature males of the tribe, although he became the natural leader of the gobs of his own age. Not only did he outweigh all of his contemporaries by at least a factor of two, but he was quick to anger and ruthless in retaliation, inflicting countless broken bones during any outbreaks of rough play. Fear being a primary influence upon goblin relationships, Ankhar's prowess made his fellows obsequious, and he was quick to take advantage of the worship he inspired. He would dispatch the young ogres to bring him food and drink, to perform his designated chores (he especially hated firewood hauling and stone breaking).

During these years the tribe moved around a lot, never settling in the same place for more than a season or two at a time. At first Bonechisel was one of many hobgoblin chiefs in the foothills around the Garnet Range, but he gradually made a name for himself as one of the most successful when it came to raiding the settlements of humans, leading his tribe in such a way that the gobs had plenty to eat—even during the waning months of winter when starvation made a rampant sweep through the bands and clans of leaders who showed less foresight.

In Ankhar's sixteenth year the War of Souls ended unnoticed by the goblin population of the Garnet Range. However, the savage creatures *did* notice that once again two moons moved through the skies. Not long after, Laka came upon a shiny green rock in a mountain cavern. She listened to the rock and heard the words of the Prince of Lies, Hiddukel. Hiddukel was pleased with her, the rock said, and she began to tell the other hobs and gobs about his wickedly successful ways.

Drawn in part by the might of the brutal chieftain, in part by the compelling words of the primitive high priestess Laka, more and more of the small goblin clans were absorbed into the Bonechisel tribe. By the time of Ankhar's eighteenth year Bonechisel's followers numbered many hundreds—and in fact was the most formidable horde along the entire circumference of the mountain range. Burly hobgoblins, seasoned veterans with scars and trophies to prove their prowess, bowed down to Bonechisel these days, and brought him gifts of food and drink and treasure. Bounty hunters stayed well away from the brutish tribe.

In the late spring following Ankhar's eighteenth winter, the gobs and hobgoblins of the Garnet Range held a great gathering during the week preceding the summer solstice. The site of the gathering was a town that had once been called Tin Cup, a formerly prosperous mining settlement of two score houses and a dozen larger buildings. Bonechisel's warriors had attacked Tin Cup the year before, slaughtering all the miners who had dared to remain. Since then, no human had visited the place.

Bonechisel held court in the upper floor of a stone mill-house. His tribemates were scattered through the houses of the town, while the clans and tribes of all the other gobs and hobs for two hundred miles around made camps in the surrounding valley and the many deep, dry mine shafts. Every night a huge bonfire raged in the village square, and the field and the narrow streets thronged with festive warriors and wenches. Alcohol flowed freely, a mixture of captured spirits brewed by human and dwarf and many vats of the vile, flat coal-beer brewed by goblin alchemists over the previous winter.

This was the year when Ankhar began to feel the pulse of the council, the dancing and the drumming and the sweat and the smell. By this time, of course, he was a well-recognized member of the tribe. By virtue of his blood parentage, he stood ten feet tall when he raised his head, a height that lifted him two or more feet above the largest of the hobgoblins in all the Garnet tribes. He was not a greedy soul, for he had not yet developed a taste for females or strong drink, and in these days there was plenty of food to go around, and he was often courted and feted at the campfires of all the lesser lords.

He was counseled in private by his foster mother. Laka spoke to him of many truths, truths that had been revealed to her by the Prince of Lies. Hearing these words, Ankhar began to see his own destiny and to think in terms of his own choices . . . his power.

Through these nights, Bonechisel watched his tribe's adopted son with increasingly narrowed eyes. A strapping hobgoblin, the aging chieftain was still no match for the young, lumbering Ankhar. The chieftain always wore a green medallion of stone formed from the first talisman of Hiddukel that his wife had discovered, and now he fondled that glowing disk, worrying. His simple mind perceived that the youth was a menace, and no doubt he regretted that he had not taken decisive action when his prospective rival had been but an infant. Now it was too late, at least for a direct confrontation.

Although he was not the most subtle of schemers, Bonechisel began to consider other ways to deal with the hulking hill giant whom most considered his adopted son. He whispered of his wishes to several lesser chieftain, suggesting that great rewards—money, liquor, gob-wenches—might come the way of one who removed the threat from his midst. The hob was not particular: poison, a knife in the back, assault by a bloodthirsty mob, all seemed workable solutions. Unfortunately, he found no takers for his schemes, not even among the most aggressive and ambitious of the sub-lords. Several even looked askance at Bonechisel when he ventured a few hints. More than one of these would-be schemers, it may be assumed, reported the chieftain's wishes to Laka or to Ankhar himself.

For his part the half-giant foster child was a good-hearted fellow, and avoided politics and other entanglements. He stayed out of Bonechisel's way out of long-established habit, remembering all too well many a bruising kick, slap, or bite that he had suffered during his younger years. Of late he noticed that the chieftain had ceased to harass him directly, though he saw the brooding glances and observed the surly attitude. Ankhar willingly accepted the hospitality of the other chieftains as he made the rounds of the vast encampment. So it was that he had become known to all of them by the the last night of the great council, when the solstice itself brightened the night. It happened to be a cloudless sky, and the silvery orb of Solinari commanded the heavens and the world.

The bonfire that night was the biggest in the memory of even the oldest gob granny. Trunks of whole pine trees were stacked into an enormous tepee, and when they were ignited the heat was such that the whole circle of watchers could not close to more than three dozen paces away from the base of the fire.

The throng of goblins, hobgoblins, and the odd ogre and draconian filled the valley, with many gathered on the hills that rose to either side of the former mining village. The moon bathed them all in pristine light, and the gobs were so thick on the ground that when they drummed and danced it seemed as though the whole landscape was thrumming with the power of the tribe.

Ankhar mingled with the throng, delighting in the drumming, raising his face and howling at the silver moon as loudly as any of the rest of them. He shook a spear over his head, a weapon he had carved himself from a straight sapling of elm. He had affixed a steel spearhead to the shaft, the hard metal treasure something that he had claimed from one of the villages overwhelmed by Bonechisel's band. Now his long arm and the even longer staff of wood raised that spearhead high above the rest of the pulsing throng, and the deep bellow emanating from the adolescent hill giant's chest roared as a steady, basso undertone to the shrill cries of several thousand drunken, frenzied warriors.

Bonechisel emerged from the front door of the large mill house. The hobgoblin was dressed in his ceremonial finest: a stiff shirt of dried bear-hide, with wide shoulder epaulets formed from the blades of captured short swords. His gleaming belt rattled with grisly trophies, a dozen human skulls that dangled from the golden links. His face was painted with white clay, except for circles of shining red around his eyes and his mouth—the crimson of fresh blood, stolen from a captive human child who had been sacrificed minutes before, simply to provide the bright facial paint. In each hand he carried a dagger with a curved blade, and he held these weapons over his head, edges crossed, and roared out a command:

"Hear me, my warriors!"

The chieftain scowled and clashed the blades of his two daggers together as the drumming continued, drowning out his words from all but the nearest of his listeners. These few ceased their dancing, facing Bonechisel in an expectant semicircle—though a few cast envious glances over their shoulders at their still reveling comrades. When the hobgoblin repeated his command, the crowd began to settle. Drums faltered, and more and more of the gobs turned their attention to their leader.

The firelight illuminated Bonechisel as he stood on a high stone porch, well above the crowd. A number of sub-chiefs crowded upon the steps leading up to the platform, jostling to be closest to the exalted one.

Finally the last of the drumming faded away, and the revelry settled to a few isolated whoops, cries, and howls. Ankhar was one of the last to settle down, so that the lofting of his spear and his deep, ululating cry stood out. Bonechisel scowled at his tribe's adopted son until even Ankhar quieted resentfully.

"My hobs and gobs!" Bonechisel roared. "I have brought you here, a great horde of warriors, and now I will tell you my plans!"

It was at that moment that the impulse came to Ankhar, and he acted without further thought. Later he would wonder if the question he had dared to ask had been inspired by Hiddukel himself.

"Why do you stay in the big house—and we sleep out here, in the rain?" Ankhar roared in a deep bellow, more commanding than any hobgoblin voice.

Bonechisel blinked in surprise and groped for a train of thought. "It has not rained all week!" he protested lamely. The crowd of gobs began to mutter among themselves, some glowering at the young giant, others echoing the question indignantly.

"We should all share the big house," retorted Ankhar, sensing the majority of the crowd was rumbling in agreement with him. Some instinct caused him to repeat the offending phrase. "The big house!"

"Big house! Big house!" The chant began as a wild whoop by some of the drunken young gobs near Ankhar, but in seconds it spread through the gathering, rising as a chorus, echoing from the surrounding hills.

"Stop!" cried Bonechisel, momentarily taken aback, holding up his hands. The crowd ignored him.

"You—Notch—you stop them!" barked the chieftain, whacking one of his under-chiefs on the side of the head—forgetting that he was still holding the curve-bladed knife.

The stricken Notch recoiled with a howl, clasping a hand to his bleeding ear. The next moment he snarled, lashing out at Bonechisel, who lifted his daggers and tried to step back. The group on the porch behind him, however, blocked his exit.

"Big house!" roared Ankhar again, relishing the squabble. The crowd surged forward, goblins on all sides pressing close, ignoring the hapless few who fell to be trampled underfoot.

The goblins behind Bonechisel were in no mood to expose themselves to Notch's fury. They pushed back, and the chieftain wobbled precariously at the lip of the porch. The bleeding sub-captain grappled with him while other lieutenants hooted and howled in amusement.

The pair fell together, vanishing into the mass on the wide stone steps. Ankhar could see only a thrashing, chaotic melee, and he pressed forward for a better look. The crowd parted almost magically before him, and he reached the base of the steps. Notch lay dead, bleeding from several deep cuts, but Bonechisel had not escaped the tumble unscathed. To judge from the bloody punctures in his legs and sides, several of his trusted lieutenants must have taken stabs at him as he rolled past them. He gasped, spitting furiously, as he looked up to see the hill giant looming over him.

Ankhar, in later years, could never reconstruct what impulse caused him to act in this fashion—but undoubtedly it had to do with the years of abuse, the vicious cruelty and bullying of his hated master. The giant abruptly brought his spear down, the steel head punching through the stiff bearskin of the hobgoblin's breastplate, through the body underneath, and into the hard ground. There it stuck, the elm shaft rising up like a flagpole, quivering from the force of the lethal blow.

For a long moment—two or three heartbeats, at least—Ankhar gaped at the dying chieftain. The crowed seemed to share his reaction, as many edged back and a murmured gasp ran through the mass, spreading outward like ripples through still water.

"Bonechisel is dead!" croaked one subchief, looking not at the slain hobgoblin but at the giant who stood like a statue over the bleeding corpse.

"Ankhar killed him!" cried another, in a tone of triumph. "Hail Ankhar!"

"Ankhar! Ankhar!" The chant started with those on the steps of the mill-house, but quickly spread through the square, down the narrow streets, through the throngs on the surrounding hillsides.

"Ankhar! Ankhar!"

Time had stopped, and now it started to move again for the half-giant. He felt liberated and empowered—two sensations wonderful and unfamiliar. He looked through the crowd, trying to spot his mother, but Laka was invisible among the sea of faces.

Slowly, with a hesitation that might be mistaken for diginity and deliberation, Ankhar reached out to grasp the stout spear shaft. He flexed his powerful mucles and drew the shaft free, lifting Bonechisel's body off the ground until he shook the weapon and the corpse dropped free.

The head of the spear was glowing, and the giant raised it curiously. He had inadvertently split the talisman of Hiddukel that the hobgoblin had worn over his heart. The vial had spilled forth its contents, an oily liquid that now slicked over the sharp, double-edged bit of his spearhead. The hard steel glowed with an emerald light that made it look as though the forged metal had just been pulled, cherry-hot, from the smith's furnace.

Wonderingly, the half-giant raised the weapon to his face, touching the sharp edge with his fingers. It was cool to the touch.

"He is the favored one of the Prince of Lies!" cried Laka. The old shaman came beside him now, shaking a rattle made from the skull of a human. "See how the god favors him with the Emerald Fire! It is the Truth! Ankhar is the Truth!"

Ankhar raised the spear over his head and relished the cheer that erupted, spontaneously from ten thousand bloodthirsty throats. Holding the weapon by the base of the shaft, he extended the glowing head high into the air, where it seemed to spark and shine with light brighter even than the full, silver moon.

CHAPTER SEVEN

CITY KNIGHTS

Y ou sure you want to do this?" Dram Feldspar asked. The dwarf was slouched in the saddle, his mare stolidly plodding along the road beside the warrior's gelding. The Garnet Mountains and the city of the same name were by now several days behind them.

The two riders were sunburned and dusty after crossing the dry plain. The previous day, the road had spanned a wide river on a splendid bridge, and here Dram had suggested they stop for a leisurely soaking, maybe an early camp. The warrior had looked across at a gaunt, burned-out structure on a bluff, a former manor house now in utter ruins, and insisted they keep going.

Now the outline of a lofty city was looming before them. A high wall of stone ramparts marked the end of the plains less than a mile away. Beyond that wall rose the houses and shops, the towers and forts, the docks and smithies, and the Gnome Ghetto of Caergoth. The great gray bulk of Castle Caergoth towered over the whole, ramparts and towers gleaming in the morning sun.

"Yes," the warrior replied, after a very long pause. "I'm sure."

Nodding and shrugging, the dwarf closed his mouth and rode along in silence—though not for long. His face brightened in inspiration.

71

"We don't both have to go into Caergoth after all—I can enter the city, and find the gnome, and bring him out to you. We can meet you in one of these little plains villages along here where no one is likely to recognize you."

"I'm going into the city, I said. Are you going to talk about it all day, or are you coming with me?"

The high wall, with its fortified gate—closed, and guarded by a full dozen Knights of Solamnia, all wearing the emblem of the Rose—stood less than half a mile away. The dwarf scowled and glowered, finally grunting his reply. "I go where you go."

They allowed their horses to amble up to the gate. The two riders tried to look inconspicuous. Though each wore a knife at his belt, their other weapons were wrapped tightly among the bundles of gear strapped behind the saddles of each of their horses.

The dwarf's eyes nervously flicked over to his companion—then adopted an air of nonchalance as they reined in before the two armored guards, who raised their halberds to block the roadway.

"State your names and your business in Caergoth," declared one of the guards. The rest of the company watched idly from the shade against the base of the lofty wall, though several men had their crossbows cocked, the deadly weapons resting casually across their knees.

"My name's Jahn Brackett," said Dram, with an easy grin. "This here's my old pal, Waler Sanction-son."

The knight scrutinized the dwarf, after a quick glance at the warrior who slouched silently in his saddle. "You're Kaolyn, aren't you?"

The dwarf nodded with a pleased smile. "Right from the heart of the Garnet Range. Always have been, always will be."

"And a Sanction-son, eh?" Coming around the head of Dram's horse, the knight looked up at Waler. "You, you're a long way from home. How're things in Sanction these days?"

The warrior shrugged. "I haven't been there for years. Still burning, last I heard."

The knight laughed at that. "Still burning! I like that—hey, fellows. This guy says that Sanction is still burning!"

Several of the other knights chuckled. "Good thing them volcanoes haven't gone out—what would they do for heat?" offered one.

"So, you two make an odd couple, to say the least," said the sentry. "Dwarves keep to dwarves and men keep to men is what I usually see. State your business in Caergoth."

"Looking for work," Dram said. "The city under the mountains is nice, but I've taken a liking to sunshine and good, steel coin. We hear the city docks are busy, figure someone can use two more strong backs for loading and unloading all these ships people are talking about."

The knight nodded approvingly. "You heard right, but you need to know about the duke's edict: There is no carrying of long blades or throwing weapons on the city streets. Violation will cost you the weapon and might mean a turn in the city dungeon."

"These little pig-stickers are all right, aren't they?" asked the dwarf innocently, gesturing to the knives he and Waler wore at their belts, the warrior pulling his cape to the side so that the guard could inspect the weapon.

"No problem with those," the sentry acknowledged. He turned and waved to someone up on the wall. A few seconds later the massive gate started to swing outward. "Good luck to you both, then—you'll find plenty of work on the docks. Just follow this main road right through town. It will take you down the bluff and right to the waterfront."

"Thank you kindly, Sir Knight!" Dram said with a bow and a flourish. His companion merely nodded and, with the gate partially open, the two riders led their horses into Caergoth.

The street was bustling with foot traffic—mostly human, though a few dwarves were swaggering about, and a whole gaggle of kender were playing some kind of game in an empty lot between two storefronts. There were only a few riders, all of them knights, visible above the heads of the pedestrians.

Here and there a freight wagon or oxcart nudged through the crowd.

A hundred paces from the gate the two riders came to a large livery stable, and here they turned into the yard. They arranged to have their horses fed and tended—a steel piece for each animal insured care for the next seven days. They rummaged through their saddlebags to remove a few items. They left bedrolls, cooking gear, and heavy clothing behind, but took their coinpurses, a spare cloak for each, and a selection of weapons.

The long-bladed knives they wore at their belts. Reluctantly Dram wrapped his battle-axe in a bedroll and left it with his saddlebag. The warrior took his long sword and wrapped the whole thing, scabbard to hilt, in a blanket. He lashed the bundle to his back as inconspicuously as possible. He wouldn't be able to sit down without unstrapping the sword, but it would serve. His twin crossbows he fastened again to his belt, relying on the long drape of his cape to conceal the contraband weapons.

"We'd better not run into any knights," said Dram, as they emerged onto the sunny street again.

"Won't encounter too many of 'em in the gnome ghetto. Here, this way."

The swordsman led his dwarven companion along a winding series of side streets, avoiding the main avenues and, surprisingly enough, making better time than they would have on the more crowded main streets.The gnome ghetto was located in the lower quarter of Caergoth, where the ancient city clung to the banks of the Garnet River. The streets were unpaved there, and recent rains had turned them into a morass of slick mud, deep ruts, and overflowing gutters. The human warrior said they should seek lodging near the squalid gnome neighborhood but not within, and Dram was more than content to go along with this plan.

"The places around the square or below the fortress will be all packed to the rafters with knights," the man explained.

"We won't be here very long, will we?" Dram asked hopefully.

The warrior smiled sardonically. "Are we ever any place for

very long? C'mon, let's go find this Brillissander Firesplasher."

"What if Cornellus was telling the truth, and Firesplasher is dead?"

"Fine by me, but then I'd like to find out exactly *how* he died."

An ashen haze blanketed the horizon as the sun dropped behind the city wall, casting not so much distinct shadows as a spreading murk that seemed to darken under the eaves of the great buildings, and to shroud the narrow alleys and walkways between the wooden buildings that made up the greater part of the city.

Even along the main avenue there remained evidence of war. The Dark Knights had taken the city during the War of Souls, and the Solamnics had recaptured it several months later. The edifice of a great marble building, which the man knew had been the meeting hall of the city's neophyte parliament in decades past, was gashed and cracked by dragon breath. Several huge columns lay where they had toppled, and weeds sprouted through cracks in the wide steps.

In the lower part of town, they passed a whole block that had burned to ashes during the battle. The blackened shells of several large inns and houses remained like gravestones, jutting from a dark expanse of crumbled stone, charred timber, and debris.

But most of the city was thriving.

They finally secured rooms at a bustling travelers' inn close to the waterfront. The landlord charged exorbitant prices but pledged easy access to the duke's palace, the great market-place, the silver and stoneworkers' districts, even the riverside stockyards that—the proprietor was quick to point out—were generally downwind of the inn, and may all the gods curse the unseasonal breeze that was currently filling the city air with the odiferous perfume of those vast, muddy corrals!

"Keep in mind, Honored Travelers," finished the fellow, a rat-faced little man who leaned uncomfortably close to them and spewed bad breath as he talked. "If there be anything else ye be wishing for, such as entertainment of the female persuasion, ye just be letting me know." He winked at Dram. "We can even fix ye up with a little dwarf-maid, if that be yer natural preference."

"I'll keep that in mind," Dram allowed, turning and hastening after the warrior, who was already crossing the crowded common room. They took the stairs to their rented room and found it to be reasonably private, with a shutter over the single window in a small parlor, which adjoined two windowless bedrooms.

After taking turns in a hot bath, the travelers shared a meal of beef stew and crusty bread. The human washed his down with a bottle of vinegar-tinged wine, while Dram drank three large bottles of ale. Finally, the pair lit the lantern in the parlor and laid the shard of marble on the sturdy, rough-hewn table.

The letters, BRILLISS, were clearly inscribed in one corner of the shard, and the stone had been broken in such a way as to suggest that the word had continued on the missing surface.

"Brillissander Firesplasher. That's the name Cornellus gave us," the swordsman said.

"Yep. That was it. Should we get started looking for him?"

"Don't see that we have any other option."

"We could wait until morning," Dram said wearily.

His companion shook his head. "If we head out in an hour or two, we'll stand a better chance of a lot of the gnomes being asleep. I prefer to take my gnomes—and my kender and gully dwarves, for that matter—by surprise, whenever possible."

The dwarf took a small lantern along as they departed the inn, and this proved wise, as the few burning streetlights in this part of Caergoth were confined to the wide avenues around the palace and treasury. As soon as they started down the narrow lanes leading toward the riverbank they found themselves surrounded by darkness.

Dram touched a match to his lamp and held it so that they could avoid the overturned barrels, sleeping drunks—human, invariably—and other refuse that seemed to be scattered haphazardly in the muddy, winding way. They passed an inn that was raucous with the sounds of fiddle music and loud conversation.

The doors burst open and a big man staggered out. He glared at the two, his eyes small and bloodshot in the midst of a flowing black beard and a mass of dark hair. With a belligerent sneer he raised his fists until, a moment later, his eyes glassed over and he collapsed, facedown, on the ground.

"Nice place," muttered the dwarf, carefully stepping around the fellow. "Let's keep it in mind for a drink afterward."

The dwarf's companion wasn't listening. Instead, he was trying to remember his way around this part of the city.

"Down here," he decided at the next intersection. For two blocks they walked close to the battered facades of two-story wooden houses, on streets that were slippery with mud and worse.

The road began to change. The mud became clean, white stones. The wetness vanished through grates. Several buildings here were made of stone, with rows of windows reaching three or four stories. Some doorways were tall enough for a man, but many were barely four feet high, with eaves hanging so low that the tall warrior would have to duck his head just to stand next to the house.

"If this is a ghetto, I like it better than the neighborhood we're staying in," the dwarf said sourly.

Lanterns bobbed here and there as individuals, mostly gnomes, bustled back and forth along the well-kept road. The warrior stepped in front of one of the lantern-carrying gnomes, a youngish-looking male with a short beard and a distracted expression. He was busy talking to himself, an earnest discussion in which he sounded as if he was trying very vigorously to press his point of view.

"Excuse me," said the warrior.

"What?" asked the gnome, blinking in confusion. "You are most certainly excused. But . . . do I know you?"

"No—I'm a stranger here," the warrior said patiently. "I'm hoping you'll help me with some directions."

"Directions?" The little fellow scratched his head. "Not my specialty, directions. What are you looking for around here?"

"Who, not what. I'm looking for a gnome named Brillissander Firesplasher, or anyone who might know something about him."

The gnome's eyes went wide. "Oh! Oh. Do you mean *the* Brillissander Firesplasher?" he asked in a tone of awe.

"I think so," the dwarf confirmed.

"Never heard of him."

With that, the earnest pedestrian was off, muttering to himself once again.

CHAPTER EIGHT

A GREAT HALL AND
A DUNGEON

The welcoming banquet was a great success, despite the absence of the dukes of Thelgaard and Solanthus. Patriarch Issel began the occasion with an overlong invocation but spoke many beautiful words in praise of the Lord Regent in Palanthas. Duke Crawford also made a splendid speech, and Lady Selinda and the duchess, Lady Martha, got a little tipsy on the bubbly wine.

"I remember Palanthas," the duchess said dreamily. "Such a beautiful city. Not like Caergoth, all walls and towers and forts."

"I suppose any place can get tiresome," Selinda replied, thinking of her private delight at getting out of her own city.

"That Golden Spire!" Martha said. "It was breathtaking! Is it true that it's your father's gold up in that tower that makes it glow like that?"

"Oh, yes. He wanted it displayed so the people could see it as a measure of our prosperity," the princess explained. "Of course, he's the only one with a key to the room!"

"Nobody ever tries to steal it?" the duchess inquired, sipping more wine.

"They couldn't possibly," Selinda replied. "Lady Coryn, the white wizard, has placed spells of protection around the tower.

No one can remove so much as a speck of the gold—not even another wizard—without my father's permission."

"They say the Duke of Solanthus is very rich, too," Martha noted, a little blearily. "Not gold, in his case."

"Yes, he has control of the Stones of Garnet," Selinda explained. "They are gems the merchants of Solanthus have gained in trade from the dwarves over more than a thousand years. Each to their own, I say, but my father prefers his riches in gold."

A little later, the hostess leaned over and whispered rather wickedly to Selinda that the dinner owed some of its success to the fact that the two argumentative lords of Solanthus and Thelgaard were absent.

"They are certainly late arriving. I do hope that nothing is seriously wrong," the princess replied. "I am looking forward to speaking with both of them."

"Be careful what you wish for," the duchess said, swallowing half of her glass of wine in one gulp. She held out the vessel for a passing steward to refill. "The fact is, I wouldn't trust either one o' them." Lady Martha blinked, as if surprised at what she had just said.

To Selinda's left, the duke was arguing loudly with one of his nobles over the manner of some criminal's execution. The duke had paid little attention to the princess after they were seated, which had given her a chance to get to know her hostess.

Now Selinda leaned over, delighted with the duchess's frankness. "Tell me more! I barely remember them. The Duke of Thelgaard . . . a big bear of a man? The Lord of the Crown . . . ?"

Frowning in concentration, Lady Martha nodded. "Yes, big Lord Jarrod. Don't let him hug you. He'll crack your ribs."

"Hug! Oh, my." Selinda was a little taken aback.

"Only after he drinks too much. He's polite enough 'til then, but he drinks every day. All day. Starts when he gets up in the morning."

"I will keep that in mind," said the princess. "Perhaps,

therefore, we should schedule the most important conferences for early in the day."

"Drinking makes him grumpy," Martha admitted, "but then, so does everything else. Not that he doesn't have a few good excuses, you know."

"For being in a bad mood?"

"Yes. After all, Rathskell in Solanthus has got all the money. That's what they say. My own Crawfish—" She gasped in mock astonishment and clapped a hand over her mouth with a glance at her husband. The duke was still engaged in his conversation, and hadn't heard his wife's use of the detested nickname. "He has this great big army. While Thelgaard is so very poor."

"What about Solanthus? You haven't said very much about him so far. Does he drink a lot, too?" Selinda wondered.

"The Duke of Solanthus," the duchess began, enunciating her words with great care, "is a scoundrel and a cad. It is whispered"—her voice dropped to a breathy whisper—"that he might even be a murderer!"

"No!" gasped Selinda. She took a small sip of her own wine. It was a southern vintage, sweeter and little more fruity than she was used to. Although she liked it very much, she made sure to drink less than her hostess. "Tell me, who is he supposed to have killed?"

"Well, the duchess, his wife—his *young* wife—was once married to a lord, subject of the duke himself. That lord perished mysteriously on a hunt in the foothills of the Garnet Mountains, a hunt where it just so happens that the duke himself was leading the riders. Of course, the duke made a great display of grief and spoke high honors about the dead man. Very convincing. Less than a year later, he took the beautiful widow as his wife."

"I should think the scandal would have cost him dearly," Selinda remarked disapprovingly.

"Well, you don't know Solanthus," Martha declared. "He took over there two years after the War of Souls. He's about as rich as the Lord Regent himself—oh, excuse me. Your papa, I mean. But Rathskell has made sure that, if you don't like the way he is doing things, you don't stay around."

"You mean, he has killed other people?"

Martha shook her head. "No, but they find reason to leave. Many of 'em left, the ones who didn't approve of his rule. Lord Lorimar was their leader—good man, Lord Lorimar," she noted sadly.

"Yes. I always admired the way he rode horseback through the streets, not like the other lords in their fancy carriages and buggies. He was very handsome, dignified. He looked you right in the eyes when he talked to you. His daughter Dara and I were friends—though she was a little older than me. Such a terrible tragedy, their deaths. And the assassin still at large!"

"That assassin—oh, he's slippery as a ghost," Martha said. "Everybody looks and looks for him. He hasn't been heard of for a time now. It's as though he's disappeared from the world!"

Selinda suppressed a shudder. Dara Lorimar had been a good-hearted, vivacious young woman. When the news of her and her father's death had reached Palanthas, the lord regent had been enraged that one of his most loyal lords had been cruelly slain. Selinda had grieved over the death of a friend.

"My father has offered a thousand steel crowns as reward!" the princess murmured.

"Whoever brings him to justice will earn their reward," Martha said, clearly a little bleary from the wine. "He's a bad one."

"My dear," the duke said sternly. He had risen, unnoticed, from his seat and was now leaning over his wife's shoulder. "I need you to come with me."

"Oh," Martha replied. She blinked her watery eyes. "I'll see you tomorrow," she said to the princess, before rising unsteadily.

"Surely you're not leaving the banquet?" Selinda objected in dismay, but Martha was ushered away, the duke holding her hand until he could pass her to the sturdy arms of several of the Ducal Guard. He returned to the table, shaking his head.

"She's a wonderful woman," he said, whispering to the princess as he took his seat, "but she always has trouble with strong wines."

"She is a delightful hostess!" insisted the guest of honor, but the duke didn't seem to be listening anymore.

Instead, he rose to his feet.

"And now . . ." the Duke of Caergoth declared, speaking over the babble of the diners, "it is my great privilege to offer a toast to our most charming, and beautiful, visitor."

The room fell reasonably silent, though Selinda couldn't help noticing that there was more talking, whispering, laughing than there would have been at a Palanthian gathering.

"We are graced by a lady whose elegance, charm, and wit can mean only great auguries for the upcoming conference of Solamnic lords. Indeed, it is my fervent prayer that her wise counsel in these talks will open the way toward a new era of peace and cooperation among the lords of the three orders.

"We stand at a crossroads now . . . an opportunity when the future beckons as never before. The Evil Ones glimmer from the shadows. The dark shadows. We of Solamnia, we bring light into those shadows. We cast that light of truth, of justice, of the Oath and the Measure into the darkest of lightless shadows. The Evil Ones can only cower as we hold true to our just and righteous course.

"This lady who is our guest, well, she is the very embodiment of that torch, that righteous light. In the name of her father, our own Lord Regent Du Chagne—who has almost single-handedly brought that light into Palanthas and helped to spread it across all the plains—we salute her and ourselves!"

The duke raised his wine glass with his right hand. "Through the dark years since the War of Souls we have struggled and strived to bring civilization back to these long-suffering lands. We of the Rose, here in Caergoth—together with the worthy nobles of the Sword in Thelgaard and of the Crown in Solanthus—ever do we look toward the great city in the north for leadership, for guidance, for good counsel. Palanthas! Aye,

Palanthas, the noble keystone in the centuries-old arch that is Solamnia. No place has stood against evil, has stood as a beacon of righteousness, more than have the great nations of Solamnia.

"To the great city of Palanthas, to the noble Lord Regent of that great city, and to his most gracious daughter who is here with us tonight: let us cry thrice hail, and drink a toast to the glory, the wisdom, and the long-standing might of Palanthas!"

"Hail! Hail, hail!"

The cry rocked the great hall, so forceful that Selinda was taken aback. It was dizzying to think that all of these people put such faith in herself and her house. Nevertheless, she stood swiftly and gracefully, very glad that she had been careful with the wine.

"My most kind and hospitable host, I thank you," she declared. "On behalf of my father, in the legacy of the Council of Whitestone, and with all our prayers for the future, I most humbly aspire to prove worthy of the many flatteries you have offered."

Selinda lifted her glass and all those present did the same, goblets clinking around the room. They all drank, and the great hall filled with cheers.

Sitting down again, the princess was amazed and delighted as a procession of servants flowed through the massive doors from the kitchen. She had been been to many banquets in Palanthas where the fare had consisted of dainty roasted fowls, or slices of ham graced with apples and plums, or bits of fish arranged fashionably on golden platters. That was not the Caergoth way: Here they brought out whole pigs roasted, and set upon massive platters carried by two burly men. Milk was poured from massive, ice-encrusted jugs, and those who wanted ale simply wandered over to one of several kegs set up in various parts of the great hall.

Selinda ate more than she ever had a single sitting before, and washed it down with the southern ale that, she decided, was smoother and less presumptuous than its Palanthian cousin.

The duke seemed to come alive as the evening progressed, chatting with Selinda about the glories of his realm, most of which seemed to center around the city's position as a natural seaport.

"Of course, we have problems, too," he admitted at one point. "The goblin crisis here isn't what it is in Thelgaard and Solanthus, closer to the Garnet Mountains, but we do find the wretches skulking about now and then. I have a prime specimen locked up in my dungeon right now!"

"Really!" said Selinda. "We never see any goblins in Palanthas!"

"Well, one day I hope to say the same thing about Caergoth," the duke professed. "My man here, Captain Reynaud, captured this one in the Garnet Mountains and brought him here for interrogation."

"Really?"

The princess leaned forward, out of the corner of her eye regarding the knight with whom the duke had earlier been arguing. The knight was a man with slick black hair and a long mustache that curled into twin prongs, like the horns of a steer. Now the man cocked an ear, hearing them and assuming a humble expression.

He waved a hand dismissively. "It was nothing, really. We had to kill a few of his comrades. They were pickets, on the ridge around a huge clan of the beggars. We chained him up and brought him back here, quick as you like." Reynaud spoke as though it were a simple business, but the princess noticed the hard edge in his eye and perceived a stern, even cruel set to his thin lips.

"I think it's really quite a thrilling story," the princess said. "Do you suppose I could see the creature? Perhaps take a tour of your dungeon?"

"Absolutely not! Out of the question!" She was surprised to have her question answered not by the duke but by a knight who had stood behind the lord during the entire meal. He was the same warrior, Sir Marckus Haum, who had met her at the docks.

85

"I beg your pardon," she said archly. "I was speaking to the duke!"

"Yes, Sir Marckus—she was talking to me!" added that worthy noble.

"Begging your Excellency's pardon, but the very idea of taking the lady into them stinking dungeons is loopy. No disrespect intended, my lady, but it's dangerous activity. The blighters will as soon bite and scratch you as glance at you. They'd spit upon you if you so much as showed your face down there!"

"I'm not worried about a little spit," Selinda retorted. Perhaps it was the ale, but she felt surprisingly indignant and more than willing to speak her mind. "I do so much want to see a goblin!"

"The risks are simply too great. Why, if your father was to hear—"

"My father is not here!" the princess responded. "Even more to the point, my father sent me here with the authority to speak his will. It is in his voice that I demand—" She paused, smiled sweetly at the duke, who was staring at her wide-eyed. "I respectfully request that your Excellency provide me with a tour of your dungeon, during which I may lay eyes upon a captured goblin or two. I shall count upon the diligence of your knights to protect safety of my person." She turned her beguiling smile upon Sir Marckus and watched the flush creep slowly across his face.

⊱⊰⊱⊰⊱⊰⊱⊰❁⊱⊰⊱⊰⊱⊰⊱

Ankhar relished his first night as leader of the great horde. He stayed in the Big House as, in fact, it rained hard on the thousands of gathered hobs and gobs. Naturally, there was insufficient space for more than a fraction of them inside the building, but they didn't seem to mind. Instead, they drank, danced, and cavorted around the great fire all through the dismal night.

It wasn't until later the next day that Laka came to see her adopted son, finding him awake and hungry—and scattering the dozen or so young gob wenches who had clamored to provide the new chieftain with whatever nourishment he needed through the night.

So tired and sore was Ankhar that he didn't even object to his mother's harangue.

"What you do with all these gobs and hobs?" she asked him, shaking the skull-totem so the pebbles inside the bony talisman rattled and hissed. "You got army here. You gotta lead them."

"Lead them where?" wondered the half-giant. He recalled Bonechisel's numerous campaigns, all of them bloody but none of them particularly momentous. "To go kill more hobs and gobs?"

Laka shook her rattle meaningfully. The black eyes gaped empty, but chiding.

"No. Go kill dwarves?"

The half-giant realized that idea made no sense. The dwarves lived in fortified cities under the ground. There was no effective way to attack them. Nor was there any reason, save a lust for the treasures that were reputedly locked away in the vaults of Kaolyn.

"No, humans. With this many gobs, we kill *lots* of humans. Maybe even a whole city."

With those words, the eyes of the skull-rattle glowed bright green, and the fleshless lips seemed to curve into an approving grin. Laka shook the rattle again, and the half-giant was more than a little impressed as words, delivered in a croaking rasp, emerged from between those bony jaws.

"Truth is in your soul,
"Justice in your blade.
"Blood is battle's toll,
"A savage empire made!"

Ankhar nodded. A savage empire made . . .

Now *that* was a Truth worth fighting for.

✕◦◑◦◑◦◑◦◐●◑◦◑◦◑◦◑◦✕

"You must do exactly as I say," huffed Sir Marckus.

"Now, now, Marckus," reassured the duke, "this is a recreational outing, not a military campaign."

"I still say, bring the creature out here and let her see it. She doesn't need to go *in* there."

"Nonsense!" replied Selinda. "The risks of an escape are much greater if you bring it outside. No, I am quite prepared to go in there to see this creature. I am not afraid."

"Then with all respect, Excellency and your highness, do consider: We are dealing with a treacherous and implacable foe. He will do anything to get hold of an example of human womanhood—begging the lady's pardon."

Sir Marckus was accompanied by a dozen sturdy knights, all more than six feet tall, broad shouldered and solidly built. Each wore a supple leather tunic that gave him good freedom of movement yet still provided protection to the torso and groin. Instead of their usual lances and great battle swords they wore short swords that looked more like overgrown knives than true swords.

Selinda was glad, thinking about it, that Captain Powell had gone back to the ships to tend to matters. He would have been every bit as stiff and protective as Sir Marckus, and she certainly didn't need two such officers clucking over her like mother hens.

"First cells won't be too bad," the knight of the Rose explained as they crossed the castle courtyard into a dark, muddy passageway between two high walls. A lone door with a swordsman standing guard stood at the end of the way. The guard saluted and opened the door as Marckus approached. "These'll be scum from the city, thieves and the like. Worthless wretches, but some of them have a chance to be paroled, so they'll be on their best behavior as we pass through."

They went through a small room with another guard, and this one unlocked the door carefully. Marckus and several of his men took torches from a rack on the wall. With the brand held high, the captain preceded the party through the second door. There was a row of cells to each side. They were tiny cages, with iron bars and a single, small door forming the front wall of each.

"Aye, Cap'n—how's the gout?" shouted a one-eyed scarecrow of a man in the first cell. "Yer lookin' fit, aye you are."

"And the lovely missus?" croaked another fellow, lurching upward from a filthy straw pallet. He came to the bars of his cell and extended an imploring hand. "You give her that bauble o' mine, I trust? I tol' ya, give it to the missus!"

"Sorry, Barthon," answered Marckus, and Selinda was surprised that he did seem genuinely regretful. "That would be against regulations. Recovered booty is to be returned to the rightful owner or turned over to the garrison's purser for recording."

"Ah, too bad." Barthon slumped in his cell, the picture of dejection. "It woulda looked nice an' sparkly on her wrist, I tell you," he said, shaking his head slowly.

The men in the other cells were not as talkative, watching the procession with a measure of apprehension or, here and there, undisguised hatred in their eyes. True to Marckus' prediction, none of them made any sound or gesture to harass them. At the end of the long, dark row of cells, the knight captain held his torch high. This batch of cells was guarded by a pair of men-at-arms. They were long armed, low-browed ruffians, so far as Selinda could tell—they looked nothing like any of the Knights of Solamnia she had known all her life. They gave a martial salute as Marckus approached. At his command, one of them opened the door while the other stood back, his sword at the ready.

"These here are a bit of a rougher crowd, my lady," the captain explained. "Rapists and murderers, mostly. More likely to feel a rope around their worthless necks than ever to breathe the free air again. I urge you to reconsider your sight-seeing."

"Nonsense," Selinda replied. "I am not afraid. Lead on, good captain."

The ranks of knights pressed annoyingly close to either side of Selina, until she elbowed one in the ribs—it hurt her elbow more than it did his leather-shielded belly—and he backed off enough that she could see smaller, dingier cages with walls of dark, wet stone.

One scowling, black-bearded fellow lurched to his feet and lunged at the door, reaching a paw of a hand through the bars, trying to strike one of the knights. The warrior was ready, rapping the prisoner's fingers with the hilt of his sword, and with a yelp the wretch pulled his fist back and shrank away. On the other side a weasel-faced fellow mumbled and cried, clutching his arms around his frail chest, rocking back and forth.

Selinda was relieved when they reached the end of this passage. The last few cells were empty, and she pressed forward with the guards, waiting as Marckus took out a large key and unlocked a portal, which, unlike the others, was made of solid iron. "Now, watch your step, my lady," said the knight captain. "We'll be going down some stairs that get kind of slippery, and down at the bottom there'll be mud and slime and nasty stuff underfoot."

"Thank you for the suggestion that I wear my boots," the princess replied. She felt a shiver of excitement as they started down the dingy stairway. Sir Marckus held his torch before him, revealing slimy, uneven slabs of limestone descending down a narrow, stone-walled shaft. Water thick with ooze trickled from step to step, gurgling toward the dark, unseen bottom.

Smoke from the torch rose along the low ceiling, stinging Selinda's eyes. She coughed and ducked her head. For the first time she wondered about the wisdom of her request, but she would not humiliate herself by changing her mind, even as Sir Marckus stopped near the bottom of the stairs and turned to regard her.

"You sure you want to go on?" he asked.

She nodded resolutely. Her foot splashed down in a puddle, and she reached out a hand to brace herself on the slippery surface. The stone of the wall was slick, mossy, and cold. Grimacing, the Princess of Palanthas continued into the dungeon.

Now there were solid doors to each side, iron doors with massive locks and narrow slots that presumably allowed the passage of food and drink. Something moved at one of those hatches, and she clasped a hand to her mouth at the sight of taloned fingers, long and flexible and tipped with curving, sharp claws, reaching out. A knight hacked down with his short sword, slicing off one of the digits before the hand disappeared. Selinda heard a deep-chested growl that made her think of a very large dog, and something banged hard into the door. The iron slab rattled in its frame, the thumping echo suddenly amplified by a piercing shriek.

"He'll remember us, that one," said the knight with the bloody sword. Despite his brash words, his tone was uneasy, and he cast a wary glance at the door as the procession came to a halt.

Selinda was about to remind the captain that she wanted to *see* a goblin when he pulled out a large key and handed it to one of his men. The fellow unlocked the metal door, pulling it back with a creak of rusty hinges to reveal a barrier of close-set iron bars.

"There's the goblin. Look all you want," said Sir Marckus. "Don't get close."

The princess stepped forward, as the captain raised his torch. Her first reaction was: What's all the fuss about?

The goblin looked wretched, pathetic, grotesque . . . but utterly harmless. It stared up at her with vacant eyes, dull even in the flaring torchlight as it squatted close to the bars. Its lower jaw hung slack, exposing the curl of a fleshy tongue. Its nostrils were wide-set, flaring outward and raised nearly flat against the low-browed skull. The goblin kept its arms wrapped around its skinny knees, clutching its bleeding hand. Glaring at her suddenly, it raised the wounded hand to suck on the stub of its severed finger.

She noticed a flare of green light in its hand, like a dull phosphorescence, and asked about the source of it.

"Ah, they call them their godstones," one knight explained. "They worship Hiddukel, lots of these ugly ones do. That green chip can't do no harm, but they fight like banshees if you tries to take it away. Easiest just to let him have it."

"Does it always glow like that?" she asked.

"Glow? I don't see no glow. Do you, Hank?"

"No," replied another knight. "The dark plays some tricks, though."

The goblin stared at Selinda as it sucked on its finger, the stone close to its black lips. In a momentary gesture—she wondered if she imagined it—she thought she saw the goblin kiss the glowing green stone. She was sure that the stone was brighter than normal, illuminated by some internal source.

Then she saw the same light, in the goblin's eyes, and it penetrated her flesh, leaving her shivering. In that look was the Truth, and Selinda gasped.

She saw herself sailing north in her galleon, departing from Caergoth on a course for home. A storm, an unnatural brew of cosmic violence, came roaring in from the west, overwhelming the ships, smashing the sturdy hulls . . . drowning them all.

It was the Truth, somehow she knew.

If she sailed from here, she would die.

CHAPTER NINE

A DETOUR

Dawn found the dwarf and the warrior sitting on the low stone wall surrounding a fountain at the intersection of four narrow, twisting streets in the Gnome Ghetto. Apparently water had once flowed from the mouth of the chubby-cheeked cherub, immortalized in bronze, who balanced on one toe in the middle of the shallow bowl. The fountain and the bowl were dry now. In fact, when Dram peered over the edge, he discovered a pair of gully dwarves curled up on the inside of the fountain, snoring loudly.

He raised his foot to thump them awake and shoo them off, then slumped onto the wall with a sigh without delivering a kick. "I guess if I don't bother them they won't bother me," the dwarf said, rubbing a gnarled hand over the back of his neck. "I just need to sit a spell and catch my breath."

Looking equally weary, the man sat beside him, nudging the blade of the concealed sword to the side so he could stretch out his long legs. They had only begun to work out the kinks when the dwarf elbowed his companion in the side. "Look—but don't look," he whispered hoarsely, indicating the narrow street to the left.

The man leaned back, from the corner of his eye catching a glimpse of two knights. Each wore the emblem of the Rose on

93

his breastplate. They sauntered side by side down the narrow way, forcing the few gnomes who were about at this early hour to scamper onto the curb or get knocked out of the way. In another dozen steps they would reach the little plaza with the fountain.

With elaborate casualness, the dwarf and the warrior rose to their feet and ambled up one of the side streets. The pair stepped into an alley, ran a short distance to a connecting alley, and ducked around the corner. They made their way through a maze of filthy hovels and twisting paths with scummy liquid puddles, finally emerging on another street—which wasn't much bigger or nicer than the alley.

"What do those Salamis have against you, anyway?" asked Dram, looking around to make sure the place was clear of knights.

The man shrugged. "It's not them, it's me. I can't stand the bastards. I see 'em, I just want to fight 'em."

"Why? Did one of them steal your girl? A couple of them beat you up in a bar? What is it? It's getting on my nerves, not knowing." The dwarf glared at his companion, but the warrior simply kept walking. With a strangled oath, Dram fell back into step, his face locked in a glower.

The narrow street took a sharp bend, and they found themselves at a small market—another wide intersection where, instead of a dry fountain, a half dozen shabby carts and tents occupied the central open space. Vendors hawked fish, eggs, and fruit. Judging from the stench, the fish and much of the produce had already passed the point of spoilage in better markets and had been brought here to the ghetto in a last attempt to unload it.

"Damn," cursed the dwarf in a husky whisper. They had already been noticed by a couple of knights among the several roaming the market, clad in leather armor, towering over the residents of the ghetto as they looked watchfully around.

"Hey, you two—what's your hurry?"

It was the same two knights from earlier, the ones they had

spent so much time trying to evade. One beckoned the pair while the other attracted the attention of the other knights in the little market. Within a few seconds, six armed men converged on them near a loosely pitched tent where a hunchbacked human was selling wrinkled, moldering apples.

"Why are you fellows so jumpy? What's that on your back—hey, are you carrying a sword?" demanded the accosting knight. His hand moved to the hilt of his own blade at his belt. "You must have been informed that goes against the duke's edict!"

Dram's eyes were wide. "Gosh, not the duke!" he said innocently.

The dwarf spun around and started to run. The warrior reached out, seized one corner of the hunchback's shabby tent in his hand, and jerked it hard. The billow of canvas came free, enveloping the advancing knights, blocking those following. The vendor screeched venomously and came after the warrior with a club, but he was gone, racing after the dwarf.

Oaths mingled with inarticulate shouts as the Solamnics stumbled and tore their way through the entanglement. Dram and his companion sprinted around the corner of the narrow lane, splashing through the scummy puddles, leaping over crates, rubble, and drunken gully dwarves. The knights could be heard shouting directions. A trumpet blared, and more shouts converged from all sides as numerous small patrols in the ghetto rallied to the sound.

Closely pursued, the two fugitives ran down one street, only to be met by several knights charging toward them. They turned in another direction, shouts and alarms sounding behind them.

"In here!" exclaimed the dwarf, skidding to a halt, tugging on the warrior's arm. Dram ducked under an overhanging section of wall. With a grimace, the warrior bent and followed, grunting as the pommel of his great sword—still wrapped and strapped to his back—caught on a timber. He and the dwarf emerged in another tight alley

Moments later they found themselves in a small courtyard,

enclosed by ramshackle buildings. The warrior spotted several flimsy looking doors, a few hanging loosely, and glanced at Dram.

"That way?" he asked dubiously.

The dwarf shook his head, bending down to grab the rusty bars of a grate that capped a drainage sewer. "Are you going stand there and watch or give me a hand?" he grunted, straining to lift the heavy grid. With the human's help, he lifted it from its frame and slid it a foot or so off to the side. The water was filthy, the stench unbearable, giving them pause

"There's a ladder on the side—follow it down," Dram urged. The warrior slid his feet and legs through the gap, located a rung on the ladder, and started down. Almost immediately one of the ladder rungs snapped, and he tumbled into blackness. The fall wasn't far. He splashed into an ankle-deep puddle of scum, his feet slipping out from under him. He landed painfully on his hip, in disgusting muck. He slowly rose to his feet, bumping his head against a low drainage pipe.

By then Dram had descended more carefully, dropping the last few feet with a splash, landing next to the human warrior.

"Damn, it stinks down here. And it's black as night," the dwarf grumbled. "Give me a minute to adjust my eyes, and we'll get going."

"Adjust?" the man replied. "Here's the way I plan to adjust." Sparks flared as he struck his flint and coaxed the glowing specks onto the wick of the small, oil lantern he had carried through the night. Quickly the flame took root, and he held the light up, illuminating a low, brick-walled pipe. The bottom was trenched and wet in the middle with thick liquid.

They couldn't keep the stench out of their nostrils. The warrior tied a kerchief around his face, while the dwarf just grimaced, wrinkling his nose. "Which way?" he asked.

"The flow goes that way, toward the bay, no doubt. If they figure out we've taken to the sewers—and they will, as soon as someone spots that grate up there—that's where they'll be waiting for us. Let's surprise them, and try the other direction."

96

The warrior began to move against the sluggish flow, bending nearly double to avoid the low ceiling hung with pipes. Dram, still scowling, came behind. Each had drawn his knife, holding the sharp-edged weapons ready in their right hands, staring through the shadows and murk.

The man held his lantern out before him. Even so, the shadows beyond the pale circle of light were dark and impenetrable, as lightless as if they were a thousand feet underground. He passed a drainage pipe to the right, a shaft only about three feet in diameter that for now was dry. They came to a similar tube on the left, one that trickled with slimy effluent.

Abruptly the dwarf gasped. The human whirled, spotting a large snakelike object emerging from a side pipe. Eyes wide with terror, Dram stumbled away, flailing with his knife at a hideous creature hissing from a grotesque, circular mouth ringed with sharp teeth.

The warrior's knife slashed out. A white tendril dropped into ooze, but suddenly there were a dozen more, all spewing from the same dark pipe. The warrior swung his lantern in a wide arc, and with fierce hissing the snake-thing—for it was one long, multi-limbed creature—retreated.

"It got my shoulder!" the dwarf hissed between clenched teeth. His left arm hung limply at his side.

The warrior stabbed again, gouged another one of the slashing tendrils, but barely pulled back before the others lashed his hand. He took a step back, as more of the creature slithered out of the drainpipe. It had numerous legs and a grotesque, segmented body, resembling a huge centipede—the size of a crocodile.

The tentacles dripped with a gummy elixir that numbed its enemies. Dram, his left arm dangling uselessly, lunged with his own blade, but the dwarf had to fall back as more tendrils flailed in his direction. One of those stroked the back of his hand, and the dwarf cursed, stumbling back.

Most of the carrion crawler's body remained in the pipe, where the man and dwarf could not reach it with their weapons. Only its forequarters were in the sewer, its head and tentacles weaving wildly. Dram, collapsing against a side of the pipe, could no longer hold onto his weapon. The blade dropped from his nerveless fingers, vanishing into the brown muck. His knees buckled slowly until the dwarf was half-squatting in the slimy liquid. His mouth opened and closed, but no sound emerged.

The carrion crawler now whirled toward the warrior and spilled the rest of its clawing legs and undulating body out of the drainage pipe. The man quickly sheathed his knife and pulled out his small crossbow. He shot a steel dart into the blur of tentacles. The carrion crawlers shrieked eerily, accelerating its charge. Angrily the man pulled out a second crossbow and fired that dart right into the monster's mouth—still it bore down upon him.

The warrior drew his dagger again and retreated, slashing back and forth, cutting several more of the grasping tentacles, but the knife was too short to strike the crawler's hateful head.

The big sword strapped to his back was a nuisance, restricting his mobility. He couldn't draw or swing the prized weapon down here. The warrior glanced at the dwarf, all but useless. Clenching his teeth, the man retreated before the lashing tendrils. The circular maw pulsed hungrily, the creature's sharp teeth flexing outward before retracting with each snap.

Holding the lamp in his left hand, the warrior managed to parry the creature's relentless attack, even though he was against the walls. Dram was motionless, half-lying in the stagnant water, his eyes wide and staring. He could only watch the battle. The warrior cast his eyes around, looking for something, anything, that would help him in this fight.

He stepped on something slippery, an eel-like fish that shot away from him, thrashing frantically through the shallow water. The carrion crawler lunged at him as the man lost his footing, and, recoiling, he tripped backwards, almost dropping the lamp. Tentacles lashed out to touch, almost gently, the side of his leather boot, and in that touch came the icy chill of paralysis.

He felt the effects instantly. In a second the tingling had spread into his calf. He kicked out viciously with his other foot, and the creature hesitated, its tendrils waving, just beneath one of the bricked archways that supported the sewer pipe.

The warrior had seconds, at the most, before more tentacles engulfed him. He hurled the ceramic lamp at the bricks just above the carrion crawler's head. The clay jar broke and the wick flamed the oil. The warrior threw up his hands, shielding himself from the explosive blast of heat as the burning liquid spilled over the front of the monster's segmented body.

The creature thrashed convulsively, bending and twisting, slashing its tentacles wildly. Hissing and clacking, it churned in the mucky liquid. With the last of his strength the human pushed himself away, his numbed foot a soggy leaden weight. The flames were quickly dying—smothered by the muck.

He collapsed onto the monster's hard-shelled, twisting body. Spotting a gap between the segments, right above the carrion crawler's mouth, he reached and drove his long dagger home with a powerful stab. In its dying frenzy the monster whipped its tentacles across the warrior, striking his hand. Bringing his left hand around, he seized the hilt of his knife and wrenched it back and forth, driving it deeper into the monster's small brain. With a final hiss and a shudder, the carrion crawler died.

The paralysis spread quickly through the human's body. He used the last of his strength to push himself off the disgusting corpse, tumbling to the sewer floor, onto his back. Moments later he was utterly helpless, though his face was above the ooze.

He didn't know how long he lay there, but he was fully conscious the whole time—and utterly incapable of moving a muscle. At last he heard someone or something approaching. The water rippled softly, lapping against his cheeks. Though he exerted every shred of his will, he could not turn his head to look around. Instead, he heard the sloshing sounds come closer and closer.

"What you sleep for?" He heard the voice, and allowed himself a small wave of relieve. A second later a strong hand grabbed his shoulder, pulled him out of the water, and dropped him unceremoniously onto some bricks. He couldn't see anything but vague shadows in the darkness of the sewer, but he caught a whiff of something that smelled even worse than the rank sewer.

The voice clucked again, critically. "Strange place to take nap. Get eaten, prob'ly—or I not Highbulp of all Caergoth."

CHAPTER TEN

<small>❦◖◗◖◗◖◗◖◗❦◖◗◖◗◖◗◖◗❦◖◗◖◗◖◗◖◗❦◖◗◖◗◖◗◖◗❦</small>

THE CAERGOTH CONFERENCE

<small>❦◖◗◖◗◖◗◖◗❦◖◗◖◗◖◗◖◗❦◖◗◖◗◖◗◖◗❦◖◗◖◗◖◗◖◗❦</small>

The man wore the robes of a duke yet prostrated himself on the floor, face pressed to the paving stones, like the most miserable servant. He bowed before one even greater than himself, one who was his master, his overseer, his lord . . . his very god.

"O Prince of Lies," intoned the man. "Weaken mine enemies, who are thine own enemies as well. Make my words your daggers, my desires your will. May the minds of thine enemies be clouded by their own greed, that greed you foster and foment with such mastery."

The Prince of Lies was Hiddukel, the god of greed and corruption. In this luxuriously appointed chamber he was represented by a merchant's scale placed on a table, the table draped with a red silk cloth. The scale was broken, one half of the balance lying on the silken covering, the other suspended in the air—mysteriously suspended, for with the broken crosspiece no counterweight was apparent on the other side of the device. The scale seemed nearly to quiver, as if eager, poised, and waiting for some weight of great value to rest upon its gleaming surface.

Now the Nightmaster stepped forward. The high priest was robed from his head to his feet in crimson, rippling cloth. His face was concealed, his hands folded into the front of his flowing garment. Stopping before the praying man, the Nightmaster looked down and asked the ritual questions.

"Are you truly a devoted servant of our most illustrious prince?" the crimson-robed priest demanded.

"I swear it upon my blood and the blood of all my kin," replied the lord, lifting his face from the floor.

"Have your efforts earned profit on our lord's behalf?"

"I have gained treasure, much treasure, for the prince's altar. This year I have turned two new souls toward his corrupt perfection." The lord was on his knees now, his posture otherwise rigid.

"How do you prove this to the Prince of Lies—for he knows the falsehood of all words, the deceit of all mortal intentions."

"I offer my own blood as proof, as sustenance for my lord." The man did not flinch. He reached up with both hands, tore away his tunic, and bared his pale, nearly hairless chest.

The Nightmaster prayed, head bowed, soft murmurs emerging from the mask of red silk. Finally he spoke aloud. "Your prayer has been heard and accepted."

One hand emerged from the red silk robe, carrying a short-bladed dagger, a knife with a blade so thin it resembled an icepick. With a sudden, precise stab the priest plunged that blade into the man's chest, through the flabby flesh and directly into his heart.

The stricken worshiper gasped from the pain, his face growing first slack, then taut. His hands never wavered from their grasp on his garment, pulling the material back, exposing his flesh. The Nightmaster pulled the blade out and reached out his other hand with a golden cup against the wound in the man's chest.

Blood—crimson, life-giving blood from the heart—poured out of the duke, spurting and swirling into the cup. Its torrent caused the man to sway, though still he bared his skin to the instruments of his religion. In five seconds the vessel was full, and the Nightmaster, who had tucked his dagger back within his robe, touched the wound and murmured an invocation, a humble plea to the healing power of his dark lord.

The bleeding stopped. The man, still swaying, did not topple. Instead, his expression changed, his grimace fading to a look of exhaustion. His face was pale, chalky white, though it brightened into a beatific smile of pure pleasure. Gently, the man closed his shirt, adjusting the flap of the collar, straightening the creases tucked within his belt.

His eyes opened, and he watched the priest turn toward the broken scale. The Nightmaster set the cup of blood on the solid half of the scale, and under its weight the scale began to shift until the disk of metal lowered to rest upon the red silk. In a flash of smoke it was gone, and in its place were several gleaming coins.

For the first time the worshiper's expression betrayed a hint of doubt. The Nightmaster took the coins in his hand, counting out three for the kneeling man, keeping the same number for himself. Each was a large disk, pure platinum, engraved with great skill to display the image of a merchant's scale on one side, and the mingled image of a Crown, a Rose, and a Sword on the other.

"Only three?" the man asked, taking his coins and studying them. He admired the beauty of each but was dismayed by the paltry total. He touched his breast, knuckles whitening as he pressed against the flesh that had, moments ago, been pierced by the steely tool of his lord's will.

The Nightmaster snorted. "Be grateful for that," he admonished sternly. "Do you expect him to be pleased that you, who have such great power and influence, a position of command among a mighty order, should have turned but two souls toward his worship in the course of a long year?"

"I must move with care—all depends upon deceit! Even my wife does not know what—"

"Silence!" hissed the priest. The cowl of his hood flared like a cobra's, and he leaned into the lord, his breath sour with the scent of raw onion. "Take the profits of your trade with our dark prince or turn your back on him—and know that he will shun you in return!"

"No!" gasped the worshiper, bending double, pressing his face to the floor. "I beg the forgiveness of my prince and of his chosen agent, the Nightmaster. Please—I spoke foolishly, in haste!"

"You are wise. Stubborn, but wise," said the priest. He stepped to the scale, pulled the silk up from the table to wrap his holy icon. "Comport yourself!" he snapped. "They come for you!"

With a murmured word the Nightmaster vanished, taking his robe, the silken bundle, and the sacred scale with him. The man pushed himself to his feet, adjusting his garments. He turned to the sound of a rap on the door. "Come in!" he barked, his tone again commanding.

His aide opened the door and bowed. "My lord duke," he said. "They are ready to begin the conference."

⊰⊹⊱⊰⊹⊱⊰⊹⊱

Lady Selinda of Palanthas was already restless and even a little disgusted. The Duke of Caergoth had been busy for the last day, leaving her in the capable but utterly uninteresting care of Sir Marckus and the duchess. The former was a stiff and formal bore, and the latter had apparently exhausted her store of entertaining gossip at the welcoming banquet. Of course, the tour of the goblin dungeon had been diverting, but other than that she was forced to conclude that Caergoth was nearly as dull as Palanthas itself.

Then there was the matter of the other two dukes. Jarrod of Thelgaard and Rathskell of Solanthus had finally arrived in the city after dark, each entering with his entourage through a different gate, going to quarters in a different palace. They would not show themselves to each other, to their host, or to the visiting princess, until protocol had been choreographed down to the precise moment of their simultaneous entry into the conference chamber.

That moment, at last, was here. Selinda sat in a cushioned chair upon a low dais installed along one wall of Castle Caergoth's great hall. Three hundred knights—exactly equal numbers (of course!) representing the orders of Crown, Sword, and Rose—stood at attention along the walls, and dozens of lesser nobles and ladies, dressed in finery, sat on the floor of the chamber. Trumpeters blared fanfare, and Selinda rose to her feet as doors in all three walls were opened by stewards just at the moment when the braying horns reached their crescendo.

One duke passed through each door. Each had his wife on his arm, each was trailed by exactly five retainers. That number had only been established, Selinda was informed by Lady Martha, after negotiations lasting most of the night. Proceeding with elaborate dignity, the three great lords advanced to their seats, which were equal in grandeur to Selinda's except they were all on a slightly lower section of dais, all four chairs forming the sides of a square.

Selinda found herself intrigued, in spite of herself, by the appearance of the two tardy lords. Duke Jarrod of Thelgaard was a huge man with a shaggy black mane of hair and a full, flowing beard of the same hue. His beard was divided into two braids, parting to reveal the emblem of the Crown upon his silver breastplate. Despite his girth, there was dignity and purpose in his long strides, and the way he carried himself proved he still boasted greater than average strength. His reputation held him to be a ferocious battle leader, contemptuous of his own safety in pursuit of a foe, and from the look of barely contained fury lurking in his dark countenance the princess had no difficulty believing this. His emblem was a stark banner, a pennant of sheer black displaying the Crown sigil in purest white.

She remembered Martha's words and wondered if the Duke of Thelgaard had been imbibing. In truth, she could see no sign of any inebriation. His wife was with him, leaning on his arm, an old crone of a woman. Her posture was stooped, as she shuffled along with his support. He was patient, walking slowly, and he showed surprising tenderness as he escorted her to a chair near his own.

Duke Rathskell of Solanthus was, in many ways, the very opposite of his rival in appearance. He was short, slender, with wiry limbs and a quick, graceful gait. His mustache was small and neat, his beard trimmed short so that it just outlined his chin and mouth. Reputedly Rathskell was a swordsman of consummate skill, and as Selinda beheld his dancer's grace and the quick, observant flashing of his eyes, she judged that this reputation, too, was accurate. She remembered Lady Martha's indiscreet gossip—that this duke had murdered his wife's former husband—and she had no trouble believing that the story might be true. A courtier carried the duke's blue banner, upon which the image of a silver sword was prominently displayed.

Rathskell's wife didn't so much walk as slither. She was very beautiful, with enormous breasts that swelled out the front of her tight-fitting gown. She smiled at the knights around her, then turned her adoring eyes to the face of her husband, who seemed to be suffering the proceedings with barely concealed contempt.

In contrast to these swaggering, warlike lords, Duke Crawford of Caergoth seemed casual and at ease. He was handsome and friendly and spoke congenially with members of the other dukes' parties. He had a joke for Thelgaard that actually caused the big man to chuckle aloud, and when he greeted Solanthus he squeezed the man's arm and leaned closer to offer a private word. Lady Martha, on his arm, glanced at Selinda and flashed a wink.

Eyeing each other, the two rival dukes arrived at their chairs at the same moment. Lady Selinda bowed to them all and took her seat. A moment later the three great nobles sat down, and the nobles, retainers, and ladies settled into their chairs. The three hundred knights and the heralds, of course, remained standing. The princess nodded to Sir Marckus, who stood behind his lord, and that worthy captain signaled to three squires. Each released a cord, and three glorious banners unfurled from the ceiling, rippling downward like silken tapestries to display the sigils of the Crown, Sword, and Rose behind their respective dukes. A moment later the fourth banner, a pure white strip of silk, unfurled behind Selinda, trailing down from the ceiling to the floor.

Patriarch Issel, the leading cleric in Caergoth—high priest of the church of Shinare—was going to give an invocation, Selinda recalled. He stood now and spoke of the importance of the knighthood and the vital coin of trade that their protection allowed to flow through the city. He got a little too bogged down in matters of debit and income for Selinda's tastes, and she was grateful when at last, after five minutes, he brought his prayer to a close.

Finally, it was time for the real work of the conference to begin. The princess rose to her feet and cleared her throat.

"Your Excellencies, lords of Solamnia, nobles and ladies, good knights and worthy squires. It is my honor to welcome you all on my father's behalf to the Council of Caergoth."

Her father had written this speech, advising her to read it loud and clear at the start of the conference. In her two days in the city she had studied it, deleted some parts that she found too bombastic, and added a few pertinent details that her father had neglected. Then she had committed it to memory, so that she could keep her eyes trained on her listeners as she made her points.

"We may well be proud of our accomplishments in the time since the end of the War of Souls. We have removed the scourge of the Dark Knights from the lands once ruled by Vinas Solamnus. We have begun to repair the depredations wrought by the Dragon Overlords, most notably the evil of the vile Khellendros—though we must all acknowledge that this task in its entirety will last well beyond any of our lifetimes. We have begun to raise the banners of justice, to restore law and order, and pride in the Oath and Measure, throughout these hallowed realms."

"Hear, hear!" The assent echoed around the chamber, a rumble of deep male voices.

"These gains have not been without sacrifice. One such sacrifice, more than any other, has added a bitter spice to this taste of freedom. My father bade, and my own heart requires, that I ask you all to bow your heads in silence as we do every Autumnul, in memory of the bold, the true, the noble Lord Lorimar."

Selinda's voice hardened, and so did her gaze. "It remains bitter medicine to us all that the assassin of Lord Lorimar still roams the lands of Solamnia—a symbol of how much work there is still to be done, restoring justice to the land. For more than three years Lorimar's assassin has evaded capture, though the unprecedented reward of a thousand Palanthian crowns lies upon his head. It is the Lord Regent's wish that this reward now be increased to twenty-five hundred crowns, paid from my father's own treasury, to the knight who captures or slays the Assassin.

"In the absence of a prisoner or a dead body, the return of Lord Lorimar's legendary sword, Giantsmiter, shall constitute proof of fulfillment. This man's identity is well known to all of you. His name is Jaymes Markham, and he was formerly a Knight of the Rose. His treachery is all the more wicked because he was the trusted leader of Lorimar's personal guards, the rest of whom perished in the attack. His treachery is a mystery, but he is known to prize the great sword, Giantsmiter, and as such is a marked man."

"My Lady, if you will forgive the interruption, I may offer a tidbit of news—perhaps too trivial and tardy to warrant urgent status—but it regards that mighty blade." The speaker was Duke Rathskell of Solanthus. The duke had risen abruptly to his feet, but now spoke respectfully, with a slight bow of his head that conveyed his apologies to the princess.

"Please—what can you tell us?" she said.

"I received word several months ago from one of my knights—Sir Percival, the captain of my scouts." The duke indicated a large Knight of the Sword with a shock of red hair and a mustache with twin plumes flowing lower than his chin. "While patrolling in the foothills of the Garnet Range, Sir Percival had occasion to inspect the stronghold of a bandit lord, a certain Cornellus, who maintains a disreputable post up there.

"Percival learned of a recent altercation in that stronghold. A warrior wielding a great, blazing sword slew many of Cornellus' attendants. No great loss there, of course, but the description of the sword matches Giantsmiter. Unfortunately, the story is now nearly four months old. Thus, I did not choose to disseminate it as an emergency bulletin."

"I quite understand," the princess said.

The duke sat back down, as the frowning princess turned the council to discussion of commerce and business concerns.

The talk started with the trading city of Garnet, the mercantile center on the plains just west of the mountain range of the same name. The free city was approximately equidistant from Solanthus and Thelgaard. Historically, it had fallen under the sway of one, than the other, of those city-states. Since the War of Souls it had been garrisoned by mixed companies of knights, dispatched by the three dukes. Though the knights guarded the city walls and gates, Garnet had successfully resisted all attempts at domination by any of the orders. Now—as both dukes apparently agreed—this was a luxury Garnet could no longer afford.

"Even the temples in Garnet are unsafe," Patriarch Issel declared. "I have learned that the shrine of Shinare was robbed there several weeks ago and the patriarch himself was murdered."

"I vouch for this report," said a Knight of the Rose. Selinda recognized him as Sir Reynaud, Duke Crawford's chief retainer, who had captured the goblin and brought it to Caergoth. "I happened to be at that temple shortly before the crime occurred."

"It's not just bandits. We have raiders coming down from the mountains, striking farmsteads and villages miles beyond their previous incursions!" proclaimed Duke Jarrod. "With Garnet to secure my southern flank, my troops could form a bulwark against the raiders' inroads to the west, I can no longer afford to send a garrison to a place that provides me with no revenue.

"Bah—it is to the north that the enemy plans to strike!" objected Duke Rathskell. "That's why Garnet is essential—essential—to the proper defense of Solanthus."

Back and forth they went throughout a long, hot day in the great hall. Selinda had almost dozed off when she heard a commotion at the back of the large room. A messenger in the livery of the Rose knights rushed in to interrupt the debate.

"The assassin of Lord Lorimar!" the messenger gasped, to general consternation. "He has been spotted in the city! The duke's agents have him cornered near the waterfront—he's in the Gnome Ghetto!"

"Evil strides the streets of my city! My men will apprehend him at once!" cried Duke Crawford, leaping to his feet, shouting orders to Sir Marckus.

"Not so fast!" objected Rathskell. "This villain is the great prize of our age—let all the orders combine for the honor of bringing him to justice!

"I pledge a hundred knights!" Duke Jarrod shouted. The others swiftly followed suit, so that it was a party of three hundred veteran Solamnics, armed and armored, that presently hastened toward the Gnome Ghetto, in pursuit of the vile murderer.

⊱⊰⊱⊰⊱⊰❀⊱⊰⊱⊰⊱⊰

Sir Mikel Horn, a veteran Knight of the Rose, had served his order in key posts for twenty years. He had guarded bands of refugees fleeing south and east to escape the depredations of the Dragon Overlord Khellendros. He had stood on the walls of Solanthus when Mina had come with her Dark Knights to sweep that ancient fortress by storm. He had led patrol after patrol against the brigands, goblins, and Dark Knight remnants that had plagued all the provinces of Solamnia since the end of the War of Souls. He helped to train the garrisons for both Solanthus and Thelgaard, earning a reputation as a man who could be trusted, a man who could think for himself, a man for whom no assignment was too difficult.

LORD OF THE ROSE

Which is why he stood here, now, on the gate-tower of the free city of Garnet, watching the last of the Solanthian knights ride away, their banners held high, their silver armor shining, amidst a fanfare of bugles. But no doubt about it, like their Crown brethren from Thelgaard, the knights of Solanthus were running away.

The goblins of the Garnet Range were on the march. All week long reports had been streaming in, describing a horde of unprecedented size—raiders who had were sweeping through small mining towns and dairy villages, plundering and killing. As the band of marauders drew closer to Garnet, many of the people had fled onto the plains while some had stayed to defend their homes. Now Sir Mikel knew that it was too late for anyone else to leave.

"Captain Horn, here are the latest reports from the scouts," said Dynrall Wickam, Mikel's squire and aide. Dynrall was his most loyal retainer, or had been up until this morning, when Mikel had ordered him to depart with the men of Solanthus.

"Will you be leaving, Captain?" Dynrall had asked.

"I cannot. By the Oath and the Measure, I stay here in Garnet until we are relieved. But you, lad—you should go!" the captain had replied.

"And leave the man who has shown me the true meaning of that Oath, and that Measure?" the squire had replied. "No, my lord, the only way I leave Garnet is if I follow you out. No sir, I refuse that order. Write it down on my record. I'm staying."

Horn had been too overcome to reply. Now he looked at the young man, one of the few steadfast warriors in the town, and all he could think of was that his own stubbornness had condemned the youngster.

"What are the reports?" he asked.

"The goblin horde has been spotted on the King's Road in the foothills," Dyrnall reported. "Still displaying surprisingly good march discipline. Best estimates are that they will be heading down the west ridge within a matter of hours. If they desire haste, they might be able to fall upon the city before nightfall."

"Then we had best take up positions on the wall. What are our numbers?"

"Some hundred knights remain, sir. Perhaps three or four times that many men of the city will stand watch. All have been directed to battle posts and will hasten there upon your signal."

"Very well. It is not so bad. It could be worse. We will acquit ourselves. Summon my bugler, and sound the alarm."

An hour later the raiders burst into view, several thousand of them blackening the summit of the low, rounded ridge that formed the eastern horizon when viewed from the town walls. They were about a mile away, standing shoulder to shoulder in silent menace.

"That big fellow there, in the middle. He's the leader," Horn said, studying the horde with a practiced eye. He indicated a massive, broad-shouldered warrior who swaggered out in front of the horde. The goblin chieftain wore a necklace of skulls, grisly trophies that rattled upon his chest when he walked. He held a massive spear in his hand, and for a moment he struck a pose, the haft of his weapon planted upon the ground as he glared down at the small, walled town nestled in its little hollow in the plains.

Abruptly, he raised the spear in a massive fist, whirling the weapon back and forth over his head. An eerie green light pulsed from that mighty spear, and when the glow washed over the men on the city ramparts their knees quaked, and their courage went sour in their mouths. A great roar rose from the horde, and the front rank of goblins surged forward. The next came behind, and soon the ground was teeming with them, a screaming, howling horde sweeping down toward the poorly defended town.

They reached the wall and the gate and barely slowed. Some goblins threw grapples over the parapet, while others formed crude ladders from posts and timbers scattered outside the walls. They swarmed up and over, striking down the few men who dared to stand against the tide. The attackers spread to the right and left, and within a few short minutes the outer wall was in their hands.

The great half giant stood at the city gate, smashing at it with his powerful fists, bashing the barrier down. Brandishing his glowing spear, he led a charge right down the main street of Garnet. Hundreds of savage, painted goblins, shrieking in blood-thirsty frenzy, thronged the street behind him.

Sir Mikel came down from the rampart and met the goblins at the head of the charge with his broadsword, killing the first two. The great half-giant loomed over him, lip curled in a sneer of contempt. The huge spear with the gleaming green tip thrust forward, and the knight made to parry, a forceful block with the hilt of his sword clutched in both hands.

But the thrust was a feint, and the hulking half-giant whipped the weapon around with startling speed. It was the haft of the weapon—a stick of wood as thick as a strong man's forearm—that struck home, shattering Sir Mikel's helmet into two pieces, crushing the man's skull.

The knight died there, mercifully, for the suffering of his city lasted through the rest of the night.

⊰⊱⊰⊱❀⊰⊱⊰⊱

"Great victory!" crowed Laka, pouring the contents of a bottle of red wine—a vintage that had been priced at more than fifty steel, just a few hours ago—into her mouth and down the front of her ragged tunic. The amulet of Hiddukel, the last shard of the green rock she had discovered so many years ago, glimmered almost with delight as the blood-red liquid spilled over it.

"Aye!" Ankhar crowed. He was leaning back on a feathered mattress in a wealthy merchant's great manor. The merchant himself lay dead in the next room, while his wife and maidservants were locked in a nearby pantry. Even now, hours later, the half-giant could hear their terrified sobs. It was a very pleasant sound. He was in no hurry to kill them. Let them beg and weep for a while.

"Many treasures," the chieftain reflected, looking at the array of gold and silver objects in the room—goblets, candlesticks, platters, and picture frames. "Food and drink for a whole year. If we want to stay here to eat."

His foster mother tossed the half empty wine bottle across the room, where it shattered against a canvas portrait that apparently portrayed the dead man who lay with his brains crushed in the next room.

"Now it look like him!" she cackled, as the crimson liquid spattered the painting and slowly trickled toward the floor. Then her eyes narrowed thoughtfully, as she closed her bony fingers around the amulet of the Prince of Lies. "You say *if* we stay here, son," she observed.

Ankhar was up, pacing around the great room, his thoughts tumbling through his mind with increasing potential, ambition, excitement. "Yes," he replied. "This fun, great victory for my army—but it only *first* victory! Now we go across plains. Take what we want. Go where we please!"

"You want war with knights?" Laka asked, her own eyes flashing.

"I *destroy* knights!" Ankhar pledged.

He stared at the pulsing light, and he saw the Truth.

CHAPTER ELEVEN

A HOUSE OF GNOMES

Not stay in sewer?" The Highbulp's lower lip quivered in a dramatic pout. "We have feast and drunk! Lots of fun—women, too!"

Dram suppressed a shudder. "Sorry, but we have business with the gnomes." He was not entirely exaggerating as he added, "We will always remember your help, though. You brought us right to the street we were looking for. Firesplasher Lane, you said, right?"

"Yep. Them Firesplashers all live here, you bet," declared the Aghar proudly.

"We'll go on ourselves from here," Dram said.

"Fine by me. Humph," sniffed the gully dwarf. "Gnome girls ugly! Gnome beer flat!"

Although Dram was inclined to agree, he knew that the standards of beauty and brewing among the Aghar were far worse. Even so, like the human, he had grown genuinely fond of the brave little fellow who had brought them through the maze of sewer tunnels unmolested, right to the short alley called Firesplasher Lane.

"Wait!" cried the Aghar with uncharacteristic emotion. "You tell me names before you go! I Highbulp Stuggleflump, Lord of Caergoth sewers. These sewers, anyway. What names yours?"

He pointed a grimy finger at the mountain dwarf.

"I'm Dram Feldspar," said the dwarf, with a stiff bow and a formal nod. "Honored to make your acquaintance, Sir Highbulp."

"Yes! Me a Sir! Call me 'Sir'!" said the filthy creature, beaming. His eyes narrowed as he glared up at the human, shifting the aim of his finger to the tall swordsman's chest. "Who is you?"

The man squinted, hesitating for just a moment.

"Jaymes. I am called Jaymes Markham," he replied. "I, too, am honored to know Sir Highbulp Stuggleflump. Now we must part ways."

The warrior started to climb up the shaft of the drain pipe, which connected to the street overhead. At the top he pushed a heavy grate to the side, then climbed to his feet and stood, watching impatiently, as the dwarf followed him up the rusty ladder and rolled onto the worn flagstones. They were in a dead-end alley that was so narrow Dram could almost stretch his arms out and touch the buildings on either side of the street.

"This is Firesplasher Lane, huh?" the dwarf noted skeptically.

Still, it did look like a gnome neighborhood, with small wooden doors leading into little stone buildings. Just a stone's throw away the alley joined a street. Several gnomes passed, glancing at the two unkempt figures, smeared with mud—and worse—from their passage through the wretched sewer

The swordsman strode up to a solid-looking door, only chest-high to the man, and knocked his fist sharply against the panel.

After a beat, an irascible voice squeaked from within, "Go away!"

The warrior repeated the pounding. A few seconds later they heard the same response, this time a higher-pitched squeak. When Jaymes knocked a third time, they heard a burst of noise—like a chair scraping across a stone floor, a jar slamming down hard onto a countertop, and muttered curses and complaints growing in volume as the speaker stomped closer.

The door swung inward, and a chubby gnome, long-bearded

and utterly bald on his scalp, stared fiercely up at the man. "Don't you understand Common? I said, 'Go away'!"

Jaymes stooped and brushed past him as he squawked. The gnome turned to glare at the warrior as the dwarf, who only had to duck his head slightly, stepped past, following Jaymes.

Despite the low ceiling, the room was quite large, though most of the floor space was given over to an assortment of tables jammed haphazardly together, in some places so closely that even the gnome must have had trouble fitting between them. Near the door was a fireplace and cook stove between a pair of chairs apparently made from salvaged bits of kindling. As crowded as the floor was with tables and counters, likewise each tabletop was covered by a clutter of miscellany: jars, tins, and boxes filled with powders, ointments, liquids, and indistinguishable substances; papers and parchments scrawled with tiny handwriting, or sprawling schematics; burners and boilers busy heating little kettles, or scorching plain-glass vials. A haze of smoke made it hard to see to the far side, and a layer of fine dust covered the floor, tables, walls, and everything else with a black coating.

"Go away!" the gnome demanded once more.

"No!" Dram declared, planting his fists on his hips and meeting the indignant gnome's eyes with a bristling glower of his own.

The little fellow shrugged, apparently undismayed by the dwarf's stubbornness. "Then stand back," he declared, "and cover your ears." The gnome followed his own instructions as he turned and dashed across the room, shouting. "Ready?"

For the first time they noticed a second gnome, almost invisible behind a large kettle on the far side of the cook stove. This one, a female, replied, "Ready!" She covered her face with the crook of one arm while, with the other hand, she extended the end of a red-hot poker into the kettle.

"What are you— "

Dram was interrupted by a *whoomph* that drove the breath from his lungs. The blast of pressure was followed immediately by an ear-stunning *crack* and a great billow of black smoke, shot through with sparks of orange fire. The cloud erupted from the black kettle, quickly filling the room with choking, gagging vapors. Eyes stinging, coughing uncontrollably, Jaymes and the dwarf had no choice but to retreat to the narrow street. They stumbled out, fanning the air, leaning over until they could breathe.

The two gnomes emerged too, though they didn't seem as discomfited. Indeed, the male seemed satisfied as he nodded and stroked his beard.

"That went well," he said to his partner.

The female was just as chubby and short as her companion. Perhaps because she had been closer to the experiment, she was still blinking, wiping soot from her face and shaking her head as if to clear her ears.

"Who are they?" she asked, as—apparently for the first time, to judge by the widening of her eyes—she caught sight of the two visitors. "Who are you?" She promptly forgot all about the human and the dwarf, turning back to the other gnome. "Make a note: I think we are still using too much sulfir, but it went pretty well. Still, I wish Pete was here to help."

"Well, of course, Pete," said the male gnome. "But he's not."

"Look," Dram interjected. "We are looking for someone you might know. We heard he might have come here."

"Nope, don't know you, don't know anyone who knows you," said the male, with a firm shake of his head. "Unless his name is Pete."

"His name is Brillissander Firesplasher," Jaymes said tersely.

The name provoked a startling reaction. Both gnomes stood at abrupt attention, the male placing his hand over his heart while his comrade let a fat tear roll through the smudge on her cheek.

"So you know him?" Dram probed.

"He was our Pap," said the male. "He's dead, though. So if he knew you, he doesn't know you any more." He blinked suddenly, as if remembering something. "Go away!" he snapped.

With a roar of exasperation, Jaymes grabbed the gnome's collar and twisted, lifting the little fellow right off of the ground. The warrior took a similar grip on the second gnome and none too gently hauled them through the door back into the still-smoky room.

"Hey! Ow! Stop!"

Ignoring their strangled protests, not to mention their flailing resistance, Jaymes and Dram firmly plopped the gnomes into a pair of chairs, both of which creaked and swayed. The man knelt so that he could confront the gnomes, leaning close into their faces, scowling.

"Now listen good. Your Pap had something that I want, and I'm not leaving here until I get it. That doesn't have to take such a long time. Or it might last until tomorrow. That's up to you."

"Pap had somethin' of yours?" snapped the bearded gnome. Abruptly, he sniffed. "Hah! Pap was no thief, and I never laid eyes on you before. How could he have something of yours?"

"Look, let's be reasonable about this," Dram said in a bluff attempt at friendliness. "What's your name? The short version?"

"Pap himself named me," said the little fellow sentimentally. "He called me Carbonfoundationremnantbasicintermixturefour partstoseven— "

"No, the *short* version of your name!" spluttered the dwarf.

"That *is* the short version. The first part of it anyway. You can call me Carbo."

"All right. Carbo." Dram turned to the female, his beard splitting into a grimace which he intended as a friendly smile. "And who are you?"

"I'm . . . well, you can call me Sulfie."

"All right, Carbo. Sulfie. I'm sorry about your Pap. Let's start with what happened to him. Tell us."

"Well, it wasn't just him. It happened to most all of Dungarden. We were just lucky that day—Pap sent us out to chop stones. Us and our brother, Salty Pete. He was working on the compound."

"Who? Pap, or Salty Pete?"

"Pap! It was Pap's compound! Usually we helped him, but

that day he sent us out to chop on the coal vein. Said he needed more black rocks, even though the hopper was still half-full. So we were gone when it happened."

"When what happened?" pressed Dram.

"Something killed your Pap?" Jaymes tried to sound sympathetic.

"Something sure did," Carbo acknowledged. "Anyway, Dungarden was gone, and so were all the gnomes."

"Except for us, and a couple of others who were down by the fishing nets."

"All gone!" said Sulfie, still fighting tears.

"Destroyed, you mean? asked Jaymes, a glimmer in his eyes.

"Completely gone," said Carbo sadly. "We heard it—like one big clap of thunder, and a huge cloud of smoke flew up into the sky. Rocks flew for a mile around the big hole in the ground. Everyone in Dungarden was dead. There was just nothing left."

"So you came here, to Caergoth?" Dram coaxed. "How long ago was this?"

"We—the Heirs of the Compound—came here three summers ago. We are just starting to make some progress recovering our Pap's work. Now, if you will be on your way, we can get back on the job!"

"Not so fast," said Jaymes. "What of this brother you mentioned—this Salty Pete? Did he come to Caergoth too?"

The two gnomes exchanged a furtive glance. "No," Carbo replied after a long pause. "Poor Pete. He didn't make it. Got killed by dracos in the Brackens."

"Why did the dracos kill Pete?" asked Dram, as gently as he could manage. "Tell us."

"We got attacked by these big dracos. They spit acid, killed two oxes, and carried Pete off into the swamp called the Brackens. We got away with one wagon. Dracos got the other one and Pete."

"The Brackens? Where's that?" asked the dwarf.

"I know," Jaymes replied. "It's a swamp, where the Upper Vingaard River meets the Kaolyn River. Nasty place."

"Yup," said Carbo. *"Real* nasty."

"Hmm. So your Pap and Salty Pete are dead. What about your Pap's work? What did you bring with you from Dungarden?" Jaymes probed.

"One wagon, the one the dracos didn't get," said Sulfie. "One of the two we rode out of the mountains."

"Picks and a scoop shovel," added Carbo, fidgeting. "Now you can go away, right?" His eyes, as if against his will, flickered anxiously toward one of the far counters.

Jaymes followed the look. "That little keg—did you bring that from Dungarden?" He rose and started across the room.

A loud knock on the door interrupted them. The warrior turned while Dram fingered his axe nervously, and the bearded gnome, with a snort of exasperation, stomped over to fling it open.

"What?" he demanded, before adding "Go away!" The gnome slammed the door shut, but a diminutive, rotund figure had already somehow slipped past Carbo to enter the room.

"You!" the new arrival said, pointing a filthy finger at Jaymes. It was an unfamiliar gully dwarf, cloaked in an even heavier—and more aromatic—layer of the scum that was the usual final layer of any Aghar's outfit. "You killed Highbulp!"

The gnomes stepped back in fear as the warrior's eyes narrowed and the dwarf stepped forward indignantly. "That's a lie!" Dram growled. "The great Highbulp was alive when we left him a half hour ago—he was going to have a drunk, I mean a drink, somewhere."

"He dead now," said the Aghar matter-of-factly.

"What! How did he die?" Jaymes asked. The gully dwarf's eyes widened, and he stepped closer to the gnomes, who were muttering anxiously to each other.

"Knight kill him. Cut him with big sword. Alla his blood come out."

"Then why did you say that my friend killed him?" demanded Dram.

"Knight was hunting human fighter—him with big sword!" The Aghar waved his finger accusingly at Jaymes.

"How do you know all this?" asked the man.

"Me watching from shadows. Gonna come to rescue when I hear him make Highbulp say 'Firesplasher Lane!' Same thing you ask Highbulp. Knight cut Highbulp then. Go tell more knights."

The dwarf and the warrior exchanged a glance. Jaymes crossed to the workbench in two long strides, snatching up the keg, shaking it once, checking to see that the stopper was securely fixed. It vanished under his cloak. The gnomes squawked in protest, but just then a violent crash rang outside, followed by shouting voices—a man's voice barking orders mingled with the higher-pitched sounds of protesting gnomes.

Dram stepped to the door, opened it a crack, and peered out.

"He's not at Number Two—but he's on this street somewhere. Take every door!" they heard.

The dwarf stepped back, closing the front door and dropping a heavy iron bar into place. Jaymes, meanwhile, fixed his eyes upon the only other door, a small hatch-like cover low in the rear wall. "Does that lead outside?" he asked the terrified Sulfie.

"After a while it does," she admitted.

"Come on." Jaymes took the squirming gnome by her wrist. Dram grabbed Carbo. The man lifted the hatch, tossed Sulfie through, held it open for the dwarf and the male gnome, then ducked through himself. "Hey, me too!" cried the gully dwarf, just before Dram slammed the hatch, leaving him behind.

They found themselves in the main room of another gnomish domicile, not quite as crowded and cluttered as Carbo's house. With a nod to her neighbors—a half-dozen gnomes regarding them with goggle-eyed stares—Sulfie led them down a narrow hallway where Jaymes, even though he was stooping, knocked his head against a low ceiling arch. They emerged at last into the street.

Many gnomes milled about, but no knights were in sight.

Castle Caergoth rose from its commanding height, and the dwarf led them away from the fortress, at a fast trot.

They hadn't even reached the first intersection when a squad of knights, all wearing the tunic emblazoned with the Crown, charged into sight. The leader, a big man with the golden epaulets of a sergeant, spotted Jaymes, who was head and shoulders taller than anyone else on the street.

"There!" cried the knight. "Stop him—Jak, go tell Captain Dayr! We've got him cornered now." Four knights advanced, shoulder to shoulder, blocking any escape. Doors slammed shut all up and down the block. Sulfie and Carbo tried to make a dash for the nearest houses but were held firm by the dwarf and the warrior.

"You two are coming with us," Dram growled. The dwarf offered his companion a questioning look. "That is, if we're going anywhere."

"Step back," snapped the warrior. He reached over his shoulder, drew the great sword in a single, smooth movement. Flames exploded from the blade. Two of the knights hesitated, awestruck at the sight of the mighty sword, but the other two charged forward, their blades upraised.

The first lost his sword, and fingers, as the fiery weapon slashed across his hands. He screamed and tumbled back as his comrade attacked, slashing back and forth with his long sword.

The second Knight of the Crown charged right onto the blazing tip of the warrior's blade and fell dead next to his wounded companion, who was kneeling, moaning and clutching the bleeding stump of his hand. The two remaining knights advanced more cautiously, shoulder to shoulder across the narrow lane.

"You might cut us down, Assassin!" hissed one of them, "but by the gods, we'll cost you time!" They rushed him.

The warrior had sheathed his sword and snatched out his crossbows. Both knights sprawled to the ground, each felled by a steel dart that punctured deep through the muscle of the thigh.

Jaymes spun and raced after Dram and the two gnomes, who were disappearing around the next corner. Another company of knights came into view. Arrows struck the flagstones behind the warrior as he darted down the connecting lanes.

"Damn them anyway!" the dwarf cursed, halting when he found himself facing of a whole rank of crossbowmen. They were Knights of the Sword arrayed in three ranks—poised for a volley, with their steel-tipped quarrels that could punch through plate mail armor.

"Down!" shouted Jaymes, tumbling into the dwarf and gnomes, bearing all of them to the pavement as the arrows whistled past just above their heads. Sulfie shrieked as one of the missiles grazed her. Dram grunted as he rose to his feet, pulling one of the short arrows from his shoulder and tossing it aside.

The bowmen were already reloading, and shouts and pounding feet could be heard coming from another direction. "Got any clever ideas?" the dwarf asked the human irritably.

A cloud of white smoke erupted around them. The murk swirled through the air, obscuring them from view. All of a sudden a woman stood before them, in a white, bright robe. Beautiful, dark-haired, she reached out to pull the gnomes, the dwarf, and the warrior near to her.

"It's . . . it's her!"gasped Dram, shocked. He stared goggle-eyed. "Lady Coryn!"

"Hurry," she snapped. "There will be plenty of time for fond reunions if we get out of here alive. Now, move!"

Even Carbo and Sulfie hastened to oblige, moving in close to either side of her billowing white robe. More arrows clattered through the alley, but the smoke made the shots go wild. The warrior was the last to join them, as he was busy slashing his blazing sword back and forth, knocking several of the threatening shots aside.

"Well?" demanded Coryn. "We're not waiting forever."

The warrior looked at her, then at the rank of knights, now reloading for their third volley. Jaymes winced, shaking his head.

"Damn," he muttered, charging into the swirl of smoke.

"Put your sword up," she suggested, with just the hint of a

wry smile. He nodded, smoothly sliding the weapon into the hilt concealed beneath his cape, then reached out to grasp the hand extended by the white-robed Coryn.

They stood in a tight circle—the dwarf, the man and woman, and the two gnomes. The lady in white chanted something guttural, and a swirl of magical power enveloped them. There was a sense of sickening disorientation, then the cloud of smoke and magic that hid them from the knights vanished.

With it went the knights, the ghetto, and in fact in the whole city of Caergoth. They blinked to find themselves still holding hands, all in a circle, now standing in the sunlit quiet of a vast plain, sheltered by a verdant, overgrown hedge. A wide river valley, marked by the silver course of a great stream, was visible below them. There were no other people anywhere in sight.

"Coryn," said the warrior. "We owe you our thanks."

She snorted, unamused. "Save that. First we have to talk."

CHAPTER TWELVE

PLEDGES OF WAR

The pursuit of the assassin of Lorimar, Lady Selinda admitted to herself, was a bright spark of excitement amid what was shaping up to be a rather tedious conference. Not that the dukes would allow her to accompany the three hundred knights who rushed to bring the villain to justice—they turned deaf ears to even her most persuasive entreaties. Even so, she felt a thrill as, with Lady Martha at her side, the Princess of Palanthas climbed to the top of the castle's gate tower, from where they could watch the progress of the knights streaming the streets of the great city.

The lady had brought a spyglass, and the two women took turns looking through the device. Selinda was amazed at the effect—when she focused the lens, she felt as though she were looking down from a low rooftop right in the neighborhood instead of from this lofty vantage high up on a castle tower.

The knights could be observed making their way in three columns. The gleaming silver armor of Caergoth's mounted finest reflected the bright sunlight as the Knights of the Rose headed down a wide avenue. The princess couldn't help but notice the Sword knights of Solanthus, and the Crown of Thelgaard, looked shabbier in comparison. Their armor, even when metal, barely glinted in the daylight, and their horses were thin, often scarred, by comparison to the huge, well-groomed war-horses of their host's detachment.

"That's Thelgaard's men in the middle," Lady Martha explained, though the black banner displaying the white crown gave clear enough proof of their allegiance. To the left, the blue pennant with the image of the silver sword flapped in the wind as the knights of Duke Rathskell swung around to the left flank.

"What is that wretched place down there?" asked Selinda, perceiving that the three detachments were encircling an area of flat-roofed shacks, lean-tos, and other hovels along a strip of waterfront.

"We call that the ghetto," Lady Martha said, a trifle embarrassed. "It *is* wretched, and no respectable human would go there. For a long time it was inhabited only by Aghar and criminal scum, though since the War of Souls it has become a sort of haven for gnomes. In fact, they've built it up a bit since going there—making stone houses, that sort of thing. Poor little folk—they suffered as much as anyone during the years of the Scourges, so my husband has been gracious enough to let them have the place. Indeed, they are better neighbors than the gully dwarves!"

"No doubt," Selinda agreed, acutely aware that her father's men had virtually eliminated the filthy little Aghar from Palanthas. Those glimpsed by her escort were seized and, she assumed, expelled from the city.

Her eyes wandered beyond the ghetto to the great docks that serviced the ocean-going galleons. She spotted her father's ships, nine in all, serenely at anchor in the great port. The tenth—her flagship, *Pride of Paladine*—was securely lashed to the wharf. The voyage from Palanthas to Caergoth had been reasonably comfortable, she recalled, and the food served to her and the few noble-ranking officers who had shared the captain's table, excellent. No trace of seasickness had bothered her, and she relished the salty breeze, even the occasional burst of spray splashing across the deck.

Yet now the prospect of re-boarding the galleon for the long return trip home suddenly terrified her. She couldn't explain her feeling, but she shuddered at the sight of the big ships, quickly pulled her eyes away, looking off to ascertain the progress of the arrest. In her heart, she knew nothing would compel her to board the vessel home. Such a trip would be disaster—this much she knew as the Truth.

It was possible to return to Palanthas overland, but how could she make that happen? Captain Powell would never understand her apprehension. She would have to give the matter some thought.

At the fringes of the ghetto, she saw, the knights were dismounting, leaving their horses in the care of squires as squads of armed and armored men deployed into the neighborhoods. They started into the squalid neighborhood streets and alleys, weapons drawn. There was no great hue and cry, however—even the bright banners were tucked away as the men started their search.

Selinda could see throngs of little people—gnomes, she guessed—prodded at sword point into the small squares and plazas that dotted the ghetto. Occasionally she heard the bark of an indistinguishable, but forceful, command. More than once she saw a gnome or some other wretched denizen squirming in the grip of a strong knight. For a long time this methodical search proceeded, as a a great many citizens of the ghetto were corralled, interrogated—sometimes roughly—then restrained in the increasingly crowded open spaces.

"They must have learned something—look!" cried Lady Martha breathlessly, as the individual parties of knights all hastened toward a small corner of the ghetto. The hapless gnomes left behind swiftly vanished into the tangled lanes, going inside and shutting their doors. Since her hostess was clutching the spyglass in her hand but not using it at the moment, Selinda grabbed the device and put it to her eye.

The knights were forming lines of battle. In addition to the gleaming swords Selinda scanned ranks of archers, less heavily armored then the swordsmen but readying their deadly crossbows. One by one the streets surrounding a small area were cordoned off, and archers deployed behind the ranks of swordsmen, all of them moving with methodical discipline. A wider ring, comprised of Caergoth's Rose knights to judge from the immaculate armor, stood back from the attacking formations, presumably to intercept the Assassin if he should try to slip through the encirclement.

Abruptly, noises of smashing wood, cries of alarm, and other sounds of violence carried upward. Selinda spied knights and gnomes running to and fro. A rank of archers raised their weapons, and sunlight reflected from the silvery darts as they arrowed down a narrow street. Overhanging roofs blocked the targets from the ladies' line of sight, but Selinda saw a small party of fugitives break for a small alley—apparently the lethal arrows had missed their targets. Focusing in more tightly, she glimpsed a dwarf. The fellow was dirty, covered in soot and brown muck, but she got a very good look at his face when he turned around to shout some imprecation at his pursuers.

Beyond him a tall swordsman came into view, and Selinda felt a tingle of recognition as she glimpsed blue flames, quickly extinguished, flickering along the edge of that mighty blade.

"Giantsmiter!" she gasped. The man turned to confront his pursuers, his face taut. Yet from the glimpse she got of him, he showed no fear. In spite of the warm sunlight on the parapet, the princess shivered with unexpected terror and excitement.

"What's that—by the gods, not a fire, I hope!" Lady Martha exclaimed, also sounding half alarmed, half titillated.

Selinda swung the glass and spotted a churning cloud of foggy vapor, swirling thickly in the middle of the street.

"White smoke," the princess noted. "Not likely from a fire."

But what was it? The cloud of mist spun and whirled, masking the fugitives. Knights closed in on the small alley from both directions, their hoarse battle cries echoing in the still, midday air. The Assassin and his accomplices were trapped, Selinda realized—there was nowhere for them to go.

Yet why were the knights milling around, now, in apparent confusion? The cloud slowly dissipated, and angry outbursts, accusatory shouts, rose from the tangled streets. Once again knights were dashing around everywhere, smashing down doors, pulling gnomes out into the street. The searching was frenzied, undisciplined. Many knights remounted, and three distinct columns—minus half their number, who remained behind to continue the search—started back up to the castle.

"Did they manage to kill him somehow?" Lady Martha asked breathlessly. "I couldn't see! I don't spot any captives!"

"I fear he may have escaped," Selinda replied.

"But how? No, that's impossible—they had him surrounded!"

"Shall we go down to the great hall and hear what happened?" suggested the princess.

The two ladies descended quickly from the lofty parapet and were waiting at the huge conference table as the doors to the hall burst open. Duke Rathskell and Jarrod were the first into the chamber, each followed by a dozen or more of his retinue.

"—your scouts must have been asleep at their posts!" snapped the thin, wiry Rathskell. "To let them slip by like that!"

"Pathetic lies!" roared Jarrod, flexing his huge arms. "It was your men who scattered at the first taste of steel!"

"Nay—they stood firm and drove the scoundrel into your line. Did your men grow faint at the sight of the blazing sword?" Rathskell demanded. His tone was quiet but menacing.

"Mine followed orders—I have one dead and three wounded to prove it!" answered Jarrod. "What blood did you spill?"

"What happened?" Lady Selinda asked, the calmness of her voice cutting through the bickering.

"We had him dead to rights, my Princess," explained Rathskell with a bow to Selinda. "Until my 'peer' "—he sneered at Jarrod of Thelgaard—"failed to perform his duty in the face of the enemy."

"Lies, I tell you!" bellowed the Duke of the Crown. "He was long gone by the time we closed in."

"My Lord, Lady Princess." The speaker was Sir Marckus, interjecting quietly. The venerable knight's calm tone seemed to soothe the level of tension in the room—at least, for the moment.

"Yes? What is it? Do you know something?" asked Caergoth eagerly.

"Not personally, Excellency, no, but I have heard whisperings among the men. One of them claims to have spotted the White Witch."

"The White Witch! Could she be in league with the killer?" Duke Crawford wondered. "Her sorcery could help explain that miraculous escape."

"If by the 'White Witch' you mean the Lady Coryn of Palanthas," Selinda said sharply. "I have heard her called thus, but I will not stand for such inferences in my presence. She has done good work in the cause of Solamnia over the last few years. She could not possibly be involved—why would she help an assassin who slew one of our most noble and esteemed lords?"

"There is no accounting for the ways of wizards," the Duke of Solanthus declared forcefully.

For the first time Selinda noticed one knight, ashen-faced and perspiring heavily, had been laid upon one of the banquet tables near the door. He held his right hand, wrapped in a bloody bandage, tightly to his chest. Two other knights were borne into the room by comrades, each of them obviously wounded in the leg.

"Duke Crawford!" the princess said at once. "Those men are injured. Surely this debate can wait. Have you not a cleric who can aid them?"

"What? Oh, of course," said the duke, looking with exaggerated concern at the wounded knights. "Patriarch Issel—see first to that fellow, there. The one with all the blood."

"My lord," said the cleric, materializing from the group of people who had suddenly crowded into the great hall. He was wearing his formal golden robe and bowed apologetically. "Of course. That is, I would if I could, but I fear the rigors of preparing for this conference have kept me from my daily meditations. I confess I lack the power to perform the necessary spells at this time. However, there are sub-priests at my temple who may be

131

capable of stanching the bleeding. They will not be able to save
the damaged hand, but they can certainly save the lives of these
noble knights. I will send word to my priests immediately."

"Yes, please do so without further delay," the princess
commanded. She could not stop herself from adding, "In my
father's city, a high priest would attend to his meditations
before worrying about the ceremonial requirements of a royal
conference."

The patriarch shot her a dark look that was noticed by everyone standing near. The dukes looked offended at her insult to the
cleric's authority. In point of fact, Selinda was not entirely sure
what priorities should guide the time of a Palanthian priest. She
kept her steely expression, even as she made a mental note to
herself: Keep an eye on that high priest.

The two men with leg wounds were carried out, but the third
man objected, shaking his head in despair.

"Leave me here," the injured knight protested. "My hand is
gone—I am no use to the Order of the Crown. Let me die!"

"Nonsense," said the cleric, with a note of spite in his voice.
"The Lady of Palanthas has decreed that your life be saved, and
so it shall if at all possible. You men, offer him your shoulders.
Bring him to my temple—it is just beyond the castle gate."

"No!" cried the knight.

"Come!" demanded the cleric. Even across the great hall,
Selinda felt the hush in the room that followed this angry shout.
There was a magic in that word.

"Bah—the fool may as well die for his failure," murmured
Duke Rathskell, as the knight was helped from the hall. "He had
the assassin before him, six swords to one."

"I tell you, it was sorcery that aided his escape!" shouted
Jarrod.

"All I'm hearing are pathetic excuses," sneered Rathskell. "If
your men were half as fast with their swords as you are with your
ale, they would have had the killer in chains by now!"

"How dare you?" barked the hulking lord. "Why, if you
handled troops anywhere nearly as well as you handle that

wench you married, we would be planning a hanging right now! Instead, the assassin of Lord Lorimar runs free!" The bearlike Jarrod balled his great hand into a fist, and thrust it toward his counterpart.

"Watch yourself, my lord," declared Rathskell, his rapier appearing in his hand as if by magic. The slender tip danced only a foot away from Jarrod's keg-sized chest.

"Stop it—both of you," demanded Selinda, stepping between them. The rapier almost brushed her cheek as Rathskell, with a grimace of irritation, yanked his weapon away. Jarrod of Thelgaard drew a deep breath and let his hands drop. She was surprised to see that the big man was trembling. His eyes were wild as he stared past the princess, as if he didn't even see her. Suddenly she felt afraid but would not allow herself to back away, not in front of these lords whose respect she required.

The tension hung in the room.

"Enough!"

The command roared through the great hall. It was Sir Marckus, the tips of his trailing mustaches quivering in rage.

"By Joli, have your Excellencies forgotten our common cause?" Sir Marckus demanded. "You should be ashamed! The Assassin is loose in the realm! You bicker among yourselves like children while he gets farther and farther away from the justice he so richly deserves! Why . . ."

Marckus finally seemed to realize that he was addressing his liege, and his liege's peers. With a visible effort he gained control of his tongue. Dukes Jarrod and Rathskell glared at him, but there had been truth in the captain's words, and the tension was broken.

"Now, now," said the Duke of Caergoth. "Let's sit down and talk about this calmly. The Assassin will turn up again—such evil-doers are nothing if not habitual. We'll get him soon enough. How about a round of drinks?" He gestured to several stewards, and they hastened to fetch bottles of wine from a nearby rack.

The dukes, with their respective entourages, withdrew toward separate tables. Selinda put her hand on Sir Marckus's arm as he started after Duke Crawford. "Thank you," she said quietly.

He surprised her by putting his large hand over her small fingers. "No, my lady. Thank *you*," he replied softly. She looked into his eyes and was pleased to note a newfound respect.

"Hurry up with that." Duke Crawford was directing his stewards as the Princess of Palanthas once more took her throne-like chair at the raised table, facing the semicircular arrangement of tables seating Solanthus, Caergoth, and Thelgaard. Jarrod and Rathskell exchanged brief, hostile glances then each huddled with his captains, whispering and muttering as the wine was poured. The Duke of Thelgaard took his glass and half-raised it to his lips, before noticing that everyone else was waiting for Selinda. Slowly, he put the vessel back onto the table.

"Lords, Knights, and Ladies," the princess began a toast. "Let us not forget the lessons of today— "

She stopped at the sounds of a disturbance. The great doors burst open, and a Knight of the Rose stumbled into the room. His breastplate was dented, his leggings gashed, and a wound on his cheek was crusted with dried blood. Dust covered him in a layer of light brown, and he advanced only far enough to lean both hands upon a table. His eyes, pleading and filled with grief, sought and found the Duke of Caergoth.

"My Lord!" he groaned. "Garnet is sacked and burned! The garrison has fallen to the last man save me. The goblins have come down from the mountains—they are invading the plains!"

"No, by Joli!" bellowed Jarrod of Thelgaard, leaping to his feet.

"When did this happen?" Selinda asked loudly.

"Three days since, my lady," the knight replied, noticing the princess among the dukes for the first time. He stood straight, seeming to find strength at the sight of her. "They came in the hour before nightfall. Thousands of them, for certain—they streamed into the town from three sides at once. We had scant warning—a half a day. Sir Mikel sent as many of the women and children away as he could, making for both Thelgaard and Solanthus."

"Take some water or wine. Then you will need to tell us more," Selinda said gently.

The knight took a deep draught. When he looked at her, his eyes filled with anguish. "Lady," he said, "I wanted to stay there with him, shoulder to shoulder with Sir Mikel and my comrades to the end. He ordered me to flee, and I refused. He bade me go upon the Oath and the Measure that word of the disaster could reach the dukes. I could not but obey."

"You did right by your captain and by the Order of the Rose," the princess replied. "Now, tell us all you know about this army. How many thousands? What manner of troops?"

The knight nodded, reflecting for several moments. "They were more a mob, Lady. No companies, regiments, brigades. Just a rampaging mob. I should guess something like four or five thousand—compared to some of the armies I saw in the War of Souls. Goblins, mostly. Some hobs, of course. Howling and screaming like madmen, tearing with claws—even feasting on the dead! They were led by a great brute, an ogre or giant I should say. They chanted his name: I will never forget it. Ankhar. Ankhar!" His tone grew bitter. "They chanted 'Ankhar!' as they swarmed in on the forlorn city and as I rode away into the night."

"Did you see the direction of their march from Garnet?"

"They followed me as far as the upper ford of the Vingaard, Lady. I don't know if they were pursuing me or if we simply traveled in the same direction. From the western bluff the next morning I could see their raiding parties extending along the bank, so I could not say where the army as a whole is going."

"The Upper Ford!" Duke Jarrod's voice was hoarse, and the color had all but drained from his face. "That places them only two days' march from my own hall. War is upon us!"

"Thelgaard be damned," cried Rathskell. "They can march up the Vingaard and reach Solanthus by tomorrow night! Captain Rankin—muster your company! Get the squires to the horses—we ride for home within the hour!"

Jarrod, too, was already spurring his knights into a frenzy of activity. Captains and sergeants ran from the hall, heralds hauled down the traveling banners. The two dukes were soon ready to leave but not before addressing Caergoth and the princess.

"Crawford—you must put your army in the field!" pleaded Jarrod of Thelgaard. "I have two thousand under my command. If you come from the west, we can smash the bastards between us."

"Yes. That is, unless they go north," Duke Crawford acknowledged.

"Then Solanthus will fall!" snapped Rathskell. "I have but two thousand swords in my own companies and twice as many villages to hold as Thelgaard. You can't leave us to the wolves!"

"No, of course not," Selinda answered for Caergoth. She looked at him earnestly. "How soon can you march?"

He blinked. "Well, I could put a force into the field, of course, but not for at least ten days. I will have to call in my own garrisons from the outlying villages. Can't leave the city unprotected, you know. Not when there's such evil afoot!"

"Ten days!" spluttered Jarrod. Rathskell narrowed his eyes coldly.

"Surely you can move more quickly than that," Selinda said encouragingly. "The goblins are hundreds of miles from Caergoth, on the very doorsteps of our two great allies. Thelgaard is right about one thing—if you bring your army east, you can be the anvil on which the enemy horde is crushed."

Her eyes swept over them as she spoke. "You must use all three of your armies, together. March in coordination, and there is no way that a 'mob' of raiders can stand against you!" She asked Caergoth, again, "How soon can you march?"

The duke gulped. "I can do my best to put the vanguard into the field by the day after tomorrow," he said. He glanced at his captain. "That is, if Sir Marckus deems it feasible."

"It is feasible, my Lord," the knight said, his face inscrutable.

It was an hour later, after the parties of both Thelgaard and Solanthus had departed, that Selinda went to look for the captain of her own escort of guards. She found Sir Powell in the duke's game room, looking over the unusual battlefield display with its thousands of miniature soldiers, and all their horses, catapults and wagons, deployed across imitation hills and streams. The knight captain snapped to attention as she entered.

"Er, I'm sorry, my lady," he said in embarrassment. "The time has passed more quickly than I realized. I should have been about my duties. I know the conference has ended unexpectedly and the dukes have gone to battle, but I lingered here, curious to see if this table really existed. People gossip about it, but it is even more elaborate than I could have imagined."

"Yes. Caergoth is quite proud of it," the princess said. "There is no need to apologize. I need to talk to you about something."

When the conference had so abruptly ended, she had thought of the galleons and of embarking on the sea voyage home, and her terror had returned and grown. She no longer debated her instincts—she had decided she was not getting aboard the ship.

"Lady," the captain was saying. "If I may be bold, your father would be proud of the way you exercised your influence today."

"Why, thank you, Sigmund," she said, pleased at the compliment. "I didn't want to waste any time, considering events. I want to change our plans for a return to Palanthas."

"Well, of course, Lady," Sir Powell said. "Of course, I immediately issued the orders. It will take a day or two to provision the ships, but we should be able to depart very soon."

"That's just it. Of course, we must dispatch the ships back to Father at once and send word about Garnet and this fellow Ankhar. But I have decided to return to Palanthas overland. On horseback."

Sir Powell looked as if he had been punched in the stomach. He blinked a few times and appeared to be straining for breath. "My lady!" he finally said. His lips continued to move, but no other words came forth.

"I am sure you will attend to the requisite security arrangements," she continued. "Of course, we can take the Westway along the foothills of the Vingaards. That will keep us far from the goblins. I don't think Father would approve if we were to follow the route of the Vingaard River. Would he?"

"No!" he croaked. "Of course not! But, my lady—"

"Oh, it will be perfectly safe. Besides, Gennard. If I am to be the Lady Regent of Solamnia someday, then I should really have a look at those fabled plains with my own eyes, should I not?"

"Yes, my lady." He already felt defeated, and she had to suppress an urge to give him a hug. He seemed impressed at her decisiveness, too, as he nodded in resignation.

"Yes, you should," he concluded.

❦

The Dukes of Solanthus and Thelgaard were gone, along with their knights. The princess and her guards would depart, traveling overland in the morning. Duke Crawford of Caergoth was back in his game room, alone with his table of miniatures—and the image of Lord Regent du Chagne in the mirror hidden in the small alcove.

"We shouldn't get too worked up about a simple band of raiders," the lord told his duke. "Garnet is small loss—they have rejected our protection, and this is their just desserts. For now, let Solanthus and Thelgaard prove themselves by handling the wretches —they weren't very cooperative at the council anyway."

"Indeed, lord. They deserve your rebuke. Though I did give them my word that I would march, with some haste."

"Bah—let them stew!" du Chagne said. "They will learn that they cannot flaunt the will of their master! Besides, an expedition to the east will be terribly expensive. Better to wait and see if they can take care of matters without you."

"Very well, my lord," said Crawford. "I will postpone my deployments."

The mirror darkened, but the duke waited until late in the evening to summon his knight captains. Sir Marckus and Sir Reynaud found their liege still in the gaming room, advancing

138

a legion of heavy cavalry against the flank of an enemy formation. If the captains noticed that the opposing formation was comprised of Thelgaard's knights rather than a goblin horde, they were wise enough to refrain from comment.

"I have been thinking . . ." the duke began, as Marckus and Reynaud stood patiently by.

"Yes, Excellency," the captains replied dutifully.

"A hasty deployment might lead to mistakes. Even disastrous mistakes."

The knights remained silent. Reynaud nodded approvingly. Marckus's eyes were unreadable below his thick bushy brows.

"The princess has announced that she will depart in the morning, escorted by one hundred knights under Captain Powell."

"Indeed, Excellency," Marckus replied. "Your own legion, nearly six thousand men, will be ready to march to the east a few hours later."

"You see. That is what has me worried. I don't want to send those men willy-nilly in one direction, only to find out that we really need them somewhere else."

"I'm afraid I don't understand, my lord. As of three days ago, we know the ogre horde was in Garnet."

"They could have withdrawn back into the mountains," Reynaud observed coolly. "Then the whole operation would be a colossal waste."

"Correct," the duke noted. "I think the legion should not march tomorrow. I have decided to wait two more days for more information. You know, so we don't make a terrible mistake."

"My lord!" said Sir Marckus, for the first time betraying an urgency in his voice. "Thelgaard and Solanthus are expecting you. They may be hard pressed! The situation is unpredictable!"

"That's exactly right. These goblins. Well, they're just evil. And unpredictable. We need to wait and see where they are headed, what they are trying to do, before we commit my legion." He looked at Marckus out of the corner of his eyes, as if to gauge his captain's level of resistance. Once again, the knight's face was an impassive mask.

"Good. Then we're understood. The legion will march two days after tomorrow." He frowned, scratching his smooth chin. "That is, unless we need more time after that. . . ."

⊰๑๑๑๑๑๑๑ᴥ๑๑๑๑๑๑⊱

The Nightmaster had agents everywhere in Caergoth, from the loftiest noble's tower to the most miserable dungeon. His spies had told him the galleons of Palanthas were reprovisioning, would leave for home within another day or two. Now came word that the ships would not be carrying their most important passenger.

The priest, shrouded in mist and wearing his masking red robe, stood on the parapet of his secret temple, peering anxiously into the cold light of dawn. The city's great gate rumbled open, and the Nightmaster watched the long column of riders depart toward the north, starting onto the wide plains of Solamnia. In the middle of that file he clearly saw the Princess of Palanthas.

One of his agents had done his job very, very well.

CHAPTER THIRTEEN

THE RUIN

"Where are we?" Dram asked, staggering slightly from the lingering disorienting effect of Coryn's magic. Sulfie and Carbo hugged each other and looked around in sheer terror, while Jaymes regarded the surroundings through narrowed eyes.

They stood in a tangle of knee-high brush, half-circled by an unkempt hedge. Flagstones marked a path around both sides of the foliage, though creepers and vines now ruled the gaps between the flat rocks, covering some completely, obscuring parts of them all.

They were on a gentle-sloped bluff just above a great river valley to the south and west. In the near foreground, a magnificent stone bridge crossed that river, a span nearly half a mile long boasting a smooth, paved highway that passed very near to their location before descending to the northern terminus. Beyond, on the south side, the highway curved sharply westward, vanishing in the distance.

"Same bridge we crossed," Dram noted, "not long ago—about two days out of Caergoth. Quite a piece of engineering, it is."

"It was built by dwarves, you know," Coryn said. "Back in the days when Solamnia was a true empire."

"Mighta known, about the dwarves I mean," replied Dram,

pleased. "It'll stand for another thousand years, at least."

The warrior stared the white wizard.

"Why did you bring us here?" he demanded.

"I brought *you* here," she said. "The others were invited along because it seemed like a better option than staying in the ghetto."

"Thanks for that," Dram said with a nod of his head. "How did you know we were in such a load of trouble?"

"Oh, I have friends in court. And in the gutters, as well," the enchantress added with the trace of a smile.

"I'm not your friend. I want to go home," Sulfie said, sniffling.

"I'm afraid you can't, for the time being," Coryn explained soothingly. "Since Jaymes was found at your house, you would be arrested by the knights as soon as you showed up. At the very least, they would want to interrogate you for a very, very long time."

That only added to the gnome's sniffling. Carbo patted her shoulder consolingly as Dram followed Jaymes over to the entrance of the overgrown ring-hedge. A tangle of vegetation covered the ground, with many clumps of wildly colored blossoms. Beyond rose a tall chimney, charred black and bereft of any surrounding structure. A few timbers and beams were distinguishable in the midst of a large area of burned wreckage.

"The gardens have suffered," Coryn said gently, coming up behind the pair. "They have had no care for more than two years now."

"What's that?" Carbo asked, intrigued. The bald-headed gnome strolled past them and right up to the ruin. He picked up a blackened board, scrutinizing it. "Nice carpentry, once. Have to allow for warping of weather. And the fire. Was this some kind of palace?"

"It was the manor house of a Solamnic nobleman. A Lord of the Rose," Jaymes said quietly. "He died here."

Carbo nodded, stroking his white beard. "Fire of natural origin—that is, not dragonbreath. Started here in the great room would be my educated guess, then spread out in all directions. It stopped for some reason, before those ends burned up."

"It started to rain," declared the warrior grimly. He turned again to Coryn, his expression cold. "Why are we here?"

"I need something, and I think you might know where it is. Lord Lorimar possessed a strongbox, a container of steel marked with his L in filigree. You have seen it, haven't you?"

"Yes, I have seen it," said the warrior.

"Well, I need that box—or rather, its contents. I thought you might know where Lorimar kept it."

"What makes you think it didn't burn in the fire?" Jaymes asked.

"Lorimar told me it was protected—it wouldn't burn. Maybe you'll help me find it, if only because I just saved your life . . ."

With a frown, Jaymes turned to Dram. "See if you can find some digging tools in what's left of the stable. A pick and a shovel should do it." He turned back to Coryn. "All right, come this way."

He led her past the remnant of a stone wall, mostly crumbled, that had once been the front of the great house. They stepped carefully between the litter of partial timbers, including trunk-sized beams that had obviously fallen from a lofty ceiling. Using the chimney as a marker, Jaymes paced off a dozen long strides along the base of a broken stairway. He knelt and brushed away the soot and muck that smeared the floor, clearing several flagstones by the time the dwarf arrived with a solid pick and a short-handled spade.

The warrior took the shovel and wedged the tool under one of the stones. With a powerful push he drove the shovel in then leaned on it to lever the stone loose. Dram pulled it out of the way while the man loosened two more of the flat sections of dark slate, revealing a layer of plaster over the red clay. When the flagstones were removed, Jaymes lifted the pick and chopped until he had broken up the plaster and the hard-packed dirt.

He dug until the tool struck something solid with a metallic *clank*. Carefully Jaymes scraped away more dirt, digging down around the edges of a rectangular box. When he knelt and brushed it clean, the ornate "L" was visible, even through the rust. Dram helped, using the shovel for leverage, as the man lifted the box.

"Looks like a pretty stout lock," the dwarf observed.

"I might have the key," said the enchantress, adding, "after a fashion."

Jaymes set it on the raised stone shelf that had once been a hearth, and Coryn, the hem of her white robe already dark with soot, knelt beside the box. She touched a finger to the latch and muttered a soft, sibilant word. A slight spark flashed from the box, and she bent with both hands to lift the lid. It rose up with a creak of rusty hinges, and, looking inside, the white robe cried, "No!"

"Not what you expected?" Jaymes asked caustically.

She stood and stared at him, her lips clenched in a tight, angry line. With one hand she gestured at the box. "It's empty!"

"What were you expecting?" asked the dwarf, his eyes shifting between the two of them as he peered into the container, feeling around with his hands to confirm Coryn's findings.

She didn't answer the dwarf. Instead, she continued to regard Jaymes with her brooding stare. Her dark eyes glinted. "Was this tampered with after the fire?" she asked. "Could someone have dug it up, opened it, then returned it to its hiding place?"

The warrior shrugged. "The soot and debris I cleaned away was like the rubble everywhere else around here. My best guess is no, it hasn't been disturbed since well before the fire."

"And the lord was dead at the time of the fire?" she prodded, as Dram eyed them. Both of the gnomes had edged closer, glancing at each other, trying to understand the mysterious conversation.

Jaymes nodded and turned away, rubbing his hand across his face. "He was already bleeding to death when the fire started."

"Then the contents of the box must have been removed before he died. That tells me something," the enchantress said.

"What in the name of Reorx is so all-fired important about this box?" fumed Dram.

"It's called the Compact of Freedom," Coryn replied, her eyes never leaving Jaymes's. "Lord Lorimar wrote it and was instrumental in getting it signed. But it bears the imprints of Lord Regent du Chagne of Palanthas, as well as all three of his dukes."

"Just a mere piece of paper?" the dwarf said skeptically.

"More than that, it's a promise agreed to by those four nobles: a pledge that Garnet will remain a free city, with none of the orders of knighthood presiding over it. It further limits the powers of the knighthood throughout the rest of the old empire, requiring that every ten years the people must approve the actions of their leaders or they will be replaced by others."

"Whoa! Du Chagne signed *that?*" Dram said with a low whistle.

"His arm was twisted slightly. All their arms were," Jaymes noted. "Lorimar used his stature—he was the only one who could broker the power of the independent merchants, and he convinced the lords that the alternative would be civil war."

"Let me get this straight. Lormimar was murdered, and this piece of paper is missing—this compact that was in this box?"

Jaymes shrugged. "That's where he usually kept it. The last time I saw it, I watched him lock it in the box. In fact"—he flashed a look at Coryn—"I helped him bury it. There was more than the compact in the box, too. Something else of great value."

"The Green Diamonds," she said. "I've heard about them, but are they mythical or real?"

"Real enough, and beautiful, each of them bigger than an eyeball," the warrior declared. He added for Dram's benefit, "In gratitude for Lorimar's loyalty and assistance, the merchants of Solamnia gave him a gift: six unique diamonds, huge, green in color. Lorimar planned to incorporate them into a crown if ever Solamnia united behind a king. The third thing in this box was another sign of that hope: He had a banner made, white silk emblazoned with gold. It depicted all three signs of the knighthood, the crown, the rose, and the sword, all on the same pennant."

"Sounds like someone figured out what Lorimar was up to and assassinated him," Dram said slowly, staring at Jaymes. "Probably a good thing—sounds like this Lorimar wanted to be the new king of Solamnia."

"No. Lorimar was content here," the swordsman replied. "I believe he wanted to live out his days in peace. Though he did have a daughter, and a marriage to her might have elevated any one of the lords toward that kingship. . . ."

"What happened to the daughter?"

A long silence prevailed, as the dwarf looked back and forth between his companions. When he perceived they were looking at each other and paying no attention to him, he grabbed the two gnomes and stomped off back to the overgrown garden.

"You need to be a little more careful," the white robe said to Jaymes, in a low, sympathetic voice. "You took a terrible risk in going to Caergoth. You were lucky I was there instead of in Palanthas. Next time you might not be so fortunate."

"I had to go there," the warrior said, his jaw set stubbornly. "I found what I was looking for. But . . . thanks for your help anyway."

"Yes, my help," she murmured.

He took off his glove, showing her the gold ring on the middle finger of his left hand. "It helped me a lot last time I came through Garnet too."

"I'm glad." She reached out a hand, brushing the stubble on his cheek tenderly. "I mean it. Be careful," she said.

"I will. You be careful, too."

Coryn nodded slowly. Looking at her, Jaymes was reminded how very beautiful she was, with her black hair fanned across the cowl of her hood, perfectly framing an oval face with high cheekbones and dark, mysterious eyes. After a moment the hint of a smile played across her full lips. She leaned forward, kissed the warrior softly. He put his rough hands on her shoulders very gently, as if afraid of dirtying her robe—which had, somehow, once again become immaculately white—and stepped away.

She whispered a word of magic and disappeared.

Jaymes stood by himself for a long time, brooding. Then he took a look around the ruins. His eyes lingered on the hulking remnant of the east wing, where the fire had been halted. The interiors of several rooms were visible, and he looked at one in particular: a chamber draped in ragged, blackened curtains that still betrayed a hint of blue silk material. The near wall had burned away, and the sagging floor barely supported the sodden, rotten remains of what had once been an elegant bed . . . a lady's bed.

"Is she gone?" Dram asked, finally coming back from the garden. "Used her magic to disappear, did she? Makes my skin crawl just to think about it!" He shuddered in the common dwarfish aversion to all things magic. "We're better off without her! Though she did give us a timely exit back there in the ghetto."

"We're lucky she bothered," the warrior said.

"Yeah. Uh, speaking of luck, we're lucky I went out to the garden just now. I got a good look at the road across the plain, and we have some visitors coming. Fast. Out of the East."

Jaymes cocked an eyebrow.

"Yes, they're riders all right, but they're not coming on horseback," Dram said. "My best guess is they're goblins on wolfback. They're spread out on both sides of the road but they aren't traveling by highway, they're moving faster on the grass."

"What about the gnomes?" asked the man.

"Last I saw they were looking around in that direction," Dram replied, indicating the shell of the manor's west wing.

The two companions made their way along the front of the house, spotting the gnomes up in the second story of the ruin, bickering in what had once been a grand hallway.

"Something put out the fire," Carbo insisted. "Rain wouldn't be enough, see. I know all about rain. Probably it was a nitrogen-sulfate mix of some kind, designed to retard combustion."

"No," Sulfie objected, "you heard them, it burned itself out. See how it got to this stone balustrade, on the big stairs? It just petered out."

"Poppycock and balderdash!" snorted the male gnome. "The stairs are wood—*they* would have burned! No, there was some kind of intervention. Perhaps a fire brigade came by and doused the flames."

"Fire brigade? Ha, ha! From where? That's just ridiculous. Maybe the stairs are fire-retardant—like ironwood! Did you think of that?"

"I thought of—"

"Rain." Jaymes said from below, staring up at the two gnomes.

"Go away!" Carbo snapped down at him.

"I told you what happened: It started to rain," the warrior continued, his tone flat. "The house was gutted in the middle, but the ends were still standing. It rained hard enough to put out the fire."

"See!" said Sulfie. "You heard him. Rain!"

"Come on," said the human, ignoring the two gnomes, who continued to debate. "We've got to get out of here—goblins are coming."

The gnomes hastened down from their high perch, moving precariously along the edge of the half-burned staircase. Once they were safely on the ground, Jaymes pointed toward the back of the once-grand manor and spoke to Dram Feldspar. "You'll find a shallow ravine just a stone's throw from the back plaza. Take the gnomes, and wait for me there."

"Aw, I don't like waiting. You're not going to do anything crazy now, are you?" asked the dwarf.

Jaymes shook his head, as Dram led the two gnomes away. Before they were out of sight, the warrior was moving forward at a crouch, concealing himself in the tangle of the overgrown garden, making his way around the hedge until he could see across the plains that extended, flat and brown, toward the eastern horizons.

He spotted the riders immediately, knew that Dram had been accurate. These were goblins riding those huge, shaggy wolves they often used as mounts. Their canine lope was unmistakable as the goblins were borne across the grassy flatland. A quick glance showed him at least two score of these outriders, with a larger column of goblins just beyond. The latter marched on foot but were making good time. All of them seemed to be verging on the ruin of Lord Lorimar's manor.

Jaymes checked the wind. It was coming from the plains, blowing toward the four companions, so they would not be betrayed that way. The warrior ducked back, watching as the leading goblins drew up to the fringe of what had once been the garden. They dismounted, turning their great wolves free to lope on the plains, while the goblins drew their wickedly curved swords and started into what had once been the rose garden, hacking the blooming branches down as if they were jungle creepers.

Jaymes withdrew to join his comrades in the low gulley. From here they could peer between the thick grasses along the rim and, as long as the wind stayed friendly, keep an eye on the goblins with little chance of being spotted themselves.

The goblins swarmed through the blackened rubble, kicking around the broken timbers, whooping and cheering as they scrambled over debris. Several squawked and barked when they came upon the fresh hole where the steel box had been removed.

A goblin tore down one of the blue silk draperies from the lady's bedchamber and threw it over his shoulders, a mockery of a regal cape. He pranced along the sagging edge of the broken floor until a rotten timber broke under his feet, plunging him unceremoniously into the tangled wreckage of the first floor. Moaning piteously, he was too injured to resist as another goblin came up to him and snatched away the material, leaving his stricken comrade pinned between two heavy, charred beams.

Gray clouds had rolled across the plains with the goblins. Now a chilly drizzle began to fall, and the marauders wearied of their unprofitable explorations. They withdrew to the garden, leaving a few pickets posted around the fringes of the ruin. As it grew dark, the orange glow of an immense bonfire brightened the interior of the hedge ring. The rain picked up, leaving the four companions stuck in their ravine soggy, miserable, and cold.

Even so, Jaymes said they should wait until dark before slipping away. Dram agreed. The two gnomes, huddled together under a single blanket with teeth chattering, had lost all their spirit. Hours later the warrior led them away, heading north behind the cover of rain and clouds and darkness blanketing the area.

Hours before dawn, they were still moving. "Those outriders are just the vanguard," Jaymes warned Dram. "I have a feeling the whole army is going to be along in another day or two."

⊰�’∘⊸∘⊸∘∘⊰●⊱∘∘⊸∘⊸∘’⊱

Mason's Ford was a nondescript town that owed its existence to a shallow stretch of the small but rapid North Garnet River. A series of small corrals and barns ringed the outer fringe of the community, which lacked the protection of a wall, tower, or any other fortification. The four travelers were foot-sore and weary as, two days after leaving the ruin of Lord Lorimar's manor, they trudged along the muddy track leading through the town and toward the river crossing that had given the place its name.

The rain had continued durng their trek, and Mason's Ford was shrouded in a soggy fog that rendered the place indistinct and dreary.

"Seems kind of crowded," Dram noticed immediately. The main street was lined by wooden buildings with long covered porches that were crowded with men, women, and children. Many of the people were huddled in blankets or tarps. A few of the men had staves, picks, and other crude weapons near to hand.

"What word of the gobs, Strangers?" asked one man, rising from the front step of an inn and ambling into the rainy street.

"Last saw 'em two days back," said the dwarf. "A patrol on worgs south of here. Dunno where they were headed."

"They burned Garnet, you know."

150

Jaymes and Dram exchanged a grim look. "No. We hadn't heard," said the swordsman.

We're just passing through, ourselves," Dram added.

The man chuckled. "Good luck," he said, before turning back to his family and companions who were watching, with interest, from the crowded porch.

"Wonder what that was about," the dwarf said. "Why in the name of Reorx are all these folks sitting around here if they're so dang worried about the goblins?"

Jaymes simply kept walking, his long strides forcing the dwarf and gnomes to hurry in order to keep up. The street started to descend toward the ford, and they noticed even more people huddled under every roof. Some had erected tarps in vacant yards, while others had taken over stables, barns, and sheds for makeshift shelters.

The reason for the crowding became apparent as they approached the river. Brown water spilled over the porches and crept up the walls of the last buildings on the street. The current surged, churning far above the banks, making the river so broad that the far bank was lost in the murky distance. Jaymes narrowed his eyes, looking toward the stout rope that anchored the auxiliary ferry, a flatboat that provided passage for those who didn't care to wade the ford. That boat was broken, hurled by the surging current against the pilings of a nearby lumber yard, where it sat with its hull cracked and open to the river's angry rise.

There would be no crossing of the Vingaard, not until the rain ceased and the flooding river fell.

⊹⊙⊱⊙⊱⊙⊱⊙⊰✿⊱⊙⊰⊙⊰⊙⊰⊙⊱

Ankhar didn't mind the rain. The water rolled easily off of his bearskin cloak, and his broad shoulders and sturdy frame were not burdened by the weight of the sodden garment. His goblins were happy to march through the mud, and the fleet-footed worgs were not hampered anywhere near as much as horses would have been.

151

Several of his outriders approached now. The half-giant halted and shook his head, casting a spray over the hobs of his personal bodyguard. The lead scout, a small, wiry goblin named Rib Chewer, sprang from the back of his lupine mount and knelt before Ankhar.

"Master, we have followed many humans to a place on this river. They cannot cross in the high water, and they have no wall to protect them. We can kill them all!"

"Good. Where this place?"

"It lies but a half-day's march to the west of here. There is no river crossing above or below for two marches."

"What about knights?" asked the hulking chieftain. "They got garrisons to north and south. They moving?"

"No, Master!" the goblin uttered a wet cackle. "They have withdrawn into their fortresses. They cower in their castles like old women. They are afraid to face us!"

Ankhar stroked his broad chin, reflecting. His horde was spread across a hundred miles, but this town was a good objective. There would be good sport in the killing, and even if they found little treasure, there was sure to be food and drink enough to satisfy his troops for several days.

"Son." It was Laka, tugging at the loop on his belt where he slung his mighty, emerald-headed spear. She waved the skull totem back and forth, and Ankhar resentfully met those dark sockets with his own eyes.

"What word of Prince?' he asked.

Instead of answering, Laka shook the head so the pebbles rattled and bounced in a wash of noise that was like the warning of a rattlesnake. No green light came into that empty visage. No words of counsel or warning emerged from the dead teeth.

"Tell god we win another victory," Ankhar said to his foster mother, his jaw jutting.

"You not tell god!" spat Laka, springing closer to the half-giant, shaking the death's-head at his face. She danced around in agitation. "The god tell you! And you listen!"

"The god tell me nothing—I see humans for the killing!" Ankhar retorted. "So we attack!"

Laka, sulking, went back to her tent—the only such structure in the whole camp, because the old shaman needed privacy for her meditations, invocations, and prayers. Ankhar tried, without success, to shake off a feeling of disquiet as he turned back to his goblin scout. That worthy lieutenant had been carefully studying the outskirts of the camp, though he had no doubt overheard the conversation between his army commander and the witch-doctor.

"You do well, Rib Chewer," the half-giant said. "Send riders to far wings of horde. March to this town today. We gather over night. Tomorrow morning we attack."

"Aye, Master!" cried the goblin, cackling again as he sprang into his saddle. The worg snapped and growled, drool slicking the long fangs, dribbling from the narrow jaws. With a howl, Rib Chewer kicked the beast in the flanks, and the wolf started across the plains at the easy lope that it could maintain for the rest of the day.

By the time it finished, the horde of Ankhar would be gathering for the attack.

CHAPTER FOURTEEN

THE BATTLE OF
MASON'S FORD

Hey, you. Come here." The speaker was a Knight of
Solamnia, Order of the Rose—the first knight the
travelers had seen in the small riverfront town where they had
been trapped for a day.

"Me?" Jaymes asked. He was seated on the ground, mostly
covered by his woolen cape as he leaned against the wall of a
store. The rain was still coming down, and he along with the
other members of his sodden little party were huddled together
under the overhanging eave of the building.

"Yeah, you," said the knight. "Come with me." He was a
young man, with a full shock of brown hair and a mustache
trimmed neatly over the upper lip of a handsome, full-lipped
mouth.

"What's going on?" Dram asked the knight, blinking himself
awake after being elbowed by the warrior.

"You'll find out soon enough, dwarf. You, human—you heard
me, come along. We don't have a lot of time."

With an indifferent shrug, and a glance at the dwarf, Jaymes
pushed himself to his feet and ambled along after the knight,
who led him around the building and along the muddy street
toward the largest inn in the main square. "Wait in there," the
knight said, pointing toward the front door. "Tell them Sir Rene

will be right there—I'm just going to make a swing past the sawmill."

Upon entering, Jaymes found the great room crowded with men: burly farmers, a dozen lanky plainsmen in buckskin, a few well-muscled woodcutters and boatwrights. A half dozen knights were standing around or seated at a large table in the front of the room. None of them paid any particular attention to Jaymes, who, after a moment's hesitation, walked up to the knights and said, "Sir Rene is coming soon—he's going to the sawmill first."

"All right. Find a place. We'll get started in a moment," said one of the knights, a gray-bearded veteran who didn't look up from a piece of parchment marked with some diagrams and numbers.

Seeing no easy way out of the situation, Jaymes went over to one side of the room and leaned against one of the stout supporting pillars. He made sure that the hilt of his sword was covered by his cape and crossed his arms over his chest, waiting.

Sir Rene, trailed by a couple more men, came in a few minutes later. The knight went to the table then turned around to face the assemblage. Rene gestured to one of his companions. "Tell us what you saw," the knight said.

The man nodded and stepped to the front of the room. He had the brown, weather-beaten face of a man who had lived his entire life out of doors. His expression was grave but unafraid.

"The goblins are coming here. They came out of the mountains and burned Garnet to the ground seven days ago. Several thousand strong, with outriders on worgs. We fought off an attack by a hundred of them outriders yesterday. We were a score of men before that fight. We are a dozen now."

"Are they coming up or down the river valley?" asked a recent arrival, a farmer with big hands and mud-spattered trousers.

"They've spread from Garnet city south to the main branch of the river," the man answered grimly. "There is no escape from them on this side of the river."

"But we can't cross the river!" objected another fellow, an older man still wearing a greasy cook's apron.

"No, we can't. Not for at least another two days, and then only if the rain stops," Sir Rene admitted. "That's why I've gathered you all here. If we are attacked—and it looks like we will be—we're going to have to fight for the lives of everyone trapped here."

"We're not warriors!" protested the man wearing the cook's apron. "We demand the protection of the knights!"

Rene gestured to the five other men—those who wore the Rose emblem—seated at the table. "Well, you have the protection of six knights. Even if there was time, we couldn't get reinforcements here across the river. So you all have the choice of waiting here to be massacred or of joining the fight."

His remarks provoked angry muttering and many apprehensive looks, as the men in the room sized each other up.

"How far away are they?" Jaymes asked in a loud voice.

Rene looked him in the eye and nodded, apparently relieved to hear a practical question. He nodded at the plainsman who had made the report. "Streamfisher here says they're already gathering just beyond the horizon. It seems likely that they'll be in position to attack by tonight, or at the latest, tomorrow morning."

He cleared his throat, planting his hands on his hips. Sir Rene might be the youngest of the knights, but the others deferred to him.

"We want to pull everyone back into a semicircle near the riverbank. The young and the old, those who can't help with the fight, we'll shelter in the ferry building, and in several of the warehouses that haven't flooded. The rest—starting with the men in this room, while including every sturdy youth, every strong woman brave enough to wield a staff or a pole—will help hold the line."

He outlined a defensive plan that was centered on the inn and another large establishment across the street. To the left of these, the flanks would be formed by the sawmill and boatyard, where unfinished hulls and overturned riverboats would form makeshift bulwarks. To the right, a stone-walled stable provided a decent strong point, and a large mill—together with its water wheel and dam on the riverbank—would form the far anchor of the line.

"We'll make firebreaks on the streets between each of these structures," Sir Rene explained. "We're lucky enough to have two score barrels of oil in one of the warehouses, so we can soak the timber enough that it should burn even in the rain. We have a little more than fifty men here, so we'll post eight or ten at each strong point, with one knight acting as captain of each group. Collect all the able-bodied people you can find. Our survival depends on driving off the attackers and inflicting enough damage on them that they lose their stomach for the fight."

A fat old man, presumably the innkeeper, brought out a couple of bottles of fiery spirits. The knight directed that they be passed around the room, so everyone who wanted might take a sip.

"I give you my knight's pledge, on the Oath and the Measure, that we will stand at Mason's Ford as long as blood flows in our veins. I ask you men to make the pledge, on this toast, that you will give us whatever aid is in your power. Together we must stand!"

Jaymes took a long pull when one bottle came to him, wincing as the fiery liquid seared down his gullet. He passed the bottle to the next man, saw that Sir Rene was watching him.

"You've got my pledge," the warrior said loud, so that the others might hear. "Where do you want me to fight?"

Dram had hung back from the crowd, listening, and now he went up to Sir Rene and volunteered to fight alongside the others. The knight looked him up and down and shrugged. "Why not?"

Meekly trailed by the two gnomes, the dwarf went with Jaymes to his assigned post at the mill. They were joined by two dozen defenders—three or four sturdy men, and a mixture of youths, old men, and a few grim-faced farm wives. They were all under the command of the weathered knight Jaymes had spoken to upon arriving at the inn. He introduced himself as Sir

Hubert and went about positioning his small force as dictated by the terrain.

The millpond was lower than the river, separated by a raised embankment that ran like a causeway along the bank of the swollen Vingaard. The pond was surrounded by a shore of dry ground, and Sir Hubert assessed it as the most likely route of attack if the goblins came along the river.

"If we had another day," the knight said in disgust, "we could dig a hole in this dam and flood out the flat. Without that luxury, we'll have to hold them at the embankment. Failing that, fall back to the wheelhouse. That will be our last redoubt."

He immediately sized up Jaymes as a capable fighter, putting him in command of a small group defending the dam, the pond, and the water wheel. The warrior posted his volunteers, assigning Dram the left flank while Jaymes himself stood on the right.

They stayed in those positions all night, through intermittent shower and drizzle. The defenders took turns sleeping. Those who stayed awake staring into the murk saw no sign of the enemy. As dawn turned the black night to a soggy gray, Jaymes spoke to the dwarf and the two gnomes.

"That keg we brought from Caergoth—we might need to give it a try here. Can you rig a fuse that will stay dry?"

Aided by Sulfie and supervised by Dram, Carbo found a small pump room, a watertight chamber located in the base of the dam. Arranging the keg in there, he ran a line of the black powder to the door of the small compartment. It was dry enough within that a spark could be struck.

Jaymes took stock of the weaponry available to his small detachment. Three of the youths claimed to have some proficiency as hunters and were armed with bows and arrows. These he posted in the top of the wheel house, with orders to hoard their precious missiles until they felt certain of hitting their targets. Apart from Dram's axe and his sword—still lashed to his back beneath his cape—they were armed with an assortment of large knives, one or two swords, and several stout poles. One burly man, a smith, had a large hammer that he flipped around deftly, pledging to crush the skull of any goblin that came within reach.

"You'll soon have an opportunity—look, there they are!" Sulfie cried, as the rain faded to a light drizzle.

The worg-riders emerged like ghostly shadows from the murk of the gray mist, loping on their fearsome mounts. There were dozens of them, riding past the dam surrounding the millpond, gazing at the steep embankment, moving on toward more favorable terrain. A few hooted at the defenders on the earthen dam, waving spears, cackling wildly. Gradually they faded from view, riding in a wide circle around the fringe of Mason's Ford.

Sir Rene came through the mill and found Jaymes on the rampart. "They're probing with their riders," the knight informed him. "They will fall upon us soon. Already we've seen a least a regiment's worth forming up to come down the main highway."

"A *formed* regiment?" the swordsman asked.

"No, not like trained troops. More like a mob. They're collecting and working themselves up for a nasty attack."

Jaymes nodded, squinting into the distance where they could begin to make out ranks of goblin infantry coming closer, marching in tight, surprisingly regular lines.

"How're you for close weapons?" Rene asked. "It won't be long before the work gets bloody."

"I have a sword," the warrior replied with a shrug. "It'll be enough for me when I need it."

Rene chuckled. "Too bad we don't have more like you. Well, good luck."

"The same," Jaymes offered. The knight made his way toward the neighboring stable, where the tethered horses had caught the scent of the worgs and were kicking and whinnying.

A detachment of mounted goblins charged, the wolves howling furiously as they skirted the fences around the stable yards. Several of the shaggy mounts leaped those barriers, racing close to the stable so their riders could cast spears at the defenders. These crude missiles lodged in the planks of the stable building or bounced off the stone foundations. A pair of huntsmen shot off arrows in response, and two of the goblins, pierced by shafts, tumbled from their saddles to lie in the muddy corrals. One worg took an arrow in the flank and yelped, limping away.

On the street between the mill and stable, orange flames surged into life as the first of the oil-soaked woodpiles was ignited. Three ranks of goblins, each several hundred strong, advanced toward the dam and the mill. Their line of march was disorganized but shoulder to shoulder, and they chanted as they drew closer. The chant became more distinct, one word repeated over and over.

"Ankhar! Ankhar! Ankhar!"

Those in the front of the first line of goblins broke into a run, whooping and howling. The defenders—including the dwarf and two gnomes—made a thin line atop the embankment, but they had the advantage of the steep slope before them. The goblins' first impetuous charge served to dissipate the shock of the large, following force.

The defenders at the mill could hear the frenzied battle on the town's main street. Weapons bashed shields, armor and, all too often, flesh. Men and goblins died. Sir Rene commanded that key sector, and his orders, calm but forceful, echoed above the fray: "Stand fast on the stairway! Advance on the left! Fire those hay-bales!"

A few goblins appeared on the riverbank beyond the mill. Over the course of an hour their numbers increased, and by the time a sizeable company had formed the battle on the main street had subsided. These goblins now rushed forward in a howling mob.

They reached the steep slope on the outside of the millpond and hurtled up the slick, grassy surface. Several of them slipped. Those that climbed did so only by clawing for traction, scrambling and pulling themselves up the steep slope. The first to reach the top had the misfortune to face Dram Feldspar. The dwarf chopped his axe in a single forceful blow, spilling brains and blood. The goblin, killed instantly, tumbled back down amidst the rank of its fellows.

The dwarf's killing blow seemed only to inflame the inhuman attackers. Bestial faces contorted in fury, and hundreds of mouths gaped wide, displaying sharp teeth. Broad nostrils flared as the gobs shrieked, brandishing their weapons, clutching at the wet grass, pulling themselves up all along the steep embankment, trying to reach the few defenders.

Carbo had fashioned a sling from a strap of leather. The bald gnome swung the weapon around his head and launched a round stone with speed and accuracy. The missile struck one goblin in the forehead, and the creature collapsed, senseless. Dram darted here and there, his axe bloody, each strike adding fresh gore to his blade. Boys and men wielded their makeshift weapons with courage and enthusiasm, if not with precise skill, and the struggling goblins were smashed back from the height of the embankment. The archers in the mill tower found targets in the mass of enemy troops.

Jaymes was everywhere along the line, wielding his sword with one hand, stabbing the long blade into the face, throat, or chest of any gob unfortunate enough to crest the slope. His eyes ranged along the position—when one youth slipped in the mud and fell backward, the warrior was there, holding the breach against three attackers who had hurled themselves into the momentary gap. Two fell from his blows, and the third retreated, shrieking and clutching its bleeding scalp.

Sulfie had armed herself with a heavy shovel, and she banged the blade against any leering face that rose above the lip of the embankment. Carbo stood close by her, launching stones into the faces of the increasingly shrill goblins.

Two boys, brothers too young to shave, fought courageously with sharpened sticks, poking the makeshift spears into the bunched attackers. A hulking hobgoblin rose from the wavering rank, seizing one of the staves in a taloned hand. With a tug, the beast pulled hard and dragged the lad from the rampart. Screaming in the terror, the youth tumbled into shrieking mob of hacking swords and biting jaws—and there his death was mercifully swift.

His brother cried out, casting his own weapon into the mob and lunging forward in a frantic effort to help his doomed sibling. Jaymes pulled the lad back by the scruff of his neck. The sobbing boy tumbled down the back of the dam while the warrior returned to chopping and slashing against the suddenly frenzied gobs.

Roused by bloodlust, the creatures threw themselves at the defenders with renewed intensity. Several more humans fell, and for a moment Jaymes, Dram, and the hammer-wielding smith faced a dozen jabbering goblins in the middle of the dam. The three drove them back, killing half, but the defense was faltering.

"The fuse—light it!" shouted Jaymes, clearing a swath around him with whistling sweeps of his bloody blade.

"All right, give me half a minute," the dwarf replied, skidding down the backside of the dam, pulling open the door to the pump room where the keg of gnomish powder was stored.

"The rest of you—back to the water wheel!" Jaymes shouted to his ragtag militia. He and the smith stood back to back, slaying any goblin that came within reach of either hammer or sword, while the rest of the defenders raced along the crest of the dam toward the shelter of the sturdy wooden structure.

Goblins spilled over the top of the dam, down to the flat, dry shore of the millpond, and they started making their way along the base of the earthen embankment. The smith staggered, dropping his hammer, groaning as he clasped a bloody wound. The warrior stepped back, giving the big man his left hand for support while, with the sword held in his other, he forced back a swarm of attackers.

"It's burning—run for it!" shouted Dram, bursting from the pump room, sprinting toward the wheel house with a pack of howling goblins pursuing him just a few steps behind.

Step by step, Jaymes edged back, still carrying the bleeding smith. When the wounded man lost his balance and slumped to one knee the warrior stood fast, hacking the head off of a goblin who charged in. The sight of the rolling head gave the next in line a moment's pause, enough for Jaymes to pull the smith to his feet again. The two of them tumbled back to the door of the wheel house just as Dram scrambled up. Willing hands pulled the wounded man inside and the dwarf dived behind.

Jaymes stood alone outside the door, holding his sword ready. The goblins paused, gathering their courage for a renewed assault. Now they spilled along the pond side. The warrior kept his eyes on the pump room, where a small puffs of smoke indicated that Dram's makeshift fuse was burning.

Abruptly, churning black vapor erupted from the pump room. Sparks shot through the murk, and red cinders scattered over nearby goblins, sending them scrambling away, swatting frantically at their burns. More and more embers shot from the pump room. The acrid cloud billowed. Bitter vapors made the goblins cough and choke, and many fell back in fear.

But that was all. The burning keg sputtered and fizzled and smoked up a storm, obscuring a large section of the dam. But it did nothing else, caused no damage to the embankment. All too soon the fire had burned itself out, and the acrid smoke was wafting away.

"By Reorx! That's not right!" Dram cried, standing in the door of the water wheel building.

Jaymes cursed and turned back to the battle with a clenched jaw.

After their momentary consternation, the goblins took stock of the situation and rushed the door of the millhouse, howling in glee.

Jaymes stood alone before the door. He held his blade in both hands, and methodically twisted the hilt in his calloused palms.

Blue fire burst from that potent blade.

⊱⊱⊷⊷⊷⊷❦⊶⊶⊶⊶⊰

Ankhar watched the panic and the retreat. He was hypnotized by the suffering of one hobgoblin, his leg severed below the knee, try to crawl back to the camp on the plains. The wretched creature bled to death within a hundred paces of the outer pickets.

The half giant felt an unfamiliar disquiet. Things had not gone well today. This town should have been easy pickings compared to the walled city of Garnet, which he had so successfully sacked.

Of course, it was all due to that wretched Blue Fire sword. Goblins had always hated that ancient weapon. The warrior who surprised them with it had wielded it well, he had to admit, singlehandedly breaking the left flank of the horde's attack.

Foremost among his regrets was the memory of that dead, silent skull, the talisman that had stared at him when he had been determined to act with or without his god's approval. This was a lesson that Ankhar would remember.

It was the lesson of Truth.

<del>⋋⊙⊙⋌⊙⊙⋌⊙⊙⊛⊙⊙⋋⊙⊙⋌⊙⊙⋌</del>

"They almost broke through at the sawmill," Sir Rene told Dram and Jaymes, as they looked around at the detritus of battle. The mill building was battered but still intact. "Sir Hubert tells me it was a very close-run affair, here. You did well to hold them."

"We did what we could," Jaymes said dryly. "I don't think we could have held out any longer if they had attacked one last time."

Rene shrugged but looked at the warrior shrewdly. "Apparently they didn't have the stomach for tremendous losses. The plainsmen report that the whole horde has moved on—apparently they're heading for Thelgaard. And the river is falling—the ford will be useable by tonight, I'm guessing."

Jaymes nodded. Sir Rene rubbed a hand across his mustache then looked at the warrior. He gestured to the more than a hundred goblin corpses scattered around the wheel house.

"Lots of burns on these bastards. That's probably one thing that scared them off."

The warrior narrowed his eyes, said nothing.

"I'm going to send a report to the dukes. They'll need to know about this battle. For one thing, first reports suggested this enemy was untrained, but I will suggest that is not the case."

Jaymes nodded. "They attacked in some semblance of rank—they could do a lot of damage, with good training."

"And I'll be telling them about the brave defense. About the warrior with the sword who stood alone before the wheelhouse and left a hundred dead goblins, many of them burned."

"That may be true enough," Jaymes replied cautiously.

"I'll be sending my report with a courier first thing in the morning," Sir Rene said, awkwardly. "Just in case . . . you know. In case you are the modest type and want to cross the river this evening and get out of here before my report arrives in Caergoth."

The warrior nodded. "We'll be on our way."

CHAPTER FIFTEEN

ENCOUNTERS AROUND
A RIVER

The lone knight spurred his horse, urging the animal to greater speed. Mud sucked at the hooves, and the animal staggered but found the strength to plunge ahead, raggedly cantering across the flat ground. Eyes bulging, nostrils flaring, the war-horse persevered, carrying the weary rider through the graying twilight. Finally the army camp materialized in the dusk, a scattering of smoky fires, sodden tents, and apprehensive troops.

The big horse slowed as it stumbled past the outer pickets. The knight guided it between the aisles of tents toward the largest canvas shelter in the encampment. The banner of Thelgaard, a white crown on a black field, hung limply from the tall staff, dripping water that pooled unnoticed among the soaked expanse.

Guardsmen made way for the rider. One, taking note of the rose emblazoned on the man's breastplate, turned and shouted, "A messenger from Caergoth arrives!"

Duke Jarrod emerged from the tent, shrugging an oilskin cape over his broad shoulders, looming above the attendants and nobles clustered around him. His beard bristled, and his huge hands were clenched, as if he sought already to strike a blow against some new foe.

"What word from your lord, man?" Jarrod demanded, his voice booming out as the horseman reined in.

"Duke Walker's vanguard is eight miles away—the bulk of his army no more than twelve, Excellency," reported the rider, slipping from the saddle and kneeling on the muddy ground before Jarrod. "He is making camp for the night but expects to cross the river first thing in the morning. He will arrive here by mid-day."

"Ah, you bring good news, at last," the huge lord said, his bearded face breaking into a broad grin, fists unclenching as he clapped his hands in relief. "With Caergoth beside us, we will bring this rabble to heel for good!" He turned to one of his officers. "Captain Dayr—send word to Duke Rathskell. We will count on him to hold the left and let Caergoth fill the middle as soon as he crosses the river. My own force shall stand here on the left, anchored on the bank of the Upper Vingaard."

"Very good, Excellency," Dayr said with a nod. He was a smaller version of his lord, bearded and swarthy, with well-muscled forearms outlined by the black silk of his soaking sleeves. He hastened away, calling for a scribe to ready pen and parchment.

More shouts came from guards at the eastern edge of the encampment, and before Dayr had even finished the flowery introduction—he was still reciting "Lord of the Sword, Master of the Garnet Spur"—the intended recipient came riding up to the headquarters tent with an entourage of a dozen officers and nobles.

"My lord!" exclaimed Thelgaard in genuine surprise, as Duke Nathias Rathskell of Solanthus slid from his saddle with a dancer's grace. His thin rapier was, as usual, balanced at his side, but he looked down in distaste as his feet sank a couple of inches into the muddy ground of his rival's camp. "I had just ordered word sent to you—we hear that Caergoth is but a half day's march away."

Rathskell's thin face brightened a bit at this news, but his familiar scowl returned. "That is indeed encouraging," Rathskell allowed, "but we must needs address the gap between our forces. I stand east of the river, in line and ready to meet the foe coming up from the south. I had expected that you would draw out your own force to meet me. We now have a gap of some two miles between our forces."

Thelgaard waved away the complaint. "That gap is Caergoth's. He will have five thousand men across the river in the morning. They will secure our center."

The Duke of Solanthus peered to the west. "How do you know he will come?" he asked.

Jarrod gestured to the recently arrived messenger, who hurried forward and repeated his lord's declaration. Still, Solanthus remained unconvinced. "My own outriders report that the horde is but a day's march south of us. If Caergoth is delayed, we leave ourselves open to defeat in detail. The gap is a danger."

"Bring your forces up to mine, then," Thelgaard said with an indifferent shrug. "I have my own right anchored on the Upper Vingaard, and I do not care to relinquish that security. If you are too timid to await developments on the plain, all you need do is march into the gap on your right, joining me here. You should have nothing to fear, then."

Rathskell glowered but managed to suppress his anger and reply. "A *simple* march, at night, in the rain, leaving my tents and baggage train exposed? I think not. Besides, I am stretched thin as it is, and if I pull too far this way I leave our whole force open to a flanking maneuver, if this Ankhar takes his troops on a wide circuit away from the river."

"You give this scoundrel, this half-giant leading the ogre horde, credit for cleverness he does not possess," said Thelgaard.

"He was clever enough to overwhelm Garnet in one afternoon," Solanthus responded. "I would have a care not to underestimate him, if I were you."

"You worry about your concerns, and I will worry about mine. Did you not hear about Mason's Ford? Five days ago, a few knights and a rabble of peasants were enough to give these wretches pause. Do not inflate your fears, my good duke."

Rathskell's face flushed at the insult, but he grimaced and once again maintained his poise. "Yes, I heard about that fight—and a noble stand it was. Perhaps this barbarian, this Ankhar, will learn from his mistakes. He has crossed the North Garnet and comes toward us swiftly enough. He may not repeat his blunt tactics again."

"You jabber like an old woman! He is a monster, an illiterate subhuman!" Thelgaard proclaimed, to the approving nods of his own entourage. Let his men see how a *real* lord infused his men with confidence!

"Surely you can spare a screening force, at least? Horsemen who could cover the gap and report on any developments?" Though Rathskell was making an effort to be reasonable, his mustache was quivering with indignation. "You have yourself in a square formation here, covering a mere quarter mile of frontage, with half your force arranged solidly on the riverbank. I have the same amount of men spread out in a line two miles long!"

"Your deployments are your own concern, of course," Jarrod of Thelgaard replied. "I have simply taken wise precautions to see that I cannot be outflanked. I do not intend to place the safety of my army in the hands of anyone other than myself."

"Suit yourself, then," Solanthus replied through clenched teeth. "You well know that I cannot close the gap, since I would place both of our forces open to a flanking run across the plains—and it would cut me off from my own city, if Ankhar moves east. We must count on Caergoth to uphold his promise. But if they come through that gap, Excellency"—he sneered at the honorific—"you understand that you will be on your own."

"That," said Thelgaard, a broad grin cracking the bristle of his great beard, "is a risk that I am well prepared to take."

He was still grinning as his noble counterpart mounted and led his party of officers back into the rainy night.

⊰∙∘⊱∘⊰∙∘⊰⦿⊱∘⊱∘⊰∙∘⊱⊱

Ankhar raised his hand, thrusting the glowing speartip high over his head in the rain-soaked night. The green light,

169

Hiddukel's blessing, stabbed through the murk and mist, a beacon to all his vast legions. The half-giant howled as he waved that enchanted weapon back and forth, feeeling the rush of power surge through his veins.

The great horde numbered more than six thousand now, with several more tribes of gobs having come down from the mountains, drawn like bees to honey as word of the sacking of Garnet spread. From the high valleys they had joined the ranks, eager and willing to obey his orders, with the promise of more pillage and plunder just ahead.

The trading center of Luinstat was to be his next target, and he knew the markets and warehouses there were stuffed with goods from across Solamnia. Three armies of knights had emerged from their cities to defend the place, but at last report the human forces remained scattered, with the largest still on the other side of the river. The two smaller armies stood nearly astride Ankhar's northward path.

"Halt!" roared the hulking commander, and the thousands of troops around him immediately came to a standstill upon that command. The half giant nodded, pleased at the increased discipline, the steadiness of march and unity of purpose that his followers had developed, improving with every passing day.

"You learn!" he crowed. "You march together now, like veteran soldiers. You attack together! Attack when Ankhar gives the order, not when you see foe. Sometimes Ankhar tell you to retreat. Sometimes retreat can turn enemy into fools!

"These my words. They are Truth!"

"Truth! Ankhar! Truth!" The cry was echoed from six thousand throats, the deep sound booming across the plains. Again and again the goblins and hobgoblins echoed the words.

"We make camp here for the night, brave ones," Ankhar roared. "Prince of Lies tells me that tomorrow we feast on blood!"

The answering roar washed across the great leader's shoulders. He didn't feel the rain, and even the thick shroud of the night was naught but a filmy barrier to his keen, dark-sensitive eyes. Now those eyes made out Laka coming towards him. The old crone grinned, making a display of her sharp teeth, shaking the rattle she had made from the skull of a human slain in the sacking of Garnet.

"Portents favorable, mighty lord," the crone cackled. "Humans have doubts. They fear Ankar's might, cunning, and courage."

"That what I hoped," he replied evenly. "Will Hiddukel aid us?"

"No doubt, son. He whisper doubts in lordly ears, shake courage of men when they sleep. He sew confusion and hesitation so you, chosen one, may reap harvest in blood."

Ankhar raised his broad nostrils, sniffed the moist air, and nodded in pleasure. "I smell wolf. Outriders approach."

His warriors were making their crude beds on the open plain—no tents and bedrolls necessary for these hearties!—as the first of the worg-riders loped into camp. The massive wolves seemed to grin with their long tongues hanging down from their fanged jaws. Several of the goblin riders slipped from their saddles and hastened to approach the hulking war-leader.

"What word of foes?" demanded Ankhar.

The captain of the scouts, the lean and wiry goblin known as Rib Chewer, knelt in the mud at the half-giant's feet. "My lord, they appear confused. There is one force solid upon the river-bank, no more than two leagues south of here. Compact like a hedgehog it is, a camp bristling with spears. But blind and stupid as a hedgehog too—with no outriders or pickets more than an arrow's flight from the main body."

"Which troops are these?"

"They fly the banner of the White Crown, lord. The other group of knights, they who flaunt the sigil of the silver sword, is a league away from the crowns, away from the river. They are poised in line on the plain, facing to the south, and very well-entrenched it seems."

"There a league of space between them?"

"Aye, lord," the goblin replied. "There is nary a picket nor a watchman in all that gap. The Sword Knights have a line at least as long, with outriders even farther toward the mountains. They gave us a merry chase, but their great steeds could not perform on the muddy ground."

"No." The half-giant nodded in satisfaction. He knew that the wolves were light and lean, steady of endurance and quick and savage in attacking. They made perfect light cavalry, especially when they were guided by the most intelligent and articulate of his scouts.

"What about other great army, Rose Lord's troops? They look so splendid and move like drunken snails." Ankhar scowled into the night. That was the force that worried him most, those gleaming knights on horseback and in chariots, the catapults and ranks of deadly crossbows. He had been dismayed to learn, from his oracle, Laka, that the mighty Rose Lord's army had marched from Caergoth, but they had approached the river at a very lack-luster pace, and he hoped that his own rapid advance would bring him to battle before the Rose Lord was on the field.

"They are nearby, lord," reported the goblin scout, "but they have yet to cross the river. They are gathered just beyond the nearest ford but made camp early, with great tentings and tarpings to hold off the rain, and fires to warm chilly human flesh. They cook and boast, even as they shiver and stare into the darkness. They are blind as moles and did not even see us as we skulked through the night.

"Good. This as I hoped. You think they stay there for long time?"

"I cannot be sure, great lord. They were not digging, as humans do when they wish to make a dirt-fort. So they may be planning to cross the river in the morning."

"We not give them time," Ankhar decided. "Rib Chewer, gather worg riders. Strike mountain flank of Sword army before dawn. Your wolves make the attack. Hold back a dozen. They beat drums. Sound like marching troops."

"Marching, O great lord? Not riding?" Rib Chewer narrowed his eyes, trying to imagine the half-giant's strategy.

"Aye. They sound like army marching around their flank, at

foot of mountains. Make lord believe you there in great numbers, that we try to go around his left and make for city. Strike quickly, then dance away. Do not let them unite strength against your fleet riders."

The goblin scout grinned, a wicked slash of sharpened teeth gleaming across his leathery face. "It shall be as you wish, my lord. They will chase and harry, but not catch us."

"Yes. Go now. Ride through the night," Ankhar said, pleased with all he had heard. "Strike before first dawn. In the darkness, humans easy to confuse."

"What of the rest of great army? Thousands of gobs and hobs, all thirsting for blood?" Laka asked, as she sidled up behind the great war leader, giving him a momentary start—he whom she had suckled at her breast when he was an orphaned babe. "You not make us wait here in the darkness, my lord?"

"No," Ankhar said, shaking his great, shaggy head in annoyance. "Important work at riverbank. Test this hedgehog. See how sharp are his quills."

ᐯᐯᐯᐯᐯᐯ ᐯᐯᐯᐯᐯᐯ

Horns blared through the darkness, shrill alarms ringing across Duke Rathskell's camp. The lord burst out of his tent, buckling on his rapier, dismayed to see it was still raining. There was no shred of daylight to break the impenetrable murk of the night.

"Curse this blackness," he snapped. "What's going on? Are we being attacked?"

"Excellency!" A torch-bearing guard ran up to him to report. In the garishly flaring light the man's eyes were wild with fear. "The pickets on the left flank report a fierce assault. Goblins on worgs, striking hard. And sounds in the night, a drumbeat of marching footsteps! It seems as though the monsters are indeed stealing a march on us, coming around the east flank!"

"Damn the enemy's cunning!" gasped the duke. "It is as I feared! The horde seeks to pass us by, to close upon Luinstat, perhaps even Solanthus itself, while all of our troops are here in the open."

173

Captain Rankin, the leader of the infantry, came running from the darkness, anxiously buckling his sword. "What are your orders, Excellency?" he asked breathlessly.

"Pull in the pickets from the right," Rathskell ordered. "Reinforce the left with everyone we have. Get the knights mounted, prepared for a countercharge! I will be boiled in oil before I let these wolf-riders get the best of veteran knights on good horses. We'll show them how a *real* army does battle!"

He frowned as he gave the last order, remembering how the heavy war-horses had bogged down the previous night when they had tried to chase off a few worg-riding goblin scouts riding close. Still, there was nothing for it—without his knights mounted, he would be going to battle like a fighter with his feet nailed to the ground.

"What about Thelgaard?" asked Rankin. "Should we send to him for aid?"

Rathskell spat on the ground. "No. The stubborn fool will only cling to his trenches. Let him rot where he sits—if he cannot hear the sounds of our trumpets, let him slumber away like a baby while we do the man's work of killing!"

A footman brought Rathskell's charger up. The duke was making ready to mount when he thought of something else. "Even so," Rathskell declared, "this Ankhar has displayed some wiles. I think we had best send a message to Caergoth and beseech his lordship to cross the river at the earliest light, to come up to the front with whatever haste he can muster,"

"Aye, lord—I will send two riders, at once! They will take separate paths to ensure that at least one of them gets through."

"Good," Rathskell said, swinging his lithe body into the saddle. In truth, he had faint hopes for Caergoth's help.

⊰∘⊱∘⊰∘⊰✪⊱∘⊱∘⊰∘⊱

The Duke of Thelgaard awakened to a gray dawn. A steady patter on his tent had kept him awake through most of the night, and his bulky frame stubbornly resisted his initial movements. Finally he was obliged to shout for his footman, and the long-suffering servant immediately entered, helped the lord to sit up on his creaking cot, and fetched his boots, cloak, and chest-armor.

His aide entered and bowed as the lord was wrestling with his heavy, brass-buckled belt.

"Any reports from the night?" asked Thelgaard, who—as usual—had left instructions he not be disturbed except in the event of an emergency.

"There were sounds of disturbance off to the east, from Rathskell's camp. Trumpets, some riders, but he sent no message."

"Bah. The old woman is chasing shadows, no doubt," grumbled the huge duke, giving his underarm a good scratching. "Our lines report no trouble?"

"No, lord. It has been a quiet night on all sides of the square."

As the duke was buckling on his heavy steel breastplate—a family heirloom pre-dating the War of the Lance—sounds reached him. Not a sentry's trumpet but the clash of steel against steel. A human voice shrieked in unmistakable agony.

"Impossible!" spat the duke. "There must be some fool making a mistake he will regret!" Thelgaard glared at his alarmed aide, who had the presence of mind to keep his mouth shut.

The huge lord snatched up his crown-emblazoned shield and lumbered from his tent, gaping in astonishment as he saw men dashing every which way. The noise of battle came from the south, along the flank of his square facing the expected goblin horde, but in the space of a few seconds the sounds had spread to the east. Torches flared, and screams rang out quite clearly from that direction.

He was under attack from two sides! Even as he tried to grasp this complicated circumstance—his mind flashed, unwillingly, to Solanthus' warning about the gap between their two armies—a trumpet blared, signaling more enemy troops had been sighted.

This trumpet warning came from the north.

"Excellency! They're striking us from three sides!" cried

Captain Dayr, racing up on his mount. "Goblins are coming against us in ranks. They've already rolled in the pickets, are hitting our main lines hard. They've got us trapped against the river and have started to penetrate the boundaries of the square!"

"Impossible!" snarled Thelgaard again, knowing it was all too possible. "How can they do that?" he asked lamely.

"They streamed through the gap in the darkness. The attacks were timed to start at first light. They strike with discipline and order, my lord, and seemed to have pinpointed the weakest links in our line. They stole a march on us!"

"What of Caergoth? Is he coming up fast?" the duke asked, feeling, almost as soon as the words were out of his mouth, that it was a vain hope. Duke Walker was a methodical man—his camp would barely be stirring at this hour, much less have completed the fording of the river, and the several-mile march needed to reach his allies.

Dayr shook his head impatiently.

"We *must* hold the lines—do you hear me?" demanded the duke.

"Aye, Excellency. We must indeed, or all will be lost!" Dayr put spurs to his horse, thundering toward the north as the sounds of battle rose to a crescendo.

"Where's my sword?" demanded the duke, as another manservant stepped forward to offer him the great blade. Thelgaard felt better as he grasped the familiar hilt. Breaking into a lumbering run, he headed toward the entrenchments that marked the fortified boundary of his camp.

The situation that greeted his eyes was worse than he could have imagined. Over a hundred shrieking goblins, many waving blood-stained blades over their heads, were already *through* the line! Knights of the Crown were reacting with seasoned competence, a score of brave men forming a makeshift rank and standing against the assault, but the goblins were hurling themselves at the knights, and swords met in a din.

The surge of battle sent men staggering back, groaning, then returning to the fight with shouts. Dozens of the attackers fell in the initial clash, but still more of their fellows poured through the breach that had been torn in the line, washing over the knights.

Thelgaard himself joined the defenders, now numbering only half of the initial twenty knights. His blade came down and hacked a gob in two, scattering several more on the back-stroke. More knights rushed into position, and standing shoulder to shoulder they finally stemmed the breach. Led by their roaring duke, the human fighters inched forward, driving the goblins back through the line of stakes that marked the camp boundary.

"Take that, you scum!" bellowed Jarrod of Thelgaard, laying about with his mighty sword. *This* was more like it—battling a savage foe toe to toe, smiting all about him, battle-blood pulsing through his veins!

A rank of archers came up beside him, crossbows snapping, silver darts plunging into the enemy. Many goblins fell, pierced by the deadly bolts that slammed their targets with more force than any arrow shot from a mere bow. The savage monsters fell back. They were surprisingly disciplined amidst the chaos. Now they halted, forming a solid line. Again and again the crossbows fired their lethal volleys, but for every goblin who fell it seemed two or three rushed to take his place.

The enemy's archers were also at work, loosing crude wooden sticks that lacked the deadly killing power of the crossbow-launched, steel-headed missiles of the knights. But they vexed the knights, these lesser arrows, puncturing exposed necks and arms, here and there striking a knight in the eye. And there were so many of them! In the face of that deadly rain the Solamnics closed ranks, raised their shields, and edged forward to try and reclaim their ruptured northern line.

Then disaster from behind. In disbelief the duke spun around, saw similar breaches on the two other fronts of his camp. Goblins were running amok through the nobles' tents, slashing through the canvas structures, knocking down poles. A few brave men stood against the onslaught but were ruthlessly cut down. Thelgaard shouted in anguish as he saw his young nephew, his sister's eldest son, run through by a goblin spear.

The vile attacker, in the frenzied rapture of his kill, stopped to dance upon the bleeding corpse, stabbing the beardless youth again and again.

With an inarticulate cry, the lord turned back toward camp, but he never even got close. The collapse on the inland front—on that cursed gap Solanthus had tried to warn him about!—was by now catastrophic. Men streamed away from the attackers, exposing both the north and south lines. With a precision that astounded Thelgaard, this rabble of savages had broken a formed defense of trained knights! A horse, trailing guts from a long gash in its belly, lumbered past. A huge hobgoblin loped after it, and Thelgaard struck the brute down with a single blow.

Arrows were flying all around. One of them struck the duke in the shoulder, drawing a cry of pain. He plucked the missile out and threw it aside but found that his left arm was nearly paralyzed. Dropping his shield, wielding his sword in his right hand, he bellowed, trying to rally his faltering army.

There were so many goblins—a dozen rushed at him in the next instant, scores more charging behind. Some of these were huge hobgoblins with fanged muzzles, snapping and growling like berserk beasts. One slashed at him with a studded sword, and the duke was barely able to parry the blow, before pulling his own weapon back and stabbing the brute through the chest. Even as the hob died, several of his comrades swarmed around, slashing at Thelgaard with an array of wicked weapons. The duke had no choice but to stumble back with the rest of his army.

At least such of his army as still survived. There were dead humans everywhere, and others who had been wounded badly crawling or limping or piteously moaning. The attackers swept past the injured for now, concentrating their efforts on knights who still wielded their weapons. Thelgaard hacked right and left, cleaved hobgoblin after hobgoblin right through their leering muzzles, but the knights couldn't stem the tide.

A flash of greenish light caught his eye, and he saw a monstrous barbarian striding among the enemy. The creature looked to be a giant, and he wielded a spear the size of a small tree trunk.

The tip of that weapon was the source of the eerie glow, and when the monster waved it above his head it seemed to inspire his brutal warriors into even greater depths of savagery.

This was Ankhar, the duke understood. Ankhar who had beaten him, humiliated him, destroying his prized army on the field of battle.

Thelgaard's crossbowmen made a last stand at the end of the tents, firing volley after volley into the horde, driving back the foe for a few precious minutes so their comrades could slip past, try to form a last line, a semicircle in the rear of the camp, adjoining the riverbank. The duke roared at the archers to retreat, but before his orders could be heeded the valiant arrow-men were taken in both flanks, goblins chopping and hacking, even biting, as they swarmed from the sides and behind. Of a hundred brave men, barely a score staggered away from the gruesome massacre.

Now the whole horde of the attackers swept against the tenuous line of ultimate defense, and in seconds the position was breached all along its front. Knights fought and died to allow a few of their comrades to escape, until there was no front, no position any more. There was only madness, a welter of bloodletting presided over by frenzied goblins and hobgoblins.

The handful of desperate men who survived had fled to the riverbank, many of them skidding down the steep dirt slope into the muddy shallows. They were pushed into the waters of the Vingaard that had become a churning mass of blood, flesh, and fear. The Duke of Thelgaard lost his sword as he skidded down the bank. He was almost trampled by a fear-maddened horse as the steed lunged past him, knocking him face down in the brown water.

The duke came up gasping, heading for deeper water. Men were casting aside their armor, seizing the manes and tails of fleeing horses, starting to swim. Those who couldn't swim, couldn't grasp some form of support, soon drowned.

Sobbing in fury and dismay, Thelgaard wriggled his way out of his heavy breastplate, the crown-emblazoned piece of armor that had been in his family for a dozen generations. It vanished into the muddy waters as the duke swam toward the far bank, strong strokes carrying him away from the deadly shore.

Behind him, the howls of thousands of triumphant goblins sang in his ears, a chorus of humiliation and shame that would echo in his memory, he knew, for every day of the rest of his life.

⊱═══════⊰

Despite the down mattress and sturdy bed that was a part of his army's equipment every time it took to the field, the Duke of Caergoth had spent an extremely restless night. Every time he drifted off to sleep, it seemed as though secret voices were whispering in his ear, warning him of dangers before, behind, to every side. Some of the whispers were lies, he knew—but others were truths!

How to tell them apart?

He awoke in a sweat, breathing hard, staring wildly around the large tent. Despite the four bright lanterns his aides kept burning through the night, it seemed terribly dark, dangerous, with unseen menace hovering in every shadowy alcove. At dawn he had a terribly upset stomach and sent immediately for his breakfast. As it arrived he had learned that two messengers had arrived from the Duke of Solanthus, but he wasn't ready to meet them, not at first. Instead, he sent even his trusted aides away and paced nervously on the lush carpets that lined the floor of his tent, leaving the two messengers from Solanthus cooling their heels outside in the rain.

Finally, he let one of his aides in and asked about the messages carried from Duke Rathskell. "They appeared most inconveniently, you know," Duke Walker sniffed, picking at his crepes and fresh oranges. "Now they disrupt my breakfast!"

"Excellency, it does seem to be a matter of some urgency," said the aide. "Captain Marckus has suggested that we muster immediately, cross the river in support. There is word of a massive goblin flanking maneuver, the horde reportedly far inland of the duke's army, coming into position to threaten the city of Luinstat."

Duke Walker had already given initial orders, and his army was gradually coming to life around him—though he would not yet authorize the striking of his grand tent. No, he needed to keep the rain off of himself while he pondered this important decision.

Where to go? Of course, to Marckus it was all so simple: just march right up to the enemy and engage in battle! The duke had to be aware of more subtle concerns—feints and deceptions, concealed intentions, even false information. Indeed, any move to cross the river, now, would inevitably expose his army to a whole host of unknown counter-moves. It seemed best to wait here, patiently awaiting word on further developments.

A half hour later, a thoroughly soaked, bloodied, and chastened Duke of Thelgaard appeared, with report of an attack on his own camp, his army routed, driven through the river. Thousands of gobs and hobs, Thelgaard said. They were too many, too disciplined, led by a canny half-giant who had struck at the knights' weaknesses.

"See!" declared Caergoth accusingly, addressing the messengers from Solanthus. "This is why I don't make hasty decisions! No, far better for us to remain here, on our side of the river and wait to see what's going to happen next!"

"Aye, Excellency," said the men.

"Now, duke, why don't you dry yourself off and get that wound looked at by one of my healers. Have some hot tea. Take a good nap. Things will look better tomorrow."

CHAPTER SIXTEEN

THE VINGAARD RANGE

The ridge cresting the Vingaard Mountains rose like an inverted sawblade across the horizon, dramatically marking the end of hundreds of miles of tabletop-flat plain. The four travelers were headed for a certain valley, where, in the middle of the range, a pair of anvil-shaped summits stood like watchtowers.

"Ah, I can smell the pines," Dram Feldspar said, drawing a luxurious breath through his ample nose. "All these weeks of trekking across the flatland is a foreign thing to a mountain dwarf. When we get into the high valleys, I'm going to take my boots off and soak my feet in an icy stream until they turn blue."

"Why would you want blue feet?" asked Sulfie. She tried to act cross, but it was obvious even the literal-minded gnome was pleased at the prospect of leaving the plains for forests and high ground.

Dram broke into a trot, with the two gnomes hastening behind. Jaymes's long strides meant he had no trouble keeping up. Of the four, he was the only one who wasn't staring in awe at the mountains. Instead, his eyes, squinting and suspicious, swept across the flatlands to the right, the left, and behind them.

They hadn't seen any other goblins or humans for the past

three weeks. The goblin raiders and the human armies apparently remained behind in the area of the Upper Vingaard River and the plains lying directly below the Garnet Mountains. The travelers had avoided small towns and farmsteads and in more than a score of days and several hundred miles had come upon no other travelers.

Nor, in the weeks since their crossing of Mason's Ford, had they seen any group of trees larger than a small copse of cottonwoods, no elevation more pronounced than the eroded bank of a stream or gully. The rains, thankfully, had finally dwindled, though that meant the landscape became a swath of dusty brown soil, scored by greenery only where the infrequent streams cut sluggishly across the featureless land. Just this morning they had skirted a small verdant grove centered around a pond, on the grounds of an abandoned and collapsing manor house, which they decided not to investigate.

They had a precise destination since leaving Mason's Ford. Jaymes wanted to get his hands on the supposedly explosive compound invented by the brilliant dead gnome Brillissander Firesplasher. How he knew about this supposed invention, Jaymes refused to say (even Dram didn't know)—but Jaymes believed it would be very useful and profitable, if such a thing really existed.

Thus far the compound, with its smoky fizzle, had proved to be a major disappointment, and Carbo and Sulfie had conflicting ideas as to the reasons for the fizzle. Both insisted that it had worked in the past, that their brother, Salty Pete, would know how and why. But Salty Pete was lost to the lizardmen in the Brackens, so it was up to them to recreate their father's formula. The first step was to find the necessary ingredients.

Sulfie had described the essential ingredient, a yellow and chalky stone that emitted a foul stench when heated, which she called "sulfir." They needed to find a store of this material; she didn't know where her father had acquired it. Dram Feldspar thought that he knew such a place, and it was he who had led them westward across the flatland.

"Yep, we're getting close," Dram said, studying the twin flat-topped mountains with a critical eye. "When I was here before I heard about this rock. There are dwarves who mine in this area, but the ones we have to keep a lookout for are not so much miners, they're more like scalawags, outlaws, who will sell anything for a price. They have lots of these yellow rocks just lying around, and as far as I know don't have any use for 'em."

Jaymes frowned. "I'm not worried about outlaws, but we've come a long way if you're wrong."

The female gnome shook her head. "Don't blame me. I told you we need to get some more of the yellow rock for a new batch of the compound, but I didn't say anything about walking a thousand miles to get it. And I don't cotton to outlaws."

"Hmph!" Dram said sourly. "It wasn't a step over four hundred miles, and if we need to find a bunch of yellow rock, then here's a likely place. The only place *I* know of, anyway. Just follow my lead and we'll get in and out of here without too much trouble."

By now the dark layer on the foothills was recognizable as lush pines sprouting in a luxuriant blanket over meadows of green grass. Wildflowers popped through the grass, blue and red and purple and white speckles waving back and forth in a cool breeze. Most delightful, clear water—in the form of a rapidly flowing brook spilling out of the narrow valley—offered welcome refreshment, a wonderful change from the brackish, muddy trickles that had marked every sluggish waterway on the whole, vast plain.

That first night in the mountains they made camp in a narrow grotto next to that stream and shared a dinner of fresh fish around a cheery fire. Not only had firewood been generally lacking on the plains, but even when they found pieces of driftwood they had been unwilling to build an evening campfire, for the light would be visible for miles. Here, steep stone walls to either side and tall trees up and down the valley masked the illumination.

As the dwarf and gnomes made themselves comfortable in mossy bowers, even Jaymes allowed himself to relax. The soft grass soothed his muscles as he lay back. The sky was bright with stars, and when he slept he wasn't troubled by dreams.

The morning dawned clear and dry. They rose quickly and started up the mountain valley, following a twisting, steeply climbing road that looked impassable to anything like a cart or wagon, and would have provided a challenge to a sure-footed mule. Dram led the way and Jaymes brought up the rear. The two gnomes were more cheerful and talkative than ever:

"This place reminds me of Dungarden," Sulfie explained. "It was like this in the Garnet Range—cool, and smelling like pines. I like the sound of the water splashing over the rocks. It would be a good place to live."

"Just be alert," Dram said, his eyes scanning the rising bluffs to either side of them. "There are those who already live here. It remains to be seen if they'll be glad to see us." He fixed Jaymes with a stare. "Are you ready to do this?"

The warrior merely nodded and continued on. Dram's hand rested on the head of his axe, but—at Jaymes's insistence—he kept the weapon tucked into his belt, instead of ready in his hand.

As the small party made its way through a narrow bottleneck between two huge boulders rising to either side of the trail, Dram came to an abrupt halt. Sulfie bumped right into him, the dwarf cursing at the impact. His hand clenched around his axe but then, with an almost visible effort, he let his arms drop to the sides.

"We've met the locals," he reported.

They found themselves confronted by a half dozen dwarves, similar in size and whiskers to Dram but wearing soft deerskin trousers and shirts instead of the dark woolens and chain shirt favored by the Kaolyn dwarf. Five of them carried crossbows, and these held their weapons leveled at the four travelers, while the sixth stood belligerently, fists planted firmly on his hips.

Small pebbles clattered down from above. Jaymes looked upward, quickly spotting another dozen or so dwarves coming into view atop the large boulders to either side of the trail. A quick glance behind showed that yet another group of the valley's guardians had slipped into position to block their retreat. All told, a good twenty or more arrows were aimed at the four of them.

"We come in peace," Dram said, holding both hands, empty, up before him. "No need for any shooting . . . Hiya Swig," he added, his tone of attempted familiarity somewhat inhibited by his clenched teeth and the fixed grimace of his expression.

"Dram Feldspar," said the dwarf called Swig, the one with his hands planted on his hips. He was grinning now, with an expression that mingled amusement with cruelty. "I never thought you'd have the guts to show yourself in these hills again. I wonder—what's to keep me from putting an arrow through your heart, right now?"

"Now, that would be a bit of an overreaction, Swig," Dram argued. "At least let us tell you why we've come."

"And delay the pleasure of watching your blood running onto the ground?"

"That would end up costing you a lot of money," Jaymes interjected, stepping forward.

Swig stared appraisingly at the warrior, who returned his wary look with a cool, neutral expression. The two gnomes looked around nervously, sidled close together, and held each others' hand. After giving a good, long impression of a person wrestling with a really difficult decision, Swig finally nodded and made a gesture. The rest of the dwarves in his party raised their weapons so that the arrows were no longer sighted directly on the travelers.

"Money, eh? Ah, you speak to my heart, stranger," the dwarf said to Jaymes. "Very well—you four will come with me. We'll share a mug around my hearth. You'll have ten, maybe fifteen minutes to tell me why I shouldn't have you killed and your bodies dumped in the garden as fertilizer for next year's hops."

Swig Frostmead was a hill dwarf chieftain, every bit as proud and vain as his cousins, the mountain dwarves. Here, north of the Newsea, the traditional rivalry of the two dwarven tribes was more removed than in Thorbardin. There, at the time of the Cataclysm, the mountain dwarves had sealed the gates of their underground fortress against their hill-dwelling kin. That perceived betrayal was a three-century-old wound that left a still-bleeding scar.

But dwarves are ever stubborn, and there was clearly no affection wasted between the hill dwarves of the Vingaard Range and the mountain dwarves of Garnet, which included Dram—one of the Feldspar clan from Kaolyn. Jaymes took note of the hostile looks exchanged between Swig and Dram as the four travelers were escorted to Swig's hall, a stone-walled house in the center of a village high in the valley of the Vingaard Mountains.

This was clearly a prosperous community. The buildings were mostly of stone, though they often had ornamental woodwork on the eaves, around the doors and windows. The narrow streets were clean, paved with cobblestones, and the few oxen they noticed in a streamside pasture were fat and sleek, clearly well fed and cared for. The mountainsides beyond the village were dotted with the dark mouths of mines, and several tall chimneys rose from an area of foundries and smelters just beyond the houses. Still, the air was clean, as the mountain wind carried the smoke up and over the adjacent ridge.

Within the hill dwarf's hall, they seated themselves on benches before a broad hearth, Jaymes made a point of sitting between Dram and Swig. The chieftain clapped his hands, and several young maids—rosy cheeked, smiling, and pleasantly plump—emerged from the kitchen, holding large mugs in each hand.

"Welcome to Meadstone. So, you tell me you have a way for me to make some money," Swig declared, after the cold mugs of bitter ale had been served to himself, his score of armed guards, and even—surprisingly enough—the four prisoners. "What's to stop me from just stealing it off your bleeding corpses?"

"Well, we don't have any money," Jaymes replied. "Not now, not yet. Of course, you could have the satisfaction of killing us today, but nothing at all after that."

"And if you live, does all this money appear like magic?"

"We came here to make a proposition. Dram here remembers you as a shrewd businessman and an intrepid miner. If we live, I offer to buy something from you—something that you can mine in great quantity, that you currently have very little use for."

Swig leaned past Jaymes to glare at Dram. "You brought this fool here? After what you did to my daughter?" he demanded.

"Now, er, Swig," Dram said, holding up his hands again. "You got the wrong impression. I didn't actually *do* anything!"

"Liar!" roared the hill dwarf, rising to his feet so quickly the thick ale in his mug almost slopped over the sides. He paused and took a long drink, so that he could gesture with no danger of wastage. "I caught you sneaking out of here with your pants in your hand! Are you claiming she ain't pretty enough for you?"

"No! She's lovely—a real treasure! A mountain flower," Dram protested. "Er, a hillside flower, I mean. But my intentions were honorable. I had split a seam, and she was mending it for me! I know how it looked. Mighty suspicious. But that's all that happened!"

"Bah—why'd you run away, then?"

"You wouldn't let me explain it at the time! If you recall, I took an arrow in my hindparts as it was! You were in no mood to listen to reason!"

Swig snorted. Still, he blinked, as if considering Dram's words. "That's the same story she gave," he grunted. "Clever, you mountain dwarf scum—even working out your lies together in advance!"

"I tell you, it's no lie!" Dram's face grew red, and his beard was twitching. Jaymes rested a hand on his companion's shoulder, exerting gentle pressure, until his dwarf companion exhaled very slowly.

Swig took another long pull, draining his mug, and sat down. Jaymes took the opportunity to steer the conversation away from reminiscence.

"I understand that you mine plenty of iron from these hills— a good, pure strain of ore."

"Aye. You understand right. So what?"

"And you do the smelting and casting, right here?"

"That we do. No sense letting a good raw material get gunked up by a bunch of amateurs."

"Commendable. Vingaard black iron is famed throughout the lands of Solamnia and beyond."

The dwarf preened a bit, warmed by the praise. "We sell it to the Solamnics at a good price. They take all we can dig and pay premium. So if that's what you're after, you might as well stop talking right now. We already got our customers."

Jaymes shook his head. "No. I have no need of iron and couldn't match prices paid by the dukes even if I did. But Dram tells me that there is another material, a waste rock of dusty yellow, that you have to cart out of the way in order to get at the iron. Is that true?"

"Sulfir?" Swig shook his head in disgust. "Oh, we haul a bit of that stinking junk off to the cities—some of the metalsmiths use it in their smelting. Most of it we pile up just to get it out of the way." Suddenly the chieftain narrowed his eyes. "You don't mean to suggest that you'd be wanting some of that useless chalk?"

"It might have a use for me, yes," Jaymes said. "I would be willing to negotiate a fee. To start, I want to arrange for the purchase of five tons."

"Five tons, eh?" Swig looked bored. "Hmm. That's a lot, that would add up. That might be possible. When do you want it?"

"I will need it in three months' time. Delivered to a place I will specify one month before delivery—some place in Solamnia."

"Delivery? Well, of course, delivery is one of our specialties, but that will cost extra."

"Of course," Jaymes agreed. "I have no desire to cheat you. If this works, it might be the start of a whole new business for you—something you'll be able to sell as fast as you can dig it out of the ground."

"What do you intend to pay for this . . ." Swig seemed to realize that "junk" was the wrong word to use in describing his newfound and apparently valuable commodity. ". . . this sulfir ore?"

"What do the dukes pay for iron?" Jaymes asked.

Swig's eyes narrowed, and he made a great show of scratching his bearded chin. "Well, that depends, depends. The finest grades fetch a thousand steel per ton, paid in gems, usually. Rough ore makes me in the neighborhood of four hundred."

"I'll match the price of low grade iron," Jaymes offered. "Say four hundred steel per ton of sulfir. But I only want the pure yellow rock—your miners will have to chop out the waste."

Now the hill dwarf looked indignant. "Of course they'll get rid of the waste! How long do you think I'd stay in business if I was selling impure product?"

"Not long—not with me, in any event. I just want to make sure we understand each other."

"I understand," Swig said. He mused for a moment then looked up at Dram, his face locked in a scowl that slowly cracked into something resembling a smile. "She was really just mending your trousers?" he asked.

"I tore 'em on a snag coming up from the south," the mountain dwarf said with a glower. "And your daughter, bless her kindness—and Reorx knows where she gets it from!—was good enough to see that I could pass on from here without the chill winds of winter blowing up my . . . well, you get the picture."

Swig tossed back his head and laughed. The two gnomes joined in, as did the other hill dwarves standing around. Even Jaymes cracked a smile, the warrior winking at the sulking Dram.

"Enough with business!" roared the Vingaard chieftain. "Brewer—bring us a fresh keg. We'll seal this suitable arrangement over a fine ale—as sacred a bond as a pledge to any god!"

The resulting feast was one of those parties that could be called the stuff of legend. Pilsy Frostmead, lovely and cherished daughter of the chieftain, emerged with several other young lasses, carrying pitchers of Special Reserve Ale, and they proceeded to see that all became better acquainted. Pilsy was a beauty by the standards of the race, with rosy cheeks and a plentitude of toothsome curves.

Dram Feldspar and Swig Frostmead, of course, proceeded to get roaring drunk. The inevitable fistfight erupted shortly after midnight and lasted for slightly less than an hour. In the end they clinched as wrestlers and, after staggering around the room with increasing unsteadiness, collapsed, utterly exhausted.

They fell asleep in each other's arms, lying in the cold ashes outside the hearth, brothers in dwarfdom . . .

And mortal proof of Reorx's blessing.

※◦◎◦◎◦◎◦◎※◎◦◎◦◎◦◎◦◎※

"You the fellow that drove the Duke of Thelgaard into the Vingaard River?"

The speaker was a human knight dressed in dark armor. He wore no emblem on his breast and carried no weapon—otherwise the guards would not have allowed him to approach Ankhar. The dark-armored knight had a companion, a man dressed in supple black leather, including gloves and a riding cape as long as a robe. The camp guards, naturally, had searched beneath that voluminous garment and pronounced the man unarmed.

These two were courageous, for they did not flinch as the half giant rose to his full height and looked down at the visitors.

"My gobs and hobs did it," Ankhar replied flatly. "Attack plan all mine."

"Nice piece of work. That bastard drove me right out of my own city. I'd like to see him spitted on a sword, myself."

"Your city? Thelgaard?"

"Well, it was for a time, a while back," the man said. "I got no place now."

"Well, duke drowned. Or swam away." Ankhar had been a trifle disappointed that his warriors had not been able to bring him the head of the enemy commander. "His army pretty much broken up. Nine out of ten men fell on field."

The half giant was more than pleased with the result of his first battle against a large force of trained knights, but it had not sated him. He hungered for more victories. That aim would not be served by fighting this man or his force of some two thousand men—including hundreds of knights in dark armor. Ankhar's scouts had reported the humans encamped just over the horizon.

The half-giant gazed at the human, sizing him up. He was handsome, by the standards of humankind, with a dueling scar on his cheek.

"You warriors? Captains of men?" Ankhar said.

The armored knight replied. "I am the leader of this brigade. My companion here is a knight of a different kind—he commands legions of magic."

The leather-clad fighter clicked his heels and bowed his head. "Sir Hoarst, Knight of the Thorn, at your service, my lord."

Ankhar chuckled, and looked back at the captain. "Why you come here, all alone and pitiful? Because I broke Thelgaard's army? I not give you his city back."

The visitor laughed with an easy self-confidence that Ankhar admired. "No," he said. "Nobody needs to give me anything. I came looking for work. I have a strong company, two hundred armored men, former Dark Knights. There are also a thousand of us on foot, all trained in knights' tactics. Sir Hoarst has two comrades of the Thorn, well-versed in battle-magic. We are looking to join your army, and we'll fight for our share of the plunder."

Ankhar scratched his broad chin. This was a surprising, pleasing development—a human offering to join and serve under a barbarian half giant. The additional troops would add considerable punch to his army. As to how battle magic could help, he had little concept, but he liked the sound of it.

"Wait here," he said, abruptly turning his back and stalking through the camp. He made his way to the conical tent that was set up for his foster mother. Not surprisingly, she awaited him, holding back the flap as he stooped to enter, then dropping it into place. They sat in semi-darkness, leaning close to speak privately.

"I like this human. Prince of Lies want him to join us?" asked Ankhar.

Laka shook her skull-totem, and immediately the eyes glowed green, the teeth chattered out a message.

"Monstrous master,

"Mankind's bane.

"Truth is righteous,

"Ankhar's reign!"

The half-giant nodded, satisfied. Without another word he rose, left the tent, and made his way back to the human visitors.

"I your general. General Ankhar. Your men welcome to join us, Captain. What your name?"

"Blackgaard. Captain Blackgaard, if you please."

"Captain Blackgaard. Come into camp. Join our feast. Soon, we march against Knights of Solamnia."

Chapter Seventeen

Apples in the Trees

"My head hurts!" protested Carbo, as the four travelers trudged out of the forest and onto the familiar flat, brown plain. "Can't we stop and camp for a day? In the mountains? By the stream?"

Sulfie, plodding behind her brother, nodded miserably in agreement. "Water and cool grass! Oh, the smells! I want to go to sleep!"

"Yeah. Can't we stop?" asked the red-eyed Dram, stumbling over a root that curled across the trail. "Ouch. Damn. Slow down, will you?"

"We have to get some miles behind us," Jaymes said, unsympathetically. If he was feeling any ill effects from the ale he had shared with them and the hill dwarves of Meadstone, the fact was not apparent to the others. "We have to cross the plains again, then return, in two months. Don't have time to waste."

He nodded at Sulfie, who had a bulging bag strapped to her backpack. "Have a care with that sulfir. It's a valuable specimen."

The little gnome woman sniffed but reached around to make sure the sack was secure. The hill dwarf had provided them with a generous sample, and Sulfie said she would embark on a study of its properties.

Jaymes turned to look at his dwarven companion, almost

smiling. "Why didn't you tell me you and Swig Frostmead had such a colorful history?"

Dram groaned. "I was hoping he wouldn't remember me, to tell you the truth."

"You should know better than that!" the warrior declared.

"Well, I've never had a daughter?" Dram snapped. "Have you?"

Jaymes' expression guarded his emotions. "No. I've never had a daughter. There was a time when I learned something about the way a father can feel toward his own flesh, though."

Dram blinked in surprise, and glanced up at his friend. When Jaymes seemed inclined to let the subject drop, the dwarf simply harrumphed and stomped along, until another question came to mind.

"Where are we going to camp, then?" he asked, pointing to the flatland sprawling before them. Blinking his bloodshot eyes, the dwarf looked around without enthusiasm. A low, mud-bottomed gulley snaked along to their right, dotted with a few thorn bushes. Other than that, they were confronted with a brown dirt and dead, brittle grass. "On the middle of the plain?"

"That's why we need to make tracks today. Remember that grove we passed when we were heading into the mountains, about ten miles away? Where the stream out of the mountains formed the pond? There were apple trees there, some of them already bearing fruit." The warrior glanced at the sun, halfway descended toward the horizon. "If we keep up the pace, we can be there before dark."

"Ten *miles?*" squawked Carbo, pitiably.

The warrior only picked up the pace, and his three unhappy, hungover companions stumbled along, doing their best to keep up. It was a long, hot day later when they finally came into sight of the trees. The trunks were gnarled and weathered, but the limbs drooped with ripe fruit. They followed a shallow, meandering stream into the apple orchard, which was overgrown with tall grass and bushes. There was plenty of fruit within easy reach of even the diminutive gnomes, and the four weary travelers munched on sweet apples as they came to the pond in the center of the grove.

"I remember this little pool for some good fishing," Jaymes remarked.

"Well, we should be able to make ourselves pretty comfortable here," Dram allowed, his sour mood lifting.

"Yes," the human agreed. "Why don't you start making camp, then drop a hook in the water? I'm going to check out that old ruin of a house, make sure we don't have any neighbors."

"All right," the dwarf said. Dram had already spotted a supple branch, which would make a perfect fishing pole, as Jaymes shrugged out of his pack and wandered off through the trees.

⊱⊶⊷⊶⊷❀⊶⊷⊶⊷⊰

"I remember this place," Princess Selinda said to Captain Powell. "My father brought me here when I was a girl—we used to watch the farmers harvest the apples from that grove in the fall."

"It looks like it's been abandoned for a long while," the knight replied. "See how the weeds have taken over the yard? The brambles are growing right out through the walls of the house. The roof is caved in over there, and I wouldn't be surprised if bats and rats have taken the place over."

"We don't need to go into the house—instead we can make our camp for tonight in the grove," the lady said. "I remember fishing in the pond there—you could hardly throw a hook in without catching something. We can have fresh fish and apples."

The captain nodded, stroking his mustache thoughtfully. "It would make a nice change from all this trail fare," he acknowledged. "I declare, it would be nice to be under the stars."

Turning in the saddle, he waved to the file of knights, nearly a hundred strong, who made up the princess's escort. "Make for the trees!" he called. "We'll camp in the grove over there! Usual drill—scouts forward to reconnoiter, knights to follow in open line."

196

With visible enthusiasm the weary riders turned their horses, several scouts dispersing as they approached the lush green trees. Already they could see the red apples beckoning here and there, growing wild and untended across the extensive grove.

During the last three weeks of riding, Selinda had grown accustomed to the smooth competency of all these knights. Captain Powell led the group with avuncular compassion, and his men responded with a loyalty and good humor that bespoke a volume of respect and affection for their leader and their own camaraderie.

Most of the knights, from the moment they rose in the morning until they went to bed at night, wore steel breastplates, helms, and other bits of armor. Indeed, when she reflected upon their seeming modesty—no doubt a reflection of their Oath and Measure—the princess wondered if some of them might not actually wear parts of their steel trappings in their bedrolls.

The scouts, who numbered only a score of knights, wore leather tunics and soft, moccasin-like boots. Shieldless, they were armed with light bows and slender swords. Mounted upon lean and leggy steeds in comparison to the broad-withered giant war-horses that carried their more heavily armored brethren, the scouts could move quickly through all kinds of terrain. Now they rode among the apple trees, making sure all was safe.

Abruptly one of the scouts held up his hand, and the rest came to an immediate halt. Several riders conferred with each other, and one of these came galloping back to the main body, reining in his horse before Captain Powell and Selinda.

"We're going to have to go in carefully—Royster smelled smoke," reported the scout. "Probably just the campfire of a few innocent travelers, but we're not going to take any chances."

"Good man," said Powell, with a nod. The scout whirled his horse and rode back to join his comrades. A minute later, the twenty men dismounted. Leaving their well-trained mounts to wait for them, they drew their swords and slipped into the grove.

"Finally," groaned Dram, leaning back on the soft grass, closing his eyes, and sighing. He had pulled off his boots, and as he let his bare feet dip into the water of the pond he began to let the weariness of the long day's trek—not to mention the lingering effects of the hill dwarf ale—fall away. He picked up the makeshift pole he had formed from a small sapling, to which he had affixed a string and hook, and inspected the worm that still wriggled on the end.

"Carbo, throw another couple sticks on that fire, will you?" he called. "This little fellow is going to catch us a fat trout, or my name isn't Dram Feldspar."

"Dram Feldspar, eh? Never heard of you."

The speaker was a stranger, and the sound of the man's voice yanked the dwarf's head around so fast that he dropped his pole into the pond. Several men emerged from the surrounding trees. They wore leather armor, and all were armed.

He noticed the emblem, the outline of a red rose, on the chest of each man's tunic. The dwarf looked around. He counted about a dozen, knew there could be more out of the sight in the surrounding trees. Carbo and Sulfie, sitting at the fire, were gaping in astonishment as the newcomers approached.

"Sorry, dwarf. Didn't mean to startle you," said one of the archers, with a nod at the ripples where Dram had dropped his fishing pole. "We smelled your smoke and just wanted to make sure who was here before we set up camp."

"Oh, uh, sure," Dram said.

It had been about an hour since Jaymes went off to inspect the ruined old house. Dram could only hope he'd notice the strangers before he blundered into their midst. As to himself and the gnomes, they had nothing to fear from a band of knights. Indeed, he reminded himself, most travelers would be delighted to have the protection of a well-armed group of honorable men. He forced himself to act gracious.

"There's plenty of room here," the dwarf said, indicating the meadow that surrounded the fishpond. "Lots of firewood and more apples than a hundred men could eat in a month!"

"That's good," said the scout. He put up his weapon and waved. "That looks about right for the size of our company. Looks like we'll be your neighbors tonight."

"Well, sure," Dram replied, smiling through clenched teeth. "Um, welcome to the neighborhood, neighbor."

✕⊶⊶⊶⊶⊶🝠⊷⊷⊷⊷✕

Jaymes crouched in the shrubbery outside the abandoned house, watching the file of horsemen make their way down from the low ridge and disappear into the apple grove. He had seen several scouts come out a few minutes earlier, reporting to their captain, then leading the rest of the party into the congenial shelter of the clustered trees.

He was certain the scouts had discovered Dram and the gnomes—even if his companions had tried to hide, the campfire would have given them away. Still he was confident that Dram would keep his mouth shut as to Jaymes's whereabouts, and his companions would not come to any harm at the hands of a band of Rose knights. He was in no hurry to test the knights' goodwill, and now their unwelcome presence would keep him from a dinner of fresh fish. Even the apples were out of reach, he realized, as his stomach rumbled. He dared not emerge from concealment, for the knight captain would have posted lookouts on the periphery.

Staying low, he made his way back through the thick bushes to the base of the old house. Evidently the former domicile of a minor Solamnic noble—one who had perished during the War of Souls—it was only about half the size of Lord Lorimar's wrecked manor, but it had been a grand enough structure in its time. He had been inspecting it when the knights had arrived, making his way through the low outbuildings, which held several large presses as well as a variety of vats and bins. He assumed that the owners had made cider, or perhaps apple wine, there.

Now he would have to make himself comfortable somewhere. He found a storage shed attached to the rear of the house, a place

199

where the roof had remained intact and where there didn't seem to be any annoying vermin. He arranged some clean straw into an approximation of a bed and forced himself to ignore the pangs of hunger and thirst that were beginning to render him fidgety. He stretched out on the pad, watching through the crack of the door as the afternoon's light faded toward dusk.

The whole area was very quiet, though he could hear skunks rustling around on the ground floor of the adjacent house. He willed himself to sleep, but his fatigue wasn't enough to bring slumber. Sitting up, leaning against the wall, he resigned himself to boredom.

Abruptly he caught his breath—a shadow moved past the door's edge! Slowly, he rose to a crouch. His eyes remained fixed on that doorway. Was this one of the knights, come to inspect the buildings with the same curiosity that had brought Jaymes here? The warrior remembered with chagrin that he had left his sword back at the camp—he was armed only with his short dagger and one small crossbow. He drew the knife and set the missile weapon to the side, hoping that the one who had cast the shadow would move on. He tried to ready himself for anything.

Even so, he was startled when the door suddenly opened, and he couldn't help but blink at the sight of another person in the fading daylight. Equally startling was the gasp of the person standing there, an intake of breath that indicated that she had spotted his hiding place.

That gasp of surprise—feminine and a little breathless— proved that this person was, beyond a doubt, a woman.

⟢�- ⟢⟣ ⟢⟣ ⟢⟣ ⟢⟣ ⟢⟣ ⟢⟣ ⟢⟢

Sir Powell strolled around the fringe of the pond. His men had made camp, and now some of them rested on the soft grass, while others explored the waters of the pond. A dozen small campfires flickered and crackled among the trees, and the weather was lovely—dry and cool, but not too cold.

Selinda's memory of good fishing had been correct. Powell's men had pulled out dozens of trout before the sun set, and the fish—wrapped in weeds and steaming in the coals of several large fires—now sent a tantalizing aroma through the evening air. The captain passed several of his men as they lounged easily with fishing poles, nodding genially in response to their greetings. These were good boys, his company, and every one was like a son to him.

He was happy that they had found such a pleasant place to camp, an oasis of water and fresh food amidst the generally barren expanse of the Solamnic Plain. Actually, this whole journey was turning out to be a rather enjoyable diversion. Lady Selinda was a pleasant companion, bright and good-humored and willing to share the discomforts of the saddle, the lash of the wind and chill of the rain, with a fortitude that would have made any knight proud. Indeed, she was probably the most uncomplaining woman it had ever been his pleasure to know. She certainly didn't fit his impression of a pampered noblewoman—if anything, she seemed grateful for the chance to get away from the luxury that had cocooned so much of her life.

What a contrast to her father, the captain allowed himself to reflect. Lord Regent du Chagne was a dour and bookish man, squinty-eyed and meticulous in details, as physically unimpressive as his daughter was beautiful. Still, du Chagne was his lord, Powell reminded himself sternly and as such deserved the respect due to his station.

Of course, the knight captain had initially balked when the princess had insisted on an overland journey back to Palanthas, but in his secret heart he was glad to have the excuse to avoid the tedious sea voyage back to the north. Selinda had been right. The goblin menace was hundreds of miles away, in the shadow of the Garnet Range, and her suggestion that they follow the Vingaard Mountains back north had been a good one. While there might be an occasional bandit or gang of thieves lurking on the plains, the presence of a hundred armed knights was enough to keep even the most rapacious highwayman far, far away.

Still, she was a headstrong lass, stubborn as a mule and a little more feisty than Powell's ideal female. Even tonight, she had insisted on going off by herself, visiting the old house that she remembered from childhood trips. Since his men had already had a good look around, the captain had sent her off with only a show of protest. In truth, he felt that she could take care of herself.

Powell came to the small camp of the dwarf and gnomes, nodding to his fellow wayfarers as they offered him wishes for a good evening. A strange lot, that trio, the captain reflected. He had never known dwarves and gnomes to have so much to do with each other. Ah well, each to his own, he told himself, strolling past their backpacks. It was a surprisingly large assortment of baggage, he noted idly, feeling a little sorry especially for the two diminutive gnomes at thought of them carrying all that stuff on some undoubtedly lengthy trek.

He stopped and looked back at the equipment. There were *four* backpacks there, you dolt, he realized. That wasn't surprising in itself. Yet he had chatted with the dwarf earlier, and indeed they had been camped nearby for several hours now. Why hadn't the fourth member of the party shown himself by now?

That fourth backpack was a large satchel suited more to a human—a *tall* human—than to any dwarf or gnome. The Captain of the Rose turned about and knelt beside the pack. Yes, indeed there was a long object there, something wrapped in a cloak.

"I say there, Cap'n? Is there something you want?" asked the dwarf, rising to his feet with hasty politeness.

Powell was already pulling aside the cloak. He saw the gilded hilt, the gold-engraved L as he revealed a weapon that he recognized instantly.

It was Giantsmiter, the sword of Lorimar. That meant the worst possible thing: the dread Assassin was nearby.

Probably hiding out in the ruin of the old house.

The old house where the Princess of Palanthas had just gone for a stroll.

Coryn's left hand clenched the edge of the table so tightly her knuckles turned as white as her pristine robe. Angrily she exhaled, a snort of sound startlingly loud in the silent chamber, then shook her head, a toss of black hair momentarily obscuring her view of the bowl of sparkling wine.

She had to watch—she knew that much—even if she hated what she was now gazing upon. In her right hand, clutched so tightly that it was bending, was the miniature golden swordsman—the talisman of Jaymes Markham, the man most of Solamnia called Assassin. She could see certain events transpire in her bowl, but they were events beyond her influence, or her will. There was destiny at work here, a future affecting all the lands of the north.

It was more than luck that brought the Princess of Palanthas to this place, she thought with a pang. It was indeed destiny, a fate woven into the very tapestry of the world. Coryn had dreaded this moment, known it might come, had known this for a long time. It was a meeting that had been foretold in certain of her auguries, even abetted by her own plans and schemes.

If not her desires.

Of course Selinda herself had made the choice to go exploring among the buildings where Jaymes had secluded himself. Coryn knew her—she was proud and inquisitive, smart and confident, but also naïve.

The wizard was startled by the flash of anger she felt. She recognized the emotion, in an intellectual sense, as jealousy even as she was startled by the flaming heat it raised in her breast.

"She is too damned *beautiful!*" snapped the wizard, shaking her head once again.

The image of Selinda du Chagne, lit from behind by the setting sun, glowed in her viewing bowl. Jaymes was dumbstruck and confused, staring at the gorgeous woman who had just discovered him, had him trapped like a cornered rat. He had a weapon, he had strength and speed. He could be past her, away from this place, in seconds.

Coryn remembered his roughness. She wanted him to use

it now against Selinda, but Jaymes wouldn't, didn't. He stood there, stock-still.

In disgust Coryn waved a hand, and the image faded from the mirror, leaving the Scrying Room in darkness. The white wizard stood and paced through the chamber, knowing the exact dimensions even though she could not see the walls, the table, or her chair in the lightless confines. With a single word she could have illuminated the place as bright as daylight, but she was unwilling to utter that word.

She would have to let things happen, she knew, let destiny take its course, but she didn't have to suffer the watching.

"You bastard," she murmured, before composing herself and slowly, carefully, opening the door.

CHAPTER EIGHTEEN

CONFRONTATION IN THE CELLAR

W ho are you?" demanded the woman. She held the door wide, allowing the full intensity of the setting sun's rays to fall upon the warrior, illuminating him like an actor on center stage. Jaymes held up a hand to shade his eyes, squinting but made no reply.

"What are you doing here?" she asked, her tone blunt.

The swordsman could tell that she was young, probably not yet twenty, and while obviously startled, was unafraid. Certainly she made no move to run away. Instead, she stood in the open doorway, peering at him through the darkness of the shed.

Jaymes shrugged, lowering the hand in which he held his dagger. "Just a wanderer," he said. "I thought this would be a comfortable place to spend the night. I was getting ready to go to sleep—I've covered a lot of ground today, and I have to admit I'm tired."

"You're lying," she said calmly. She surprised him by stepping into the shed and, even more shocking, pulling the door shut behind her. "You're traveling with that dwarf and those gnomes, the ones camping in the apple grove, aren't you?"

He peered at her silhouette against the faint steak of daylight coming through the crack in the door frame. He could make out a halo of golden hair. Beyond that he could discern few details: She was taller than average for a woman, and though she had a cape hanging off of her shoulders he guessed that she was slender.

She was courageous. Foolish, perhaps, but also very brave— of that there could be no doubt.

Her voice was confident, even arrogant and a little amused. It was the voice of a person who was used to issuing orders without having to worry whether or not those commands would be obeyed. It was the voice of a noblewoman.

Jaymes guessed she was traveling with the company of knights he had earlier observed. It occurred to him that she might be the reason for that large company, that she was important enough to warrant a sizeable and well-armed escort.

But she was still youthful, and acted as though this was some kind of thrilling adventure for her. She was overconfident in the way of one who had never experienced anything terrible. She conveyed a sense of secret delight, as if it pleased her mightily to be away from her escort, and to have discovered him here.

It was altogether confusing, and he felt at a loss. A part of him wanted to rush past her, throw open the door, and race away into the gathering dusk. He wasn't entirely sure why he declined that course of action, but the greater part of him felt no urge to run.

With what he hoped was a subtle gesture, he slipped his knife through his belt at the small of his back and held out his empty hands, palms displayed, before him. Still, he said nothing

"I asked you, what are you doing here, why are you hiding?" she said.

"I don't know what you mean," he replied. "Is it so incredible that I'd simply prefer a roof over my head?"

She sniffed. "There are lots of roofs around here. Why would you choose a place that smells so bad to make your bed? Or is that *you* I smell?" she added.

He blinked. "My turn. Who are you?" he asked.

She shrugged. "Just a traveler, like you. I know this place— my father used to send me here when I was a girl. My mother and I would take trips to the plains. We would come here to the apple farm, then go to Lord Lorimar's estate to stay for a fortnight at the end of summer. Of course, that was a long time ago, but when we came back through here and made camp in the grove, I felt a pang of nostalgia and decided I wanted to have a look around."

His vision, temporarily obscured by the brightness when she first opened the door, had begun to make out a beautiful woman with rounded cheeks and large, inquisitive eyes. The sunlight striking her hair colored it like spun gold. The swelling of her bosom beneath the cape suggested a pleasing form. Her head was held high as she stepped toward him.

"You said your father would send you from your home to the plains? From where is that, may I ask?" he asked.

"I live in Palanthas."

"He did not bring you himself? Why not?"

She shrugged, and for the first time there appeared a slight fissure in that self-confident façade. "I don't know. He had important business in the city—he always has work that keeps him busy. That didn't prevent me from doing some traveling. I had a good friend who lived in a manor on these plains. I would visit Dara Lorimar every summer."

"You are more than a mere traveler, Lady," Jaymes ventured. "You carry yourself like royalty. You are certainly brave—for all you know, I could be a robber, a common thief, or even worse."

"There are some who say you are worse. *Much* worse," she said dryly.

Jaymes shifted warily. Somehow she knew who he was, though how she had made that identification was beyond him.

"Oh, I recognized that dwarf," she explained. "I saw him before, in the Gnome Ghetto of Caergoth. I was watching through a spyglass when the knights tried to capture you there. When Coryn the White whisked you away. When you killed that knight, cut off the hand of another one. They say it was you who killed Lord Lorimar and his daughter—my friend. Oh, I know exactly who you are or who you are supposed to be. You are the Assassin."

"You know all that, and you're not afraid?" Jaymes asked. "What makes you think I won't kill you then?"

She stood blocking the door. Every muscle in the warrior's body was twitching, urging him to make a dash, attack, hide, do *something*. Yet he stood there like a trapped deer, quivering, nostrils flaring. The woman before him was a slender reed, beautiful, truly, but obviously he could overcome her. Yet the warrior was unwilling to shove her aside and make his escape.

"Maybe you will kill me yet," she said, her voice even, still unafraid. "Then we will surely know, won't we? We'll know that you're a cold-blooded murderer who would shed the blood of a woman with no regret. Who will do whatever he needs to do to get what he wants. 'This is the Assassin,' they will all cry, and Captain Powell and his men will hunt you down and kill you."

"That would be a little late for you, don't you think?"

She shrugged. "I say to myself, what if they are wrong? What if you are not the one who killed the lord and Dara?"

"I'm afraid I don't understand."

"Lady Coryn. I know her, and I saw her help you in Caergoth, help you escape the very knights who serve the nobility of Solamnia. For ten years she has been an ally of our noble houses, helping to make this land strong and righteous again. She has risked her life many times to drive the Dark Knights out of Palanthas, to banish the beasts of Khellendros from the northern coasts. I have wondered why she would help you."

"Well, she was my lover, once," he said harshly, more harshly than he intended. "She has a tender spot for me."

"Oh." Finally something seemed to take her by surprise. Those large eyes widened, then narrowed. Her voice, when next she spoke, was cold. "Except I don't believe you."

"Believe what you want," he said. "I don't care."

He was eyeing the door, again considering the notion of pushing her out of the way and making a run for it, when loud male voices reached them. Many knights were approaching.

"Lady Selinda!"

"Your Highness?"

"Princess! Where are you?"

"What, you're the daughter of Du Chagne?" he asked, astonished. "You are the Princess of Palanthas?"

She looked around in alarm then fastened her large eyes on the warrior. She was still remarkably unafraid. He stared back at her, waiting to see what this surprising creature was going to do next.

"Come here!" she said, pulling open the door and gesturing to him. "I know a place where you'll be safe—trust me."

Jaymes hesitated. Why should he trust her? The answer was obvious: With a single scream, she could bring doom down upon him.

"This way," she said urgently. "Hurry!"

With those words to prod him, he followed her through the door. They emerged from the shed to see that none of the knights had reached the rear of the building yet. "This way!" she said, ducking her head and running. She moved with speed and grace in her leggings, and the warrior had to hurry to keep up with her.

Selinda led him along the back of the house, ignoring the shouts that grew more insistent—and nearer. They came upon a horizontal trapdoor, leading into a compartment underneath the rear of the house. There was a rusty iron bolt atop the door, which the young woman kicked open then reached down to pull up the hatch.

"This is a wine cellar," the princess said. "There is a way out of here. You can escape through a tunnel, a long passage, that leads down to the bank of the stream. Hurry!"

He paused, his natural wariness balking at the sight of the shadowy flight of steps. "How do you know that?" he asked.

"I told you—I used to play here as a child. It was my favorite part of the whole estate. Now, go!"

Jaymes looked at her, frowning. After only a moment's further hesitation he plunged into the dark space beneath the trapdoor, slipping down the steep wooden set of stairs and coming to rest on his rump on a dusty floor. The momentary flash of light around him vanished as she dropped the door of the hatch back into place.

He listened, expecting to hear the sound of approaching knights. Instead, he heard a metallic clunk and knew that the princess had fastened the outside lock on the door.

"Don't be such an old maid," Selinda said, shaking her head in the face of Captain Powell's anger—anger, she knew very well, fueled by his genuine concern for her.

The knights had brought her hastily back to the camp, swords drawn, eyes wide as they explored the shadows to all sides. Despite her protests that she had not seen anything untoward, they acted as if they had snatched her from a menace in hot pursuit. They jostled her along so roughly that she arrived in the safety of the camp huffing for breath, her hair and garments in disarray.

Fortunately, in their eagerness to get her away from the ruins none of them had examined the rear of the house. She had been able to slip away from the trapdoor before she met her "rescuers," so none of them spotted a hatch, its rusty iron bolt in place. The Assassin, as she had known he would, had refrained from making any noise that would have attracted their attention.

"This is the Sword of Lorimar!" the Captain of the Rose spluttered, gesturing to the tall blade that now lay on the table in his command tent. "That means that the Assassin is nearby somewhere! By Joli, if you had met him near that old ruin, you could have suffered the same fate as Lorimar's daughter!"

"I appreciate your diligence, Captain. Your men made haste to find me and bring me to safety. Surely the crisis is past."

"That is not the point—nor is the danger past," fumed Powell. "From now on, you will stay safely behind in the camp where we can keep an eye on you. As to that wretched murderer, I can only suspect he's miles away by now. A cur like that would certainly flee at the approach of a company of knights."

"What about those you suspect of being his companions—the dwarf and gnomes? Surely he would not abandon them?"

The captain of knights shook his head. "That was my failing, Princess. When I found the sword, my thoughts were all of you and your immediate peril. I led the men to seek you and bring you back. I left only a skelton few on guard here. By the time we returned, those rascals had slipped away into the dusk. I can't spare the men to chase after them in the dark, not when the real villain is out there somewhere."

"He *is* the real villain, that warrior?" Selinda inquired. "Has the evidence been presented to a lord or a knightly council?"

"The evidence is plain, my lady!" Powell declared in exasperation, pointing to the sword. "That is the mark of Lorimar on the hilt. Giantsmiter is a unique weapon—the flaming blade of the gods, it has been called. When that fire is blazing, it can cut through stone, metal, anything. Witness how it felled the knights in Caergoth who went to arrest him!"

She frowned, thinking of that episode and its consequences. "Still, the circumstances of Lorimar's death, and of his daughter's, all the circumstances are somewhat murky, are they not? Is it known why this particular warrior wanted to slay them?"

The captain looked serious, and very tired. He appeared ready to brush away her question but apparently decided upon frankness. "I myself knew of Sir Jaymes Markham, when Lorimar was still alive. He was a maverick Knight of the Rose, but for many years presumed to be loyal. For some reason he wormed his way into Lorimar's confidence and into a position of responsibility in the lord's House Guards. He is the only one to survive that dark evening—his badge and breastplate were found at the scene. He stole the sword, Giantsmiter. If he is innocent, why did he do that? Why wouldn't he come forth to bear witness against the true killer?"

Selinda frowned again, shrugging her shapely shoulders. "Perhaps you are right, or perhaps he had his reasons. There were others who desired Lorimar's death, were there not?"

Captain Powell winced. "There are stories, my lady, circulating all through the knighthood, of course. Lorimar was a wealthy man, and he was hated by some in the knighthood for writing the Compact of the Free and coercing the signatures of many powerful lords."

"I remember even my father complaining about it," the princess noted.

"Rathskell of Solanthus hated Lorimar. He wanted to court Lorimar's daughter, but Lankford refused the match. He humiliated Thelgaard, too, when that lord tried to claim Garnet with some concocted fiction—Lorimar made him look like a fool."

"I always had the impression Lorimar was greatly admired," Selinda said.

"True, my lady, greatly admired by some. He had allies among the Crowns and Swords. He was a fair-minded man, and the rank and file held him in the highest esteem. The people looked to him, even more than to your father—if you will forgive me saying so—as the hope of their future. There was even that nonsense about the prophecy—every two-bit charlatan preacher spread that around."

"Dara, 'Princess of the Plains'?" the young woman remembered. "That one day she would be the queen of a restored kingdom? I knew her very well. She laughed about that prophecy."

"Perhaps, but the prophecy was widespread—that she would wed some mysterious Lord of No Sign. Who can blame the people for dreaming of the old days of empire? There's not a veteran knight who hasn't. But I think Lankford bore no illusions that it would happen during his, or even his daughter's, lifetimes."

"Why do you think he was killed?" Selinda probed uneasily.

"The long and short of it is he was a threat to others. Both the dukes of the Crown and the Sword had vowed to block his more liberal-minded ideas. I know for a fact that Caergoth was outraged when Lorimar also sought the hand of his daughter in marriage and was flatly denied."

"What, Crawford wanted to marry Dara? How do you know this?"

"Your father himself told me. He doesn't trust either of those lords. That was one reason he had such high hopes for the recent council."

She turned around, apparently confused and distraught. "Yes, the goblins! They'll wreck everything! They are a worse threat than this Assassin."

"Ah, my lady, don't worry. Goblins are a threat we knights can handle. Indeed, our orders live for such a challenge. Between Thelgaard, Solanthus, and Caergoth, those wretches will be wiped out—or so badly smashed that it will be a generation before they dare to show their faces on the plains again!"

"Indeed. Well, at least there is some comfort there," Selinda said, regaining her composure. "Now, if you will excuse me, I will retire to my tent. All of this excitement has me utterly exhausted.

It was much later, when most of the camp was asleep, that Selinda rose from her cot, wrapped herself in a warm shawl, and slipped out of her tent. She had taken note of where the guards were posted and had no difficulty slipping past them, unseen as she started back toward the abandoned house.

And the Assassin.

❦ ❦ ❦ ❦ ❦ ❦ ❦ ❦

Jaymes had nothing with which to make a light, so he blundered around the surprisingly large room in the darkness, groping with his hands, seeking any indication of the tunnel Selinda had told him about. The wine cellar was lined with massive kegs, most of which unfortunately sounded empty when he tapped them lightly with his knuckles. After several circuits of the room, he was convinced the place was surrounded by solid walls, the only entrance being the trapdoor through which he had entered.

Jaymes examined the stone wall behind the massive wine kegs but was unable to find a weakness, any crack or flaw in the solid masonry that might indicate a secret door. The princess had lied to him—there was no tunnel out of here, no secret passage connecting the wine cellar to the stream.

He had already tried the trapdoor and found, as he suspected, that it had been firmly latched from the outside. It rattled slightly but was solidly constructed and showed no signs of rot or decay. With the awkward angle forced by the narrow stairway and the fact that he was pushing almost straight up, he couldn't budge the barrier. Perhaps a series of smashing blows might have eventually forced the door up, but the inevitable noise would bring a platoon of knights down on him long before he could shatter the latch.

He was slumped on the floor in disgust, leaning against the cold stone wall, when he heard the catch on the trapdoor released. Moving quickly and silently, he was waiting at the bottom of the stairs when Selinda stepped inside. He was ready to spring upward, to charge through the door and make his escape, but again something made him hesitate. He waited as she started down the steps, watched as she stopped to close the heavy door behind her.

Only when she had joined him on the cellar floor did she touch spark to the wick of a small lantern, finally casting some light around the dusty, moldy room.

"Come on," she said. "I'll help you get away from here now."

"If there was ever a tunnel out of here, it's been covered over since the time you knew it as a girl," he warned.

She merely smiled and went to one of the massive wine kegs, the last one along the far wall of the room. Reaching down, she twisted the spigot, and pulled. Jaymes felt chagrin as the front of the cask swiveled away, revealing a small dark passage.

"Follow me," she invited.

"You should stay here," he urged.

"No," she demurred. "I'll take the light. Besides, you might need help at the other end. Come this way."

She started into the narrow passage, and he had little choice but to follow. He had to stoop to pass under the low ceiling, but the well-made tunnel was surprisingly dry. They padded along in silence for several minutes, and Jaymes found himself pondering many things about this puzzling woman before him. When they stopped for a short rest, he asked her a question.

"You were a friend of Dara Lorimar's?" he said. "Why are you trying to help the man who is accused of killing her?"

"Because," she said, after a few seconds thought. "Someday I hope to find out the truth."

Selinda wouldn't say any more, instead leading him along at a rapid pace. Finally they came to the end of the tunnel, where an old wooden ladder led up a shaft toward a sturdy trapdoor.

"That's covered with a layer of dirt on the outside," she said. "You'll have to pound a bit, but it should open up and let you out."

He ascended the ladder and did as she suggested, thumping with his fist until he felt the trapdoor loosen and shift. Placing his shoulder against the barrier, he heaved upward, heard the tearing of grass as the thing gave way. With a final heave, he pushed himself upward, rolling onto soft turf.

He wasn't at the stream bank. Instead, he was in the apple grove, surrounded by a dozen knights who had no doubt been alerted by the thumping under where they stood. They surrounded him in a circle, weapons drawn, as Selinda came up behind him.

"Fetch Captain Powell," she said. "I have brought him the Assassin."

CHAPTER NINETEEN

THE PRISONER

We should execute the fiend immediately!" declared Sir Powell, the roar of his voice thundering through the camp. He glared at Selinda, eyes bulging, veins throbbing in his forehead. He was as worked up as she had ever seen him. "Burning him at the stake would be only fitting justice for the crimes he committed against Lord Lorimar and his family. You've seen it yourself—the proof of his guilt is right there, in that purloined fabled sword!"

"I will thank you to watch your tone," Selinda replied coldly. "You will not win this argument by shouting me into submission!" The two of them stood alone in the dark night, away from the men of the company. Wind rustled through the apple trees, and a bright campfire crackled nearby.

The captain, his mustache quivering with indignation, stepped closer to the princess. With a visible effort he lowered his voice. "We have him in chains, now, thanks to you, Princess, but he has already killed one man in Caergoth, trying to escape. Then, too, he carried with him the sword of Lord Lorimar—the weapon that vanished at the time of that noble lord's assassination! I told you that he had renounced the knighthood—took off the breastplate of the Rose and cast it aside! What more proof of his guilt do you need? These are crimes that cry out for justice—and that justice can only be served by putting him to death!"

"You make a damning case, Captain," she replied. "I am merely suggesting—no, insisting—that the decision to execute be deferred until the prisoner can be taken to Palanthas so that my father can make that choice with the aid of a proper court of law!"

"The man is wily, desperate—a killer! The road to Palanthas is long and trying, as you well know. We are not set up for such a task, keeping a desperate prisoner. What if he escapes, does more harm? Will you accept the responsibility if he gets free and kills again?"

"What about the Oath and the Measure?" she retorted. "What kind of justice do the Solamnic Knights stand for? Killing a man merely because it's inconvenient to arrange a trial?"

"Pardon me for saying this, but need I remind you, my lady, Lord Lorimar was a great friend of your family? Is it not unseemly for you to make such a vigorous defense on his assassin's behalf?"

"You do not need to remind me of *anything*, sir!" Selinda hissed, her face flushing. "Dara Lorimar was a playmate of mine since childhood. Do not *dare* to presume that I wish her killer to have any special favors!"

"Then why take chances?" Powell pressed, shaking his head in confusion. "We can hang him right here! Or lop off his head. Even burn him at the stake—your lady's preference, of course."

"My preference, sir, is that he be bound, and delivered to Palanthas. There in the great city of Solamnia, justice may be served under the watchful eyes of the lords and the gods," the princess stated. She turned and walked a few steps away, trying to bring her raging emotions under control.

"But the risks—"

"Truth is worth risk!" she shot back. "There are still mysteries here, mysteries about this man and about the murders! Why did Coryn the White aid him, as I've told you, if he is an enemy of Solamnia? You yourself have admitted there were others who had cause to hate, to fear Lord Lorimar. What if one of them ordered the killing? Even if Jaymes Markham performed the deed, it might have been at the bidding of another! Who would be happier than that man to see the assassin executed, his secrets destroyed with him. No, Captain, we need to discover the whole truth!"

She circled around the silent, fuming Powell in the firelit clearing. In truth, Selinda wasn't certain why she thought an immediate execution was such a bad idea. When she thought of Dara Lorimar, bleeding to death beside her father's savagely battered corpse, her hands clenched and bitter tears came to her eyes.

It was true that this man, Jaymes Markham, had borne the dead man's sword away from his ruined mansion.

She looked at Sir Powell, who, though he glared at her, had apparently exhausted his arsenal of opposition. Indeed, the veteran officer looked old, weary, dejected. Selinda felt sorry for him.

He straightened to full attention as she resumed the argument, his demeanor frosty but obviously, now, resigned.

"Don't you wonder *why* the Lorimars were killed?" she asked.

"Yes. Yes, I often think about it," Powell admitted. "But what makes you think this villain is capable of telling the truth?"

"At least in Palanthas he can be questioned by all the experts in my father's realm! Clerics and mages can query him, and maybe their unique skills will ferret out the truth!"

"That may be so, but the danger! The chance of escape, or rescue. Remember, he has three accomplices still at large, need I remind you? There are too many risks involved—"

"Oh, come on, Uncle Siggy," she said, employing the pet name she had lavished on him when, as a little girl, she had bounced on Sir Sigmund Powell's knee. "Do you think a dwarf and two gnomes are a threat to a hundred worthy knights?"

She sighed, put her hands on his arms, felt the strength there and the loyalty for which she loved him. "I know you only have my best interests at heart, and I don't mean to cause you any more grief." She raised her hands to his shoulders, squeezing. "Really!"

His posture remained rigid, but she saw the gradual softening in his eyes. Slowly, he relaxed, finally raising one of his hands to cover her own. "The man is a villain! A treacherous assassin, and who knows what else he has done as an outlaw?" he said. "If he should bring any harm to you—"

"He won't," Selinda said firmly. She smiled slyly. "Just think, if we had returned to Palanthas by sea, as you had planned, we never would have found him. You should be congratulating me for bringing us this way, allowing you to capture the most celebrated fugitive in all Solamnia! The least you can do is obey my wishes in this one simple matter."

"Ah, my lady. As ever, I obey you. But this matter is far from simple. I remind you again: What if he should escape?"

"That is something, dear Uncle Siggy, I shall count on you to prevent!"

⊱✧⊰

Jaymes felt the rough bark of the apple tree chafing against his back. His arms were shackled behind him and around the trunk of the tree, so there was little he could do to ease the pain. When he twisted his head, he could see the big fire, glowing between a ring of trees, and he sensed that the princess was over there, talking about him with the leader of the knights. The knights had found the sword, Giantsmiter, and of course they had taken away his crossbow and dagger. His magic ring, a gift from Coryn, remained on his middle finger of his right hand, all but useless behind his back.

It didn't take any great stretch of imagination to realize that Princess Selinda had played him for a fool, lulling him into a sense of security before springing her trap. Why had he listened to her? If he had simply knocked her over the head, he would be far away from here by now, across the stream and safely onto the plains. Instead, he had followed her like a bumbling puppy.

How Jaymes had underestimated the princess—to think he had been so busy admiring her courage, her cool assessment of risk and danger, when all the while she had been playing a game, pulling him around like a pet with a ring through its nose.

Still, regrets were a waste of time. What was done was done. He wondered about Dram and the two gnomes—there was no sign of them. They must have escaped in the confusion. The loyal dwarf, no doubt, would remain nearby for a while, looking for an opportunity to stage a rescue. Jaymes shifted, counting ten knights within sight of where he was sitting. Half were watching him. The rest were staring into the surrounding darkness. A whole regiment of dwarves couldn't rescue him under the circumstances. Far better to hope that Dram, Carbo, and Sulfie were far away and safe.

He heard a stirring among the guards, saw several of them straightening to attention as someone approached.

"My lady!" one protested. "You should not come near the villain!"

"Nonsense." He recognized Lady Selinda's curt, confident voice. "He is well restrained, I'm sure."

"Well, yes, but—"

"Then I am perfectly safe, Wendell. Of course, you may keep an eye on us, but please do so from over there. I would like a few words with the prisoner, in private."

"But—my lady!"

"In *private*, Wendell." Her tone was gentle but steely at the same time.

The knight called Wendell stalked over to Jaymes and glared daggers at him. "Not a hint of any threat to the lady—not a gesture, the merest expression, of disrespect—do you understand? Or I will be only to happy to cut out your black heart and feed it to the crows!"

Jaymes met the knight's murderous stare but made no reply. Wendell's hands twitched, and he looked ready to deliver a sharp kick with his iron-shod boot. Instead his face contorted, and he spun about, taking a dozen steps away. He stood there at attention, his eyes fastened on the prisoner with furious intensity.

Selinda came over and sat on a stump of wood. She wore a sturdy leather skirt split up the middle, with woolen leggings and an unadorned shirt. Her blonde hair was looped into a ponytail behind her. She sat easily, leaning her elbows on her knees as she studied Jaymes. She had a curious expression in her eyes—amusement, mingled with wariness and contempt—and her slender fingers interlocked as she joined her hands before her.

"I told you Dara Lorimar was my friend," she said quietly. "Her father was like an uncle to me. If you killed them, you will suffer their fate. How did they die? Did they suffer?"

Jaymes winced, looking away. He drew a breath, felt her eyes boring into the side of his head. "Tell me the truth now. Do you know how they died?"

"She died with a sword in her hand," he said, finally. "I think the first blow killed her—she did not suffer long in any event. The lord . . . it was worse for him. His leg was broken, he was bleeding from several stabs. In the end it was the fire that killed him."

He looked, saw that her eyes were shining, wet with tears that did not spill onto her cheeks. Her fingers were taut, the knuckles white. "And the Sword of Lorimar? How came you to bear it?"

Jaymes met her look. "He dropped it when he fell. It was too valuable to consign to the flames, so I took it away," he answered.

"Thank you for your honesty," she said, her voice hoarse, and, for the first time, absent its usual quality of confidence and command.

"Why do you pick at these scars?" he asked.

She snorted. "These are things I want to know. I have *many* questions," she added, noncommittally. "After they execute you, I fear it will be too late to find out some of the answers."

"Are they going to kill me this very night?" he asked, trying to keep his voice level, uncertain he wanted to know the answer.

"Captain Powell wanted to get on with it, yes, but I have

persuaded him to wait until you can be taken to Palanthas for a proper trial." She stood up now, and there was no sense of hesitation, regret, or amusement as she stared down at him. Her eyes might have been fire, but her voice was ice. "When the high court finds you guilty—*then* I will be ready to watch you die."

❦❦❦❦❦❦❦❦❦

Dram Feldspar's belly was wet, but he dared not raise himself out of the muck. He glared over at Carbo and Sulfie, but the two gnomes needed no warning—they, too, had flattened themselves along the stream bank, all but buried in the mud, concealed by a dense clump of cat-tailed reeds as the file of knights rode past.

The three of them had spent a cold night here, a mile or more from the grove where they had initially made such a pleasant camp. Dram had seen the knight's captain as he found Jaymes' sword. The officer had called out an alarm, summoning his men, sending them toward the abandoned house where the dwarf was certain that his companion was hiding. All of the captain's attention was focused on that ruined manor.

Dram had wasted no time collecting the two gnomes, snatching up a few possessions easy to grab—including the bag of sulfir Sulfie had been carrying—and slipping past the sentries.

The dwarf and the two gnomes had been able to crawl away from the grove unseen, into the muddy stream. They crawled some distance away from the Solamnic camp. Late at night they heard some commotion, and Dram had inched back close enough to overhear the conversation between a couple of guards. They referred to "the prisoner," and the dwarf knew his old friend was doomed.

Just an hour past dawn, a few scouts had emerged from the apple grove, cantering northward, splashing through the stream a hundred paces from where the three of them were dug in. Shortly thereafter, the rest of the company rode by, several outriders flanking either side of the main body. Dram and his companions burrowed into the reeds as one of the outriders came dangerously close.

At last the dwarf dared to raise his head, watching the troops pass. He spotted Jaymes, the warrior's hands shackled to a saddle, another set of chains linking his ankles under the belly of a steed. He rode in the middle of a dozen knights, every one riding with one hand on the hilt of his weapon, one eye on the prisoner.

A moment later the dwarf spotted someone else who stood out from the bulk of stern knights. This person was indisputably a female, a woman who rode astride her horse, not sidesaddle, her posture every bit as proud and capable as any knight. Her golden hair streamed in a plume behind her head as she dug her spurs into her horse, joining the pace of the swiftly cantering knights.

All rode through the stream without breaking stride, the horses surging up the far bank, thundering onto the plains, heading north. In a few minutes they had vanished from sight, but Dram gestured to the gnomes to stay put. Sure enough, the last scouts emerged from the grove some ten minutes after the main body had departed, spreading out, riding watchfully behind.

Once again the three squeezed down amidst the reeds as the last knights passed. The leather-clad scouts on their light horses headed north in the wake of the column, eyes roving from side to side. It seemed to take forever before they dwindled to specks.

Only then did Dram struggle to his feet, muttering and cursing as he tried to wipe the stinking mud off his tunic. He settled for rinsing most of it from his beard. Finally, with the two miserable, complaining gnomes in tow, he too started northward, following the easily distinguishable spoor of the knightly column.

CHAPTER TWENTY

PROFIT AND LOSS

Ankhar had initial difficulties integrating the human soldiers into the ranks of his goblin horde. The two races possessed an instinctive antipathy that resisted his most persuasive efforts to tame. They were forced to set up their camps some distance from each other. Yet many a passing glance, sneer or curled lip escalated into blows, bloodshed, even a few fatalities.

Ankhar had a brainstorm on the day when Blackgaard came to him and complained that two of his men, suspected of some slight, had been ambushed and severely injured by their allies.

Actually, it was Laka—and Hiddukel, Prince of Lies—who gave her adopted son the idea. She whispered it to him in the dark of the night. At first light the next day, Ankhar asked for a demonstration of battle magic from Hoarst and his compatriots. The half-giant suggested a broad, flat-bottomed valley for the occasion. The many thousands of gobs and hobs assembled in more or less regular ranks on the slopes to watch, while the half giant, together with Laka, Captain Blackgaard, and Rib Chewer, sat upon a low hilltop with a good view of the target zone.

The half giant roared with delight as the Thorn Knights spewed blazing fireballs, searing lightning bolts, and thunderous hailstorms against hapless thickets of thornbushes, a beaver dam, and a clump of cottonwoods. When these had all been reduced to charred pulp, the three wizards demonstrated other talents. One launched from his fingertips a blazing spear that struck down a hapless prisoner staked nearly a mile away. Another, a female elf, vanished from sight and startled the hill giant by appearing behind him. She handed him a conjured rose with the hint of a smile.

Hoarst himself performed the most spectacular spell, calling down a swarm of meteors that apparently obliterated the Thorn Knight, as well as pummeling and cratering a large section of the plain. Only when the dust settled did the viewers see that Hoarst was alive, strolling casually out of the ruined swath of ground. He saluted Ankhar with a little click of his heels and bowed as the half-giant and his companions applauded.

After a moment, the hobs and gobs of Ankhar's army added a massive roar of approval, awed—just like their half-giant leader—by what they had witnessed. As Laka had predicted, the goblin-kind were more amenable to their human compatriots after that.

"When next we meet knights, there new kind of Truth upon the battlefield!" crowed the commander, clapping the former dark knight Blackgaard on the back. Ankhar was impressed that the man wasn't staggered by the blow, though the human did murmur something unintelligible underneath his breath.

"What you say?" the half giant asked with a scowl.

"*Est Sudanus oth Nikkas,*" the Dark Knight captain replied.

"What that mean?"

"Perhaps you know that the Solamnics pledge *Est Sularus oth Mithas*—My honor is my life?" the human suggested.

"I hear this," Ankhar lied, starting to lose his patience.

"*Est Sudanus oth Nikkas* means 'My power is my Truth.' "

The half-giant thought about that saying for a moment, then laughed, a dull rumble of amusement slowly bubbling from his chest. "Yes," he agreed. "That the way of my army."

He looked to Laka, who bobbed her skull rattle. The eyes glowed bright green in approval.

"Yes, my power is my Truth," he repeated.

"Look at these figures!" snapped Bakkard du Chagne, waving the parchments in the general direction of Baron Dekage. "It's as if the miners are purposely slowing down production—merely to spite me!"

"I am sure that is not the case, my lord," the aide de camp tried to reassure him. "After all, the rains have been intense during this season. You recall, a score of workers lost their lives when the north dam burst and they were unable to escape their flooding tunnels. Surely that is more a cause of the production drop than any recalcitrance on the part of the common laborers."

"Bah! You know what those towns are like, there along the north coast! Barely getting on their feet again since the Scourge! So twenty men lost their lives? A hundred should be willing to step forward and take their places! Where else in all Solamnia might they expect to earn that kind of money?"

"Quite right, Excellency. Their ingratitude almost boggles the mind. Er, what action would you like to direct on this matter?"

Du Chagne grimaced and turned to the tall window. As usual, the sun was streaming in, the azure waters of the Bay of Branchala glittering like a million sapphires. Ships plied these waters in increasing numbers, a dozen or more tall-masted galleons arriving in the port. Several massive galleys were just now rounding the point, no doubt bearing tin and spices from the east. The Lord Regent nodded—his share of the docking taxes alone would add more than a hundred steel to his ledgers, for *each* of the newly arriving ships.

He glanced at the conspicuously empty docks, near the smelting yards. He knew that the coal reserves on the Norlund peninsula were extensive and only now being tapped after long years of wastage under the Dragon Overlords. Every day, those mines should be able to produce enough of their black fuel to send at least one, and soon enough two, heavily laden barges down the coastline. In truth, his smelters, his forges—all his industries!—clamored for the fuel like hungry chicks in an eagle's nest.

Yet coal production continued to decline. The last barge had arrived three days ago and had already been emptied and towed back to the mines. There were no coal barges in sight in that direction, and the reserve of coal piled near the waterfront had dwindled from the dozen or more mountainous cones that were the norm to a couple of pathetic hillocks that would barely last the week. He thought of his mountain of gold, secure in his towertop high above, and he dreaded the thought that he would have to dip into it to help the city pay for routine operations.

"I won't stand for it, do you hear!" snapped the Lord Regent. "It is completely unacceptable!"

"Indeed, Excellency. I merely await your orders," DeKage said patiently.

"Bah—enough of coal headaches for now. Tell me, have any interesting dispatches arrived in the morning pouch?"

"Yes, there is one here, sent by Captain Powell. I believe it arrived by pigeon, shortly after dawn. It has been transcribed for you and is ready for your perusal."

"Very well—that might be distracting. Let me have it."

The aide handed it over, and the lord regent perched his spectacles upon his blunt nose. He hated to wear the damned things, they were a sign of weakness, but in truth his eyes were not what they used to be. He certainly could not read the finely printed foolscap of a messenger pigeon's paper, if it hadn't already been transcribed into large letters in solid, dark ink. He read the missive quickly.

"Well, this is big news. They have caught the bastard—the Assassin of Lorimar!" He crumpled the short missive and glared at DeKage. "They are bringing him here!"

"Indeed!" The baron allowed himself the luxury of a thin smile. "Good news indeed, is it not, my lord?"

Du Chagne was looking out the window, thinking. It never failed—things always became more complicated. He nodded. "Yes, very good news, of course," he agreed. "Now, moving on—what else is on the agenda?"

"Very good, my lord. Now, there is the matter of the wheat

harvest. As you can see from the charts, it has been a good year on the northern plains. Unfortunately, the late rains have caused two deleterious effects. First, some of the stockpiles have been flooded in the yards on the eastern end of the High Clerist's Pass. Secondly, some of the road through the pass remains washed out, and it is apparently beyond the ability of the local residents to repair—at least in a timely fashion. I have here a series of messages, urgent requests for assistance from the city."

"Why must I do *everything* for these people? Are they too lazy to lift a pick and shovel?" Du Chagne slumped into his leather-padded chair, putting a hand over his face. He was starting to get a headache. He pictured the cost in more gold: gravel purchased from local quarries, teamsters to haul the fill, lazy workers who would siphon off his hard-earned fortune.

Just then, du Chagne's attention was drawn by a knock at the door. He scowled; his councils with his aide de camp were inviolate unless something significant warranted an interruption.

"What is it?" he barked.

A liveried doorman hesitantly opened the portal and stood at attention. "Begging your pardon, Excellency, but you have a visitor. I told her you were in conference, but she was really quite insistent."

"She? A woman. Most inconvenient. Who the devil is it, man?"

"The White Wit—that is, the Lady Coryn."

Du Chagne almost groaned audibly. He didn't have time for this! "Tell her to come back next week!"

"Er, I can't, my lord. That is, she's not here. She spoke to me, and said . . . let me see, she said, 'Tell the Lord Regent I await him at his highest counsel.' Then she blinked out of sight, Excellency."

"Damn it." Du Chagne left the baron and his servant, running out the door and up the spiraling stairs to the top of his loftiest tower. His stocky legs propelled him toward the gold that was his only, and thus his highest, counsel. He arrived at the glass-walled room, panting, fumbling for his key at the landing,

228

and when the door opened he stumbled inside, terrified of what he might find.

His gold was still there, every bar of it, stacked just as it had been when he left it that morning. A quick glance across the neat stacks confirmed that not a single ingot had been stolen.

Coryn the White emerged from behind one huge pile of gold bars. Her robe, as pure alabaster as a layer of new fallen snow, glistened in the sun-brightened hall. Silver symbols, etched in thread-thin wire, winked and sparkled as the light shone on the robe.

"How did you get up here?" the duke croaked before glancing again at the gold. With a strangled gasp he lunged forward, running his hands over the bars, insuring that it was not some cruel illusion. "Are you threatening my treasure?" he demanded.

"Of course not!" the white wizard replied. "If you'll remember, the magic protection I cast upon it makes it proof against theft. Even from myself. I am not interested in your gold."

"That spell is still in effect?"

"It is permanent—it will outlast me, and you. Your gold cannot be stolen so long as you keep it in this room," assured Coryn.

"What do you want here then?"

"I come to bargain with you." She let her fingers trail across several smooth, gleaming bars. He resisted the urge to rush over and wipe off the smudges he was sure her touch had left.

"Now, Lady Coryn. As always, it is a pleasure to see you, even if I would prefer that your visits take place in another, er, locale. Also, I am in the midst of pressing affairs. May I ask you to be as direct as I know you are capable of being?"

"Of course, Excellency," Coryn said, bowing slightly. Her black hair gleamed like satin, falling over her shoulders, framing her face and matching the indigo of her eyes. She was very beautiful, the Lord Regent reflected idly. He respected the fact that she did not use this beauty as a weapon, as so many women did. While he himself, of course, was immune to such charms, he knew they reduced many men to whimpering fools.

Still, Coryn the White had other weapons at her disposal, and the regent resolved to remain alert. Once a useful ally during his reclamation of Palanthas, she had an increasingly annoying way of sticking her nose into matters where it didn't belong. More than once she had insisted upon courses of action that had had serious repercussions for the regent's profit margins. She had proven herself to be a populist at heart, and du Chagne had no fondness for populists. Bad for business, bad for maintaining law and order, bad for progress, they were troublemakers, every one of them.

"I have been to the estate of Lord Lorimar," she said without preamble, causing his eyes to widen. "I went to retrieve a document that should have been there—the Compact of the Free. No doubt you recall it, as you, yourself, were one of the signatories. He kept it in a strongbox with the six green diamonds."

"Yes, of course I recall it," said the Lord Regent, trying to keep his tone neutral even as he felt a surge of irritation. The compact was a populist document if ever there was such a thing! "He also had that ancient banner of the three orders. We all know it was his goal to restore a united Solamnia—he would use the diamonds in the crown, and the banner of the Crown, the Rose, and the Sword would be the new royal sigil. So what about all this?"

"The compact, the six green stones, and the pennant are all missing. That is, I could not locate them in the ruin, where they should have been, and I come to ask if you know what happened to them."

Du Chagne's jaw flapped, and he stammered like a peasant before he gathered his wits and replied. "It was a parchment document, by Shinare! Why, that place burned to the ground! What makes you think it could possibly have survived?"

"Because I know where the lord secretly kept it, and it was proofed against fire. Furthermore, he told me that only two other people knew where it was kept. One of those people was you."

"My dear Lady Coryn, I assure you I have no idea what you are talking about!" protested the regent. "I once saw his strongbox—knew that he wanted to make those six stones into a new crown—but it's ridiculous to assert that I knew where it was hidden! Now, if you will excuse me, I have matters in the *real* world to address! Mundane things like road repairs—if you want the people of Palanthas to have anything to eat this winter! And those repairs will cost me more of this gold than I should like to part with."

That last statement was true.

"No doubt," Coryn replied. "If you insist you know nothing about the lost compact, then I shall ask the same question of your dukes. Do you think they know where it is? And the green diamonds?"

"They're gone, I tell you!" Du Chagne blurted.

"Gone?" Coryn blinked, and he wondered if she was stupid—or was mocking him. "You mean, just like *that?*"

She snapped her fingers, and all the gold, the more than twelve thousand bars in the treasure room, vanished. Du Chagne screamed in horror and spun around, staring in disbelief at the room that was utterly empty. There was no longer any brilliant reflection, no warmth—suddenly it felt very chilly and looked very dark in here.

"What did you do?" shrieked the lord regent. "Where did it go?"

"Oh, your gold is still here," Coryn said. "I told you, it can't be stolen."

"Where is it then?" he demanded, taking an angry step toward her, his fingers clenched.

"Here," she said, apparently unafraid.

Du Chagne groped around, feeeling a solid mass of a block of golden bars. He fumbled, lifted one, felt the solid weight of an ingot. He hefted it but could see right through it—as if it wasn't there!

"I can't see it!" he whined.

"Neither can anybody else," the wizard told him. "It's invisible."

"I can't trade with invisible gold!" cried the lord regent.

"Perhaps not. Perhaps your partners will take payment on trust?"

"Nobody takes payment in trust, as you well know!" snapped the duke. He glared at her, breathing hard, trying to gain control of himself. "What do you want?" he asked.

"I want to find that compact and the missing strongbox. I want to know who killed Lord Lorimar," the white wizard answered.

"I don't know where any of it is!" protested du Chagne. "The Assassin killed Lord Lorimar! We all know that!"

"Perhaps your invisible gold will help you rethink these events," Coryn said calmly.

"How can it do that?" he demanded.

Instead of answering, the enchantress murmured another word, a strange-sounding utterance that echoed in the air for several seconds after she disappeared.

⊰◦⊱◦⊰◦⊰◦⊰◉⊱◦⊱◦⊰◦⊱◦⊱

"My dear!" cried Lady Martha, embracing her husband, Duke Walker, as he came striding through the doors of the castle. The troops of his Ducal Guard were still filing into the courtyard, and the streets beyond rumbled from the weight of heavy wheels as the freight wagons of Walker's personal baggage train rolled across the drawbridge and into the castle's yard. "I did not expect to see you back so soon! Have the goblins been vanquished?"

"Not entirely," the duke said with a dismissive shake of his handsome head. "There were difficulties between Solanthus and Thelgaard—not too surprising—and I was unable to force them to cooperate."

"But Thelgaard—is he all right? I heard there was a terrible battle?"

"He is a moron!" snapped Walker. "He lost the better part of his army and came in to my camp like a drowned rat after swimming the Upper Vingaard. If I hadn't provided him with an escort, I doubt that he would have made it back to his keep in one piece!"

232

"He went back to Thelgaard?" Martha was perplexed. "So the war is over, then?"

"No, I keep telling you," snapped the duke, growing more vexed. His sleep had been troubled by terrible dreams during the whole expedition "Thelgaard lost a battle. He is back in his keep with such few survivors as got away with him. I doubt they will be sallying forth any time soon. After Duke Jarrod's men and the Crown knights were defeated, Duke Rathskell and his own force fell back to Solanthus. They are quite safe there—for you know that is the mightiest fortress anywhere on the plains."

"Yes, my duke. But what of the goblins—they have retired to the mountains then?" asked Martha, her pretty brow wrinkling.

"I'm quite sure I don't know," said the duke. "They probably have taken Luinstat by now. I had to order the place evacuated, since Solanthus absolutely refused—refused, I tell you!—to stand before it."

"But . . . that's way over by the Garnet Mountains! Why did you bring the army back here?" the lady pressed.

"Damn it, woman! It's not the whole army—just my personal guard and my own wagons! The army is posted by the Kingsbridge, ready to move when need be. I have bigger problems than that! I haven't had a good night's sleep since I took to the field, and if this problem is going to get solved, I'll have to get some rest! Now, have my servants draw me a bath!"

"But . . . what about the goblins?" Lady Martha wasn't the smartest duchess ever to don a tiara, but she knew that something about her lord's grand strategy didn't sound quite right.

"If they create more problems, Joli knows one of those tiresome fools will let me know about it. As for now, I'm hungry as well as tired. Go tell the chefs that I would like something fresh for dinner as soon as I am done with my bath. I have been on the plains for too long—have them make something from the sea!"

The Nightmaster stood on a high tower alongside the bulk of Castle Caergoth. His temple was far below here, but he borrowed this lookout whenever he wanted to look at the night sky. No one had ever spotted him here—at least, no one who had lived to tell of their discovery.

From here the priest had watched the Ducal Guard return to the city, saw the knights stabling their horses, going to the houses of their wives and mistresses. This meant that Caergoth's army was inactive, no doubt gone into bivouac somewhere on the plains.

The cleric of Hiddukel knew that his god should be pleased with his labors. In truth, many of his plans had worked out as he desired. His goblin agent, sequestered in the dungeon below the castle, had been able to reach the mind of the Princess of Palanthas, had ensured that she would return across the plains instead of by ship. His crystal visions had revealed to the dark priest that the detour was working exactly as he and his master wished. The auguries were right—indeed, she had stumbled upon the Assassin!

If only the Assassin had been killed. Instead, the fugitive was captured! The dark priest felt a shiver creep along his spine, for this was *not* what his immortal master desired. The Prince of Lies needed his most dramatic deceit to remain undiscovered, and that required that the man called the Assassin must die.

That interfering bitch of a princess had seen to it that the man would live, for several more weeks at least. Each passing day was too long.

It was necessary to prod events along, which he could do with the whisper of a dream that would carry through the evening's dusk. . . .

⊰◦◎◦◦◦◦◎◦◉◦◎◦◦◦◎◦◎◦⊱

The Lord Regent's palace was dark, save for the torches at the front doors and the lanterns carried by the watchmen who patrolled the outer wall and the upper parapets. Bakkard Du Chagne looked out from the lonely bedroom on the upper floor—his wife had long ago been banished to her own chamber on the far end of the royal wing—watching not the lights but the darkness. It was near morning, but he had been unable to sleep since a terrifying dream had roused him before midnight. In the wake of that nightmare, he had sent a secret message into the darker quarter of his city. Now he watched and waited.

A memory, unbidden, provoked a shiver of terror. He recalled the empty-looking vault, all his vast treasure treacherously concealed by the White Witch. How dare she? And how could he force her to remove her spell. That, unfortunately, was not a problem he could solve tonight.

There! He saw a shadow moving along the base of the wall, staying well concealed from the guards. The shadow followed a zig zag course through the garden, avoiding the hounds and even the servants' quarters. When the shadow came to the base of the palace, it started up a trellis, climbing silently. This trellis was usually lit by several bright lanterns, but tonight the Lord Regent, claiming difficulty in sleeping, had ordered them extinguished.

When the shadowy figure reached the top of the trellis, he slipped over the railing, crossed the balcony and entered the door that was being held open by Lord Regent Bakkard Du Chagne.

"Excellency," said the man, kneeling, "I await your order."

"Yes, of course," said the regent. "Show your face."

The visitor pulled back the cowl of his dark hood. His visage was that of a Knight of Solamnia, right down to the bushy, but carefully trimmed, mustache.

"Good, yes, that disguise will work."

"What are your orders, my lord?"

"There is a file of knights approaching the city from the plains. They are led by Captain Powell, chief of my palace guard. A good man. Loyal, and true to the Oath and the Measure."

The man nodded, as the noble continued.

"They will be entering the pass of the High Clerist within the week. They are bringing a prisoner with them, a notorious assassin they recently captured. I wish you to meet this party—I will send some message for you to convey, some missive for Powell to explain your trip. Call yourself . . . Sir Dupuy."

"It shall be as you command, my lord," pledged the man. He bowed tentatively, sensing there was more to come.

"Your payment . . . I cannot pay you in gold, not this time."

"No gold, my lord?" The man had the audacity to sound disappointed.

"No, but here is a bag of good steel coins," snapped du Chagne. "Convert them to gold yourself if you desire! You know where the moneychangers are! First, do this job for me."

"Of course, my lord. As to the job. . . ?"

"You will ride with the column of knights as they return to the city," the regent said. "You will locate the captive. And, Sir Dupuy?"

"Excellency?"

"It is my express wish that this prisoner should not reach the city alive."

CHAPTER TWENTY-ONE

TRACKER AND TRAPPER

For long days Jaymes was chained to the saddle, his ankles shackled beneath the belly of the old, swaybacked mare. The mare's reins were held securely in the fist of a knight riding just ahead of him. Two or more knights, their hands resting on the hilts of their swords, were never more than an arm's length away.

Captain Powell was taking no chances. Even so, while he and his men treated the prisoner with stiff contempt, they did not display any outright cruelty. They paid him scant attention, actually, except to make sure he was securely bound. He was fed indifferently, usually after the rest of the party ate, but not starved.

As to the princess, she ignored her prize utterly. Despite her earlier apparent fascination with him, now she seemed content to ride along with the knights and wait for justice to run its course. Though Captain Powell switched from the head to the tail of the column at will, Selinda du Chagne always rode among the first rank. So far as Jaymes could see, she never even cast a backward glance at the outlaw she had contrived to snare.

The knights made good time on their journey. The terrain was smooth, the midsummer weather tolerable, though it rained a lot. Within ten days, a fortnight at the most, they would arrive in Palanthas.

Where the gallows awaited.

The dwarf slogged along well behind the knights, pulling his shawl tightly around his shoulders, cursing the rain that soaked his beard, trailed down his chest, chilled him through his garments and his armor, down to his very bones. He cast a look back at the two gnomes, for Sulfie and Carbo always plodded behind him, every bit as sodden and weary and miserable as himself.

"How much farther?" asked the female, plaintively raising her hood enough to look at Dram. "I say we should give up!"

"How in blazes should I know how much farther?" groused the dwarf. "We're going to follow those knights until I say we stop! And we won't stop until they stop! So shut up, keep going!"

Dram dropped his head and pushed forward, ignoring the whispered complaints exchanged by the two trail-weary gnomes. He was determined, implacable! He was a mountain dwarf, dammit!

In the depths of his heart, though, his determination was beginning to flag. Dram didn't have the slightest idea how they could possibly rescue Jaymes.

For one thing, the knights, on horseback, made much better time than the three short-legged pursuers. Only by pushing on into the dark of each night, and starting off with the first glimmer of dawn, had Dram been able to keep on their trail.

On yesterday's trek, it had been nearly sunset by the time they reached the camp which the Knights of Solamnia and their prisoner had departed from twelve hours earlier. Now they were a full day behind the column of knights.

"Why does that guy mean so much to you, anyway?" Carbo had asked the night before in the moments before they fell asleep. "Why do we have to catch up to them and try to save him?"

"He saved my life once," Dram had said—simply, and truthfully. Only to himself did he admit there was more to it than that. There was a destiny laid upon Jaymes Markham, a cause that propelled him. He was a man in search of vengeance, but it was more than that. The dwarf had embraced the man and his destiny. Win or lose, he was determined to share his friend's fate.

It was the tenth day following Jaymes's capture. The jagged crest of the Vingaard Mountains had formed the western horizon, with its skyline to their left. Now the trail of the knights abruptly veered, with those peaks rising before them. The knights were heading west, straight into the mountain range.

"We're not going to *climb* those, are we?" asked Carbo hesitantly, as Dram stopped to take a drink from his water flask.

"Nah," the dwarf said with a lot more assurance than he felt. "There's a pass right through 'em—High Clerist's Pass. They're heading to Palanthas, I'm pretty sure, and it's a good short cut."

Of course, he had never taken that road, but he had heard of it. He knew it was guarded by an ancient fortress and tower, the site of many a crucial battle during past wars. How they would pass that castle undetected was a question that bothered him. Perhaps, as some had said, the fortress had fallen into ruin and disrepair. In any event, first they had to navigate the long, winding road leading up to the summit. Dram was certain that it would involve a lot more climbing than the gnomes were accustomed to. Of course he, being a mountain dwarf, was not deterred by the thought of a few miles of steep, uphill walking.

At least there would be the cover of trees, he told himself, as they approached the foothills. He could see that the party of knights had moved onto an old flagstone road, probably one of the ancient highways dating back to the days of the Solamnic Empire. There was plenty of proof that their horses had passed by.

The sun had already set behind the crest of the mountains as the roadway entered a region of forest. They were following a river valley, the highway just a few paces above a rapid, clear stream that spilled between a bracket of frowning cliffs. When Sulfie spotted a patch of blackberry bushes down near the water, Dram agreed to a brief halt, even though they still had perhaps an hour of daylight left. A little rest, coupled with some fresh fruit, might give them the energy to make up some lost ground the next day.

The clouds broke up as the made camp, and the dwarf decided to indulge in the luxury of a fire, hoping to dry out some of their possessions and keep the mountain chill away. The companions camped in a narrow grotto with steep stone walls on two sides. Dram was able to find lots of dry wood under the thick branches of the evergreens. Piling sticks in a makeshift firepit, he struck a spark into dry pine needles and soon had a crackling blaze.

"We can dry out a few of these wet clothes, before they start rotting right onto our bodies," he remarked, stripping off his woolen shirt and leggings, propping them on a makeshift rack of branches. He settled back, munching a handful of berries that the gnomes had collected, and feeling a measure of satisfaction. His eyelids grew heavy, and he leaned back against a grassy hummock.

"Hey!"

Sulfie's exclamation had Dram jumping to his feet even before his eyes opened. He looked around, crouching beside the campfire, his stout axe raised, and saw a most unexpected visitor.

"Lady Coryn!" he gasped, as the enchantress in her glimmering white robe materialized out of the surrounding underbrush. His first feeling was of immense relief.

His second was that he was darned near naked.

With a muttered curse he dove behind the drying rack, slipping into his pants while he used the draped shirt as a dressing screen. The wizard smiled and glanced away. The two gnomes, eyes agog, stood near the hem of the woman's robe, touching it as they reached up at her with slack-jawed amazement.

"Hey, you're that magician who made the white smoke," Carbo said, remembering. "Where did you come from, now?"

Her eyes met Dram's as the dwarf's head popped through the neck of his tunic. Still flustered, he hastened to pull a stout log up to the fire, wiping the moss and bark off as much as possible.

"Here, my lady. It's not much, but won't you use it for a chair?" he asked. He returned to his hummock as she thanked him and sat down.

240

"Why don't you go and get some berries for the lady," Dram suggested to the still-gaping Sulfie. "Carbo, try working your net in the stream. See if you can get us some fish, all right?"

The two gnomes hurried off, and the dwarf turned to gaze upon Coryn. He was surprised at how happy he was to see her.

"So you know about Jaymes?" he asked.

She nodded. "I come from Palanthas. The Lord Regent has just learned of his capture, and I learned about it, as well."

"Do you know—is he still, well, safe and sound?" the dwarf wondered.

"I have not actually seen him, but it is my understanding that he is perfectly well. Though he is most certainly not safe."

"What do you mean?"

Coryn closed her eyes and drew a breath through her nose. She looked as weary as he felt, thought the dwarf. And so terribly young. Awkwardly, he reached out a big hand and patted her on the knee. She took his hand in hers and smiled.

"You're a good friend to him, you know that?" she said pensively.

He shrugged, embarrassed. "Well, I try to be a friend," he said. "He's been a good one to me. I know if someone was hauling me around in chains, he'd do what he could to get me out of there."

"Tell me. You never talk about it. How did you meet him?" asked the white wizard.

Dram leaned forward. "I was bounty hunting in the Garnet foothills, going after goblins wherever I could find the bast— excuse me, the little runts. I was damned good at it, too. Had me over a hundred ears I was going to take to Thelgaard for the reward.

"Only thing was, I went there with my ears, and the duke's purser said the goblins weren't their problem anymore. I was expected to go all the way to Solanthus—a hundred miles away—and get the bounty there! Well, I sorta took offense to that, and one thing led to another, and a couple of these knights—the Crown fellows, who follow Thelgaard—got their

241

arms or legs broke. They had me clapped in arms, sentenced to hang, when Jaymes came along and sprang me from the dungeon. Disguised himself as a Rose Knight, he did, and he made a pretty convincing show of it."

"That was, what, almost two years ago?" Coryn said. "I remember you were with him when I ran into you both down at the Newsea."

"Yep, been together like salt and pepper ever since. We were doing some pretty good goblin hunting, too, though it was like holding back a tide. Nobody was paying the same bounty anymore. Then, of course, there was this business of the gnomes."

He glanced over toward the stream, saw that Carbo was busy fishing some distance away. Sulfie's head popped up from the blackberry bushes then vanished as she cheerfully went back to her pickings. "You started him on that, you know. With that letter that came over the water from your friend in Solace."

"Oh, Palin is not really my friend," Coryn said. "I barely know him, but he was kind enough to answer some of my questions, which is why I told Jaymes about Dungarden. These gnomes, I presume, must be the next step in the puzzle."

"Yes." Dram shook his head. "Though I'm not sure this is a puzzle with all the pieces fitting together." He told her about the failure of the compound when they had tried to use it to destroy the dike at Mason's Ford. "A lot of spark and sizzle, but not much else," he admitted. "The gnomes are all right. They've been good companions, I must admit. They say that their brother, Salty Pete, knew one part of their father's compound—an elusive component, but he was killed by lizardmen when they crossed the Vingaard River. They're going to try and recreate the ingredients on their own, but Reorx only knows how long it will take."

"Tell me, the small party of gnomes who departed after the explosion at Dungarden, did they cross at the Brackens?" Coryn asked. "Is that where Salty Pete disappeared?"

"Yep—that's the place they mentioned." Dram frowned at her. "Why do you ask?"

"Have faith," Coryn said. "There may yet be some good news. Although from what Palin told me, his son spent years working on the same problem. He also cautioned me that some secrets are better kept forever. I agree with him, but I also feel that we don't have much choice right now."

"Tell me, how did you meet our mutual friend?" the dwarf asked. "He gave you such a hug on the shore of the Newsea, at first I was thinking you must be his long lost sister or something!"

Coryn smiled, savoring a secret memory. "Not his sister. *Hardly,*" she admitted. Her expression grew serious, even sad.

"Actually, I met him on the night Lord Lorimar was murdered," she said. "The Lord was a good friend of mine—I had been giving him advice and information on matters in Solamnia, since shortly after the First Conclave. In Palanthas I caught wind of a plot building against him—but I was too late—and arrived at his manor to find the place already in flames. The lord and his daughter were dead, and Jaymes was there, holding that great sword. He wore the emblem of a Knight of the Rose then, too."

"His favorite disguise, once upon a time," Dram admitted awkwardly. The dwarf had never probed his human friend for more details about that night—but he didn't like to have to hear from Coryn that Jaymes was indeed at the scene of the crime.

"I watched him take off his tunic, that proud rose glowing red as blood. He threw it into the flames and stood there, watching, as the blaze surged around him. He was already burned on his shoulders and face, but I got the impression he wasn't going to move, Finally I cast a spell, a cone of cold, and brought him out of the fire. He just followed me when I took his hand."

"Why would you help a man who just killed your friend?" Dram asked bluntly.

Coryn looked at him for a long time, her expression enigmatic. The gnomes called out as they started back from the stream, and the dwarf wondered if she even heard his question. Perhaps it was impertinent, anyway.

Only then did he catch her words, barely whispered above the friendly wash of the mountain stream.

"I wouldn't," she said.

⟨◦⟩◦⟩◦◦⟨◦⟩◦⟩◦◦⟨◦⟩

Jaymes was, as always at night, chained to a stout iron stake driven deep into the ground. He was almost getting used it, and—though he had watched carefully for any variance, any weakness in the diligence of his guards—he had seen not such much as a glimmer of a chance at escape. Even if the knights had not guarded him constantly, the stake was too strong, too deep

Right now he was trying to use his manacled hands to slurp from the usual bowl of gruel that served as his evening meal. A cry of challenge and answering password attracted his attention, and he watched idly as a Knight of Solamnia, wearing the emblem of the Rose, came riding on a lathered, blowing horse, into camp from the direction they were headed.

The newcomer dismounted and was directed to Sir Powell, who was having his meal nearby with Lady Selinda and several officers. The Rose knight was apparently a messenger, for he knelt respectfully and handed a scroll to Powell.

Selinda asked a question, and the knight captain shrugged, passing her the parchment.

"I don't know why he didn't just wait until we get to Palanthas to tell me that," Powell said, loud enough for Jaymes to overhear. "But if he wants to transfer the Third Regiment to the coast, who am I to stop him?"

"Strange," Selinda agreed, after scanning the message. "My father usually doesn't concern himself with minor deployments." She looked at the messenger, who still knelt before them. "Thank you for making the journey, Sir Dupuy. Please, help yourself to our trail fare. Do you need to return at once, or did my father give you other instructions?"

"If I may beg the indulgence of Your Ladyship and the captain's approval, the Lord Regent suggested that I accompany your party on the ride over the pass and back to Palanthas. There is some damage to the road, washouts caused by the spring rains. As I have just come over that route, I will at least be able to warn you when these obstacles are coming up."

"By all means," Sir Powell said, heartily. "Take up a bowl and join the men. We rise with the dawn and ride an hour later."

"Thank you, sir. My lady," the knight called Sir Dupuy said, rising to his feet. He looked around, apparently seeking the cook fire.

Jaymes would have sworn that the man's eyes lingered far longer than necessary upon the chained prisoner.

⊱✦⊰

Dram was awake as the first glimmers of dawn were brightening the sky over the eastern plains. His body ached, but he was looking forward to entering the good air of the mountains again.

The two gnomes were still slumbering, and he let them rest a little longer as he stirred the faded coals and rekindled the fire. He looked up to see that Coryn was already awake. Though she had slept on the ground, her white robe showed not the slightest stain of grass or mud. Not even the blackberries, of which they had all eaten plentifully the night before, had left a mark.

"The white moon was full last night, and Solinari favored me. I learned something that might be important to you," she whispered. "There is a prisoner held by the lizardmen in the Brackens . . . a gnome. He has been kept there for more than a year."

"A gnome?" Dram immediately understood. He nodded toward Carbo and Sulfie, who snored contentedly, arm in arm, beyond the fire. "You think it might be their brother, Pete?"

"It could very well be," she said.

If Coryn had been off checking on the status of captured gnomes during the previous night, Dram had had no clue. He nodded, reflecting on the strange ways of wizards, and decided to take her at her word—he didn't *want* any more details. Besides, there remained a more pressing concern: the rescue of Jaymes.

245

"Yes," Coryn said grimly, as though she had been reading his mind. "You have to get Jaymes away from those knights as soon as possible. I meant what I told you last night. He is in danger—terrible and immediate danger."

He grimaced, shaking his head. "What can I do?" he said. " I can't even catch up to those riders, much less get him out of such a tight spot. Isn't that your specialty?"

She sighed. "I can't afford to take the chance of being identified—it was risky enough in Caergoth, and I fear that I was spotted. But I might be able to help you with this potion."

She reached into a pocket of her robe and came out with three small bottles. "I have become rather good at brewing such helpful magics, if I say so myself. Of course, I have the benefit of being able to roam about Jenna's laboratory while she is in Wayreth. I think you might find these useful."

Coryn extended her hand and, after a moment's hesitation, Dram opened his own burly paw and let her drop the bottles onto his calloused palm. He looked at the potions reluctantly. "Magic makes my skin break out, you know," he said.

She smiled sympathetically. "You might have to put up with some blemishes, then, if you're going to help your friend. I suggest you leave the gnomes here—have them camp out of sight somewhere and wait for you. They'll only slow you down."

"Aye, I'm sorry to say, but I'd been thinking along the same lines myself," Dram admitted. He scowled at the small bottles, each of which seemed to hold only a shot or two of clear liquid.

"This blue bottle is a potion of haste," the enchantress explained. "Use just enough so that you feel a little tingle. You'll be able to cover twice as much distance today as the knights can ride."

"Haste, huh?" Dram held up that bottle, which was the largest of the three, and inspected the liquid sloshing inside. "All right," he said. "So I might catch up to them. What then?"

She explained about the other two potions.

CHAPTER TWENTY-TWO

THE GORGE

Jaymes shifted uncomfortably for seemingly the hundredth time of the night. Sleeping with his hands manacled at his waist allowed him precious little room to maneuver. His wrists were raw.

He stared up at the sky, the white moon near zenith. Since that moon had risen at sunset, he knew it was not much later than midnight.

At least the evenings gave some respite to the pain of riding a horse all day. His legs cramped so much he was unable to stand when they finally allowed him to dismount at the end of the day. Though the other knights took breaks, including a midday meal, climbing down from their saddles to stretch, they didn't go to the trouble—or risk—of letting their prisoner do the same.

Wriggling around, he tried to ease a kink that had formed in the muscles of his back. He couldn't do much about it. Cursing softly, the prisoner was on the verge on closing his eyes when he spotted a cloaked figure moving stealthily through the darkness.

This figure, though bent low, moved more like a human than a dwarf. Immediately the warrior thought of the lone knight, Sir Dupuy, who had arrived bearing a message from Lord Regent du Chagne. The man had been watching Jaymes surreptitiously all evening. Sitting around a fire with several fellows, the stranger's cold, hard eyes had frequently shifted over to the chained man.

Now the prisoner stared at the cloaked figure as it scuttled towards him, evidently on his hands and knees. Jaymes closed his eyes to narrow slits so the other man wouldn't guess he was awake and pondered what to do. The menacing knight was perhaps ten paces away, his eyes fixed upon the prisoner. Jaymes felt helpless. The chains binding his hands were so tight, he would have little ability to defend himself.

"Say there, friend," Jaymes suddenly called out, opening his eyes and sitting up straight. He made a great show of trying to stretch. His voice rang out in the slumbering camp, and several knights grunted in their sleep or shifted and opened their eyes. "How about helping a thirsty man with a drink of water?"

He was not surprised when the cloaked man—indeed Sir Dupuy—rose smoothly, letting his cape fall to the ground. The man looked around, saw that a sleepy sentry was staring at them and other knights were stirring. Several watched as Sir Dupuy came up to Jaymes, extending his canteen.

"Just a quick sip," the man said gruffly. "And then be still!"

The prisoner took the proffered vessel, drank, then handed it back. He replied loudly. "Thank you kindly, good sir knight."

The hilt of a dagger protruded from the man's belt. Without another word Sir Dupuy turned to walk away, stopping to pick up his cloak as if he had just happened to spot it lying on the ground. He went over to his bedroll and lay down, but his eyes, glittering with fury and frustration, remained fixed upon Jaymes.

Wrestling himself around to a sitting position, the warrior met the stranger's glare. Cramps froze his muscles, pain rippled through his legs, hips, and back, but he had to remain awake, and he watched the knight, watched and waited patiently as the moon, with excruciating slowness, crept through the western sky.

He maintained his vigil until dawn brightened the sky and the camp began to wake up around him. Only when there were a dozen knights up, kindling fires, putting kettles on to warm, did he allow himself to close his eyes for a few precious minutes. He woke when they came with the crowbar to pull his stake out of the ground and prod him into the saddle of a horse.

One of the knights watching the operation, already seated on his horse, was Sir Dupuy.

Throughout the morning the file of mounted knights climbed into the Vingaard Range, along the winding road leading up to the High Clerist's Pass. Jaymes had traveled this road often in the past, and he saw that the rainy summer had taken a grievous toll on the ancient highway. In places half the surface had eroded away, much of the gravel tumbling down into the precipitous gorge. Here and there erosion left only a narrow trail for the riders to negotiate, and in single file their horses skittered past drops of several hundred feet. Far below, Jaymes could see the whitewater rapids, a headwater of the West Vingaard River, flowing over and around jagged rocks and fallen timbers.

Jaymes rode along in silence. The nearby knights made no attempt to converse with him, and he avoided attracting attention as much as possible. Sir Dupuy had taken up a position near the head of the column—while the prisoner was in the middle. As the morning progressed, however, Dupuy fell farther and farther back in the line. Finally, as the noon hour approached, the rider from Palanthas was just ahead of the brace of guards near Jaymes, one of whom was always holding the ancient mare's reins.

Once again the column reached a washout, where the heavy rains had eroded a great section of the roadway. The remaining path barely qualified as a thin ledge above the cliff below. The first knights dismounted and one by one led their horses across, as the rest of the column came to a halt, each man waiting his turn. Dupuy, standing at the edge, extended his hand as Jayme's escort slipped out of his saddle to get ready to make the narrow crossing.

"I'll lead this one," Dupuy said, reaching for the reins of the prisoner's mount.

"Wait—you're going to let me dismount, aren't you?" Jaymes spoke to his main escort, a knight who had treated him humanely through most of the journey. "That looks a little too slippery there—you might lose a good horse, if I overbalance him."

"Sure. Makes sense to me." The knight addressed one of his comrades. "Darron, keep a hand on your sword and an eye on the prisoner, while I let him down." He released the shackles around Jaymes's ankles as Dupuy watched impassively. When the manacles were loose, the warrior slowly, carefully lowered himself from the saddle. The resulting cramps paralyzed his legs, and he held on to the reins for a few seconds, trying to regain some strength, eyeing the dangerous passage before him.

"Come on—let's get moving," urged one of the knights.

"I'll take the horse—you can make your own way," Sir Dupuy said pleasantly, but his eyes were cold. He stepped back from the narrow, mud-streaked ledge, pulling Jaymes's horse to the side.

Moving awkwardly on the narrow muddy path, with his hands tightly manacled, Jaymes had no choice but to step past Sir Dupuy, with the sheer drop directly beneath him to his left. The prisoner tried to brush by quickly. Sir Dupuy bumped him slightly, a movement no doubt invisible to the other knights behind them. Jaymes slipped and lost his balance—but not before grabbing the other man's belt with his fingers.

"Let go, damn you!" hissed the knight, but the prisoner's powerful grip made sure that both of them slipped from the steep heights.

Together, they fell toward the raging river below.

⊰∘⊙∘⊙∘⊙∘⦿∘⊙∘⊙∘⊙⊱

Dram had ordered the gnomes to stay near the riverside camp, feasting on blackberries and fish until he returned. Unaware of his plan, they were grateful for the chance to rest. Starting off by himself, Dram put Coryn's magic to the test immediately.

He took a small sip from the blue bottle. The haste spell worked as well as the wizard claimed—although dwarven legs were not made for speed—Dram churned up the mountain road as fast as a galloping horse and much faster than a column of horses proceeding at a cautious pace. Consequently, the dwarf had caught up to the column of knights and concealed himself behind a nearby shoulder of the mountain ridge by the time they drew up to pass, single file, around a washout in the road. The dwarf was feeling a bit shaky from the lingering effects of the potion but deduced from the look on Jaymes's face that he had little time to waste.

He acted swiftly, swallowing the second potion, and was stunned and a little taken aback as his body, rendered utterly invisible, vanished even from his own sight. Looking down, he saw only the ground where his feet ought to be. He took a few teetering steps and gulped as he saw footprints pressed into a patch of the soft ground. The strange sight gave him the shudders.

Taking care to step on solid ground, so that he wouldn't leave telltale footprints, he approached the rear of the column and started making his way past those knights and their horses who were still waiting to move across the bottleneck. He leaned away from the horses, nervous that one of them would smell him and spook or that one of the knights would see a telltale puff of dust or other clue to his presence. Fortunately the attention of men and horses alike seemed fixed upon the taut spectacle of the perilous crossing.

Edging around one of the knight's steeds—the mount of the company captain—he paused in astonishment. He found himself staring at Jayme's great sword, Giantsmiter, lashed to the saddlebag. The dwarf's fingers tingled—he had to grab that sword somehow, return it to Jaymes! Remembering what Coryn had told him about the second potion, he recalled that anything he held or wore while he was concealed by the magic would also vanish.

No one was looking in his direction as Dram reached up, unlashed the rope, and pulled the long sword away. The mighty weapon immediately became as invisible as the rest of him.

Suddenly his attention was riveted on his friend. Jaymes had started across the narrow ledge, moving past another knight who stood against the uphill side behind him, when the two men grappled for some reason, slipped, teetered, and fell over the brink.

Praying to Reorx that he was not too late, Dram reached for the third potion.

❦

Jutting rock struck Jaymes in the ribs, knocking the air from his lungs. Still, the warrior retained his vise-like grip on the squirming Dupuy. For a sickening instant they went into a free fall. The warrior's head snapped back as the knight's elbow, then fist, jabbed at him. Dizzyingly they spun through the air.

They slammed on top of a boulder and caught, just for a moment, before straddling a knob over a sheer drop of a hundred feet or more. Jaymes stared downward for a brief moment, seeing a terrifying array of jagged rocks below. Only the outcrop of this flat-topped shelf had saved them from certain death. Now, both men, after smashing hard onto the ledge, struggled to reclaim their breath. Wedging a hip onto the narrow space for better balance, the prisoner finally released his hold on his enemy's belt.

Dupuy squirmed away from him and half-rose, clutching for the knife in his belt. With his hands still bound, Jaymes kicked out, trying to dislodge his opponent, as he wriggled around for greater security. Loose rocks scattered and tumbled away.

The other man was strong, and agile as a monkey. Dupuy avoided two powerful kicks and gained a crouching position, the knife in his hand. He glanced up, sneering in satisfaction.

"Those fools can't see us. They are masked by the overhang. I can cut your heart out, and they'll never know what happened."

Jaymes scrambled back.

Dupuy grinned and leaned closer, the knife outstretched.

It was a move Jaymes had anticipated. The chained man kicked hard at some loose rock on the inside of the ledge. A large stone exploded out of the mass, striking Dupuy on one kneecap. The man's face went white, and he gasped in pain as he crumpled.

Jaymes brought one bootheel down hard on the knight's outstretched right hand. He heard the cracking of small bones, as he kicked out hard with the other foot. Sir Dupuy screamed as he went off the ledge. The scream trailed off pathetically, ending in a sickening crunch.

Gasping for air, with sweat streaming into his eyes, the warrior slumped back on the narrow ledge. His hands were still secured by a steel chain. There was no way he could climb up or down, but the bastard hadn't killed him. He could savor that triumph.

Finally, his weariness overtook him. It was peaceful here, beyond the reach of his captors. He let his head loll back against the sun-warmed cliff . . . perhaps it was time for a well-earned nap.

His eyes had barely closed when he heard a scuffing noise, sitting up in alarm as dust flew from a pair of unseen boots.

"Who's there?" he demanded, squinting to see who it was that had dropped on the ledge. The air was clear, his eyesight was perfect, yet he saw no one. Cursing, he strained against his cuffs.

"Hold on, old friend," said Dram, slowly coming into view. The dwarf was grinning, and—even more amazingly—holding the sword of Lorimar.

"By . . . by all the gods. . . ." Jaymes said, feeling numb with shock as much as pain.

"If I recall correctly, this thing will cut through steel, right?" asked the dwarf cheerfully.

The warrior nodded mutely, wondering if he was losing his mind. What was Dram doing, appearing like magic? Was he perhaps already dead? Well, fine, he felt tired enough to be dead.

Yet by the time his manacles were cut loose—the painful burns on his wrist made by the flaming sword would make scars he would treasure—he knew that he was alive. Before he could ask Dram how in the world he had been saved, the dwarf brought out a small bottle and took the first sip.

"It's my last potion. This one's for flying," he said matter-of-factly. "I saved enough for you to have a drink, too."

CHAPTER TWENTY-THREE

ROYAL RAGE

"Y ou mean he's gone? How did it happen?" the princess demanded furiously of Captain Powell. In vain, she had been trying to figure out what happened. The first men she had encountered told her such conflicting tales—the prisoner had escaped, had killed a man, had plunged into the gorge. The most ridiculous claim had come from a shaken young knight who had insisted the prisoner had sprouted wings and flown away!

Powell stood at the edge of the drop. His face was flushed, his eyes wild, his voice cracked like a whip, but the knight captain shook his head in exasperation at the princess's approach.

"Tell me! Did he escape? Did he die? What?"

"All we know for sure is that he killed Sir Dupuy, the knight who came from Palanthas, even as the poor man was trying to help him across the narrow ledge," Captain Powell declared through clenched teeth. "They both toppled over. We lost sight of them past the overhang. Some men report they saw him flying through the gorge, carrying the Sword of Lorimar! Ridiculous, I don't have to tell you. I have sent men to see if they can get a look down into the gorge, to see if he ended up on the rocks or in the river."

"What about the other man, Sir Dupuy? Are you sure he's dead?"

"Both of them ought to be dead, by Joli—there's no way anyone could survive that fall!" said the captain in disgust and frustration. "But the Sword of Lorimar is missing from my saddlebag! So far we haven't been able to get a clear look at that part of the river directly below us—the overhang juts out too far!"

"Well, get someone down there to check!" ordered Selinda.

"Perhaps we should lose our lives too? Haven't you noticed the raging river with all the jagged rocks at the bottom?" The captain's tone was furious, his eyes bulging in his head. The young princess suddenly understood the depth of his emotions: not just anger at the escape of a prisoner but humiliation for his own failure, and grief for the loss of a good man. "I've sent some men down the road—that they might get a look from the next bend."

The princess bit her lip, turning away. She drew a deep breath. "I'm sorry," she said quietly. "Yes—I see the danger, and I should have realized you would have acted at once if things were otherwise. The man who died—who was he? It seems strange that he was involved."

"Yes, that's a little strange," Powell admitted. "He belongs to my order, yet I've never made his acquaintance before. I asked some of the other men—you know, family details, that sort of thing—and none of them claim to know him either."

"Is that so unusual? The Rose is a large order, is it not?"

"Yes, of course. There are chapters all across Solamnia, even on Ergoth and points west. But the man had a Palanthian accent, which is home to most of the men in this company, and we have all served together or trained in Sanction at some time or other in the past decade. It seems odd he could be a stranger to us all."

"Sir!" called a knight, riding up the trail as quickly as safety would allow. "We got a good look at the river. There is a body down there, wearing the tunic of the Rose. Sadly, it would seem to be Sir Dupuy."

"Just one body?" demanded Powell.

"Aye, sir. Just the one we spotted. But . . . sir!"

"What is it, man? Speak!"

"I did see the prisoner flying, sir. Pardon me for saying so, but I swear this on the Oath and the Measure. He was carrying that great long sword and soaring down the gorge like an eagle, heading back toward the east. I may be going mad, Sir, but that's what my eyes told me I saw."

"Very well, then." Powell declared crisply. "Who else supposedly saw the prisoner flying?"

Several more knights spoke up sheepishly, all of them claiming to have witnessed the impossible. Several added that they saw two flying figures, one of whom resembled a dwarf.

"Flying dwarves, now?" the captain groaned. "By Joli, what next?" He turned away, rode a little way up the widening road as Selinda spurred her horse to his side.

"Do you believe such lies? How can it be possible that the Assassin *flew* away from here?"

"You heard them. Either they're all lying, or bewitched by some kind of illusion magic. They saw a dwarf, too—maybe that dwarf we allowed to escape. Well, obviously there's some kind of sorcery at work—but from what source and how he worked these wonders I have no idea." Suddenly Powell smashed his fist into the rocky hillside above the road. Trembling with rage, he had to turn away from Selinda and compose himself. If I had let the prisoner be executed as was proper, he thought, this wouldn't have happened.

The princess, understanding his shame, hung her head.

"I'm sorry," she said again. "This is my fault."

He turned back, his expression stiff and controlled as usual. "No," he said. "The responsibility lies with me, and I will tell your father that."

"What about pursuing him, er, or them?" she asked hesitantly. "Not that we can fly after him, of course."

"I have already dispatched fifty men to the east," Powell said, pointing down the road they had traversed this morning, the treacherous way back to the plains. "They are riding as fast as they dare, and will disperse to scout the area when they reach the flatlands. They are pledged to search for the villain, as long as it takes, but I doubt they have much chance of success—even fleet horses can't fly! But we must make a commendable effort."

"Perhaps we should all go after him?" Selinda suggested.

She shut her mouth and stepped back as she saw the flush of rage once again start to color the captain's features.

"No, princess," he declared in a deep, powerful voice. "The rest of the company is the minimum necessary to properly protect you. We must stay together now, and we must make haste to get you safely back into your father's palace, where you belong."

⊱⋅☼⋅⊰

The mountain fortress rose against the backdrop of the looming Garnet Range. Draconions lined the walls and the gate, glaring in a mixture of suspicion and fear at the horde that had appeared with the dawn on their very doorstep. The stronghold bristled with spears and swords clutched in clawed talons, with rustling leather wings quivering in agitation. The scaly, fanged defenders hissed and growled along every battlement.

The many thousands of goblins and hobgoblins, arrayed in battle order, with regiments of growling worgs and poised riders on both flanks, made an impressive threat. The ranks of human soldiers were also neat, tight, seemingly prepared to advance at the word of their commander. The Dark Knights formed a broad front, their great steeds snorting and ready, lances upraised. The massive horses stood beside their monstrous comrades, steady as steel.

Fresh from the sacking of wealthy, abandoned Luinstat, the warriors of Ankhar's horde were spoiling for a fresh fight. They roared ugly challenges, banged their spears against their shields, stomped their feet, and raised a din that easily over-whelmed the sibilant taunting of the draconian defenders of the stronghold.

Ankhar swaggered forward out of the front ranks of his army, one brawny fist braced upon his hip while the other clenched his spear, waving the glowing tip back and forth over his head. He raised the weapon as high as he could, and his glare swept the battlements, seeking the draconian clad in the most gold.

The half-giant finally fixed his eyes upon that one—an aurak naturally—and his voice bellowed across the valley.

"Let me in! I talk with master, Cornellus the Strong!"

"Go away!" barked the aurak. "He doesn't want to see you."

Ankhar flexed his massive fists. He eyed the gate, pretty certain he could bash it down personally, with just a few strong punches. The thousands of gobs and hobs arrayed behind him would swarm over this place within minutes. His troops outnumbered the defenders three or four to one.

However, he had learned a few things about leadership during the course of this summer's campaign—and he had not come here to shed the blood of a lot of draconians or to lose more of his own troops. He turned his tusked face upwards, allowed a bland, unthreatening expression to fall across his features. He lowered the spear, and the green light faded—*almost* completely—from view in the bright afternoon sun.

"You ask mighty Cornellus again," the half-giant said calmly. "Tell him Ankhar, Speaker of the Truth, seeks audience with great Cornellus. Want to discuss something of profit and power for both."

The aurak bristled, his great wings flaring from his shoulders. His taloned forepaws, clutching the sharpened timbers at the top of the wall, dug into the wood. He was anxious to fight, but with a conscious effort he considered Ankhar's words.

"We can always fight later, if that what your master want," prodded the half-giant Ankhar cheerfully. "We kill you by night or all day—whichever you want. Right now, we talk. Go tell lord."

"Very well," the big draconian said, finally. His wings buzzed audibly, but he nodded his head in a token, albeit a minimal gesture, of respect. "I will go and inform Cornellus."

An hour later, the hulking half-giant and the obese ogre

were seated together in the great hall. The place was charred and smelled of soot, and several holes were burned through its thatched roof, but it was still a large chamber swirling with the motion of many attendants.

"Belated warm greetings, Goblin-Master," began Cornellus, as slaves poured them huge mugs of mulled wine. The half-ogre swelled across his huge chair, his short, golden tusks gleaming in the torchlight. Sweat glistened on his round head, and slaves blotted at his smelly wetness with cloth towels. He was a huge creature, but even seated on his grand throne he found himself looking up at this half-giant called the Speaker of the Truth.

"I fear I do not have lodgings for all the guests you bring to my lodge," said the bandit-lord, waving a pudgy hand toward the unseen horde that, as yet, waited outside the walls of his stronghold.

Ankhar chuckled, deeply amused. "Goblins say you got room for ears of their cousins to stay here. They say you pay for those ears."

The grotesque ogre flushed and choked, spilling some of his wine across his massive belly. He shook his head, heavy lids slamming down over his eyes in a practiced expression of boredom that attempted—without much success—to mask his fear.

Ankhar could see that his opening shot had struck home.

"I am afraid my esteemed guest has been misinformed," Cornellus declared sanctimoniously, his voice rising. "I make bounty hunters pay for their killings! I do not pay them!"

"Of course," Ankhar replied, his deep voice genial. He paused, slurping at length of the sweet, spicy wine. "Not important, anyway. Gobs can be pests. Filthy little runts. They like trapped furies when got good leaders."

"So I hear," the bandit lord allowed.

"Oh?" The half-giant raised a bushy eyebrow. "You hear about us defeat Thelgaard? Drove whole army of knights into river. Killed hundreds, drowned hundreds? Got whole baggage train?"

259

"Yes, word of that battle reached us even here, high in the mountains. I did not know if the stories were exaggerated, or not," Cornellus said carefully.

"Of course, Thelgaard not such a wealthy duke. Not like in Solanthus! In Solanthus they got vaults filled to ceilings with treasures. But, Thelgaard not poor man. At least, not poor at start of day!"

Ankhar reached into his spacious belt pouch and pulled out a long strand of dazzling silver links, pouring the gleaming metal from one massive hand into the other. Laying the treasure on the table, his blunt fingers gently stretching the links apart, the half-giant revealed a chain holding a large disk emblazoned with diamonds and rubies.

The bandit lord's eyes grew wide.

"This one of many tokens carried by Solamnic duke into battle," the half-giant chieftain said with a belly-rumbling chuckle. "Don't know why. Maybe he try to bribe us."

"It is quite splendid," Cornellus allowed, all but drooling as he leaned forward, probing at the gleaming necklace with one of his sausage-sized fingers. "May I hoist it?" he asked hesitantly.

Ankhar looked astonished. "You may *have* it! I bring it as gift for you. You like this stuff?"

"My honored guest, I am humbled by your generosity!" exclaimed the half-ogre, snatching up the chain, pouring the links between his massive hands. "It is truly a splendid gift."

The grotesque Cornellus looked at Ankhar with an expression of almost tragic regret. "Would that I could offer something even a fraction as valuable in return. Alas . . . ."

Ankhar waved away the offer, a magnanimous gesture of one massive paw. "I knew you like trinket," he said. "Besides, I got no use for such treasures. I want other stuff. Not gold. Not gem. Not precious metal . . . "

Cornellus, ever the alert merchant, smelled a deal. "Tell me, O mighty war chief, what is it that you most wish for?"

"Ah," Ankhar said, with another chuckle. "Maybe dusky

giantess with big breasts—that rare treasure! Or maybe palace in the sky, on top of clouds. Of course, can't have these . . . "

"No," Cornellus agreed, with some relief. "Though I can inquire as to the matter of a giantess. . . ."

"I tell you what make me happy right now, you know?"

The half ogre raised an eyebrow, listening.

"I want regiment of draconions. Back up my goblins. Then I *take* what I want, burn rest!"

"A regiment of draconions? With that, yours would be a force of raiders such as the plain has not seen in many years," Cornellus agreed, thinking it over, imagining the plunder.

"Raiders?" scoffed the half-giant. "They more than raiders— they an army!"

"What would you do with such an army, may I ask?"

"With army like that, Ogre, I tear down walls of Solanthus itself. Open up vaults, where treasures piled to sky."

"I wonder . . . is it possible? Would the draconians fight their best under your command?" The bandit lord's eyes flashed.

"Est Sudanus oth Nikkas," murmured the half-giant, watching his counterpart carefully.

"Eh? What does that mean?"

"They follow me, friend, and city, any city, can be taken. My power is my Truth."

⟆⊛⟆⊛⟆⊛⟆⊛⟆⊛⟆⊛⟆⊛⟆⊛⟆

"Do you mean to say that you had him in chains? That you brought him all the way from the southern plains? And that he escaped on the very doorstep of the High Clerist's Tower?"

Bakkard du Chagne's voice was strangely hushed, almost a hoarse whisper, as he spoke to the captain of his guards. Even so, Selinda, who was off to the side of her father and Captain Powell, was certain that she had never heard him so bottled up with fury.

"Yes, Excellency. That is exactly what happened. It was a monumental failure, and the fault is naught but my own. My men acted bravely and competently throughout the long journey. I can only offer up my sword and my epaulets as penance."

"You can offer more than that!" The Lord Regent's voice rose, becoming shrill. "You can offer your blood, your life!"

"Father!" Selinda declared, stepping forward and raising her own voice.

"You stay out of this!" du Chagne snarled, turning to glare at her. His expression blazed, almost causing her to falter, but she raised her chin and met his fury with her own fierce determination.

"I won't! Captain Powell's behavior and his leadership were exemplary. The fault, such as it is, lies with me and with that wretched Assassin. The captain would have executed the prisoner at once, and I now see—too late—that this would have been in accordance with the situation. Instead, I insisted he be brought here to stand trial. I overruled the captain's strenuous objections, invoking my own rank in imposing my will. I see that this was a mistake, and as a result of my mistake, not only has the fugitive escaped once more, but a good, brave knight has perished."

Her father's face turned a most disquieting shade of purple. His mouth moved wordlessly. Captain Powell broke the awkward silence.

"No, I cannot allow your daughter to accept fault in this matter, Excellency," the knight said stiffly. "Though 'tis an expression of her noble nature that she does." He softened slightly as he looked at Selinda, and she saw the gratitude in his eyes.

He abruptly snapped to attention, looking at some place on the windowed wall beyond the lord regent's shoulder. "If your Excellency wishes some miserable portion of my unworthy flesh as just retribution, I offer myself willingly. Though it would not make amend for my failing, it is only justice I should suffer such fate."

"Bah—get away from here, both of you!" snapped du Chagne. "This bastard has already cost me too many men—I cannot afford to lose even an incompetent, Captain! Go and supervise the stabling of the horses—I shall send for you at some point in the future."

"Aye, Excellency." Powell turned on his heel and with as much dignity as he could muster marched out of the vast chamber.

Selinda, steeling herself in the face of the lord regent's anger, spoke softly. "Father. . . ?"

"What is it now?" he snapped, then softened his voice. "What now?"

"The man who died . . . Sir Dupuy. Did he have a family? I should like to offer what comfort and recompense I could to his widow, see to the future of his children. It is only fair."

Du Chagne's eyes narrowed, boring into her. "I have problems of my own!" he declared. "You know nothing about my problems—about a room that looks like it's full of nothing! Coal and fuel and the rising price of everything! And you dare to bother me with trivial questions about some fool of a *knight?*"

She was taken aback—he looked positively cruel!

"Such concerns are preposterous!" he continued. "He was a knight—he knew the risks he took, as do all knights. He didn't have a family. He leaves no one who cares for him. Now go!"

Selinda turned and departed the great room, nodding absently to the guard who held open the door. What did her father mean: "A room that looks like it's full of nothing"? He had been in a foul state from the moment of their arrival a few hours earlier, and at first she thought he was upset about the prisoner's escape. She had noticed, with surprise, the treasure room atop the Golden Spire was closed and shuttered—something she had never seen before—and now wondered if that had something to do with her father's mood.

Her mind was awhirl with questions and guilty awareness and a sense that things were even more troubling than previously imagined.

⟨∘⊙⊙∘⊙∘⊙⊙𝕏⊙⊙∘⊙∘⊙⊙∘⟩

The duke knelt at the altar of his immortal lord. The dread scale teetered before him, the balance hanging in peril, until once again his blood was added to the measure. Finally the crimson fluid drained from the lord's veins equaled the weight

263

of a great pile of golden coins, and Hiddukel, the Prince of Lies, was pleased.

Now the Nightmaster stood over the nobleman. The priest's mask was as black as the surrounding night, his words even darker. They were in the temple beneath the city, in the dampness and the dark.

"The young woman, the princess of all Solamnia, has returned safely to her home. She awaits the pleasure of the gods and the man who will claim her. She is the key, for the one who claims her will claim all Solamnia."

"Aye, Master."

"That man must make her his wife. He must take her as his bride. That man must be you, my lord duke."

The kneeling duke looked up in confusion mingled with fear. "But Master—I already have a wife! How can I take another?"

"You cannot. Not so long as your present wife lives." The Nightmaster leaned forward, holding out a piece of gauzy cloth to the kneeling duke. "Take this," commanded the cleric.

The nobleman did. "What is it?" he asked nervously.

"It is a shroud of silence. You can drape it above your bed. When the curtains hang down, nothing that happens beneath it will make any sound. It is the will of Hiddukel that some things remain secret."

"But. . . " The duke's face grew pale, and he slumped, his knees buckling until his hands came to rest upon the floor. He had given so much blood to this dark god, so much trust and devotion, and now this.

"There are reports the Assassin escaped from the knights who captured him on the plains . . . that he is once again at large."

"Aye, Master . . . I know these reports."

"He could be anywhere . . . he could strike in the north . . . or the east. He could strike here."

"He is a menace to all Solamnia!" the noble agreed.

"A menace . . . or an alibi. Think, my lord duke. Do you understand what must be done?" asked the Nightmaster. "Sometimes a lie can be seen as the Truth."

For long moments the nobleman held his face to the floor, trembling. Only after considerable reflection did he gasp, raise his eyes in an expression of comprehension—and of horror.

"Yes. Yes, I understand . . . I know what you command," he replied.

"Tell me!" insisted the dark cleric, his voice bubbling like lava.

"That my own dear wife must die at my hand—but that my people must believe the Assassin has killed her."

CHAPTER TWENTY-FOUR

THE BRACKENS

From the lip of the escarpment, looking down into the wide, flat river valley formed by the junction of the Upper Vingaard and Kaolyn Rivers, the Brackens presented a depressing vista. The forested swamp sprawled across the sodden lowlands in a tangle of hummocks, marshes, fetid ponds and sluggish streams, all broken by dense copses of moss-draped trees that rose from the mist like gaunt guardians. The hum of mosquitoes was omnipresent, an audible drone across the whole territory. Eerie birdcalls echoed.

The four travelers stood on the rim of the grassy bluff some fifty feet above the swamp and swatted at a few of the buzzing insects who rose to greet them, knowing that the pests would be far more numerous once they climbed down the steep hillside.

The Brackens extended as far as they could see in either direction. The shiny open water marking the main channel of the Upper Vingaard was just barely visible, three or four miles away. The escarpment extended along the entire length of the river valley, and the tangled, forbidding swamp was a constant barrier between the base of the bluff and the river. The distant trail of the plains road and the ford the gnomes—and many travelers—had used was far away, below the place where the two rivers merged.

"Do we have to go in there?" Dram asked, scowling.

"We came this far," Jaymes drawled, scratching his chin. "Why not see things through to the main event?"

"The white lady said Salty Pete might still be alive in there?" Carbo asked dubiously. "How can she know such things? We saw him get dragged off by the big black draco!"

"The White Lady told me she'd heard of a gnome held captive in there," the dwarf said bluntly. "She didn't know his name—but thought it might be your brother. Said he's been there for a couple of years. The timing is about right."

"Yeah. We lost Pete two years ago," Sulfie said hopefully.

"I've learned to trust her," Jaymes said with a shrug. "She's surprised me more than once." He glanced at the sun, which had cleared the eastern horizon. "We should get moving—if we're fast, and lucky, we might be in and out of there before sunset."

By now, the four travelers were fit, well fed, and reasonably well-rested. After leaving the Vingaard Range, they had spent a few weeks evading the patrols of knights that rode vigilantly across the plains. Traveling by darkness and finding hiding places—a herdsman's hut, a clump of brambles, streamside caves—before each dawn, they made their way eastward and south from the Vingaard Mountains down to the river of the same name. Then they had followed the flow south until they reached this broad convergence.

The two gnomes remembered the route they had followed when they departed Dungarden, and now they found themselves in the same fateful area. Their goal lay before them, in all its unappetizing sprawl and decay. Even the smells were daunting—the stench was more than just the miasma of rot and stagnancy. There was a metallic, smoky overlay to the odor that bespoke of something more sinister than death.

"The ford we crossed is over there, to the left," Carbo noted. "We didn't go into this swampy stuff when we came from Dungarden. The wagon would have sunk right down, without a decent track, you know, but the road goes past the swamp, not into it." He mopped his bald pate with a grimy rag, shaking his head at the ugly memories.

"Tell us about the attack," the warrior said.

"Well, there's the road. You see it coming down from the far bank? We trundled down that hill, twenty gnomes on two wagons, each pulled by two oxen. We came to where the road goes into the river there, then we crossed. It's a good ford, shallow with a gravel bottom. Then the road comes into the woods along the edge of the swamp down there—it's kind of built up with a stone bed, so the wagon was doing all right. That is, until the dracos attacked."

"You keep calling them that. You mean draconians?" Dram pressed.

"Well, they made me think of draconians, but they were bigger—not dragons, but sort of like a composite of dragons and draconians. They spat acid, though, and killed the two oxen hauling the first wagon. We all raced to get into the second wagon and ran away, but Pete didn't make it out."

As he recounted the tale, tears glimmered in his eyes, and listening nearby, Sulfie shivered.

"Dragon spawn?" Dram guessed, shaking his head, looking at Jaymes.

"Likely," the warrior agreed. He looked at Carbo. "Were they all black?"

"Yep," the gnome recalled with a shudder. "They were the blackest, scariest things I ever saw! They hissed and roared, and that spit—it burned the fur and the skin right off the poor old oxen."

"But your brother—you didn't see him get killed?"

"No. One big draco—you called it a dragon spawn?—grabbed him up by the neck and ran off. He cried out just one time. The others came after us, and we had to flee. As soon as we got out of the trees they stopped chasing us, but Pete wasn't making any more noise, so we concluded that he was killed."

Sulfie spoke up, finally. "If they have Pete, then we have to go get him out of there. I'm not afraid of any big lizard!"

"Yeah, let's go," Carbo agreed. He went over to his sister, looked at her seriously. "Don't be getting all hopeful. Remember what we saw."

"Yes," the female agreed, but she raised her chin in determination. "Remember the White Lady, too. *She* wouldn't lie!" she declared, glancing at Jaymes and Dram, emphasizing that her assessment did not necessarily extend to present company.

"You guys coming too?" she asked.

"Yes," Jaymes replied with a small nod.

Dram huffed and scowled. "Well, if Pete knows how to finish the damned compound so it can do something besides fizzle and smoke, then I'd like to hear about it. But I do hate mosquitoes."

The human grinned. "Once the dracos start swarming, I guarantee you won't even noticed the bugs," he remarked.

Sulfie's eyes were wide, but she wrapped her little arms around herself and started down the grassy bluff. The others followed and approached the moss-draped trees that marked the edge of the Brackens. The sunlight seemed to dim, and a thick, grayish haze lingered in the air, masking the brightness—though not the warmth—of the sun. If anything it was even hotter at the base of the hill, and the air was thick and steamy.

The mosquitoes were thick here too, a steady whining drone in their ears. The companions also heard birds cawing angrily to each other and a chorus of croaking frogs. A myriad of smells greeted them, none of them pleasant. The sooty, metallic stench seemed almost asphyxiating. The swamp was a green-black wall of dark, mossy trunks, vines and creepers, with thick ferns sprouting from the ground.

No obvious path presented itself, but Sulfie led the way, pushing away some vines and stepping between two ancient tree trunks. The others followed. In single file they plunged into the trees, trying to move soundlessly, surprised as the noisy frogs abruptly fell silent. The ground was wet everywhere with pools of stagnant water, and sometimes they had to hop from one gnarled tree root to the next. A large snake slithered across their path. Something bigger splashed in the water nearby, and they hurried on.

Deeper and deeper into the swamp they progressed, pushing vines out of the way, ducking under creepers, edging past hooked thorns. By the time they had advanced two dozen paces, sunlight was but a distant memory. Now they couldn't see more than a few feet in any direction. The mosquitoes swarmed over them.

They came across another snake—this one a black, venomous viper that coiled menacingly and raised its wedge-shape head, hissing. Jaymes pulled Giantsmiter from the scabbard on his back and brought the huge blade down with a single chop, cutting the snake into two wriggling segments. They pressed on in the sucking mud. The warrior held his weapon upraised.

Sulfie slipped off the gnarled root of an ancient cypress, sliding into what looked like shallow pool. With a little gasp of dismay she sank to her waist and began to settle deeper. She clawed at the root, then grasped Dram's strong hand. Grimacing, the dwarf set his feet and pulled the gnome free. She was covered in mud and nearly gagged at the leeches wriggling on her leggings—but swatted them off. Grimly she rose to her feet, nodding when the dwarf said he would take the lead.

The smells grew stronger, swamp gas rising in choking clouds as their feet disturbed long-dormant layers of rot. A stink like carrion made Jaymes gag, and he held a handkerchief across his mouth, blinking away tears as he strained to see through the murk. Still that metal-smoke scent permeated everything, growing stronger as they penetrated deeper into the Brackens.

"Hsst!" said Carbo, drawing a big sniff through his wide nostrils. "Do you smell that smell?"

Jaymes nodded, his nostrils twitching. "Yes. Smoke, but not from wood." Indeed, the vapor smelled bitter, acrid, more like something raised from a foundry than a campfire.

"That's Pete!" cried Sulfie. "I'd know that stink anywhere! He's busy cooking his stuff!"

"Stuff?" Dram asked.

"Yep. We each had one kind of stuff, Pap taught us about.

Like my specialty is the yellow rock." She gestured at the dirty sack on her back, which was filled with the samples of sulfir.

Carbo nodded. "Mine is charcoal. Pete's stuff is the strangest of all, and he was very secretive about it—we don't really know that much about it. He was always doing funny things with fire. But I know that smell! It means he's still alive—it *has* to! This way!"

The gnome made to crash through the underbrush, but Dram placed a restraining hand on his shoulder. "Easy does it," the dwarf whispered. "The dracos are probably still alive, too."

With visible reluctance, Carbo nodded and moved on more cautiously, soon stepping out from the trees onto a narrow, muddy path of sorts. The others emerged after him, and without hesitation Carbo started toward the direction that seemed to lead deeper into the swamp and from which the strong smell emanated.

The new trail was narrow and muddy, twisting around the larger trees, but even Jaymes had enough headroom, as the vines and low branches had disappeared.

"You thinking what I am?" asked Dram, with a glance at his human companion.

"Yes," Jaymes said. Who—or whatever—used this path was tall enough to clear it to a height of better than six feet above the ground.

The acrid scent grew steadily thicker. After a few minutes, the path opened into a shadowy, narrow clearing. Trees draped with moss and vines enclosed the space, with a tiny patch of sky overhead. That glimpse of blue only seemed to emphasize the gloom of this fetid place.

"There!" cried Carbo, pointing toward a gaping pit in the center of the small open space. The hole in the ground was dark, lined with mud, and venting an assortment of noxious gases. Greenish vapors were visible in narrow tendrils rising from the pit and wafting through the dense air. "He's going to be down there!"

The gnome darted toward the pit. He didn't hear the leathery wings flapping loudly overhead, but his companions were more alert.

"Duck!" cried Sulfie, leaping forward to tackle her brother. They tumbled to the muddy ground as a shadow flashed by. A black serpent swooped past, diving from overhead, barely missing the two gnomes. The creature's large wings flared as it alit. It was not armed with any weapon, but its claws and fangs gleamed as it crouched and eyed the two gnomes. It looked like a small dragon. Crocodilian jaws gaped to reveal a forked, thrusting tongue, and its leathery wings buzzed.

Carbo sprang to his feet. He pulled his little dagger and was about to charge the strange serpent when, once again, his sister bowled into him, knocking him to the side just before a stream of yellow liquid spurted from the monster's maw. The two gnomes rolled away, barely avoiding the lethal strike. The reptilian creature lashed its head on its long neck, following the course of the rolling gnomes, and started forward. It was indeed dragon-like, though more like the size of a large—and winged!—alligator than a truly monstrous wyrm.

With a strangled shout, Dram charged the creature from behind. The dwarf's axe split the spawn's head open, and it collapsed, one wing flopping into the pool of acid left from its earlier blast. Carbo and Sulfie climbed to their feet, wide-eyed and trembling.

Jaymes had his sword in his hand and was looking up at where the dragon spawn had been lurking. He spotted a platform high up in a sturdy tree. Another black, reptilian form crouched there with slitted eyes—then the second dragon spawn leaped at him, spitting acid. He twisted away so that only a few drops landed on his cape and trousers, foaming on the woolen cloth.

The spawn landed a few feet away, hissing and flapping in menace. Glowering, Jaymes twisted the hilt of the sword in his hands. Immediately the weapon blazed to life, blue flames running up and down its keen steel edge. The dragon spawn recoiled, rearing onto its hind legs—but its reaction was too slow. With twin slashes, the warrior gashed its breast, then cut its head from its lashing neck. He stepped on the acid that hissed and bubbled on the ground but quickly wiped his boots on some ferns. The acid ate away at the plants, spewing foul gas as it soaked into the dirt.

Both spawn bled greenish, viscous blood from their wounds. Jaymes scanned the treetops. The swamp was utterly silent—no longer were the birds cawing and frogs croaking. For the moment, there was no sign of another threat.

"Quick—into the pit!" whispered Dram. "Get out of sight!"

He uncoiled his rope and tied it to a tree, tossing the other end across the mud and into a hole nearby the others had not noticed. It looked to be about thirty feet deep. Carbo descended quickly, hand over hand, followed by Sulfie, and Jaymes. They all scaled downward until their feet struck the bottom of a muddy chamber. Dram came last.

Enough daylight filtered down for Jaymes to make out several tunnels branching outward from this round subterranean lair. The air smelled terrible, and they had to strain not to choke or cough, blinking watery eyes, covering their noses as best they could. The human found that if he bent, he could breath a little easier—the worst of the vapors seemed to rise toward the damp and dripping ceiling, flowing up and out the vent hole.

"Does this smell like your brother too?" Dram asked.

"Yep. Follow the stink," Carbo urged. "I can't see!"

Jaymes drew the sword he had sheathed during the descent, and once again flames flickered along the blade. The blue light was faint but enough for them to make out a few details. The chamber showed signs of crude excavation, as if animals had burrowed it out of the soft dirt. There were no shoring timbers supporting the ceiling or arching above the tunnel mouths for four small passages leading deeper.

"Over here," Sulfie said, sniffing at one of the passages. "Pete's over here, somewhere!"

They moved into the passage that boasted the worst stink, straining to see in the murk. The flickering sword helped a little.

273

At least the side passage had a high enough ceiling that even Jaymes could walk upright. Roots and tendrils dangling down looked, in the blue illumination, like furry, wriggling tentacles, and they eyed these warily as they progressed.

Shortly they came to a fork, where the wide passage began a gradual descent and a smaller corridor continued on another level. The two gnomes sniffed carefully but could not reach a consensus.

"Might as well try the wide one," Dram suggested. "It gets more use, seems like."

Jaymes took the lead, holding the sword at his shoulder so the others could see better. The floor was slimy with rivulets of water. With each forward step the path seemed to get steeper, and Jaymes began to slip and slide.

The warrior paused, squinting ahead.

"Unless Salty Pete has grown gills, this is the wrong way," he declared. "There's more and more water down there, filling the whole tunnel. Looks like this might be an underwater bolt-hole."

"No gills—so let's try the other way," Sulfie said. Dram extended a hand to help the warrior back up the steep, slick slope. Soon they reached the previous juncture and this time took the narrower corridor.

They had not gone far before they spotted the glow of firelight ahead, spilling into the corridor from a large room off to a side. Jaymes doused the sword-fire, and they all crept forward.

They came to a chamber that looked like a crude blacksmith's shop, with a mound of coals glowing in a huge pit and several cluttered benches along the far wall. A small figure bustled about, tossing logs onto the fire, then running back to stir something in a large cauldron.

"Pete!" shouted Sulfie, rushing forward.

The gnome looked up, gaping in surprise, then wrapped his arms around his sister and brother in a frantic hug. He was bearded like Carbo, though with a shock of graying hair where his brother was bald.

"No! Yes! You guys!" he declared. "Wow—I can't believe it! After all this time. Have I got a story to tell you! You'd never believe—" He paused, looking around in confusion. "Wait," he said. "How come Sheedra let you in here?"

"Who's Sheedra?" Dram asked.

A slithering figure with dark scales, invisible in the shadows, slid past the doorway. Something huge and black.

Jaymes spun, his sword in his hands, but he was too late. A large, gray rock tumbled into place, blocking the doorway as neatly as a cork in a bottle.

They were trapped.

CHAPTER TWENTY-FIVE

SHEEDRA

Jaymes and Dram hurled themselves at the boulder, driving their shoulders against the slick stone surface, legs pumping, boots churning on the muddy floor as they strained to move it out of the way. They gasped and grunted, strained and cursed, finally collapsing.

The rock hadn't budged an inch.

"It weighs too much. You'll never be able to get it out of there. Even the dragon spawn can't move it. Only Sheedra can," Salty Pete explained.

"Who in Reorx's name is Sheedra!" demanded Dram, between gasps for air. He sat in the mud, his back against the immovable rock.

"She's the black dragon who lives here. She uses that rock to keep me locked in when she goes away. Now I guess she's using it to keep you guys locked in here too."

"Why hasn't she killed you?" Jaymes asked, shaking his head. "Two years in a dragon's lair must be some kind of record."

"Oh, she protects me, actually. The spawns would have pulled me apart and eaten me up right away, if not for her," Pete admitted.

"Why?" asked Sulfie, as she glanced at the various kettles and cauldrons around the firepit.

"I think she wanted someone to talk to. She even sings, a little, and the spawns don't care about singing or talking. They're pretty stupid."

"Great. Violent and stupid, too. How many spawn are there around here anyway?" asked Dram.

Pete shrugged. "Maybe twelve. Or a few more. They all look alike, so it's hard to count them, and some are in the lair while others are always prowling around in the swamp. I never see the whole group of them all together."

"It's so terrible, you being kept prisoner down here," said Carbo.

"Well, it hasn't been so bad. Sheedra lets me eat better than her spawn," Salty Pete explained. "Probably because I keep her fire going, and I make her stuff. I think that's why she had the dragon spawn capture me. They can't build and can't cook either. Like I say, they're pretty stupid."

The little gnome's face brightened proudly. "She really likes my frog chowder." Then his expression darkened, and he shook his head sadly. "Not that I would recommend it. Nothing like the carrots and lettuce we used to get in Dungarden. And beef! Oh, I remember beef!"

"Tell us more about Sheedra," Dram encouraged.

"Well, she's a black dragon, like I said. I think she's been living here a long time—one of her songs is about fighting the Golden General in the Lance War. Her friends all got killed in some big battle, and she got her wing burned off and crawled into the Brackens and made this her hideout. She's lived here since then."

Salty Pete scratched his head. "Let's see. She's enormous. And mean as a snake. Except that she brings me stuff, so I can work. She's taken a liking to me, I guess. She got me these cauldrons and kettles and sends the spawn to bring me plenty of firewood. The spawn frighten me, but they're more scared of her, so they don't hurt me. They bring me plenty of frogs, so I can cook them up. I've grown partial to frogs."

"Dragon spawn're left over from the days of the Overlords.

Came here to hide, maybe during the war, maybe before," the dwarf guessed, looking grimly at Jaymes.

The warrior nodded. "You guess there are about a dozen of them close by, maybe more?"

"Yep. They come and go. Sheedra does too. Like I said, she likes to sing her songs. She tells us that we're all her children, but the spawns don't listen much. I admit I do, though. Passes the time."

Pete sighed, slumping his shoulders. "After she sings, she puts that rock there."

Jaymes had been studying the massive boulder. He crossed the room to poke around the long workbench. He found a sturdy iron bar, as tall as he was, and went back over to the barrier. Dram followed him, bringing a stout kettle, which he inverted to serve as a fulcrum. The warrior jammed the edge of the pry bar under the rock, then balanced it on the upturned pot, trying to exert some leverage. Even with both of them leaning on the bar, straining with every sinew, the huge stone wouldn't budge.

"We'll never pry it loose, not without this Sheedra's help," Dram said in disgust, backing away from the boulder and glaring at the big stone in fury. Jaymes, his face slick with sweat, agreed.

"Peteeeeey?"

The voice, soft and yet thunderous, rising musically at the end, penetrated through the rock to fill the smoky air in the workshop. The companions all looked to Salty Pete, whose eyes had grown very wide. He gulped and cleared his throat.

"Um . . . yes, Mistress Sheedra? I'm in here," the gnome called out in an exaggerated sing-tong tone.

"Yes, Petey, but who is in there with you? Are they bothering you? Are you afraid of them?"

"No, I'm not afraid, Mistress. These are . . . . these are some old friends, who have come to see me."

"Petey. . . remember, I am your best friend. You remember, don't you?"

"Oh, yes Mistress Sheedra. I certainly always remember that you are my friend. My very best friend!"

"Other friends are not true friends. Others are nasties . . . do you have nasties in there with you?"

The gnome looked helplessly at his siblings, at the human and dwarf. "No, Mistress Sheedra . . . not nasties! Good friends. Um, not as good as you, though."

"*Sheedra* is Petey's best friend. Not nasties who come through swamp. Not friends, nasties."

"No . . . nasties are not my friends," Pete answered, with an apologetic look at his would-be rescuers.

"Petey? Sheedra is Petey's best friend. Only Sheedra."

"Um, yes Mistress Sheedra. That's right, my only best friend."

"Others are nasties. Will you kill them? Or shall I?"

"Good idea, but maybe you should leave the killing to me," the gnome stammered. "Um, yes. Give me a little time. I'll . . . um . . . I'll kill them all. Or else let you know if I need help."

"That's so sweet of you. I'll wait right here, Petey . . . . you tell me if you need me to help you kill them."

"I'll tell you, for sure!" promised the gnome. "Now I've got work to do. I have to get busy, um, killing my frien— I mean, killing the nasties?"

"All right, Petey. . . you are such a good worker. I will wait here and perhaps slumber a little as I wait."

Salty Pete turned back to his visitors. "We have a problem," he whispered. "Of course, I really don't want to kill you."

"That's a relief!" Dram muttered. He shook his fist at the obstinate boulder. "We gotta figure out a way to move this rock! We have to get out of here!"

"You'll never move it," Salty Pete confirmed, whispering back. "It would take an earthquake, an explosion, or something."

Carbo looked up suddenly, glancing from his brother to his sister. "Now there's an idea. . . ."

"Do you think we could try?" Sulfie asked, shivering.

"We can make some of the old reliable compound. If we get ·

the mixture right, that would set her back on her heels," Carbo said.

"Pap's compound?" Pete said. "I thought about that already. I've been thinking about that for years, but I don't have any yellow rock."

"Hey, guess what? We brought some sulfir with us," Sulfie said. She held up the bag she had carried since they had departed the hill dwarf valley, nearly a month before. "There's lots more coming, but this might be enough for a small batch. Let's put our heads together and give it a try!"

"There's charcoal over there, plenty of it," said Carbo. "What about you, Pete? You got your necessary stuff? I though we smelled the familiar smell, coming through the swamp."

"What do you think I've been so busy making all this time?" asked their long-lost brother, crossly. "Of course—I have kettles and kettles of the saltpeter over there. Nothing much else to do, except cooking frogs into batches of chowder. So let me see that sulfir."

"Here!" Sulfie encouraged.

"How long do you think it will take?" Dram asked, nervously glancing at the boulder in the doorway.

Carbo shrugged. "Not long. A couple hours, maybe."

"How soon until Sheedra's likely to, er, wake up or lose patience and come in and check on us?" Jaymes asked.

Pete looked up. "Could be any minute. More likely days, but we'll hear her when she starts to move that boulder, that's for sure."

"Right," agreed the warrior. "Best get to work, then."

Quickly the three gnomes got started. Pete selected an empty cauldron for the final product, while Carbo collected a series of measuring cups, and assembled a small balance scale. Sulfie started to grind some of her yellow rock into powder, using a large mortar and pestle, while Carbo scraped charcoal from several charred logs, and Salty Pete added small portions of his saltpeter from one of his kettles. Dram and Jaymes warily watched the boulder at the door, which fortunately exhibited no signs of movement.

For a long time the gnomes worked in busy contentment, grinding and sifting, measuring and weighing, adding carefully determined amounts of the three ingredients to the large kettle. They took turns stirring, re-sifting, and thoroughly mixing, increasing the amount until they had used up nearly all of their supply of sulfir.

"Yep," Carbo said finally, peering into the cauldron after they had mixed and remixed it extensively. He reached down, critically examining the black powder within. "That certainly resembles the stuff Pap used to make."

"Well, the other batch looked like the old stuff, too," Dram noted sourly. "It just fizzled and smoked, if you recall."

"We didn't have Pete's help when we made that version, did we?" Carbo retorted.

"What next?" Jaymes asked impatiently.

"We put it in something, fill it up, and seal it. One of those casks will do. We jam that down by the rock, then set a fuse, light it, and . . . I guess we'd better hide real good, too," Pete said. "We want to blow the rock up but not ourselves. Right?"

"Right," Dram agreed.

"Petey?" The bustling activity froze at the sound of Sheedra's voice. They all looked at Salty Pete.

"What is it, Mistress?" he asked, with a gulp.

"Did you kill the nasties yet? Do you need my help?"

"Um, no, Mistress. Soon. I am figuring out an especially painful way to do it."

"Oh, that's good."

"I will tell you when they're real dead. Soon, all right?"

"All right, best friend."

There turned out to be enough powder to fill three casks, right to the top, so they did so, sealing all of them tightly with wax. "The tighter the seal, the better the blast, Pap always used to say," Carbo said approvingly. "I think one of these will be enough."

"What about the other two?" asked Pete.

"We take 'em with us," Jaymes suggested. "Let's pile some dirt around them over in the corner."

Finally they had one keg positioned, while the other two were, hopefully, insulated from the anticipated explosion.

"Let's light the fuse, and then go down that hallway and around the corner, far into my room. There's a storage closet in the back where we can shut the door and hide," Carbo said. "You might want to put your hands over your ears, too."

Pete turned his face to the massive rock. "Oh, Mistress?" he called. "Mistress Sheedra?"

"Yes, Petey?" came the sibilant response.

"Put your ear real close to the rock. You will hear me torture the nasties before you hear their dying screams."

"Oh, Petey. I like that."

They quickly made a fuse out of the same black powder. After a final examination of the keg, Pete touched a spark to the line of powder, which immediately began to fizzle and pop, burning toward the keg. The companions dashed into the hall, around the corner, and down the narrow hallway into Pete's small sleeping chamber. They were barely able to jam themselves into the small closet and pull the door shut, lacing their hands over their ears, before they heard a stunning explosion that rocked the closet, knocked the wind from their lungs, and left their ears ringing.

The closet door sagged inward but held. Jaymes was the first to recover, staggering to his feet, pulling the gnomes and dwarf up too. He charged out of the room and up the hall with his sword in his hand. The shop was revealed as a mess of wreckage and choking smoke. Large cauldrons had been overturned, the benches smashed, with smoldering bits of debris everywhere. The smoke was thick, but he saw that the blast had worked and the heavy boulder had been expelled into the outer corridor by the explosion.

Wasting no time, he charged into the hall and looked around, waving his hand to clear away the smoke. The rock had been tossed six or eight feet. A taloned foot and a slinky black body stuck out from under it, twitching. Its huge head was out of sight.

Dram came out and joined him, chuckling at the sight.

"Musta been listening 'real close' at the door, like Pete suggested. I guess she got popped over the head."

"Let's get going—come on!" Jaymes barked.

By then the three gnomes had emerged into the hallway, Carbo and Salty Pete each carrying one of the extra kegs of powder they had prepared. Together the companions raced up the muddy corridor, into the adjoining passage, back to the pit. With profound relief Jaymes saw the rope still dangled from the opening overhead.

"Quick!" Dram urged, racing to the rope, taking hold of the bottom to brace it for the gnomes. Overhead the sky was a hazy blue, a promise of freedom and fresh air awaiting them.

The daylight vanished, replaced by a shadow darker than night. The black dragon loomed above them, the bulk of her massive body blocking out the light.

"Uh-oh!" Pete cried suddenly, pointing upward. "It's Sheedra. She must have gotten out from under the boulder, and slipped out her bolt hole, and come around here. I think she's mad!"

"Right, back the way we came!" cried Dram. He pushed Carbo and Sulfie, who had just reached the bottom of the rope, then followed them, sprinting back toward Pete's workshop.

Sheedra slithered down through the hole like a monstrous snake diving into a rabbit's burrow. She was immense, black, and scaly, with muscular shoulders and a wedge of a head that lashed from side to side, yellow eyes staring into the darkness. Her huge wings flapped, completely filling the round chamber, and she hissed with a sound of a volcanic steam leak.

"Petey!" she called, her voice stern, crackling. "Nasties tried to kill me!"

"Run!" screamed Sulfie, sprinting as fast as her little legs could carry her. Her brothers, and Dram, came behind. Jaymes, however, stepped into the darkness of a side corridor, crouching low, his blade—flames extinguished—held low.

"There are the nasties—hssst!" spat the monstrous serpent, her forked tongue flashing in the darkness.

Serpentine jaws gaped. The warrior heard a gurgle of bubbling pressure, then a gout of caustic acid streamed past him. Someone screamed loudly down the twisting passage.

Jaymes twisted the hilt of his sword in his two hands, outlining him and the weapon in blue flame. The dragon took no notice of him, however, slithering after the fleeing gnomes and dwarf.

The warrior raised the sword before him, flames surging brightly from the blade. Another stream of acid spewed down the corridor, away from him—the mere vapors brought tears to his eyes.

Jaymes stepped into the corridor and from behind charged the black dragon, which was coiling to fling herself after the gnomes. She roared loudly as the flaming sword pierced her skin. Sheedra's head snapped around, like a striking cobra, but the swordsman was already beside her, and with one brutal slash he chopped through her neck. Drooling acid, jaws gaping, the black head tumbled free. Sheedra's body thrashed wildly, its huge tail smashing Jaymes to the side. By the time he sat up, however, the corpse was gurgling, and the black dragon was dead.

"Carbo's burned!" Sulfie was sobbing, as she and Pete carried the stricken gnome back into the chamber. Carbo's tunic was half dissolved, and the upper part of his body and his head were covered with terrible wounds.

"There'll be more spawn coming," Pete warned, as Dram scrambled up the rope. "We gotta get him out of here fast!"

"Then climb for all you're worth!" the human said. "I'll take Carbo."

As gently as possible Jaymes picked up the wounded gnome, who was moaning in pain, his beard singed away by the blast. The warrior held him under one arm and tugged on the line with the other, relying on the dwarf to haul him up

At the lip of the hole Sulfie and Salty Pete grabbed their brother. Jaymes pulled himself out, and all the companions were on the ground.

"We've got to move!" snapped the human, once again snatching up the injured gnome.

They sprinted for the trail, Dram and Sulfie leading the way, Salty Pete close behind. They darted around the mossy trees, making for the scent of air and glimpse of daylight at the edge of the swamp. Carbo lost consciousness sometime before they reached the edge of the Brackens, but still they ran, splashing through puddles, pushing through the foliage that closed in when the trail petered out. They didn't slow down until they had burst from the swamp, scaled the embankment, and once again could look down upon the Brackens from the arid safety of the plain.

CHAPTER TWENTY-SIX

SOLANTHUS

Ankhar slept on the ground, just like the rest of his army—no tent or cot to distinguish the leader of the horde from his rugged troops. The long march from Cornellus's stronghold had made his limbs and eyelids feel heavy. Wrapped in a great bearskin sleeping robe—a gift from Blackgaard's lancers—he was already bedded down for the night when Laka came to see him.

The half giant welcomed the counsel of his foster mother. They crouched beside the dying embers of his fire, while a dozen painted hobgoblins stood in a ring around them, facing outward and guarding against any approach.

The old crone waved her rattle at Ankhar, the skull talisman she had made from the head of the dead captain of the Garnet knights. The eyes glowed green, and Ankhar watched the bony jaw, still studded with immaculate white teeth, start to move.

"The Crowns are now broken," hissed the death's head.

"Shattered and lost.

"They wait for your justice,

"While dreading the cost."

"Listen to the prince!" said Laka, shaking the skull-on-a-stick so that the teeth clattered.

"Crowns have returned to Thelgaard," the half-giant noted,

scratching his massive jaw. "That place ripe for taking. Keep is strong, but city walls low and incomplete. Too many Crowns die at the Battle of the Crossings. Not be many fighters there. What you think mother? Does Prince wish me to attack Thelgaard?"

In reply, the old shaman shook the skull again, a rattle so vigorous it looked as though she was trying to shake the firmly mounted trophy off of the end of her wand. The ghastly face merely bobbed, once again its jaw clattering.

"Treasures piled high
" 'yond walls that are thick,
"Take your war there,
" 'Ere trophies, they slip."

Laka shook the talisman some more, but no more words emerged, and gradually the emerald light faded from the eye-sockets.

"What he mean? Thelgaard's walls not thick—little treasure there, if we believe Cornellus."

"These words of Prince," the crone said, reaching up bony fingers to caress the broad jowl of her adopted son. "You must understand."

The commander turned away from the warmth of the fire, from the tenderness of the old witch. He stroked his chin, looking at the vast plains spreading below. When he spoke next, Laka could discern his words, but she sensed that Ankhar was speaking more to himself. He raised a hand, pointed generally to the west.

"Thelgaard there. Three days march away."

He swivelled to the right, pointing toward that horizon. "Solanthus there. Five days march away. Solanthus got great, thick walls. Much treasure."

He chuckled, like a rumble of distant thunder.

"I understand the Prince. Crowns have been defeated. Time we destroy Swords and take riches." Ankhar turned to his foster mother, who was regarding him through eyes that were brighter than the red moon nearly full in the night sky. She licked her lips, nodding happily.

"Tomorrow we march on Solanthus," the commander said, with a self-satisfied nod.

⋘◦◖◦◖◦◖◦◖◦◖ ✦ ◗◦◗◦◗◦◗◦◗◦⋙

Duke Rathskell of Solanthus was a brave man, but now he lay awake and whimpered into the darkness of his bedchamber like a terrified child. Never in his life had a dream terrified him so much as the nightmare that had just shook his mind. He found himself trembling, drenched in a chilly sweat, and everywhere he looked in his candlelit bedchamber he spotted the shadows of bogeymen, horrific monsters, and cruel, tormenting assassins.

He knew Ankhar was coming, the enemy horde marching out of the mountains toward Solanthus, but, strangely, that wasn't the worst aspect of the threat. He could barely remember what it was exactly that had terrified him so. He only recalled some vague threat regarding his trove of gleaming gems, the great chests of his treasure, full of the fabled Stones of Garnet.

Had somebody threatened his treasures? Surely that would not have caused him such intense terror! He felt as though more than his treasure was at stake; his life, his very soul, was imperiled.

Only then did he hear the humming, the persistent drone that augured a summons from the sacred mirror. He knew where to find the source of that sound: It would be glimmering in the secret alcove of his bedroom. Alarmed at how loud the humming was, the duke looked to his side, breathing a sigh of relief.

The duchess, his lovely young plaything, slept soundly beside him in the great bed, snoring gently as the duke, his heart pounding, slipped from beneath his covers and went over to the alcove where the magical artifact was gradually coming to life. He pushed the panel to open the hidden door. Nervously glancing over his shoulder, the nobleman—a Knight of the Sword, a veteran of wars and revolution—pulled shut the door so that his wife would not wake and discover his secrets.

Only then did he take a seat on the cushioned chair, striking a match and lighting a pair of candles—not so that he could see the mirror but so that the mirror could see him.

Composing himself, mopping the sweat from his brow, he pulled down the velvet cloth that covered the mirror. He confronted an image there that was not a reflection.

"My lord duke," said His Excellency, Lord Regent Bakkard du Chagne. "My time is valuable—you have kept me waiting too long! Didn't you hear my summons?"

"I beg your Excellency's pardon," said Rathskell, trying to keep a calm expression, even as new drops of sweat formed on his forehead. He dared not mop them away, could only hope that his image in the mirror would not reveal every imperfection. "I was sleeping and needed a few moments' time to wake up."

"Sleeping? It is not yet midnight! Bah, I am two decades older than you, and my work keeps me busy into the small hours of the night. You would do well to take that lesson from me, Duke."

"Indeed, Excellency. I shall try to exercise greater diligence. It's just that there is so much to do. . . ." This time Rathskell was unable to stop himself from mopping his trickling sweat. "I most humbly apologize. It shall not happen again! If only I did not need to conceal my activities from the one who shares my chambers . . ."

"You know women are not to be trusted, not with such secrets as we possess. If the slut is not capable of restraining her curiosity, you must see that she sleeps elsewhere!"

"Yes, of course, my lord!" If the duke was distressed by the regent's characterization of his wife, he gave no hint.

"Let us turn our attention to your responsibilities, then," said the Lord Regent. "Are you aware that the forces of the Crown are defeated, cowering within the walls of Thelgaard. That Caergoth, too, has retired, taken his army south of the Garnet River again?"

"Indeed, my lord? I knew Thelgaard was routed most ignobly by the horde of the half-giant. Half his men killed, the rest falling back to the walls of his city. He refused, my lord—absolutely refused—to cooperate with me on a rational plan of defense.

Caergoth was still on the field with a considerable force, while I was compelled to return to my own bastion—I did not want the barbaric rascals to get between me and my own fortifications."

"Good course, that. Prudent, in the event. Thelgaard is a fool, and our path to empire will only be paved when he has been replaced by someone more capable and reliable. You should not risk your own army until the others' forces have been exhausted. At the same time, you should encourage them to inflict damage upon the enemy."

"Indeed, lord. Though it seems that Thelgaard inflicted precious little upon the foe. Have your agents informed you how Caergoth is faring?"

"Yes. He has retired to his city, driven by timidity and indecision. Your own city will be the next target of the enemy."

The duke mumbled his agreement, shivering—for this was the very revelation that had stalked him in his most recent dream. The Lord Regent's next words surprised him, however.

"If Solanthus falls to the goblins, it is no loss—we can retake it when we desire. However, it is important that the treasures of the vault be retained, for the good of the knighthood. Therefore, you must empty your treasury and bring the Stones of Garnet to safety. I hereby order you to bring those stones to Palanthas for safekeeping."

"My lord!" Solanthus was appalled. "The risks of such a journey!"

He remembered what it was that had shaken him to the core. In his dream he had been trapped with the stones, here in the city! Both he *and* his treasure had been doomed by the surrounding horde! Surely that was the meaning of the dream. The Lord Regent was right—he needed to get them out of here for safekeeping!

"Very well, Excellency." The duke tried to conceal how unsettled he was. In the face of such dire portents it seemed that fleeing with his riches was the only way to preserve his life and his fortune.

"Be quick and secretive about this," instructed the lord. "You know the White Witch has been asking persistent questions, making a pest of herself, as usual. Give her wide berth."

"She is wily, the Lady Coryn," agreed Rathskell. "If she presses me, I do not know if I can thwart her."

"You *must!* " Du Chagne's voice was a hiss. "Do whatever it takes to stop her! Do you understand?"

"Anything?" the duke asked, with a gulp. "Her powers are daunting, my lord! But I shall do what I can—"

"Rathsky?" The voice—a familiar nasal whine—came from the bedroom. He could picture the duchess sitting up in bed, looking around in confusion. How much had she heard?

"I must go!" the duke said urgently.

The Lord Regent scowled darkly, but the voice rose— "Rathsky! Rathsky!" She was out of bed now, approaching the alcove!

Rathskell dropped the cloth across the mirror and blew out one of the candles. He took the other in his hand as he pulled the secret door aside to find his wife, blinking sleepily, with her hair in a tousled mess, just outside the alcove.

"Oh, there you are. What are you doing?" she asked. "Where were you?"

"Just a little meditation in my private closet," he said. "I have so many problems of state to worry about."

"Well, I can't sleep very well if you are jumping up and meditating all the time," she said, grumpily, stumbling back toward the quilts. "Why don't you come back to bed?"

The duke's eyes narrowed as he watched her. That was close.

"Yes, dear," he said quietly. "It is time."

⊱⋇⊰⊱⋇⊰⊱⋇⊰❀⊱⋇⊰⊱⋇⊰⊱⋇⊰

They could no longer be described as a horde. Ankhar and his followers moved out of the Garnet Mountains and onto the plains—not as any rag-tag barbarian force but as a formidable army.

Even before the worg-riders emerged from the forested foothills, the commander had dispatched a dozen auraks—the only draconians capable of true flight—on aerial reconnaissance of the lands across the planned route. They reported universally that the knights seemed to have withdrawn into their great fortresses and were patrolling only in the immediate vicinity of each city's walls.

Even so, the half-giant enforced strict discipline as his army swept across the plain. He had hundreds of lupine cavalry covering the ground before and to either side of his mighty columns. His footsoldiers marched in thunderous cadence. His regiments teemed with goblin spearmen and swords. There were huge phalanxes of archers, draconians advancing with wings furled, including companies of kapaks and baaz, commanded by snarling, whip-cracking sivaks.

Riding in the midst were the heavily armored knights of the Blackgaard's Brigade, forming a solid block, a crushing hammer to be wielded in accordance with the army commander's will. The legions of humans, mercenaries and brigands who had joined together marched shoulder to shoulder with gobs and draconians that had been their lifelong enemies. It was an impressive tide of martial power, driving across the landscape like a force of nature.

Over the course of five days the army made steady progress toward the great, walled fortress city of Solanthus. As they drew near all of the human outposts retreated within those lofty battlements—"Like turtle pulling in legs and head!" Laka cackled—and Ankhar's troops were not even subjected to harassing attacks as they spread in a vast semicircle around the city.

Of course, Solanthus was not an easy target. It stood at the northern terminus of the Garnet range, on a commanding bluff overlooking the plains to the east, north, and west. Gentle ramps had been excavated in all three directions, carrying wide, smooth roads up to the city's massive gates. Yet each gatehouse was a small castle in its own right, and each road passed directly beneath the parapets of the city wall for a good quarter mile before reaching the gates, so any attacker would have to run a lethal gauntlet before coming close to those massive, ancient barriers.

The city's great landmark, its Cleft Spires, rose above the walls, the towers, everything else. This great natural pillar, cloven in half by a blast of lightning many centuries before the city was founded, loomed hundreds of feet high. The two halves bent away from each other, curving above the great marketplace at the heart of Solanthus.

Ankhar knew all this, and knew to be patient.

His army made a sprawling camp outside those three plains roads. There was another, much narrower, track leading out of the city to the south, climbing through a perilous series of switchbacks as it ascended along the front ridge of the mountain range. That was no path for an army or for the flight of a panicked populace. Instead, the commander knew to keep his eyes and his army trained on the three great gates, intimidating the enemy army and the lord huddling behind those high, thick walls.

He was standing in the middle of his camp, staring up at the north gate, when one of the guards came up to him in the late twilight hours. "Lord Ankhar?" said the hobgoblin, snuffling loudly. "An ogre is here to see you."

The half giant nodded. He followed the guard through the camp toward the darkening expanse of plains. To the south the vast bulk of Solanthus rose against the sky. The walls and towers of that ancient bastion were already aglitter with torchlight.

The half giant shook his head at such foolishness. Didn't the knights know those flames only served to night-blind their own men and provided no defense against the great army before their city?

At the edge of the camp, the hulking chieftain could not disguise his surprise. There was not just "an ogre" to see him, but a feathered and painted ogre chieftain of strapping sinew and size. Even more significant, this visitor stood at the head of a vast column of his fellow ogres and another great host of hobgoblins and gobs. There were at least two thousand fresh warriors, and all of them pressed forward, casting admiring eyes toward the huge war leader.

"Lord Ankhar?" asked the ogre, prostrating himself on the ground at the half-giant's feet. Behind him, the great company of savages knelt in unison.

"I Ankhar."

"I am Bloodgutter, chief of the Lemish vales. Even beyond the mountains we have heard tales of your deeds among the plains of men. You have battled the knighthood on the open field and defeated them! Your victories are the birth of legend, and you give us hope against our hated foe. We hurried here over many days of marching to offer you our swords, and our blood."

"Aye. Lemish long way. You a bold ogre."

"In truth, lord, Lemish is a poor country now. We were driven there in ages past by the armies of the knights. For years we have waited for a chance at vengeance. We ask only a fair position in your army, lord Ankhar. For that, we will gladly give you our trust, our lives."

"Est Sudanus oth Nikkas," the half giant said. "My power is my Truth."

"I pledge my tribe to the Truth that is Ankhar," the ogre said, bowing his head.

"You serve me? Only me?" asked the half-giant.

"To the death, lord!"

"Very good," said the war chief, pleased by the surprise reinforcements. "Make camp with ours. Welcome. Bloodgutter valued sub-captain. Rest and eat. We attack humans soon."

><@∘<@∘<@∘@∘❀∘@∘<@∘<@∘<

The duke gazed at the Cleft Spires, which rose higher than the loftiest castle tower and broader even than the great gatehouses that stood astride the three highways leading from the city.

Solanthus was a plains city, though it stood in the shadow of the mountains. Now the plains were lost, taken by the horde—the army—of Ankhar. Who knew how long the city itself would last?

The duke felt a stranglehold of fear, like a fist clamped on his throat. He had to get away from here—he had to flee!

"What is it?" The Duchess of Solanthus, her face pale, confronted her husband as he paced back and forth in his private offices. She was a beautiful woman, much younger than her husband, but now her face was drawn, almost haggard with worry. Duke Rathskell's obvious fear only made her more terrified.

The Duke of Solanthus was wringing his hands, as he had been doing throughout the night. Couriers had been bringing him a steady stream of reports, and he knew that his city was nearly surrounded. The last news—that a great brigade of ogres had joined the foe—had driven him to an uncharacteristic burst of profanity. That outburst, emerging from beyond the closed door of his chamber, had brought his wife running in concern. He glared at her, then back at the message. Abruptly the duke crumpled the sheet and cast it aside with a furious gesture.

"I must get the Stones of Garnet away from here!" he declared. "The Lord Regent commands it—he needs them to bolster the knighthood across Solamnia!"

"But . . . Rathsky? You always said those stones were yours, to be used as you see fit! Not for Bakkard du Chagne or the other dukes. Isn't that right?" she asked, as sweetly as she dared.

"I see fit now to take them away from here!" he snapped.

"But the goblins!" gasped the duchess, waving in the general direction of the city walls. "They have ogres and draconians with them too! There must be ten thousand of them out there! They could attack at any moment! Should we really be worrying about the stones"

"No . . . I mean yes, my dear," said the rail-thin duke, as he glowered at the walls, the floor, at everything in sight, including his wife. Still, he forced himself to speak calmly. "I must save the stones, and of course that means I must leave the city with them."

"What are you going to do?" the woman asked breathlessly.

"Well, I have no choice," snapped Rathskell, decisively. "I will place the most portable of my treasury—the gems and jewelry—into strongboxes and have them loaded onto a wagon and personally drive that wagon up the mountain road. I will head for Caergoth. That way, at least I will be able to exert my influence on Duke Crawford—he *will* bring his troops to the city's aid!"

"How will you—I mean, we—get out? The road to Thelgaard and Caergoth is blocked by that terrible army of savages!"

"I told you—the mountain road, my dear. And not we—just me. It is rough, but with a good team and driver, I should be able to get up into the foothills before the wretches know what I am about. With luck, I can reach Caergoth in three days and be back with a relief force within a week in plenty of time to rescue you."

"But—what about the city? Your castle?" The duchess sniffled. "What about me?"

"Captain Rankin will be in charge. As long as he keeps the gates closed and the walls manned, you will be safe here. I can't ask you to take the risks of the road, my dear. If we can keep those wretches focused on Solanthus, it may be that Caergoth will be able to fall upon them from behind. Yes, that is my plan, and if I so say so myself, a brilliant plan, with bright hopes for success!"

"Do you really think so?"

The duke fixed his wife with a withering glare.

CHAPTER TWENTY-SEVEN

TREASURE ROAD

Horribly seared by the black dragon's acid, Carbo writhed in pain as Jaymes bore him along, the bluff above the broad Vingaard. They made camp at the first shelter they reached in a grass-lined ravine, and Dram gave his small flask of dwarf spirits to their injured companion. The strong drink seemed to alleviate the little fellow's pain, but it couldn't do anything to heal his grievous wounds. The acid had burned his flesh away and blinded him. They stretched him on a blanket on the ground. He held his brother's and sister's hands, as, gradually, his labored breathing grew quieter, more relaxed.

Carbo died shortly after sunset, and the companions laid him to rest in a small grave, watered by the tears of his sister and his long-lost brother. Jaymes and Dram, having dug the grave, stood uncomfortably by as the bereaved pair sobbed out their farewells.

"You should never have come for me," cried Salty Pete, his narrow shoulders quivering. "This wouldn't have happened— he'd still be with us!"

"No," Sulfie said, sniffling, wiping her large nose with a handkerchief. "He wanted to come and find you. He was so brave."

Jaymes cleared his throat, touched his chin, his heart. "I think he's proud that he helped to get you out. He was a hero."

"But he's dead! Sheedra killed him, called him a 'nasty'! I hate her!" Pete proclaimed.

"Well, she's dead too. Jaymes and his sword took care of her," Dram said.

"I'm sorry it was too late for your brother," the swordsman said.

Jaymes turned and stalked to the edge of the ravine. He looked at the murky waters of the Upper Vingaard, his fists clenched into white-knuckled knots in the gathering darkness.

≈⊙⊙⊙⊙⊙⊛⊙⊙⊙⊙⊙≈

"Jaymes—wake up."

The warrior was awake in an instant, sitting up, reaching for his sword, until he recognized the white-robed enchantress who had suddenly appeared, as she so often did, without warning.

"What is it?" he asked, throwing off his blanket and rising to his feet. "You have news?"

He and his three companions were camped on the open plains, several days march south of the Brackens and the grave where they had buried Carbo. Sulfie, Pete, and the dwarf still slept. Nearby, two casks stood with their gear, containing the rest of the explosive compound they had been able to ferret away from Sheedra's lair.

"The Duke of Solanthus is moving the contents of his vault to Caergoth or Palanthas. He will take it on the road himself. If our suspicions are correct—if he is the one who ordered the murder of Lord Lorimar—the green diamonds will be among that treasure."

"Do you really think it was him?"

Coryn shook her head and shrugged her shoulders. "I don't know what to think. Remember what you told me: The house was attacked by six knights, none wearing the sign of an order."

"But they were Solamnics, I'm sure of that," the warrior asserted. "One of them was standing over Dara's body and muttering, reciting that foul pledge—*Est Sularus oth Mithas.*"

"And she was already dead?"

298

"Yes, I told you. I was in another part of the house, I heard the commotion and came running. Dara had been stabbed through the heart. The lord was bleeding, his leg nearly sliced off."

"And the attackers?"

Jaymes shook his head. "I've told you all this before . . . more than once."

"Be patient. Tell me again," said the wizard.

"I can't remember details. I lost my head, to be honest. I was in such a rage, I killed them all. Five of them, and quickly. The last one talked a bit—only told me his lord would be pleased."

"Could they have been bandits?"

"No, there was discipline in their attack, like knights. That vow—I will swear on what's left of my honor that they weren't Dark Knights. They were Solamnics."

"Then it must have been Rathskell," the enchantress said. "We know he was furious when Lorimar denied him the right to seek Dara's hand in marriage. Thelgaard strikes me as too stupid for such deviousness, so I think Solanthus is the one. He will be leaving with his treasure before the dawn."

"Why? Isn't the safest place for his treasure within the walls of his own castle?"

Coryn gave him a sly half-smile. "Let's just say that all of the lords are having an attack of nerves. The Lord Regent feels he is short of funds. Perhaps I had a little something to do with that."

"What, you stole his gold?" Jaymes asked.

"Of course not!" The white robe feigned shock. "I did fix it so that he might be a little reluctant to spend it. In any event, Solanthus plans to ride even before the dawn. He will take the mountain road to the south so he can avoid the horde on the plains."

The warrior frowned. "I'll never get there in time," he said, shaking his head. "Even with a fleet horse—"

She cut him off, her smile broadening. "Well, there are more expeditious ways to travel than even astride the fastest horse."

He looked at her questioningly.

"Let me have your ring," she said.

Puzzled, he pulled the golden band off of his finger and handed it to her. She held it up and murmured an incantation, repeating the quiet words three more times. When Coryn handed the ring back to him, it felt slightly warm.

"Go ahead, put it back on," she instructed. "You will be able to use it to teleport four times—you must picture the place you wish to go. Turn the ring twice around your finger, and it will take you there."

A shiver ran down his back as Jaymes slipped it over his finger. The warmth it emanated felt pleasant, comforting.

"Do you know the mountain road south out of Solanthus?" she asked him.

"Yes. I know it well from my goblin-hunting days. Dram and I just traveled that way to meet with Cornellus."

"Good." Coryn handed him a small leather bag. "Here," she said, answering his raised eyebrows, "this is a magic bag. In case," she added with her sly half-smile, "you find yourself with a few more treasures than you can easily carry in your pockets."

He nodded. "It should come in handy," he said.

By now Dram had awakened, and the two gnomes were also stirring. Jaymes filled them in. "You should make for the Vingaard Mountains with all haste," he said. "I will catch up as soon as I can. Tell Swig Frostmead I'll be bringing his money."

After a hasty goodbye, the White Witch wrapped them both in the cocoon of her magic, and they were gone.

⊹⊙⊙⊙⊙⊙⊙⊙⊙⊙⊙⊙⊙⊙⊹

The wagon rumbled along the narrow mountain way, skirting the steep foothills of the Garnet Range. The Duke of Solanthus and his driver clung to the rails and the reins, trying to stay perched on the jolting seat. A column of a dozen Knights of the Crown clattered along ahead of the four sturdy workhorses pulling the wagon, while a similar detachment followed close behind.

The road was dangerous. To their right, the slope spilled down to a cliff, which hung over a dry ravine some two or three hundred feet below. To the left, the land rose sharply.

They had departed through a little-used gate in the very south of the city walls, far from the main roads connecting Solanthus to the rest of Solamnia. Fortunately, there were no goblins near this route. Leaving before dawn, they had been able to travel high into the mountains before the sun rose. Behind them now they could see the ogre army sprawled across the plains like locusts, a dark smudge extending for miles in three directions around the walled city dominated by the stark landmark of the Cleft Spires.

Duke Rathskell glanced over his shoulder, not at his besieged city but at the four strongboxes lashed into the wagon's cargo bed. They were all filled with jewels. Probably enough jewels to ransom his city, he reflected sourly, but they were bound elsewhere.

"My lord duke!"

Rathskell saw one of the men from his trailing escort galloping forward, waving for his attention. He kept his grip on the side rail, gritting his teeth at every wrenching bounce, waiting for the man to catch up to the rumbling wagon.

"What is it?" snapped the duke, even as the driver, at his orders, kept urging the team of horses onward.

"Goblins, my lord," said the knight. "A large number have moved onto the road behind us. They seem bent on giving chase."

"How many of them?" he asked.

"A detachment. A good-sized group, to be sure—maybe a thousand of the bastards. We didn't spot them at first, and now they are but a few miles behind us."

Rathskell cursed. "Are any of them mounted?" he demanded.

"No, sir. The party appears to be on foot."

"Good. We should be able to outrun the wretches. Now go back to your post, and keep an eye on them! Let me know if you see any sign of worg-riders or if they appear to be closing the gap."

"Aye, lord!" The knight snapped off a salute and turned to ride away. Rathskell was still watching him when he was stunned by the loudest explosion he had ever heard. Dust and smoke

301

rmixed with gouts of fire billowed across the road behind the wagon. The duke watched in disbelief as the man and horse, propelled by the blast, went soaring into space and tumbled toward the base of the rocky precipice along which the road skirted.

The team of horses bucked and surged ahead in sudden panic, lurching the heavy vehicle forward over the bumpy road—until, moments later, a second blast obliterated a great section of that roadway, right in the path of the advancing wagon. The lead horse fell, part of its head torn away by the explosion, while another steed shrieked piteously and went down with a broken leg.

"What's happening?" demanded Rathskell, panic setting in as he stood up and drew his sword. The driver didn't answer. Instead, he clasped both hands to his bleeding forehead where a shard of rock had smashed him, then slumped, unconscious, in his seat.

The wagon was trapped, the duke could see—two sections had been blown out of the cliff-side road, blocking passage forward and back. The two blasts had neatly separated the duke from his escort of knights. Some of those men had recovered their senses but were forced to rein in at the edges of the gaps. There was no way for the mounted men to reach their lord.

"Are you all right, Excellency?" called one captain, astride an agitated horse at the edge of the forward gap. "Are you hurt?"

Rathskell shook his head, still trying to grasp what had happened. Was it magic that had torn the very roadway off of the mountain? He didn't think so—not from the ogres.

"Stay there, lord! We'll try to reach you!" cried the captain, the leader of the detachment at the front of the column.

One brave rider volunteered. The knight urged his horse into a gallop and tried to leap the still-smoking breach in the road. The distance was too great, and both horse and rider tumbled over and bounced down the cliff, finally settling in gruesomely distorted poses among the broken rocks below. Wincing, the duke looked away toward the rear. He saw the knights there taking a defensive posture down the road, dismounting, drawing weapons. Several of the men were hauling fallen timbers out of the woods, making an impromptu breastwork. With a sickening sense of apprehension, the duke remembered the goblins—"maybe a thousand of the bastards"—coming at them hard and fast from that direction.

Only then did Duke Rathskell notice a lone swordsman step into sight, on the island of road with the duke and his trapped wagon. The man's weapon, a mighty blade, was gripped in both his hands, as he approached the disabled wagon.

He wore a cape, and his whiskered face was devoid of any emotion. But his eyes were dark, and smoldered with contempt.

"I know you. You are the Assassin!" spat the duke, as Giantsmiter blazed even brighter than the sun on that bright mountainside. The duke whipped out his own slender rapier and jumped down to the road.

"I've been called that," Jaymes said, "but I'm no assassin, and I didn't kill Lorimar. You, of all people, should know that."

"What's that supposed to mean?" demanded Rathskell. "You killed him, and you slew his bitch of a daughter, too!"

Jaymes lunged at the duke, nearly gutting him. The nobleman, though taken by surprise, fell back. The knights on both sides of the gap in the road shouted curses and warnings.

"Be careful how you talk about the Lady Dara," Jaymes hissed. "You don't want to have too many lies on your lips when you go to meet the gods."

A master swordsman, the Duke of Solanthus was grim now and circled warily. Jaymes brought Giantsmiter over his head in a whistling smash, then swiftly chopped from the right and the left, advancing remorselessly against his foe. The smaller man leaped back, using the edge of the wagon as a shield, stepping around the two restless horses remaining from his team.

Rathskell charged into Jaymes's attack with parries and thrusts, forcing the taller man away from the wagon, backing him to the edge of the precipice. The warrior stopped at the edge, driving his own blade with powerful overhand blows, again and again knocking aside the duke's slender weapon.

Changing tactics, Rathskell scrambled up into the bed of his wagon, swinging wildly down at Jaymes's head until the warrior jumped up next to him, forcing him back. For several moments they slashed and cut at each other, both standing in the wagon, their blows whistling over the four strongboxes resting there. Finally, Jaymes made a rush, and the duke half jumped, half fell off the wagon, again retreating to the edge of the slope.

With a sinking feeling the duke saw with a glance that the knights of his rearguard were engaged at their roadblock with a mass of goblins. The ogres were howling with bloodlust, while he was engaged in a fight for his life. He stabbed at Jaymes's legs as the tall man neared, then turned and ran to the far end of the broken shelf of isolated road.

Here the men of the duke's forward guard had dismounted and were trying to make their way along the precipitous gap on foot. One man had already plunged to his death and lay in a heap next to the horse and rider who had failed the earlier attempt. The rest of the men were busily coiling rope to belay the next climber.

Rathskell knew they would not reach him in time. He was a skilled swordsman—once he'd thought himself the best in the world—but he could see that he was no match for the Assassin. The duke's sword was first-rate but useless against the legendary Giantsmiter. He screamed his frustration as he attacked.

Giantsmiter blocked his best efforts again, this time smashing his rapier, the loose shards of steel shattering and tumbling down the mountainside. Rathskell turned to flee, and Jaymes made a swift slash through his enemy's hamstring. The wound exploded in blood. The duke collapsed, his right leg nearly severed. He groaned in pain and fear as the fiery Giantsmiter brushed his immaculately trimmed mustache.

"Which one has the green diamonds?" asked the swordsman, indicating the four strongboxes.

"I don't know what you mean—I have never heard of green diamonds!" protested the stricken nobleman.

Jaymes scowled and cut him on his other leg. "Don't be a fool. You'll get nowhere lying to me!"

"I'm not lying!"

Jaymes squinted. He turned and slashed the locks off of the four strongboxes, one after the other, then searched through the piles of glittering diamonds and rubies.

"I'm going to ask you one more time. The green diamonds?" he demanded.

"I'm telling the truth—I've never heard of any such diamonds!" cried the duke.

Shouts came from behind them, cries of alarm mingling with the clash of steel. "The goblins are closing in," Jaymes noted. "They'll be able to scramble along the cliff easily enough. They're not as encumbered with armor, as your knights."

Rathskell groaned in pain as he twisted to look in horror. His rear detachment was fighting bravely, but the odds were overwhelming. Each knight had killed six or eight goblins, but there were only a few dozen men back there, and they were facing hundreds of attackers. One by one, the knights were falling, slain or grievously wounded or, in some cases, simply pushed from the cliff by the press of goblin bodies.

Jaymes pulled out the plain leather sack Coryn had given him. He picked up the gems and jewels from one strongbox—and, though the box was several times larger than the bag—he poured the contents in. He repeated the process with each of the other three boxes, and when he was done the sack bulged only slightly.

"Wait! Please, you can't leave me here!" begged the lord. "The goblins—"

He looked back and saw that only a few of his defenders remained on their feet. It wouldn't be long now. Already several of the brutal attackers were starting to scale across the sheer cliff. The duke couldn't stand, couldn't even crawl for all the pain he was suffering. His one leg was utterly useless.

When he turned back to plead again for his life, he could only moan in despair. The mysterious attacker, with his satchel full of a city's worth of jewels, had disappeared.

CHAPTER TWENTY-EIGHT

COMMERCE AND A COMPOUND

S wig Frostmead let the stream of glittering gems flow from one calloused palm to the other. The gleam in his eyes was, if anything, even brighter than the myriad speckles of light that sparkled and glinted from the cascading jewels. He looked up at Jaymes and flashed a grin so broad it was almost a leer.

He coughed, growing serious. Frowning, he looked at a gem closely, examined another, then set them aside, his face now a mask of bored disinterest. Jaymes knew these Stones of Garnet were impeccable, perfectly cut by master jewelers, large and pure, but the warrior said nothing, his own face as empty as the dwarf's.

"Er, yes," Swig admitted, his tone grudging. "I think these will cover the agreed-upon costs. Of course, I will have to have my appraisers go over them with an eyeglass. Just to confirm, though the cut certainly looks acceptable to my unpracticed eye. Not that I suspect anything amiss, but a fellow can't be too careful in matters like this."

"No," Jaymes said calmly. "A fellow can't."

He wondered what the dwarf would think if he knew the fortune in stones he had been offered was only a fraction of the wealth the warrior had expropriated from Duke Rathskell's strongboxes. He had used the second teleport spell to take him to a place that nobody would suspect, where he had buried most of the gems. Of course, Swig Frostmead didn't need to know all the details, and Jaymes smiled to himself, knowing that whenever he needed to buy more sulfir, he would always have plenty of stones.

After all, a fellow couldn't be too careful in matters like this. . . .

"Now, as to delivery . . ." The dwarf was ready to see the deal through. "We'll have to charge a standard fee for that, of course, but I have willing dwarves, with strong backs, available for the work. Just depends on how far you want them to haul the stuff."

"Actually, I was hoping you might suggest a place," the warrior said. "Perhaps some land nearby that you'd be willing to lease to me? I'll be setting up a rather large operation and will need the lease for some time. We could perhaps arrange for, say, ten years use, with a clause allowing for extension if things work out. Of course, I'll want to contract with your clan exclusively—with probably some assistance on security, and other odds and ends. Not to mention we'll be needing regular supplies."

"Eh, what? You don't say. Ten years. Just for starters? Hmmm. That kind of takes me by surprise. What will you be doing on this land?" asked the dwarf, his eyes glimmering.

"That has to remain a secret, for the time being."

"Huh. A secret. What will you be needing security for?"

"Privacy. I'll need plenty of water and a good source of nearby timber. I'll want to hire some more of your fellows—at top wages, of course—to do some logging, building, and such."

"For good wages, I can probably find you some workers. I like the way you do business, my friend, and I know just the place to set up your operation. I think things can be arranged without difficulty. Of course, there's always plenty of work for us deep in the mines, but some dwarves are willing to work under the open sky."

"Well, then," said the dwarf chieftain. "Let's take a walk, shall we?"

They emerged from Swig's lodge into the breathless clarity

of a mountain morning. It had been more than two months since Jaymes's earlier visit, and now he saw the aspen forests of the Vingaard Range were brightened with the gold foliage of autumn.

Unlike his previous crossings of the plains, however, his journey here had been instantaneous. Using the second magical charge in the ring Coryn had given him, Jaymes had arrived in Meadstone only a few hours before. He had surprised Swig at his breakfast table, but the dwarf had gleefully set aside his porridge for a look at the precious stones that he now, very carefully, wrapped up in a soft cloth and secured in his pocket. "It's just over this ridge, here. Private, like you wanted, but not too far to haul the sulfir. Hope you don't mind a little stroll."

"In this mountain air? What could be better?"

They passed the mouths of numerous mineshafts on their way out of the village. Jaymes was impressed to see the mountainous piles of yellow stone that Swig Frostmead's miners had been able to excavate in the weeks since they had made their deal.

For a long while they climbed through an open forest on a gentle ascent, heading companionably upward on a smooth, wide trail. They crossed the crest of the ridge by midmorning and about two hours later reached the base of the next valley. After spending another hour walking back and forth, pacing off the dimensions of a clearing, studying the flowage of water in the stream, the dwarf and the warrior agreed that this area would suit their agreement.

They worked out the terms of the lease with a handshake and another few gems. "Ten years," Swig said, clearly pleased with the deal. "Don't worry—we'll keep the Salamis off your back."

Jaymes narrowed his eyes. "I don't recall mentioning the knighthood."

Swig chortled. "You didn't have to. We'll keep everyone else off your back, too—you can count on it!"

In truth, Jaymes knew the hill dwarves had no legal property rights to this valley. He could have built his operation here and hired dwarf laborers without paying Swig so much as one steel.

Now, however, he had made the greedy hill dwarf a vested partner in his plans, and Swig and his doughty fighters would help guard this place against outsiders.

The very next morning Jaymes paid a score of newly hired dwarves to clear the trees away from a flat stretch of ground. The tall, straight trunks they would trim and stack to use as building timbers; everything else would go into a massive firewood pile that would provide the raw material for charcoal. A few extra gems sprinkled among the workers proved an invaluable recruiting tool, and by the next day he had all the workers he could possibly use—that was not even counting the dozens of dwarves who were busy hauling sulfir over the ridge and down into the place Jaymes decided to call, simply, Compound.

He knew it would take Dram, Sulfie, and Salty Pete a good long time yet to reach the Vingaard Mountains, since they were coming on foot, but there was plenty Jaymes could do to get the place ready. Within another few days, hill dwarves were busily erecting timber-walled buildings to serve as a factory, storage sheds, and outbuildings. The water from the fresh stream was diverted into a holding pond. After a week the reservoir was full, and they allowed the stream to resume its plainsward course.

By the time the dwarf and the gnomes arrived, a fortnight after Jaymes, the area was transformed. A score of hill dwarves were busy making charcoal. Others were busy grinding the sulfir into a fine powder, using cauldrons and large rocks in lieu of the mortar and pestle Sulfie had demonstrated in Sheedra's lair.

After Jaymes brought Dram up to date on everything, the dwarf took over as foreman, supervising the preparation of the sulfir and charcoal while Sulfie and Pete made saltpeter. Within a matter of days they had stores of all three materials, and soon the black powder was being produced and collected in stout kegs.

When, one day, Swig Frostmead's lovely daughter, Pilsy, came over the mountain to inspect the work, Dram strutted with pride and showed her all their progress. Jaymes watched, amused. Even the gruff Frostmead himself finally seemed to approve of the match—anyone who consorted with a man of such wealth could not, in the hill dwarf's eyes, be all rotten

Jaymes stayed until he was certain all aspects of the work were proceeding well. Casks were being filled with the black powder every day, safely stored in an underground bunker that was well insulated against fire as well as wetness. After the first six days of full production, the warrior went to find Dram overseeing the great charcoal fires. The dwarf was sooty and unkempt, but he flashed a fierce grin when Jaymes asked him how things were going.

"We'll have all the charcoal we can use—for the rest of the year—within the next week," the dwarf proclaimed. "Sulfie is doing a good job overseeing those fires—says it's for her brother."

"Good," said the warrior. "I must leave this in your hands."

"You're off again?" Dram asked, raising his eyebrows. "Let me guess: Thelgaard?"

"I have an important rendezvous with the duke," said the warrior. "It has to be him—if Solanthus was telling the truth about the green diamonds. I told you, he said had never heard of them."

"You can't be sure he was telling the truth," the dwarf said.

Jaymes shrugged. "The treasure—and the Compact of Freedom—were taken by the agents of one of the lords. Lorimar was a lord of the Rose, so that tends to cast suspicion upon the lords of the Crown and the Sword. The Sword Duke is dead . . ."

"So you'll be seeing the Crown," Dram agreed. "Good luck, and be careful."

"Always," Jaymes replied. He flexed his finger on which he wore the golden ring, and in a glimmer he disappeared.

"My Lord?"

Duke Crawford spoke to the mirror in a hush and looked over his shoulder. Though Lady Martha was elsewhere, he could not get over the impression someone was sneaking up on him.

He had a bad feeling that time was running out.

After a seemingly interminable delay, the mirror glimmered to life, and Lord Regent Bakkard du Chagne glared at him. "What is it?" he demanded

"Duke Rathskell of Solanthus is dead. His treasure was stolen before he could bring it to Caergoth."

"Damn that fool! He lost the Stones of Garnet?" cursed the regent. "Did the goblins take him? That villain Ankhar?"

"No, lord. I am afraid the news is even worse. Solanthus departed his city with his treasure loaded into a wagon, as you had ordered. He was pursued by goblins, but they didn't catch him. Instead, he was ambushed by the Assassin himself—with some kind of blasting magic. The Assassin tore the roadway up, killed the duke, took his treasure, and vanished just as miraculously as he appeared. Those knights of his escort who survived rode on to Caergoth and just yesterday informed me of these facts."

"The Assassin? I tell you, the man is the greatest menace we face. He must be destroyed!"

"I understand, lord!" Indeed, Duke Crawford *did* understand. What he did not understand was how he could possibly catch a man who never seemed to be where he was supposed to be, who appeared at the most inconvenient locales then simply disappeared, and who was now, apparently, capable of some kind of new and destructive brand of magic.

"Enough of that wretch—talking about him gives me a headache," growled the regent. He stared into Crawford's eyes, and it seemed as though his vision bored right into the duke's skull. "You will need to join your army in the field, you know."

"But . . . my lord. They are doing quite well, guarding the Kingsbridge. I am needed here in the city."

"You have important work to do, my good duke—and it is time that you take matters into your own hands!"

Crawford's blood turned cold at the threatening tone. The Lord Regent adopted a more genial look, almost avuncular.

"You know, my daughter says that she was rather struck by

you during her recent visit. She carried on quite a bit about your city, your banquet, your grace and manners. Too bad you're married—else you'd have the prospect of a splendid match there!"

Crawford nodded, not trusting himself to reply. He remembered the words of the Nightmaster, commanding just such a union. The words had seemed mad at the time. Du Chagne was speaking again, once more stern and commanding.

"Take care that our Assassin is found! Beware that he does not strike at the very heart of your stronghold!"

"Er, yes, lord. I shall!" The duke all but quivered at the prospect of such an occurrence. The Assassin, striking right in Castle Caergoth?

"My lord." Crawford bowed his head, humbly. "I shall do everything in my power to see that events remain under control."

<hr />

"So this head of famous Rathskell?" asked Ankhar, admiring the grisly trophy that was proudly proffered by Dirtborn, the hobgoblin sub-chief who had led the pursuit of the duke's wagon that had tried to slip out the back gates of Solanthus.

"Yep!" declared the tusked warrior, beaming. "We kilt a bunch of his knights too, but we thought you'd want th' duke's head."

"Treasure it," declared the half-giant. "See head of duke!" he roared to his fighters, holding it up and showing it around. "This fate of enemies of Ankhar!"

Dirtborn bowed deeply, shivering in delight.

"What about duke's treasure? Spy told me it on that wagon. You got it for me?"

For the first time, the hob looked crestfallen, even a little fearful. "Sad to say, lord, there was no treasure when we reached the duke. It was taken by another man—we saw him pour it into a magic bag."

"Who this man?" demanded Ankhar, glowering.

"I do not know, lord. He had a sword that blazed with a blue flame." The sub-chieftain was about to say more but abruptly looked down, clearing his throat with a low growl. "And . . . well . . ."

"Speak truth to me! You bring me head. Now tell me what happened!"

"Lord, it was this man with the fire sword who first struck the duke, not us. He did not kill the duke but crippled him so that we could take him after we slew all the knights of his guard."

"Very well. I glad you tell me this Truth."

Ankhar hefted the head, which fit easily into his palm. The duke's thin mustache was frozen in a curl that might have been disdain or amusement. The half-giant was about to call for his foster mother to admire this trophy when he heard her dry cackle close behind him. He turned and offered the head, which she snatched up eagerly and mounted on the stick rattle—she must have been expecting this prize, for she had already discarded the skull she had carried since the sacking of Garnet.

Still cackling, Laka shook the head on its stick. Ankhar watched, saw the green glow come into those eyes. He was not surprised when the jaw started to move, the words a croak and hiss.

"Walls too tall and gates too thick,

"Will break an army's will,

"Seek the softer target hence,

"In greener pastures kill."

The half-giant looked toward the stout, tall walls of Solanthus. The city was still defended by many knights, he knew—and now there was little treasure and no lord, within those walls. Certainly an attack against that place would entail considerable risk, and there was little to be gained by wasting his army.

Nodding to himself, Ankhar made his decision.

"Rib-Chewer!" He summoned his reliable goblin scout.

"Yes, lord?"

"We will leave Solanthus. Great treasure no longer here."

"What are your orders, lord?"

"Riders charge walls—make great charge. Humans cower, scared of you and your wars. Rest of army march away."

"It shall be as you command, lord. What, then, after the army has marched away?"

"You follow me. We go to Thelgaard. Remember: *Est Sudanus oth Nikkas.*"

"Aye, lord," said the goblin with a cackling laugh. "Your power is your Truth!"

⊱∘⊶∘⊷∘⊶❀⊷∘⊶∘⊷∘⊰

"Guards! Come quickly!" shrieked Duke Crawford, bursting from his bedroom wearing only his dressing gown. Dawn was a pale fluff in the eastern sky. Most of the castle was dark and quiet.

"Help!"

Immediately, Sir Marckus, who was rarely far from his master's side, burst into the ducal apartments. "What is it, my lord?" demanded the knight captain, his eyes widening as he saw the blood on Crawford's garments. "Are you hurt?"

"Not me!" cried the duke, "but the Assassin was here—Lady Martha has been slain!"

Marckus went into the sleeping chamber, his sword in his hand. His eyes widened in horror at the sight of the duchess, her throat slit, lying in bed and staring sightlessly at the ceiling. Her face was locked in a death-mask of shock.

The captain turned around, once again regarding the blood-spattered duke. "Tell me, what happened, lord?" he asked soberly. "When was she killed?"

"Moments ago, I should think," the duke said. "I was strolling on the balcony, taking the morning sun. I went over to the main keep, and that's when the wretched villain must have acted. I returned to see someone in a black cloak running along the parapet, in the other direction. He had a sword in his hand—a sword that was burning with blue flames! It can only have been the Assassin!"

"What is it?" Captain Reynaud, buckling on his sword, came charging in. "What happened?"

The duke repeated his story, his voice growing more steady as he recited the same horrifying tale.

"Oh, Marckus—Reynaud! It's too horrible!"

"Indeed, lord, quite tragic and shocking. Won't you have a seat?" The senior captain ushered his lord to one of the padded chairs in the royal anteroom. Other guards, drawn by the commotion, came in now, and Marckus sent one of them to get some wine for the duke. Reynaud organized a search, dispatching knights in teams of two to comb the castle, the nearby passages, the courtyards, and even niches in the moats below.

Others were sent to search the surrounding streets, the buildings and temples nearby, all told to seek a man with a large sword wearing a black cloak. Marckus pressed the duke for more details, but Crawford admitted he hadn't even seen enough to be certain even that the killer was male, not female. Only one thing was he sure of: The sword had burned with an enchanted blue flame.

Servants helped the duke change from his bloody garments. Others carefully wrapped the body of the duchess, and hauled the corpse away with as much dignity as they could muster.

In the midst of al this activity Marckus stood at the doorway to the balcony. His eyes roamed along the clean flagstones, seeking some trace of blood, but there was nothing, no signs or clues. Nor did there seem to be any singeing or charring, not even on the bedding where Lady Martha had been struck by the burning blade.

Instead, the captain found his eyes drawn back to his master. The duke, taking a sip of wine, seemed calmer now.

Indeed, he almost looked pleased about something.

CHAPTER TWENTY-NINE

THELGAARD UNCLOTHED

Thelgaard—the duke himself and his army was hard pressed. That much was obvious to Jaymes immediately as he released the ring of teleportation for the last time. He had brought himself to one of the high ramparts of the castle that rose in the heart of that once-thriving city. He found himself alone upon the dark wall and could spot no guards on any of the adjacent ramparts. There were no weapons stockpiles, nor watchfires set—in short, nothing indicated this ancient fortress was ready for war.

Yet war was coming to Thelgaard.

It was night, and the swordsman could see thousands of campfires spread nearby across the plains. Ankhar's army had come and laid siege to the duke's city. When Jaymes considered the size of the enemy force he had seen at Mason's Ford, he realized the horde had grown considerably, tripling in size since that battle four months earlier. Now the army's fires were like a thousand constellations across the plains, tiny starlike specks flickering in the blackness of the night.

In contrast, the city seemed bleak and deserted. The city gates along the King's Road leading out of the city were shut, but at first glance Jaymes couldn't spot any guards. As he looked more carefully, he saw a half dozen men slouched in the shadows on the parapets, hardly enough to demonstrate a defense, let alone stop a determined attack. They looked more like stealthy bandits or starving beggars than bold knights in the service of an ancient order.

Across the sprawl of the city a few chimneys emitted puffs of smoke, but the narrow and winding streets of Thelgaard were quiet. A few people scuttled quickly from one place to the next, but there was no raucous activity, no inns doing bustling business, no merchants or craftsmen laboring late into the night.

No streetlights burned, either. Jaymes wondered, at first, if this was because the oil was being conserved for battle, but even on the ramparts, the platforms where catapults and ballistae should have been positioned were bare. Nor did he see any cauldrons filled with oil and left to heat in preparation for a battle.

A door opened a few dozen paces away from him, and Jaymes shrank into the shadows of the crenellated battlement as a pair of watchmen emerged from a darkened tower. Both were speaking in hushed whispers, staring at the enemy camp. Jaymes remained silent as the two men peered at the enemy horde, whispering.

They were walking in his direction along the battlement, and soon he could make out a few of their words.

"Died in her sleep, they say . . . old woman . . . surprised she hung on this long."

"Duke is heartbroken . . . hasn't been the same since the Crossings Battle . . . do you think he'll fight stoutly?"

"Who knows?"

The guards paused a half dozen steps away from Jaymes, one lighting a pipe while the other took a drink from a small flask. Their attention remained on the vast army spread out on the plains.

Sticking to the shadows, he slipped away from the guards, and quickly came to a stairway that led down into the interior courtyards. He had the sword of Lorimar strapped to his belt now and guessed that if he walked about normally he might be mistaken for someone who belonged here. This theory was put to the test immediately as at the base of the steps he came upon several scullery maids carrying buckets of water to the kitchen.

"Beg your pardon, Sir Knight," said one of them as the maids quickly bowed and stepped out of his way. He nodded as he passed, suppressing a amused smile—he wore no uniform armor, no knightly insignia, and yet they still assumed he was one of the fighters in their duke's employ. Perhaps they were grateful for every able-bodied man in the city and weren't about to quibble.

He made his way past a sprawling barracks that seemed abandoned. The doors stood open, revealing an empty common room. Jaymes remembered places like this—always centers of gambling and music and merriment when a company of soldiers was in residence. Now, the barracks looked forlorn.

Strange, thought Jaymes, it is almost as if the duke has surrendered without a hope.

Nearby was a stable, the doors standing open, not a horse to be seen. He remembered the stories of Thelgaard's defeat on the bank of the Vingaard north of here and wondered if it was true that most of the duke's men had been lost. Certainly that could explain the lack of catapults and other war machines. If the duke's army had been routed, they would have had to leave all of their heavy equipment behind. Horses, too, would have been trapped against the river, most likely captured or drowned.

Making his way to the castle chapel, he shrugged away the inconsistencies. Aside from the fact there seemed to be few guards about, and therefore fewer obstacles to his mission on this night, it didn't matter to him whether the knights were busy drinking in the city's beer halls, had fled the impending battle, or had indeed been badly decimated in their initial conflict with the horde of Ankhar.

Jaymes found the chapel and entered the sanctuary through the massive wooden doors, which were unlocked. This temple, like so many in Solamnia, was dedicated to Shinare, mistress of the Scales. Several priests were busy counting coins, stacking them on the large golden scale that was the symbol of their mistress. One glanced at Jaymes as he walked in but offered neither greeting nor objection as he passed through another door and found himself in a hallway connecting the temple to the great hall of the keep.

Only then, when he reached a pair of tall, arched doors that led into a cavernous chamber, did he finally encounter a sentry who appeared to take his duties seriously. The man held a spear across his chest and blocked the door as Jaymes approached.

"His Excellency the duke is in council with Captain Dayr and his officers," declared the guard. "You cannot enter."

"His Excellency will want to hear from me—I bring word of developments in the enemy camp," Jaymes reported, standing at ease.

The sentry, a young knight—his mustache, which valiantly tried to emulate the long handlebar shape of a veteran's, was a wispy thing of straggling hairs—scowled as he digested Jayme's words. He clearly had his orders, but after all how could this lone man inside the very walls of Thelgaard Keep possibly be a threat?

"Why don't you ask him yourself?" the warrior encouraged.

Nodding, as if that had been his intention all along, the young knight turned, knocked once at the great door, and pulled it open. "I apologize for the interruption, my lord. There is a knight here who claims to have brought information on developments within the enemy camp."

"Send him in!" ordered Thelgaard, the words booming from his massive barrel chest. Jaymes strode past the guard and advanced across the great hall. Despite the warmth of the night, a great fire blazed on the hearth, as if the duke needed some tangible evidence of life and vitality within his tomblike fortress. Thelgaard was huddled with four other men, all Knights of the Crown, examining a map that had been spread out on the table nearest the fire. The duke was the largest man in the room, looming over his soldiers. Indeed, thought Jaymes, the man was bulky to the point of fat.

"What is your name, Sir Knight?" asked the duke, frowning as he studied the advancing warrior. "I do not recognize you."

"Perhaps my sword will serve as a reminder," Jaymes said casually, drawing his weapon with a smooth gesture. "You must have seen it before, in Lord Lorimar's house!" he declared, as blue flames burst from the gleaming steel blade.

"By Joli—it is the Assassin!" gasped the duke, taking several steps backward. "Stop him! Kill him!" he cried.

Jaymes heard a rush of sound from behind. He whirled and slashed, cutting in two the spear held by the young guard who was charging to his master's aid. With a lunge and a stab, the warrior drove the man back through the door, knocking him onto his back in the hallway. Quickly Jaymes stepped back inside and pushed that massive portal shut. With one hand he dropped the heavy latch into place. He heard the guard calling for help, pounding on the stout barrier, but there was no immediate threat from that quarter.

By then the four captains with the duke had drawn their own swords. Protecting their lord, who shrank behind them, they fanned out and approached Jaymes with varying degrees of aggressiveness. One, a dashing knight with red hair and tiny, glittering eyes, was careless enough to rush ahead of his fellows. It was the last mistake he ever made—the Sword of Lorimar eviscerated him with one swipe. His scream died and he flopped face forward in the puddle of his own gore.

The other three knights, all seasoned combatants, advanced in unison, forcing Jaymes back to the door. He parried a blow from the left, a stab from the right, a slash from the middle. Smoke swirled around him as the legendary sword slashed through the air. The scent of ozone lingered in the air, bittersweet in his nostrils, and the blue flames trembled as though eager for blood.

"Dayr—kill him!" cried the duke.

The officer in the middle, who was trying to do just that, snapped through clenched teeth, "Yes, my lord!" Dayr was thickly bearded, short but nimble. He charged Jaymes, who parried his thrusts with several savage blows of Giantsmiter. Dayr's two comrades hesitated. With several blocks and a counterattack, the warrior seized the initiative, driving all three Crown knights back.

The men were deft, however, dodging his deadly blade—until Jaymes sidestepped. A backhand cut sliced right through the blade of the nearest captain, and a twisting forehand blow gashed the man's forearm. Dropping the hilt of his sword, gasping in pain, the wounded knight sank to his knees, moaning.

Dayr and the other one angled away from the determined Jaymes. They stayed close together until they came up against a heavy banquet table. With a brazen rush, Jaymes drove his weapon against both their swords, shattering the blades and knocking the men to the floor. They glared up at him as he raised his sword.

"Take your companion!" Jaymes snapped, gesturing with his head toward the man with the wounded arm. "Leave here—now! I intend to have a private conference with your duke."

"No—don't leave me with him!" cried Thelgaard, aghast.

Unable to challenge Giantsmiter, the two officers, averting their eyes from their pleading lord, helped their wounded comrade to his feet, and bore him to the great doors. Jaymes followed, pushing them out then latching the door tightly again.

The warrior closed in on the duke, who stumbled backward until he was almost crouching in the fireplace. "Please—don't kill me!" he begged, dropping to his knees.

The warrior squeezed the hilt of the sword, waiting until the flames died away. "I could kill you," he said calmly. "Just like *that.*" He brought the blade down upon a nearby bench, splintering the heavy oak planks. Kicking the shards of wood aside he stood over the blubbering Thelgaard.

"I know!" cried the duke. "Please—don't!"

"I'll spare you if you tell me the truth," Jaymes said, his voice low and level.

"I will—ask me anything!"

"Where are the green diamonds and the Compact of Freedom?"

the warrior demanded, holding the tip of his mighty weapon close to the huge duke. "Where did you hide them?"

The look of utter confusion on Thelgaard's face was almost convincing. Tears welled in his eyes, and he shook his head wildly. "I know of no such diamonds!" he gasped, his voice a craven whisper. "I haven't seen the Compact since I signed it—two years ago! Please—I swear, I am telling you the truth!"

The warrior smashed the sword again into the stout table, hacking off the end of it. "Your wife, the duchess, just passed away mysteriously, didn't she?" he said coldly, taking a step closer.

Thelgaard, for a moment, seemed to recover his composure. He stopped his wailing and looked at the Assassin with an expression of genuine grief. "I loved my dear wife, as is well known," the duke said. "She perished in her sleep last night—Joli was merciful to spare her the sight of her city's fall."

"I don't care about your city. I care about those green diamonds and that Compact. And about the men who took them when they killed Lord Lorimar. The men *you* sent to kill him," Jaymes said.

"No! That's a lie!" blubbered the huge duke.

Jaymes lifted Giantsmiter threateningly. "Tell me what you did with the stones and why you ordered Lorimar killed!"

"I don't know anything about green diamonds—I've never seen them. And I don't know why Lorimar was murdered! By Joli, I thought *you* killed him! That's the truth!"

"Liar!" spat the swordsman. "Tell me! Those were your men who killed Lorimar, weren't they? Did you send the badgeless knights to Lord Lorimar's house, to steal the document, and the gemstones?"

"No!" cried Thelgaard. "I swear it upon a thousand gods!"

"The *truth!*" snarled Jaymes, bringing the blade down on the floor, shattering the flagstones in front of the cringing, kneeling duke.

That sudden violence seemed to help Thelgaard recover some of his composure. Still on his knees, he drew his bulky body upward and glared at Jaymes. His expression was calm, even peaceful.

"I swear upon upon the tomb of my wife that it wasn't me."

Jaymes was taken back. He had expected the man to lie, was fully prepared to kill him, but all his instincts told him that the terrified lord was telling the truth.

With a sudden retch, the duke toppled forward, vomiting violently, gasping and spewing until he was a sweating, shivering mess.

Jaymes turned and left him like that, a broken lord, kneeling in his own spew.

⚬⚬⚬⚬⚬⚬◉⚬⚬⚬⚬⚬⚬

Lady Selinda found life in Palanthas as boring as ever. She spent a lot of time on the upper parapets of her father's great palace, gazing at the mountains, the bay, the sky, and the clouds. Almost with fondness she thought of the desolate plains, the long ride that had brought her back home. No longer did she fear sea voyages—indeed, the notion of salt air and an ocean wind struck a romantic chord in her breast, as never it had done before.

Her father was more irascible than ever. His fury at the escape of the Assassin had remained at a fever pitch, and neither Captain Powell nor the regent's daughter had been inclined to seek his company. Even his treasure room didn't seem to soothe him. He ordered shades pulled over all the great glass windows, so the Golden Spire no longer gleamed over Palanthas. He was far too unpleasant about the whole topic for his daughter even to think about asking him why he rarely visited that once favorite refuge.

In her heart, she blamed the escape of Jaymes Markham for casting a vile spell on her father and the whole castle, and she knew that she had only herself to blame for that episode.

It was early in the evening, and Selinda was looking forward unenthusiastically to dining alone, when she was startled by a knock on the door of her private chambers.

"Who is it?" she asked.

"The one called the White Witch," came the answer.

"Coryn!" Selinda threw open the door and embraced the enchantress, then quickly pulled her into the room and closed the door. "I have been hoping you would turn up sooner or later—though my father tells me you have been terribly busy this summer."

"So, I understand, have you," said the black-haired wizard, looking at her.

"Oh, Coryn—you know everything! So you know I captured the Assassin, and we were bringing him here, but he escaped."

"Yes, I know you've met him. I have too." Coryn looked closely at the princess. "Do you really think he killed Dara and her father?"

"He's certainly capable of murder," Selinda said, a little defensively. "He killed a brave knight of my escort, Sir Dupuy. Dragged him right over the edge of a cliff."

"Well, then you would be interested to know they claim he has struck again. Another murder."

"The Assassin has murdered someone else?" The princess felt a twinge of confusion and dismay. "Whom did he kill?"

Coryn shrugged, strangely noncommittal. "I didn't say he murdered someone. I said, people claim that he did."

"Who is claiming?" Selinda pressed? "Who was killed?"

"The Duchess Martha of Caergoth. Duke Crawford claims that the Assassin, identified by his burning sword Giantsmiter, came into his chambers and struck down his wife in her bed."

"Lady Martha!" Selinda gasped. "But she was . . . harmless!" Only after a moment did she shake her head. "Wait, that doesn't sound like him, not at all. He's a dangerous killer, but why would he kill the wife of Duke Crawford? Was the duke hurt, also?"

"Strangely enough, no," answered the mage. "He was present and witnessed the killing, but the Assassin did him no harm."

"That makes no sense," Selinda said.

"No, it doesn't," Coryn agreed. "But that's what they are claiming. They're tearing about Caergoth in a frenzy, looking for him."

"It seems a bizarre mystery," the princess admitted. "Why would the Assassin kill harmless Martha?"

"Why, indeed," Coryn said, turning to leave. "I wanted to warn you. Be careful."

"You too. Good bye," said the noblewoman.

It was only an hour after the white wizard had gone, that Selinda found Captain Powell at the waterfront. The Palanthian flagship, *Pride of Paladine,* was tied to the wharf and was being provisioned and made ready to sail. She told the veteran knight what Coryn had told her.

"The duchess? Killed in her bed, in the palace?" Powell said, frowning.

"The duke was there, but unhurt."

"It seems . . . it seems very unlikely indeed, my lady," the captain observed cautiously.

"I think so also. *Too* strange." In that instant, Selinda made up her mind. "Captain. I have a mind to return to Caergoth. Leaving as soon as possible and going by ship. Will you accompany me?"

"My lady princess, I would be delighted."

"Good. I'll tell my father." She realized as she said it that she meant *tell*, not *ask*. It was a good feeling. "We can sail on the morning tide."

⋊⊙⊚⊶⊙⊶⊙⊙ 🜂 ⊙⊙⊶⊙⊶⊙⊙⋉

Ankhar raised the mighty spear over his head. The green tip glowed ever more brightly, despite the sun that was just beginning to poke above the eastern horizon, casting the tall keep of Thelgaard into long shadows across the plain. The horde covered a vast ring of plains, the landscape dark with their numbers.

All awaited his command.

He knew that much of the population of the city had fled even before his army had arrived on the scene. Long files of refugees made their way south, toward Caergoth, and Ankhar had let them go—he and his army no longer killed for killing's sake.

Now the half-giant stood for a long while and admired the

325

ranks of horses and wolves and their riders, of broad-backed ogres and wing-stiff draconians, the legions of gobs and hobs extending to the far horizon in orderly lines. It was dawn, and the light of the sun glinted on the brass roof of the keep.

"Charge!" cried the Ankhar. His ordinary shout was loud as thunder, but the power of the Prince of Lies amplified its volume. As the green light pulsed from the spearhead in his hand, the commander's words were not just heard by every single one of his soldiers, no matter how far away they stood—each word was felt as a visceral impulse to work the will of their leader and his god.

The goblins surged toward the low walls of Thelgaard. Archers filled the sky with arrows that rained down upon the few men who dared to defend the city. Ogres marched forward to the beat of heavy drums that echoed through the ground and the city walls. Teams of humans rushed to the walls, scrambling up crude ladders. Brandishing swords, they swept along the battlements and dropped down the inside walls to spread out through the tangled slums.

The brigade of ogres from Lemish carried a heavy trunk as a ram and battered down the weakly manned city gates. Thousands of attackers followed them, swarming into the main avenues. Draconians scrambled up the walls and launched themselves from the heights, gliding on their wings to outflank the small bands of defenders who tried to make valiant stands.

Hoarst and the other two Thorn Knight spellcasters concentrated on the army barracks and armory, igniting the wooden structures with fireballs, blasting with lightning and ice the panicked soldiers who stampeded for safety. The killing would have been greater except Thelgaard's army was so depleted that the strongholds were already largely abandoned.

Gobs and hobs and all the other invaders rushed through the streets of Thelgaard, right up to the great keep, the castle that had stood for more than a thousand years. Its walls were high, but flying draconians seized key towers, quickly dropping ropes to their comrades swarming through the moats. Within an hour the curtain wall had been cleared, and the attack swept through the courtyards, penetrating into each barracks and stable, every corner.

The army of Ankhar was an unstoppable tide. They plundered and killed, burned and looted. Pockets of knights fought to the death, while those citizens who had lingered tried to escape and mostly died. Fierce battles raged here and there, while other parts of the city, bereft of defenders, were, gleefully looted.

Finally the attackers arrived at the great hall of Thelgaard Keep. Here the mass halted, parting ranks so that the commander could have the honor of the ultimate moment. Ankhar strode forward, stopping before the stout entry to the keep.

"Est Sudanus oth Nikkas!" he roared.

The half-giant bashed open the doors to the hall with one mighty blow of his own fist. He charged in with his gleaming green spearhead poised, ready to drive death through the heart of the lord.

The Duke of Thelgaard was already dead, the blood still draining from the cuts he had made on his own wrists.

<⊙◦⊙◦⊙◦⊙ ❀ ⊙◦⊙◦⊙◦⊙>

Captain Dayr looked back at Thelgaard Keep. The invaders had claimed the entire city in a few hours of savage assualt. Dayr and two score men had held out in the west gatehouse for a full day, watching as the rest of the city was overrun. The attackers had taunted them with word of the duke's suicide, but the forty men in the gatehouse—all knights—had inflicted grievous losses at the cost of only two dead.

Finally, as night had fallen, Dayr led the group on a bold escape. They seized horses from a corral outside the walls and rode bareback onto the plains. Some of the worgs and riders gave chase, but they were exhausted from the day of battle while the knights' horses were fresh. The knights had soon left their pursuers behind.

"Est Sularus oth Mithas," Dayr murmured, seeing the banner of the Crown torn down from the castle's highest tower.

His honor was his life, but that honor did not require him to die, not in the service of a lord who lacked even the spirit to wield a weapon in his own defense. Dayr thought bitterly of all the men who had died in the Battle of the Crossings and here because of the ignobility of the Duke of Thelgaard. The captain himself had ordered men to their death based on his master's foolish commands. It was a mistake that Dayr vowed never to repeat.

Sometimes honor required that a fighting man retreat so that he could live to fight another day.

CHAPTER THIRTY

THE IMMACULATE ARMY

Early on a cool autumn morning the whole city of Caergoth was astir. Although most of the duke's great army remained in the field, camped just south of the Garnet River, Duke Crawford had kept his personal guard, nearly a thousand knights, with him in the city. For a week those knights, and every courtier, noble, and priest had been involved with the pageantry attending the Duchess Martha's funeral.

The duke, in fact, was rather taken aback at the evidence of his late wife's popularity. For all her simplicity and faults, she apparently had struck a chord with the common people of Caergoth, who demonstrated their genuine grief. Patriarch Issel had delivered a stirring eulogy, and six of his stout clerics had borne her casket to the royal vaults, in the catacombs of Temple of Shinare below the city.

Now, at last, the funeral was over. Knights and squires bustled to prepare for an expedition. Wagons filled with freight lumbered through the streets, starting for the camp of the army some thirty miles away. Great herds of fresh horses to replace battlefield losses and cattle to feed the hungry troops were driven eastward through the city gates and out across the plains.

Finally, after an interval for one last civilized breakfast, it was time for the duke himself to depart. The thousand knights of his personal guard would escort him into the field, where he would take command of the larger force. The companies of the Ducal Guard were organized by the colors of their mounts. First came the blacks, then the chestnuts, followed by the grays, and finally the whites. Each rider was clad in gleaming armor, the silver outline of the rose visible upon every breastplate. The horses trotted in formation, as precisely as if they were leading a coronation parade. They proceeded out of the gates of Caergoth in ranks of four, proudly leading down the long, swept pavement of the King's Road.

The duke himself rode in a carriage, with Sir Marckus and Sir Reynaud on their chargers beside the open vehicle. The lord accepted the cheers of his adoring populace as he rode through the streets and out the gates, enjoying the accolades so much that it seemed considerably dull once they left the city and were left merely trundling along the road—good, paved highway though it was.

Because of that road they made very good time, and in two days they rode all the way to the crossing of the Garnet River. Here the army was camped beside one of the engineering wonders of the Solamnic Realm: the King's Bridge. The span of white marble had stood for hundreds of years, since long before the Cataclysm. Indeed, it had been erected by dwarven masons under the auspices of Istar's Kingpriest and had once been called the Kingpriest's Bridge. After the fall of that great city and the convulsions of the Age of Despair, the people of Solamnia had chosen the shorter appellation.

Lord Lorimar had erected his manor in the shadow of this bridge on the north bank of the great river, and the ruins of that once-splendid house could be glimpsed from the crossing. The duke felt his eyes drawn to the charred site, even as he shuddered in horror. Dara Lorimar had been such a beautiful woman . . . what a shame she had to die that way.

More relevant to Crawford's immediate future—and a relief to his distracted mind—was the spectacle of the great army, more than ten thousand men encamped along the south bank.

The men exploded with cheers as their lord rolled through the vast tent city.

The next day the duke led his entire army across the bridge, which was nearly a quarter mile long. At the north end, where the road started across the vast plain, he climbed one of the two watchtowers, and relished the sight of his great army flowing over the gleaming span, and forming into neatly organized columns on the north side of the river.

The Garnet River was not as great a waterway as the mighty Vingaard, which lay to the north and drained the vast swath of the plains through the port of Kalaman into the northern ocean. But the Garnet was still deep and fast-moving and bore snowmelt and rainwater from the mountains of the same name through the fertile bottomlands of Caergoth into the Strait of Ergoth. Marshy banks kept the troops away from the river's edge. Like the road itself, the bridge was paved in granite slabs, and stood as proof of the greatness of the Solamnics.

First across were the knights of the Ducal Guard on their uniformly colored horses. Next came the ranks of pikemen marching in crisp formation, the silver tips of their tall weapons glimmering like a field of diamonds. This column alone stretched more than a mile long. The pikemen were followed by legions of men armed with sword and shield, with more long ranks of those carrying crossbows. Finally the catapults and ballistae rumbled along, the great war machines pulled by straining oxen—even those ponderous beasts had been combed and brushed to a sheen, their tack polished and buckles shined to a dazzling brilliance.

Duke Crawford stood atop the bridge tower and watched the mighty column as it marched past. He allowed himself a moment of pride, reflecting that no force on all of Krynn could stand against his multitude on the battlefield. His captains saluted him, their horses prancing with heads held high. Trumpeters brayed, and festive banners and pennants snapped in the breeze.

In all, the column was more than ten miles long, each detachment formed of men loyal to him, sworn to the Oath and the Measure. They had come from Sancrist, Sanction, and Palanthas, from even farther outposts across the continent of Ansalon, but they would obey *his* orders alone. Every polished piece of equipment, each steel blade and razor-edged arrowhead, had been provided for such cause as he deemed right and proper. His great power almost made him swoon in his saddle.

"Why the glum face?" the duke asked Captain Marckus, who stood in the position of top honor on Crawford's right. "Does it not look like a splendid army?"

"Aye, lord. There is no more splendid looking army. Please forgive my melancholy—I was but reflecting that the late duchess would have been delighted by the pageantry."

"Ah, yes, the Lady Martha was always one to relish a display," the duke allowed, grimacing. Marckus was always reminding him of the last thing he wanted to remember. As a practical man, he had come to see the death of his wife—distasteful as the whole affair had been—as a blessing. Now he was free to seek a truly worthy wife!

His mind wandered to the Princess Selinda. He recalled the golden sheen of her hair, the breathtaking swell of her breasts beneath her velvet gown. Now *that* was a woman who would make a proper wife! Not only that—by virtue of her own rank, she could raise a duke to the status of a king. The duke imagined Selinda's certain delight when he communicated to her, hopefully in person, news of the great victory he was about to win. He wished she could be there to welcome him when he returned, victorious, from the field of battle—what a perfect moment!

Now, as the duke stood on the tower and watched, it took more than three hours for his army to make the crossing. In fact, he stepped back from the brink several times for refreshment, and once even enjoyed a short nap under the shade of a hand-held awning. When he awoke, his troops were still marching past! They gave a hearty cheer as he again appeared at the battlement and offered them an encouraging wave.

Impatient at last, he climbed down the many steps from the tower, mounted his charger, and started to ride away. He passed uncomfortably close to the ruined manor of Lord Lorimar—the blackened, burned structure seemed to stare ominously at him. He spurred his horse forward, cantered along the side of the great column as it advanced northward. He knew that he cut a dashing figure as he rode his stallion, trailed by a dozen or so men of his entourage.

Caergoth was going to war! He felt a twinge of nervousness, suddenly conscious that this was *real* war. The news from the east was dire. The horde of Ankhar had sacked Thelgaard. Solanthus was isolated, the duke slain. Crown and Sword had been humbled by a mere barbarian chieftain. It was time for the Knights of the Rose to set matters right. The Lord of that order, Duke Crawford of Caergoth, was just the man to command the forces of good.

The excitement of the march diminished considerably in the following days as they steadily moved northward along the road. One the second day the Garnet Mountains rose into view on the eastern horizon, but the force passed only within a dozen miles of the outlying foothills.

The great body of the infantry, the foot soldiers who were the backbone of this and every other army, plodded along stolidly in the center of the great formation. The individual units were spread out in a fan-like pattern so they could respond to a threat from either flank. A strong screen of heavy cavalry brought up the rear. The baggage train and war machines were in the middle of the infantry columns, securely protected against threat from any side.

Caergoth's outriders, his light cavalry, swept the plains ahead of his army. Soon reports began to arrive, and they were exactly as the duke had anticipated: The horde of Ankhar was heading south to meet them. The enemy, too, was closing his ranks, massing his great army into a single phalanx.

The army of Caergoth slowed as it continued north. No longer was the army spread along a ten-mile stretch of the road. Now they marched in block formations, covering a half-mile frontage. Only a small portion of the army could actually use the paved roadway. At least the catapults and other war machines, as well as the wagon trains hauling supplies, ammunition, and everything from portable smithies to huge stocks of coal, could still roll along the highway dating back to the days of the Empire.

It was when they passed the border of Southlund that they began to smell the nearby Garnet Mountains. The ruin of the city of Garnet, scene of Ankhar's first conquest, appeared like a blackened scar, and the troops grew quiet, deadly serious, as they marched past. It was only a few miles north of the devastated fortress-city and a similar distance west of the mountains that they finally got scouting reports of the army of Ankhar.

The outriders rode as close as they could, though they were driven back by sweeping charges of goblins on their worg mounts. The light cavalry of the knights exchanged battle with these lupine riders in a number of sharp skirmishes, with neither side prevailing. The duke knew his horsemen were feeling the size of the enemy, gathering information on its dispositions, its line of march, and its order of battle.

There were whole regiments of battle-hardened hobgoblins, huge swaths of ground covered by the winged draconians, and more and more goblins spilling down from the mountains.

Finally the duke called a halt. His army camped in a broad front, all units facing the north. The catapults and ballistae were positioned among the infantry, with archers dispersed along the great line. Crawford ordered his men to dig a deep, steep-walled trench more than three miles long that would defend the northern edge of his position. This ditch was lined with spiked poles, while the artillery captains drilled the catapults, studying the ranges on the field, even going so far as to stake out distance markers so that, when the enemy attacked, they would be able to shoot accurately.

The wooded slopes of the Garnet foothills anchored the right side of the line, while the vast left, where the plains allowed maneuvering room, was protected by more than a thousand knights on horseback.

A mile to the north, the barbaric warriors of Ankhar made their own camp, and the two armies spent an uneasy night staring across the gap at each others' campfires, and wondering if the morning would bring a dawn of bloodshed and death, or victory.

‹‹○◊›‹◊›‹◊›‹○◊ ✦ ◊○›‹◊›‹◊›‹◊›

Jaymes traveled south from Thelgaard, avoiding the patrols of goblins and draconions that roamed everywhere. He wended his way through the separated camps of Ankhar's army. The next morning he saw the black ranks surge forward and knew the city would fall under the onslaught of Ankhar's army.

He was unpleasantly surprised by how quickly that army moved southward after their victory. He had taken it as a matter of certainty that such a makeshift force would stay many days to plunder and pillage Thelgaard. Instead, their leader propelled them on the move again, the day after the battle.

Meanwhile, Jaymes was forced to enter the Garnet foothills for cover. He was able to slip through the forests without being detected, but the going was much slower than if he had remained on the flatlands. He followed the roughest terrain he could find, scaling rocky bluffs, plunging through tangled ravines.

Approaching the ruins of Garnet, he crossed over a ridge and caught the first glimpses of outriders—silver knights with pennants and fast horses—and knew the duke of Caergoth had brought his army into the field. Patrols from both side were sweeping into the Garnet valleys, so Jaymes found a tall hilltop, with sides too steep for horses or wolves, and climbed to the top. He looked out over the plain and saw the two great forces assembled, facing each other.

With the Sword of Lorimar over his lap and his back resting against a sun-warmed stone, Jaymes settled down to watch.

‹‹○◊›‹◊›‹◊›‹○◊ ✦ ◊○›‹◊›‹◊›‹◊›

Selinda sailed to Caergoth in the same stout galleon, the *Pride of Paladine*, which had carried her to Duke Crawford's fortress earlier in the year. The spring excursion had been so balmy and peaceful it was almost boring. Now, in the autumn, great gray mountains of water loomed on all sides, and the ship pitched and rolled violently through the whole of the ten-day voyage. When at last they arrived in the port of Caergoth, she was bedraggled, sick to her stomach, and anxious to regain her footing on solid land.

Although once again the city guard came out to salute her, the city some offered some contrast to her previous visit. Captain Powell, riding at her side, was the first to remark upon it.

"The place looks empty," he said, approvingly. "All the troops must be in the field."

"At last," Selinda agreed, knowing how reluctant Duke Crawford had been to send his men to war—even when they were so sorely needed to defend the realm. "There's something more to the odd quiet, I gather . . . the place is still in mourning."

They heard tales of the murder from the servants, as they were shown to their sumptuous guest quarters. Powell talked to the few knights, old or disabled, who had remained in their barracks as the bulk of the army went to war. Selinda chatted with several ladies of the court. They compared the versions they heard from various parties of what happened: the Assassin had struck in the early morning, slaying the duchess and leaving the duke alive.

Selinda still felt a personal responsibility for every crime that villain committed, but she had a hard time seeing Jaymes Markham as the perpetrator of this senseless crime.

Captain Powell voiced the same doubts when the two met for a quiet dinner.

"It stinks. There's not a bit of logic to the story," he said to the Princess of Palanthas. "Why would he break into a castle to slay a helpless silly fool of a duchess—begging your lady's pardon, of course."

"That's quite all right," Selinda replied. "Why, indeed?"

The more she thought about the man she had met, the man she helped to capture, and the man who had escaped from her party of knights, the more she shared Powell's view: Such a man had no motive or cause to kill a hapless innocent like the Duchess of Caergoth.

Her suspicions, growing to a certainty as she tossed in bed that night, made her sleep as fitful as during her turbulent voyage.

⊱⸱⸱⸱⸱⸱⸱⸱⊰

It was early evening as Coryn the White stalked through the camp of Caergoth's army, seeking the command tent. The knights she encountered bowed or salute, but all looked at her fearfully after she passed. She knew they called her the White Witch behind her back, and for now she was content to know she provoked their fears.

She found the duke before his tent, enjoying a savory steak served on rare and delicate china. He was dining with a half dozen of his currently favored officers. Several bottles of wine—an excellent vintage from Qualinesti, she noted idly—stood on the table.

"My lord duke," she said, ignoring the cross look upon Caergoth's face as he greeted her. "I am pleased to find you here."

"Of course, a visit from the Lady Coryn is always a welcome diversion," he said warily. "Please, will you join us for the meal?"

"Thank you, but I cannot," she replied, half-smiling at the look of relief that passed across his features. Indeed, the thought of dining with this pompous peacock was enough to put her off her appetite.

"I have been observing the camp of the enemy," she said. "I believe they are preparing to move north, perhaps as soon as tomorrow. Some of the northernmost units have already extinguished their fires and seem to be readying for a fast march."

"Ah!" crowed the duke, gesturing to his men. "It is as we suspected—the wretches have no stomach for a fight with a real army!"

"Perhaps," Coryn acknowledged. "Though I have seen no signs of fear or disquiet in the enemy camp."

"But you just said—"

"I said they were preparing to move. I said nothing about retreat. I suspect Ankhar intends further maneuvering—after all, anyone can see it would be foolish to attack you here, behind the great ditch you have created as a barrier, with all your ballistae and catapults safely sited on one side of the ditch, aimed across the plain. One thing this Ankhar has shown, my lord duke, is that he is not a dolt."

"What are you suggesting?" pressed Caergoth.

"Simply that if you know they are on the move you might consider attacking in the morning and catch the enemy unawares as they prepare to march. Come out of your entrenchments, and attack at once! If you act quickly—strike by dawn, you might seize an opportunity."

"Attack?" The duke looked at her as though she were mad. She showed no emotion, though his response made her heart fall. "We are solidly entrenched here! No, my fortifications are good, my deployments cautious. My lady Coryn, we intend to stand as a wall here and let the enemy break himself upon our rock-hard surface!"

A chorus of assenting ayes rose from his captains, though one knight—Coryn recognized him as Sir Marckus—stared down at his plate, obviously troubled.

"And what if he is marching away?" The duke posed the question, rhetorically. He was obviously thinking aloud. "Then it is my opinion that he has chosen to fall back. Therefore, he is as good as beaten!"

"My lord duke—that is not the case! He marches for some mysterious purpose. If he slips away, he will fight elsewhere."

"Ah, but my lady Coryn, you are not a tactician. He has obviously had a good look at my army and does not like what he sees! I appreciate your advice, as always, but urge you to study military strategy in your spare time. This discussion is concluded. Now, if you cannot join us for dinner, please allow me to enjoy my food while it is still at least a bit warm."

In the morning, the vast army of Caergoth watched from its camp as the enemy army turned its back on them and marched away. Coryn didn't see this—she was already gone.

CHAPTER THIRTY-ONE

SHATTERED RANKS

Jaymes stayed in his hilltop position until full darkness had descended. He watched Ankhar's formations begin to break camp at sunset, companies starting to slip away to the north or move into the Garnet foothills. The first of the horde's detachments to leave were those to the rear, so unless the duke had observers posted high in the hills—and Jaymes knew he did not—Caergoth would never guess his enemy's slow, methodical withdrawal.

Watching the barbarian army's movements, the warrior deduced there would be no battle in the morning—or at least, no battle along the lines Caergoth had planned—but that was not his concern. Jaymes had one more appointment with a duke at nightfall.

He made his way silently down through the pine forest layering the foothills, thinking about his confrontations with Thelgaard and Solanthus. In each case he had been reasonably certain he was going after the man who had ordered the death of Lorimar. But when each man had faced the swordsman's vengeance, they had pleaded their innocence convincingly enough.

That left Duke Crawford of Caergoth, the least likely suspect. Jaymes tried to figure out his motives: a Rose lord ordering the removal of another of his order. The duke was secure in the greatest city-state in the plains, the key link between Palanthas and Sanction. Perhaps he couldn't tolerate the presence of an independent-minded lord on the periphery of his domain . . . that might be why he hired assassins to kill a noble, and a beautiful young woman.

Of course, Duke Crawford, too, had wanted to marry Dara Lorimar, Jaymes recalled.

Possibly it was a mere matter of money. Jealous of du Chagne's and Rathskell's massive fortunes, the Duke of Caergoth simply might have coveted a treasure of his own.

The periphery of the duke's camp was well-marked, with pickets and bright campfires posted every fifty feet. Along the north edge was the deep ditch and hastily constructed breastwork, so the warrior elected to approach from the south. There were pickets posted everywhere, and entering the camp on foot was foolhardy. In fact, his feet were tired, and he had another idea.

He picked out a spot where three men stood around a blazing fire, a single horse tethered nearby. Jaymes walked up to them, waving his hand as he came into the glow from the fire.

"Ho, knights," he said calmly, as the three men saw him and reflexively reached for their swords.

"Who goes?" asked one, a sergeant.

"A friend," Jaymes said, still approaching at an easy pace. "I come from yonder Garnet, where those bastards up there burned me out. Looking to join up and fight," he added.

The guards relaxed a bit. "Reckon we can use another man. Let me send for Captain Reynaud," the sergeant said.

"Sure. Or you can tell me where to find him," the swordsman replied.

Something in the suggestion must have aroused suspicion. "Wait right here, stranger," the knight declared. He gestured at the great hilt of Giantsmiter, jutting into view over Jaymes' shoulder. "While you're at it, let me have a look at your blade there."

The other two pickets had sensed the leader's sudden wariness and once again placed their hands on the hilts of their swords. The warrior nodded, starting to reach for his sword.

Instead, he delivered a sharp kick to the gut of the suspicious sergeant, crumpling the fellow to the ground. With two sharp punches he bloodied the noses of the other two guards, before they could draw their weapons. Then he raced over to the horse, pulled the reins, and vaulted into the saddle.

By then the three guards were shouting, lunging after him, calling for help. Jaymes kicked his heels, and the animal took off like a shot, streaking into the darkness. The warrior lay low across the animal's neck and heard the *pffft* sounds of arrows slicing past his ear. In a few seconds he was out of range but allowed the steed to race south until the night had swallowed them.

A backward glance confirmed that the knights weren't mounting any pursuit of a lone horse thief, not when they were near ten thousand warriors of Ankhar's horde. Jaymes circled back to the ruins of Garnet at a trot, and made a solitary camp in the hollow stone frame of a house that had lost its roof to fire.

Coryn joined him there, emerging from the darkness in a twinkling of sparkles. Placing her hands on his chest, she looked at him with her eyebrows raised questioningly.

"It looks hopeless," he said bitterly. "They have the camp and the duke guarded like a sacred vault. I can't reach him inside there, but he's the one we seek. I'm certain of it now."

She sat down beside him, took one of his strong hands in both of hers. "Crawford has murdered his own wife, you know."

His eyes narrowed. "When?"

"A fortnight ago, perhaps. Claimed it was you, of course."

He spat into the darkness. "Do you have a potion . . . or something that would let me reach him? Invisibility, or something?"

Coryn shook her head. "If I did, I'm not sure I would give it to you. Even if you found out the truth, you'd never get away alive."

"Well, the duke might die tomorrow anyway—along with a *lot* of other folks."

The white wizard shook her head, black hair cascading across her face, tears welling in her eyes. "There is so much *good* in the knights," she said softly. "They're the hope of the future for Solamnia—perhaps for all the world. Why does their order attract such fools?"

"I was one of those fools, once," Jaymes said. "Listen, if you have anything that will help me, you've got to give it to me!"

"I told you—even if you made it to the duke, you'd never get out of there alive!"

He shrugged. "I don't much care."

"I believe you—I known you don't care. But *I* do," she whispered, pulling his head down, bringing his lips to hers. She was shaking as he held her close. They found solace, as so often before, in each other's arms. Their embrace lasted much longer than their passion, which carried them intertwined to restful sleep, so that they lay together in the roofless house as the stars paled and dawn slowly brightened the sky.

⋉⊙⊙⋊⊙⊙⋊⊙⊙⋊⋇⊙⊙⋊⊙⊙⋊⊙⊙⋊

"My lord—we must pursue! We cannot let Ankhar get away."

The urgent speaker was Captain Marckus. Like everyone else in the camp, he had awakened to see the enemy army had almost completely withdrawn from the battlefield. By now there was only a screen of wolf-riding goblins out there, a half mile away, and a few large regiments still marching northward beyond.

Duke Crawford shook his head, trying to be patient with the exasperating Marckus. He still trembled from the terrifying dream he had been having—his army routed, destroyed, himself spitted upon a huge, green-glowing spear. That vivid image stuck in his mind. Though his eyes were wide open, it was seared into his consciousness. Still Captain Marckus droned on.

He couldn't tell Marckus he was staying put because of a dream. He knew that the veteran Knight of the Rose would expect a more logical military explanation.

"Captain, the evil ones are fleeing before us, fearful even of our shadows. If we can break his army thus, without even the shedding of blood then is not our victory all the more sweet?"

"This is no victory, lord! It is an opportunity squandered! Who knows where they will go, what mischief they will wreak?"

"Well, they will wreak no mischief on my army today!" replied the duke smugly. He found himself wishing for a consultation, a soothing prayer from Patriarch Issel, and he regretted his decision to allow the priest to remain behind in Caergoth.

Marckus snorted, biting his tongue.

Crawford shrugged. "We offered battle here, and they declined. Captain Reynaud has scouted the nearby hills and assures me there is no danger from that direction. What more proof of our supremacy do you need? Now, I will thank you to obey your lord in this matter. Perhaps there is some area of training or discipline requiring your attention? Captain Reynaud is busy inspecting the catapults. Maybe you can see the horses are fed."

"Aye, Lord," Marckus agreed. "I am sure they are hungry."

⊱⊶⊷⊶⊷⊶❋⊷⊶⊷⊶⊷⊰

The bored sentry climbed toward his lonely perch on top of the rocky ridge, one of the lowest and westernmost of Garnet's foothills. He didn't like being stationed so far from his fellows—and their cookfires—but his captain had posted him on this ridge in the unlikely event that the enemy tried to make a flanking maneuver through the rough terrain.

Not that any army could move very fast or easily down there, he thought, looking at the tangle of rock and scrub pine in the narrow, carved valleys below, a maze of cliffs and deadfalls. Anyone could see how unlikely it was that an army would take this path.

But he was used to obeying bad orders. He settled on a sun-warmed rock, noting that it was slightly after noonday, and took out the small flask he carried in his belt pouch. There was one advantage to being out here by himself, he acknowledged. No pesky sergeants or officers were around to see him drink his fill!

He didn't hear the slightest rustle, much less the goblin that had climbed the cliff below him, quietly pulling a razor-sharp knife from a leather scabbard. By the time the lone sentry had opened his mouth to shout an alarm, the blade was slicing through his throat.

The only sound that emerged was a dying gurgle.

⊰⊹⊱⊹⊰⊹⊰❂⊱⊹⊰⊹⊱⊹⊱

The worg riders came down from the mountains in the middle of the afternoon, sweeping like a summer squall, black as oily smoke, piercing the army of Caergoth. They emerged from a series of valleys that were *behind* the long ditch, the prepared entrenchments, the carefully measured fields of fire for the catapults. The wolves roared in unison as they charged, with thousands of lupine paws pounding the ground simultaneously, and growls and snarls erupting from fanged, drooling jaws.

They struck the army in its exposed flank, which was anchored on the foothills of the Garnet Mountains. A secure area; a direction from which no army could attack—Captain Reynaud had assured the duke—after his horse had been unable to make headway into the hills.

Ankhar's army had threaded through those hills, and all the more impressive, it had done it silently over only a few hours' time The goblins and their sleek, powerful wolves bypassed the limited roads and trails that restricted the movement of knights and horses. Ankhar's army had no wagons, no war machines, no baggage except that carried by each barbaric warrior in his small kit. With that startling tactic, they negated every advantage of Caergoth's meticulous deployment, his steadfast preparation, and the expectations of his veteran officers and boldest captains.

The wolf-riders were only the first wave of the attack, but they came so suddenly and fiercely that they had spread through half the ranks before the other half even knew they were under attack. Canine jaws tore the throats of men who were looking up

344

from their afternoon chores. Horses were bitten and hamstrung in their corrals, and the great supply wagons of the baggage train were quickly put to the torch, burned by mounted goblins who didn't even slow down to admire their destructive handiwork.

Here and there a company of humans stood armed and ready, and these men formed squares of resistance, weapons and shields turned outward, valiantly defending their ground. The lupine cavalry simply gave them wide berth, leaving them for the second wave. Most of Caergoth's cavalry had been posted on his left, near the open plain. Now these knights rode toward the sound of the fighting, great waves of charging horsemen—and in the process wreaking even worse chaos through the ranks of infantry who were desperately trying to form up along the whole of the reeling front.

In the wake of the worg riders came the draconians. The reptilian warriors, more than two thousand of them who had joined at the bidding of Cornellus, appeared along the high crests of the foothills. They howled and barked, making a ghastly song of death—then they launched their assault. Though most are incapable of true flight, all draconians can glide, and they used this ability to great advantage. Spreading leathery wings, they embarked from the high ramparts, descending from the heights with terrifying speed. Even in the air they maintained formation, so that they landed in groups of one hundred or more, spreading out through the increasingly confused ranks of Caergoth's army.

They shredded the formations of pike and sword. Even in death they wrought havoc: a kapak glided down to perish on upraised spears and, dying, became a shower of acid spilling across a dozen men, blinding, choking, causing unspeakable pain. When a baaz perished it became a statue, and as it fell the killing weapon was frozen into its petrified flesh, torn from the human's hands to leave the wielder unarmed in the face of the next brutal assailant.

Goblins and hobgoblins, the great mass of Ankhar's army, came as the third wave. They poured out of the mountains in seeming infinite numbers. Their archers halted at the periphery, showering the vast camp with deadly missiles. Droves of arrows filled the sky, spilling downward over great swaths of land. In many places the brave squares of defenders, those who had seized weapon and shield and stood back to back with comrades, holding ground, were slaughtered by this deadly shower. If a few arrows went astray, wounded or killed some goblins, that was no matter—Ankhar's army had many goblins and a limitless supply of arrows.

The Thorn Knights assembled and rode forward to aid the onslaught. Sir Hoarst and his two comrades delivered a crushing meteor swarm into the midst of Caergoth's camp, barely missing the duke and his entourage. They sent hailstorms sweeping across the lines, ignited supplies with blazing fireballs, and sent powerful gusts of wind racing, which kicked up clouds of dust that blinded the defenders and further confused the situation.

Deep into their charge, the leading goblin regiments converged on the great war machines of Caergoth's army. Brave artillerists were struggling to bring these big weapons into play, pulling up the stakes that had anchored them facing to the north, wheeling the cumbersome devices around so they could face an enemy that was converging from behind. As often as not, by the time these weapons were oriented toward the east a hundred goblins had overrun the crew, butchering those men who tried to stand by their machines, setting fire to the great structures of timber and steel. One did manage to lob a few big rocks against the enemy, only to be shattered by a well-aimed lightning bolt from Sir Hoarst.

Much of the right wing of the Caergoth army was annihilated, destroyed before the men could even react to the sudden disaster. A few knights and footmen survived by fleeing south, and they never turned back. The pockets of resistance became fewer and fewer. Those groups too small to be efficiently targeted by archery were overrun by the countless goblins who hurled themselves in a rapturous frenzy at the humans.

Farther from the foothills, the ranks had had more time—the

warning of one or two minutes was enough to save a hundred lives—and here whole companies of armored knights deployed quickly under the commands of their veteran captains and sergeants-major. The duke himself fell back to safety, escorted by Captain Marckus and a small detachment of the Ducal Guard.

Two score knights rode down a regiment of goblins, leaving hundreds of the attackers dead and dying in their bloody wake. These riders pulled back, and more knights joined the first brave but now depleted unit, their horses surging around the blocks of human infantry, the footmen standing in lines and unbreakable squares while more and more horsemen collected. Gradually the rush of Ankhar's attack slowed, ebbed, and ground to a halt.

There was cause for some hope. More than half the army had survived the initial attack and had regrouped magnificently, holding a line at right angles to the position it had originally staked out. Captains shouted themselves hoarse, and as the enemy paused—even hardy goblins knew fatigue—the moment arrived.

Later, no one would remember which captain organized the decisive charge. Reynaud was there, along with several others. Most likely it was everyone, recognizing the enemy's faltering and their last opportunity. The mounted knights mustered a stirring charge between the ranks of their own infantry, companies overlapping, hundreds of horses starting at a trot, accelerating to a canter, and finally into a mad gallop.

They surged over the goblins and draconians as though they were sand formations on a beach—and clashed with the worgs, more than a thousand riders on each side. Horses and men, goblins and wolves, bit and gouged, slew and died. There was no semblance of rank or order—it was a cacophony of death, with every steed trying to keep its feet, every rider lashing out to all sides at any and every enemy who came within reach.

Inevitably in this fight, the heavy horses and their armored riders prevailed against fleet, but smaller and lighter, opponents. At first only a few worgs broke from the fight, then more of them, until at last the whole mass of Ankhar's cavalry wheeled and streamed away, racing through the broken camp, past the burning catapults and wrecked wagons. Those who could not run away fast enough were ridden down and trampled by the vengeful knights. Even the knights' horses seemed caught up in the bloodlust as, nostrils flaring and lungs heaving, they bore forward.

The three Thorn Knights stood firm for a long time, magic spells blazing and crackling against the riders, knocking Solamnic Knights from their saddles, destroying horses. But they were unable to break the great charge, and when the line of armored cavalry smashed through, Sir Hoarst teleported to a Garnet hilltop. His two fellow mages, however, were trampled and stabbed.

Now, at last, the tide seemed to have turned. The wolves and their riders fled headlong in a route the knights could not follow for very long, back toward the foothills. They sped into a narrow valley, a steep cut between two frowning cliffs. The wolves bounded and leaped and loped on the rough ground, climbing slowly up from the plain, and the knights, crowded together, came after. The Solamnics hacked at the stragglers, as the rougher ground took its toll on wolves and horses both.

At last the goblins and their canine steeds turned and made a stand, and the horsemen converged on them, packed so tightly between the two cliffs that they could barely move, they could only press ahead. The goblins dismounted, took up positions on large boulders and in narrow draws. Still the horsemen plodded on, packing into the valley, knights and their horses frantic for vengeance.

It was then that Ankhar sprang his greatest trap. The half-giant materialized atop one of the highest cliffs, hefting a huge boulder in his hands. Raising the heavy stone over his head, he cast it into the first of the tightly packed ranks of mounted knights. Two men and a horse died under that massive boulder.

That was but the beginning of a rain of death. Archers, this time the human mercenaries of Blackgaard's Brigade, appeared on the cliffs, gleefully shooting down into the pinned ranks of the horsemen. A hundred ogres, the surly brutes who had accompanied Bloodgutter from Lemish, took their place beside their chieftain and added a steady barrage of large rocks to the fray. In the press below, most of the knights could not even turn their horses around, much less make an escape from the lethal mess.

Countless boulders tumbled from the heights, crushing knights, breaking the backs and legs of terrified horses. Ankhar himself heaved over one hundred boulders. More than a thousand archers showered the knights with their arrows until it became a killing ground such as Krynn had hardly known.

At the start of the charge, a thousand proud knights rode into the valley. After an hour of slaughter, less than a hundred straggled out.

❧❧❧❧❧❧❧

"Rally to me, men! Hold the bastards here!" Sir Marckus cried, leading his charger back and forth along the line of swordsmen he had scrounged from the remnants of broken units. They were terrified, but his voice steadied them, made them remember that their best chance to live was to hold together.

"Stand and fight, man!" Marckus called, when a wild-eyed captain, one of Crawford's aides, came thundering past on a panicked steed.

"Make way!" screamed the man. "Fall back to the south! Every man for himself!"

Marckus grimaced as he turned away, but not before he saw the man fall, pierced through the back by a plunging arrow. He spared no time on regret—better to try and save the lives of those who faced the foe than to worry about the fate of those who died trying to flee.

The cause was hopeless. The entire right wing of the army had been shattered, and their most powerful striking force, the armored knights, had been lost in the foolhardy charge into the narrow valley. The barbarian half giant, Marckus knew, had outgeneraled the Duke of Caergoth at every turn.

The captain found his duke, ashen faced and trembling,

349

astride his stallion at the rear of the army. Reynaud, grim-faced and furious, was with him. Marckus glared for a moment at his fellow captain. It was Reynaud who had scouted the hills, reporting them impassable for a flanking maneuver. It was too late for recriminations—now, survival was all that mattered.

"Take the duke to safety!" ordered Marckus. "I'll lead a fighting withdrawal."

Without a word, the other captain slapped the hindquarters of the duke's horse, setting the steed to flight. Reynaud joined him, the two of them galloping southward across the plains.

Marckus did the best he could, trying to hold the men together in retreat. When the line was intact, at least each man could draw on his comrades. They battled stubbornly, giving up ground. In doing so they gave the majority of the survivors a chance at escape.

Glancing back, the captain could see the catapults and ballistae, the wealth of supplies and cargo in the great baggage train. All were overrun by goblins and draconians. The enemy swarmed around the artillery pieces, hacking at the wooden frameworks, igniting them with oil and torches. At least they wouldn't be able to turn those captured weapons against the army of Caergoth.

That was slight consolation, and the retreat continued. By late in the day, the army of Caergoth, those who remained, had left the field, and the goblins only ceased their pursuit when they were too tired to kill any more.

CHAPTER THIRTY-TWO

A NEW AGE OF WAR

Things have gone very badly." Coryn announced calmly, but Jaymes sensed disaster in the uncharacteristic way she bit her lip as she spoke.

She met him in the skeletal gatehouse of ruined Garnet. They had spent most of the day in the abandoned city, hearing the sounds of battle, seeing the smoke smudging the northern sky. Neither had wanted to go and witness the slaughter, but late in the afternoon Coryn had departed for a reconnaissance.

"So Ankhar pulled a surprise and attacked out of the hills?" Jaymes asked.

"Yes. Come, you can almost see from up here." She led him up the damaged stairway to the top of the gatehouse. Staying low, they looked across the western plains.

They could see troops streaming past. The nearest were a mile or two away from them, and all were heading south as fast as they could march. A few horses, including one that looked like the duke's proud stallion bearing a whip-wielding rider, raced among those afoot, quickly outdistancing them.

"They all have to cross the King's Bridge," Jaymes said. "If they're closely pursued, it will be a slaughter."

"Is there something we should do? Something to help?" Coryn asked, her face drawn.

"Why should we do anything?" challenged the warrior. "This isn't our fight."

"Decent men are dying out there!" snapped the wizard. "Men who are paying for their lord's hubris, his stupidity, with their lives! It isn't Duke Crawford I'm concerned about—it's those brave soldiers and their widows, their fatherless children!"

Jaymes scowled, rubbing a hand across his face, and made no reply.

"Dammit! You wait here and watch then," Coryn said contemptuously. "I have to do what I can!"

The warrior winced as though she had struck him. "I can think of one thing we could do that might be useful," he said.

"What?"

He explained his idea, and she agreed. "I'll go to the Vingaard Range. I'll see if I can find Dram—if so, I'll meet you at the bridge."

"All right."

After a fervent embrace, Coryn departed with a magical word, and Jaymes rode out onto the plain astride the horse he had stolen from the camp pickets the night before.

The scope of the disaster was immediately apparent. The swordsman fell in with the retreating army—no longer did he need to try and slip past vigilant sentries or bluff his way through checkpoints. He rode past footmen fleeing south as fast as they could run, then encountered a solitary captain, a weathered old veteran who wore the crest of the Rose, struggling to command a disorganized rear guard. The man welcomed Jaymes's arrival with an appraising look and a nod of approval.

"Help steady these lads in the middle, if you can," said the captain.

When a small group of goblins rushed them from behind Jaymes charged them singlehandedly, drawing and waving his sword—though he didn't make it flame. Even so, the gobs fell back, and his example seemed to inspire the troops, who started taunting and jeering the enemy. The pursuers kept up the pressure, staying in sight but out of arrow range as they followed the retreat.

Every once in a while, a few goblins would rush forward, and the rearguard line would fight stubbornly. By sunset they had managed to hold off the pursuit long enough that the bulk of the army could make for their distant city. All the survivors would still have to pass over the long bottleneck formed by the King's Bridge.

Jaymes and the Rose captain rode at opposite ends of the last remaining line. The makeshift brigade included men who bore crossbows. Others were armed with pikes or swords. The goblins came after, almost desultorily. The goblin strikes were usually beaten off, but on each occasion several more valiant soldiers fell.

Some worg riders and their wolves also rode forward in daring assaults. Once, Jaymes's horse reared at one of these sallies and brought its heavy forehooves down hard, crushing the skull of the leading worg. After that, the enemy cavalry stayed away.

Jaymes's leadership was of far more value than his sword in the retreat.

"Drop those pikes!" he urged at one point, seeing that the long poles wielded by some men—designed for tight ranks—were of little use now. "Pick up swords and shields. Stand fast, men!"

There were plenty of weapons available. Many of the troops, as they fled south, had simply cast aside their swords, crossbows, and shields. The rout was as chaotic as any Jaymes had ever seen.

At one point he came upon an overturned armorer's wagon. Among the litter of blades and spear shafts he spotted a crate that had burst open to reveal several small, single-handed crossbows. He took only a few seconds to dismount, pick a couple of his favorite weapons, and snatch up several quivers of the small, lethal darts that served as ammunition. With the crossbows cocked and loaded, suspended beneath his cape, he felt better.

After dusk they got a brief respite as, at last, the pursuing army seemed to be sapped by the day-long battle. The humans were tired, too—dead weary, in fact—but the knowledge that survival depended on continuing southward provided powerful motivation, kept them moving long past the point of exhaustion.

During one of these lulls the Rose officer introduced himself to Jaymes as Captain Marckus, in the service of the Duke of Caergoth.

"Where's your commander?" the swordsman asked.

"I saw him ride past, earlier," Marckus remarked dryly. "He had a good horse under him." The captain leaned over in his saddle and spat onto the ground. Then he squinted, staring at Jaymes.

"You look like you've held a command in your life," he said. "Perhaps, as I have noticed, you know how to make ordinary men stand, to give courage with a word and a look. That's not a thing that comes to many men. Tell me, were you once a knight?"

Jaymes scowled darkly. The question stung more than he had anticipated. "I did stand with the knights at Mason's Ford," he replied. "We held these bastards off over a long, bloody day."

"Fair enough," said Marckus, with a nod. He turned to ride back toward his end of the line, but his eyes lingered over the embossed hilt of Jaymes's sword, now hanging at his side. "Nice weapon," he said, before spurring his horse away.

The retreaters kept moving during the long, surprisingly cold night. The fighting faded away owing to the enemy's fatigue, and the men kept marching southward in silent ranks. No one wanted to stop—and everyone understood that to fall behind was to die.

Near dawn, gray light suffused the plains, and the mass of men waiting to cross the bridge was visible even from two miles away. In a panicked throng, terrified soldiers scrambled, begged and pleaded for a chance to move onto the long span of white stone.

When Jaymes looked to the north, he saw that the army of Ankhar had made good use of the night's rest. The goblins and other troops were refreshed, moving quickly, converging on the mass of terrified and disorganized humanity thronging at the entry to the bridge. Once again the worgs were in the lead, but now ogres and draconians were plainly visible, hastening to keep up with their mounted brethren. A company of armored men, apparently Dark Knights, rode at both flanks of the pursuing force.

The warrior rode over to Captain Marckus, who was staring at the scene. The veteran knight's mustaches drooped, and his face was lined, as though he had aged ten years overnight.

"You should go down there," Jaymes encouraged, pointing at the knot of disorder at the very terminus of the bridge. "Try to get them moving in some semblance of order—as fast as possible. They need an officer, someone to steady them. I'll try to get our boys here to make a stand and gain for the rest a chance to get across."

Marckus seemed ready to argue—no doubt he felt his place was here at the rear, facing the enemy.

"These men know you," Jaymes argued. "You wear the crest of their duke. If they obey anyone, it will be you."

The captain nodded, then offered a salute. "You're a brave man," he said.

"See you on the other side," Jaymes replied.

He put the spurs to his horse's heaving flanks and rode along before the line of swordsmen. The first rank of goblins on fleet wolves was bearing down rapidly, barely a mile away now.

"All right, lads," Jaymes called out, assuming command. "The fools still haven't learned their lesson. Let's see if we can teach them how the men of Solamnia make war."

⋉⊙⊶⊙⊷⊙⊶⊙⊛⊙⊶⊙⊷⊙⊷⊙⊷

"Chase!" roared Ankhar, striding back and forth through the increasingly ragged ranks of his mighty army.

His troops had won the great battle, he knew, but the full work was not done. If they could keep up the pressure, smash the remnants of Caergoth's army on this side of the Garnet River, his would be a victory for the ages. If not, the humans would regroup.

Unfortunately, Rib Chewer's worg riders were sadly depleted,

355

many killed or wounded, the rest worn out and spread across twenty miles of foothill and plains. Blackgaard's Dark Knights had done a great deal of killing in the early stages of the retreat, but now the huge horses were exhausted, barely capable of a staggering walk. He had two small companies of armored knights still fresh, and these were posted on the flanks of his pursuit force.

Yet Ankhar knew he was on the brink of an historic victory. If he could annihilate his enemy, the power of the knighthood would be broken across all Solamnia. The half-giant was determined to make that riverbank a killing ground.

He himself was so weary he could hardly stand, but he would not let that fatigue show.

Ankhar looked around, wishing he could have Laka's counsel, but he couldn't find her. He had told her to stay back from the fighting once it began, and her feeble legs would not allow her to keep pace with the pursuing army. Well, she would hear about the victory soon enough, and she would have to be satisfied.

"Come!" he roared, waving the emerald spearhead, the enchanted talisman of Hiddukel, over his head.

It may have been his imagination—or the bright sunlight—but it seemed the glow was not as intense as it had been at the start of the day.

✕⊶⊷⊶⊷⊶❀⊷⊶⊷⊶✕

Selinda had been restless for five days after arriving in Caergoth, but there was nothing to do but wait. For a time there had been no news. Then, yesterday, the rumors began to trickle in. She picked up from her servants and even from several courtiers of the duke's court distressing rumors of invincible enemy hordes, a crushing defeat.

She proposed to Powell that they ride out onto the plains to see what was really going on. When he had suggested, not joking, that he would clap her in chains before allowing her to ride beyond Caergoth's high walls, she had agreed to stay and wait.

Still, she sprang to her feet when she heard the first herald's cry, and she was already down in the great hall when the Duke of Caergoth came striding through the doors of his mighty keep, flanked by Captain Reynaud. The nobleman stopped, shocked and a little confused, seeing Selinda waiting for him.

"How fared the battle?" she asked.

"Oh, fine," he said. "I . . . I am so glad to see you. Can I offer you a glass of wine?"

"Aren't there more important things right now?" she asked, stunned at his nonchalance.

"None that I can think of," he said, snapping his fingers and sending a steward hurrying to the wine closet.

"I was terribly sorry to hear about the Duchess Martha," the princess said. "Her death must be awful to bear."

"These things happen," he said, shrugging. "A small thing, compared to the killing out on the plains."

"Was it a victory, then?" Selinda asked hopefully.

"Hard to say. Too soon to tell," the duke replied dismissively before taking a large gulp of the wine the steward had just handed him. "I need to see my priest," he added, "but then we'll be having dinner—something splendid, to be sure. Can you join us?"

The princess frowned but saw she wasn't going to get more information out of the duke, not right now. "Very well," she said. "Thank you. When?"

Duke Crawford didn't reply. He had already exited, heading for the temple of Shinare at a most undignified trot.

⊰⊱⊰⊱⊰⊱❀⊰⊱⊰⊱⊰⊱

Through the long, dry morning the throng made its way across the bridge in steady ranks, paced by Captain Marckus's steady voice and confident air. Jaymes and his diminishing company held the line against constant attacks. The goblins found renewed energy when they sensed the survivors were on the verge of escape.

For two hours the men of Solamnia fought a pitched battle at the north end of the long bridge. Jaymes commanded the soldiers

357

at the rear, as Marckus moved others across the span as quickly as possible. Archers in the bridge towers added to the defense, and Ankhar's troops were not able to rupture the determined front.

Finally, the rear guard was the last unit, standing in a tiny knot between the towers at the northern end. Leaving the ground littered with their dead, the pursuing goblins had fallen back slightly beyond the reach of the deadly crossbows on the bridge towers.

They waited as though to see what these last humans would do next. No need to fight and die in such close quarters, after all.

"Let us face the enemy here, men," Jaymes announced. "Stand shoulder to shoulder, and don't let them onto the bridge."

"How long must we hold out?" asked a young, wounded soldier plaintively. He looked with longing at the south shore, a quarter mile away.

"As long as it takes," Jaymes said, trying not to let his anxiety show as he glanced around. Where was Coryn? Would she find Dram and bring him back in time to help?

"Just have faith, lad," said Captain Marckus, who had come back to stand with the rear guard. "Your officers won't let any more harm come to you."

Not half a mile away, the ground was black with the gathering mass of Ankhar's army. "If they cross the bridge, there's nothing to stop them between here and Caergoth," the veteran captain muttered quietly.

"I know. I might have a plan, but I'm waiting for a wizard to get here and help out."

As they set up positions, Jaymes dismounted, sending his horse across to the other side of the bridge with a couple of wounded men lashed to the saddle. The first rank of the enemy, a line of huge hobgoblins, rushed forward with a roar.

The warrior drew the sword of Lorimar and twisted the hilt in his hands. Immediately bright blue fire erupted along the keen edge. In the face of those flames, the hobgoblins faltered.

In a flash of white smoke Coryn was there beside him. With her arrived Dram Feldspar and the two gnomes of Dungarden. They bore four stout casks.

Growling and pointing, the goblins balked again at the sudden display of magic. Soon they would deploy archers, Jaymes guessed. He gave instructions to the newcomers. Glancing at the goblins, they saw the urgency.

"So, I should have guessed. Is this your wizard?" asked Marckus, regarding the enchantress, the dwarf, and the gnomes. "Hello, Lady Coryn," he said, with a formal little bow.

"Hello Marckus," she replied. "You look spent."

"Just doing my job," he said. "I had help—from your friend, here."

"Yeah, yeah. Will one of you help me put these under the bridge?" Dram cut in. "One at each of the four northern supports."

Several knights helped lower the dwarf, supported by ropes, until he could crawl along the pillar that supported the marble slabs of the bridge. He lodged the first cask in place, then crawled out, trailing a piece of string that, he explained to Jaymes, was a refined version of their earlier fuses. "Leave it be for now," the dwarf counseled.

In short order, the rest of the casks were placed underneath the span, with the shortest fuse at the south end, increasingly longer lines toward the north. With the touch of matches, the long fuses were fired. Immediately they started to sputter and flame.

"Run!" cried Jaymes, ordering the rest of his men away. Seeing the fire dance along the fuses, they needed little urging to sprint for the south bank. Dram and the gnomes followed.

Jaymes brought up the rear, but as soon as the humans started to flee, goblins and draconians surged onto the bridge, howling. A great, painted hobgoblin led the way, waving a studded mace. The span vibrated under the pounding of hundreds of boots.

That first hob disappeared as a towering explosion lifted a whole section of the bridge into the air. Smoke and fire billowed skyward, soaring up hundreds of feet, sending shards of white marble cascading down into the Garnet River.

The subsequent explosions came in staggered sequence. Each one of the four casks of powder blasted out another portion of the bridge, and with each section a score or more of enemy warriors were blown to pieces, or hurled through the air and into the river. Many goblins were trapped on standing parts of the bridge or pinned under wreckage. Without their connecting supports, the last parts of the bridge swayed and, one by one, toppled into · the river.

When the last blast had sounded, and the smoke began to clear away, the King's Bridge was a ruin. Fully half of its length was gone.

No army would be crossing to the south of the river any time soon.

CHAPTER THIRTY-THREE

THE ROSE HAS THORNS

G o along bank! Swim! Get after them! Kill them!"
Spittle flew from Ankhar's jaw as he roared commands at the mass of his troops milling around on the north bank of the Garnet River. His frustration was so great he was trembling. Pacing in agitation, he kicked more than one slow-moving goblin so hard he broke its bones.

The smoke had drifted away by now, revealing huge gaps in the bridge that had stood for more than a dozen centuries. At least four of the vast support pillars were smoking wrecks. He didn't know how many of his troops had perished in the hellish eruptions, but certainly many hundreds. What kind of terrible magic had these cursed knights used against him? He looked around, wanting to shake an explanation out of Hoarst, but the Thorn Knight was missing.

"Move!" he bellowed, waving his spear at a group of hobgoblins hesitantly probing the marshy bank. Three of them leaped into the water and were carried downstream by the current. Flailing and splashing, they tried to return to the shore, but only one—aided by the clasping hands of his comrades—was able to reach safety. The other two went under and didn't come up.

"Wait!" The voice came to him as though from a distance,

familiar, but irritating him like a bug that wouldn't go away. "My son—wait!"

Ankhar heard the cry only after Laka had repeated it many times. He ordered his units to spread out along the bank, to seek a crossing of the Garnet River so he could continue the campaign against the shattered Solamnic Army. Finally the half giant turned to glare down at his foster mother.

"See—bridge gone!" he roared. He gestured to the long, ragged files of weary soldiers on the far bank, shuffling in the direction of Caergoth. "That army beaten—but it getting away! I must destroy!"

His frenzied anger would have driven any other member of his army into panicked retreat, but not his wizened foster-mother. Laka put a frail hand on the half-giant's great paw, and—though he wanted to brush her away—he could not ignore her insistent touch.

"Listen to prince!" the old she-hob said, shaking the rattle she had made from Duke Rathskell's head.

The eyes glowed, and the jaw spoke. Ankhar scowled at the talisman but knew that he must listen—he *had* to listen.

"Enough of blood," came the hissing commands.

"For now did fall,
"The river stands
"A fortress wall."

"But . . ." He waved his hand at the escaping Solamnic formations.

"Listen to Prince of Lies," Laka repeated. "To you, he speaks Truth. Remember: Truth!"

The half-giant rubbed his fingers across his eyes, trying to hold back the headache that was starting to throb. He hated this Truth, but he knew that his mother and their dark god must be right.

"One time before you make war without prince's blessing," Laka reminded him unnecessarily.

Indeed, Mason's Ford stuck in his memory like a thorn. On that occasion he had attacked merely because he felt the impulse to do so. He had ignored his own warriors' disorganization and fatigue and hurled his troops against a feeble defense that had, nonetheless, inflicted the only defeat Ankhar had suffered. It was a defeat that would have been avoided if he had taken the counsel of Hiddukel and Laka.

"You win so much!" his foster mother reminded him in a whisper, her eyes glowing with pride. "You shatter cities of knighthood! You break their armies. You have surrounded city of Cleft Spires—now you lay siege to it! You not need to drown army in river."

Ankhar nodded. His agitation melted away.

"You right," he said. He raised his voice, shouting to his captains—Bloodgutter, Rib Chewer, Dirtborn, Blackgaard, and the rest—who stood nervously nearby, waiting for his orders.

"Stop attack. Camp here. We rest. Enjoy spoils."

And those spoils, he admitted with some pride, were great. Not just the treasures and provisions they had gained in sacking Garnet, Thelgaard, Luinstat. No . . . his gains were greater than all that.

"Est Sudanus oth Nikkas." He murmured the phrase quietly, looking to the north and relishing the great Truth:

All that vast plain belonged to him.

⊱⊰⊱⊰⊱❀⊰⊱⊰⊱⊰

The city gates stood open, and the few knights still on duty actually flinched away from Jaymes as he rode into Caergoth at full gallop. Everywhere he saw signs of the defeat—wounded men on porches, in alleys, even stableyards. Sergeants-major shouted and cajoled. Shamefaced men—many lacking the weapons they had dropped on the long retreat—took positions on the walls, in the gatehouse. Others marched with lackluster gait but with some semblance of discipline toward the castle or other defense points.

The exhausted men were fearful of pursuit, but Jaymes knew they were safe, for now. Following the destruction of the bridge, the army of Ankhar would be stopped at the Garnet River for a long time. Dram, Sulfie, and Salty Pete were not far behind him, making their way to the city as fast as their legs could carry them. Coryn had flown to destinations of her own, riding the wings of magic.

Within the city, Jaymes paid little attention to the disorganized army as he guided the horse along the city's wide central avenue. A great plaza that had been the site of a teeming marketplace was now so empty he could cross it at full speed. The hooves of his horse clattered across the flagstones as, finally, he rode past the Temple of Shinare, with the great golden scales on the doors, and drew up before the gate of Castle Caergoth itself.

The great drawbridge was down, but several guards hurried into position to block his path. Two of them carried long halberds while the third drew his sword and stood firmly in the middle of the wooden span. Jaymes pulled his own weapon and waved it high.

"Get out of my way!" he snarled, sweeping the great weapon in a circle. "I have business with your duke!"

This proved persuasive, and the men cleared out of his path. One shouted a warning across the courtyard as Jaymes continued toward the keep, his horse stumbling and only gradually slowing.

"Guards! It's the Assassin! Take him!"

The cry came from Captain Reynaud, who stood with drawn sword before the door of the keep. His black, curling mustache quivered as he glared at the rider. Several knights emerged from a door at the side of the courtyard, but like the guards at the drawbridge they displayed a marked lack of enthusiasm.

"You men—stand fast!" barked the officer. "See that he doesn't get out of here!"

More men came running, blocking off the drawbridge. Others dropped a portcullis, closing access to the courtyards deeper in the castle complex. After a quick glance to make sure no archers were drawing a bead on his back, Jaymes dismounted smoothly.

"You returned quickly from the battle," he drawled to Reynaud, still holding the sword in one hand. "You and your boss should have stayed around for the real fighting."

The captain came forward, holding a great sword in both his hands. "Drop your weapon or die!" he challenged.

Jaymes merely laughed.

"Murderous bastard! How dare you!" spat the captain, dropping into a fighting crouch.

The man called the Assassin took the hilt of his own weapon in both hands. He twisted, and Giantsmiter flared brightly in the castle courtyard. Reynaud put up his left hand to shield his eyes, but he didn't retreat one step. He waited, his sword extended.

Jaymes advanced and took a swing. The flaming blade hissed and crackled through the air, and there was no mistaking the fear that flashed in Reynaud's eyes. Jaymes stepped closer, slashed again and again, each blow forcing his opponent back.

"Attack him, you fools!" cried the officer, gesturing to the half dozen men standing before the portcullis. They started forward cautiously, as Jaymes attacked Reynaud.

The captain turned and sprinted for the door of the keep as the other knights closed in—then backed away as Jaymes wheeled to face them, swinging the flaming sword in their direction. Unimpeded, the swordsman stalked up to heavy doors of the keep, doors Reynaud had just slammed shut.

A tremendous blow from the sword of Lorimar smote the barrier in two. Stepping through their smoldering wreckage, he found himself in the entryway of the vaulted great hall.

"You may not come here!"

These words were spoken by a cleric, a surprisingly youthful-looking man in a gold robe who stepped from a side room and held up one hand, gesturing for the warrior to stop. The cleric was handsome—but his expression was curled into a sneer of hatred.

"Get out of my way, priest," declared Jaymes. "The scales of Shinare will not protect you from this accounting!"

"Perhaps not," said the priest, the sneer curving into a cruel smile, "but my strength comes from a secret source. Stop where you are!"

The patriarch shouted words of command. Magic coursed through the hall, but Jaymes kept walking. The ring pulsed on his finger, grew warm as it absorbed the cleric's spell.

"Slay him, my prince!" cried the priest. He brought one fist down into the palm of his hand, his eyes flashing. Jaymes heard a noise and looked up, saw the ghostly image of a hammer swirling in the air above his head. That conjured weapon smashed downward then vanished as soon as it touched its intended target. Again, the ring pulsed with warmth.

"Impossible!" croaked the priest, staring in disbelief.

Jaymes took another step closer to the wide-eyed priest. "Maybe your god has taken a vacation," he said calmly.

"You dare to blaspheme—you'll pay for that heresy!"

The priest retreated into the side room. Jaymes followed, saw the man push on a panel of the wall, opening a dark passage. He ducked inside, and the secret door swished shut behind him.

Jaymes sprinted after him, splintering the wooden door with a single blow, revealing a small landing and steps leading steeply downward into darkness. His sword burned, illuminating the way. He followed quickly, descending a spiraling stair for a long way down. At the bottom he raced through a dark tunnel, hearing footsteps scuffing rapidly along in front of him.

The swordsman's fiery blade revealed a narrow passage with brick walls and frequent overhead arches of stone. These arches separated the segments of the tunnel into individual vaults. Several side passages beckoned, but Jaymes continued straight ahead, still following the footsteps.

Coming to a partially opened door, he saw it was fitted for a lock bar on both sides. Pushing through, Jaymes charged into a place where, very suddenly, he found himself groping through utter darkness. He wondered if Giantsmiter had faltered, but when he raised it up he felt the warmth of the flames against his face.

This was magical darkness, he realized, and his ring was apparently useless to dispel this effect.

A heavy blow from the sharpened corner of a solid object smashed the back of his head.

The darkness swallowed him completely.

⊱❖❀❖❀❖❀❖❀❖❀❖❀❖⊰

"Where did the bastard go?" demanded Captain Powell.

Captains Marckus and Dayr, together with a young knight named Sir Rene, rushed into the courtyard. They had all heard the urgent shouts claiming that the Assassin was on the premises.

Marckus had returned to the officers' barracks after brooding on his lord's behavior and on many other things, during the long retreat. He had been pondering his next course of action with Dayr, who was bitter about his own duke's failings, when the commotion in the courtyard had drawn their attention and brought them out.

"What has happened?" demanded the grizzled veteran.

"Reynaud claimed the Assassin came through here," Powell replied. "It looks like he shattered the door and entered the keep."

"We've got to find him—but don't kill him!" Marckus declared urgently.

Powell flashed him a look of surprise—even understanding—then nodded. "Yes, you're right."

The four knights raced into the keep to find terrified servants milling about.

"Where did he go?" asked Marckus.

"Captain Reynaud ran upstairs to find the duke," reported a doorman, pointing to a side room. "The Assassin ran in there."

"Why?" asked Powell, confused.

"He was chasing the priest back to the temple!" stammered a young maid.

"There's no temple inside the castle walls!" declared Marckus

"Patriarch Issel uses that way—it connects to Shinare's

367

temple outside the walls! There's a door in there that looks like a part of the wall, but you can see it now. The Assassin smashed it open."

The four knights raced over to the dark passage, hesitating at the top of the dark stairs. "Captains!" said Dayr. "We need to split up. Sir Rene and I will go after him in this tunnel, but the two of you should get up to the living quarters to see to the duke."

Marckus was ready to argue, but he could see the wisdom of the Crown Knight's words. "All right—get after him, and we'll get upstairs." He turned to Powell, saw the Palanthian was already moving toward the large staircase leading up from the great hall.

"Good luck!" called Marckus as Dayr and Rene ducked into the secret passage. He turned and ran after Powell.

Privately he wondered: Was he going to protect Duke Crawford?

Or to demand an explanation?

⋈⊙⋗⊙⋗⊙⋗⊙⋗🛡⊙⋗⊙⋗⊙⋗⊙⋈

Coryn drifted along the corridor of Caergoth Castle, unseen and silent. She had taken the form of a cloud of gas, the potion tingling magically in her senses, allowing her to fly, slip under doors, and evade detection. She glided swiftly as she sought her destination: the inner sanctuary of the duke himself.

She was going to have a talk with Crawford of Caergoth.

The wizard would have transported herself directly, but she did not know the precise location of his apartment, never having visited there, and that fact made any attempted teleporting very dangerous. Instead, she had appeared in the public hall of the castle, materializing to startle several servants who were sweeping the floor. They had fled, and Coryn had proceeded to float up several flights of stairs, passing galleries and parlors in her search.

Now, in this wide hallway, she probed underneath a few doors, finding mostly unused guest rooms until she noticed the chamber at the end of the hall, where a Knight of the Rose stood guard. Guessing that his presence marked her destination, she drifted past the knight, unseen, and flowed beneath the door.

Duke Crawford was alone in his bedchambers, pacing back and forth. He was wearing a dressing down of silvery silk. Coryn dispelled the magic to appear in front of the man, her white robe bright, her dark hair cascading over her shoulders, down her back.

"Hello, my lord duke," she said coldly.

"Get out of here!" Crawford squawked, paling.

"No. I came here for some answers," she replied, advancing into the luxuriously appointed chamber, which boasted multiple wardrobes, several dressing tables, and a set of tall glass doors leading onto a balcony. A massive four-poster bed with a gauzy canopy tied up above a quilted surface was at the far end.

"How dare you?" demanded the duke. "I am lord here—and I command you to leave at once!"

Coryn had been prepared to be calm and reasonable, but she felt her temper rise. Stepping towards him, she fixed her dark eyes upon his face.

"Does being lord mean that you can commit murder at will?" she snapped.

"You mean—the duchess?" he cried. "Don't be ridiculous! That was the Assassin!"

"It may have been an assassin," she said with a shrug, "but I don't believe it was Jaymes Markham."

The duke edged away from her, interposing the great bed between himself and the white wizard.

"What reason could you possibly have for killing her?" she demanded, taking another step closer, pointing an accusing finger.

"You'd never understand!" Crawford snapped. He glanced up at the large curtain over the bed, but the wizard was not distracted.

"Is this where you killed her?" she asked, indicating the huge mattress. "In the very bed she shared with you?" Trembling with rage, Coryn felt a flicker of magic spark at her finger, a lethal lightning bolt that she felt tempted to release. Angrily she shook the deadly impulse away—she wouldn't strike him down, not like that, but she wouldn't let him go, either.

He stared at her, fidgeting on the other side of the bed, as the wizard took another step nearer, stopping on her side of the large, four-posted mattress. She leaned forward, trembling with fury.

Her mind conjured the perfect spell to capture and immobilize the man. With her left hand she found a bit of spider web in one pocket. She pulled it out, chanting the simple incantation:

"Aracnis—"

She was momentarily taken aback as Crawford lunged toward a bell-rope and pulled. She tried to continue casting her web spell, but the gauzy net above the bed fell down, covering her head. Immediately the sound of her voice ceased, swallowed by magic.

The wizard recognized a spell of silence, and—though she didn't know how the duke had cast it—understood her own spell was wasted. She was even more startled when the duke dived across the bed, seized her by her wrist, and pulled her down onto the soft mattress.

She wrestled, but he was startlingly strong. Intense fury took over. A dangerous spell came into her mind, one that would burn him badly but leave him alive, but when she tried to bark the single necessary word of command, still she could make no sound.

Now, for the first time, she felt afraid. The filmy gauze shrouded them in silence—no doubt the same silence that had muffled any sounds of Lady Martha's murder. Coryn struggled, kicking and flailing. She clawed at the duke's face as he pushed her down. His fingers closed around her throat, choking her, strangling her. Her lungs strained desperately for air.

Coryn felt the world go dark.

Finally the duke released his grip. She coughed and gasped, but her violent gagging was eerily soundless under the magical silence.

Shaking her head, drawing ragged breaths, Coryn didn't have the strength to resist anymore as he lashed her wrists together with a braided cord. He tore a pillowcase and roughly gagged her, tying it around her so tightly it cut her cheeks and forced her jaws open.

Only then did Crawford rise and once more pull the bell-rope. The silence dispelled, and he chuckled, almost a giggle.

"Yes, she died right here!" the duke cried triumphantly. "You were right—it *was* me. Now I will kill you too!"

CHAPTER THIRTY-FOUR

THE GAME ROOM

Jaymes recovered consciousness. He could see again—the magical darkness had been dispelled, and he realized several torches crackled and flared in wall sconces. He was in an underground room, apparently some kind of shrine. His skull felt as though it was about to implode, and there was sticky wet blood on the back of his head.

The next thing he saw was Giantsmiter, across the room from him, upright with the tip of the great sword resting on the floor. The blade reflected the bright torchlight, and at first that was all the swordsman noticed. Only gradually did he realize a priest was here, standing with both of his hands on the hilt of the blade. Unlike the cleric Jaymes had chased down here, however, this priest was dressed in a tight-fitting cloak of red, which included a mask of the same color that concealed his identity.

The warrior's head throbbed. Trying to focus through slitted eyes, he looked around the oval-shaped chamber, which, remembering his long run down the dark tunnel, he judged to be located under the Temple of Shinare. Besides the door he had come through, several other doors led into dark passages. He saw a set of golden merchant scales in an alcove at one end. The chain supporting one balance was broken, and that half of the scale lay on the stone floor. The other half, apparently counterbalanced by nothing, swayed in the air.

"I see that my blow did not kill you—more's the pity," the priest remarked. A studded mace, gleaming with inlaid gemstones, swung from his belt. No doubt this was the weapon that had knocked Jaymes out and left his head ringing like the inside of a gong.

"What kind of temple is this?" Jaymes asked, feeling as though he were talking through a mouthful of cotton. Pushing himself up to a sitting position, he leaned his back against a damp stone wall. His hand went to his scalp, rubbing a bloody bump.

"This is the temple to my true god, the Immortal One who will soon become the master of all Solamnia."

Although the words came from behind the red mask, Jaymes was fairly certain it was the voice of the Patriarch, but this priest was not wearing the garb of Shinare. Instead, the swordsman was reminded of Hiddekel, the god of thieves and brigands.

"Hiding out in the dungeon under your regular church?" he asked.

"I serve Shinare during the day, but my true lord is the Prince of Lies," said the cleric. "I am the Nightmaster! Let Shinare collect her tolls and her tithes—I measure my wealth in the souls of men!"

"Do you serve the duke as well?"

"Let the mirror in his game room lead him!" declared the priest, with a harsh, dry laugh. "He knows that we serve the same master. He has recruited others to our cause, as well. He knows I am the Truth to him!"

The priest started to pick up the great sword then rested it on the floor again, cocking his head, listening.

"Hmm, visitors," he said calmly. "No doubt the arrival of a killer such as yourself caused some consternation in the castle."

Jaymes could hear the sounds, too—footsteps of running men, mingled with clinking armor, creaking straps. Some of the knights in the keep had finally chased him into the darkness. The sounds came closer, but the priest made no move to shut the door.

Moments later, two knights charged into the secret shrine, as the cleric held up a commanding hand.

"Halt!" he cried, and both running men froze, as though their feet were stuck to the stone floor. Magic tingled in the air.

Jaymes recognized the two—one was Sir Dayr, formerly a captain in the service of the Duke of Thelgaard, and the other was Sir Rene, who had commanded the defense of Mason's Ford. They glared at the masked cleric and struggled but could not budge.

The warrior's head throbbed, and he leaned back against the wall, trying to marshal some strength.

"By Joli—who in the Abyss are you?" demanded Dayr, waving his sword at the masked priest.

"He wants to be called the Nightmaster," Jaymes said wearily.

"I *am* the Nightmaster!" the cleric insisted.

"It seems the duke and one or two of his cronies are secretly working on behalf of the Prince of Lies," the warrior explained. His vision had cleared. He flexed his fingers, feeling strength slowly return.

"What do you mean—hey, that's the Assassin!" gasped Dayr, finally noticing the bleeding swordsman.

"Correct!" crowed the priest. "Now he will meet his due justice on the weapon he has used to such ill effect!"

With visible effort the Nightmaster lifted the heavy blade, taking a step toward Jaymes. He twisted his hands on the hilt, but the familiar fire did not burst forth from Giantsmiter. Shaking his head, the priest muttered in disgust. "The steel will slip into your belly cold as well as hot," he growled, advancing another step.

Jaymes struggled to reach under his cape. The two small crossbows he had picked up on the battlefield had been jabbing him in the belly. His right hand closed around the handle of one and, grimacing, he pulled it out. The trigger was cocked, the steel tip aimed at the front of the red silk robe.

The Nightmaster lunged, driving the sword downward, but the bolt from the crossbow flew much faster through the air to punch through his robe, through his skin. With a strangled gasp the man slumped to his knees, spilling the big sword at Jaymes's feet with a resounding clang. The priest clutched frantically at the wound, but his fingers couldn't get a grip on the tail of the deadly metal dart, and he uttered a long sigh as he toppled sideways to the floor.

With the Nightmaster's death, the spell binding the two knights was broken, and they both stumbled forward, toward the sword that lay just beyond Jaymes's boots.

By now the second crossbow was in the warrior's hand, leveled at Captain Dayr. "No! Stop right there," the warrior said.

Eyes narrowed, the Knight of the Crown halted, watching warily as Jaymes pushed himself to his feet. The warrior almost blacked out from the surge of pain he felt, but he growled, reached down, and picked up the sword. He slid the weapon into his empty scabbard, keeping the crossbow leveled at the knights.

"You won't get away this time, you know—this whole city knows you're here," the captain warned him.

"I'm not trying to get away," Jaymes replied. He limped to the door, keeping the crossbow trained on the two knights. Backing out of the shrine, he slammed the door shut and dropped the bar into place.

They pounded and shouted as he limped into the darkness, but Jaymes knew it would take them a long time to break the door down.

⊱✦⊰

Coryn could hear again. The only noise, at first, was her own strained breathing through flaring nostrils—the tight cloth gag not only had prevented her from speaking, it made it almost impossible to breathe through her mouth.

"Come with me," ordered the nobleman, jerking the wizard to her feet by her bound wrists. She tugged angrily against him and he abruptly punched her on the cheek, knocking her off the bed and onto the floor. Her head spun, and she tasted fresh blood as he lifted her by her bonds again. This time she stumblingly maintained her balance, leaning weakly against one bedpost.

Dragging her behind him, the duke started across the room. "Guard!" he called, as he approached the door.

"Yes, my lord duke?"

"Go to the kitchen—tell them I want my tea delivered to the game room! Have Captain Reynaud bring it."

"Right away, lord."

The young sentry clomped away. As soon as the sounds faded, the duke opened the door, and pulled Coryn out into the hall. There were no other people in sight, as he prodded her along the corridor in a different direction. She felt the tip of a knife press against the small of her back.

"This is the same blade that cut the Duchess Martha's throat," the duke calmly. "It was not very hard to kill her, you know, and it won't be very hard to kill you."

Coryn said nothing. The duke took the lead, pulling on the rope. She lurched along, the knots cutting into her wrists. She tried to bite through the gag without success. She couldn't talk, couldn't move her hands—couldn't wield her magic. He was in front of her now, and she could see the knife, an ornately jeweled dagger, in his hand. Her anger mingled with a growing sense of helplessness.

Crawford stopped and opened a door, pushing her into a large, wood-paneled room. There was a table in the middle draped with green cloth, and as she stumbled against the table she saw that it was covered with hundreds of miniature soldiers, painted and poised in martial action. A battle was in progress, though she had inadvertently knocked down a good number of the tiny soldiers.

Duke Crawford didn't seem to care. Instead, with another sudden shove, he sent her sprawling against the wall. Her head banged on the stones. As she slumped to the floor he pulled open a side door, revealing an alcove. There was nobody else in there, but she was vaguely surprised to hear him speaking.

"My lord? My lord!" said Crawford. "I have the White Witch—she is bound and gagged, but alive—at least, for the moment!"

Jaymes raced down the corridor, holding his sword in both hands. He had retraced his steps out of the hidden tunnel and the secret temple, emerging back through the shattered panel into the great hall of Caergoth keep. There he scattered a dozen servants and started onto the stairs leading up to the duke's quarters.

Now he heard someone coming and ducked into a side door, watching as a young knight hurried past. When that man headed down a nearby stairway, the warrior ran in the direction the knight had come from. He climbed another flight of stairs, darted around a corner, and halted suddenly in front of a pair of veteran, stern-faced knights.

Jaymes froze, his sword ready, though not yet aflame. The two knight captains glared at him coldly. Eyes narrowing, the warrior recognized one of the officers, then the other.

"Captain Powell," he said tersely. "I sincerely hoped never to see you again."

"I am sure of that," said the Knight of the Rose, "after you killed a good, loyal knight, escaping from me."

"And Captain Marckus." Jaymes nodded coolly to the other knight. "I am glad to see you survived the battle at the bridge."

"Yourself, as well," the grizzled officer admitted grudgingly. At Powell's puzzled look, he explained. "This man held the rear-guard together all the way to the bridge. Then he and a dwarf, with some help from the White Witch, destroyed the bridge before the enemy could cross the span and ravage our retreat.

"I just left two of your comrades—Captain Dayr and Sir Rene—down in the temple of Hiddukel, only a few minutes ago. I hasten to add that I left them alive," Jaymes said.

"What temple of Hiddukel?" demanded Marckus. "Here? In Caergoth?"

"Right under the Temple of Shinare. It seems the Patriarch was working nights, serving the Prince of Lies. I *didn't* leave him alive, however," the warrior explained, still holding his sword warily. "When you go down there and remove the Nightmaster's mask from his body, I think you'll see a distinct resemblance to

Patriarch Issel. He's the one who persuaded the duke to kill his wife."

"How dare you utter such an accusation!" declared Sir Marckus. "You're a brave enough fighter—I'll give you that—but I won't have you slandering a Lord of the Rose!" His hand tightened around the hilt of his sword as he stepped forward.

"Lord?" spat Jaymes, contemptuously. "I'm only slandering killers and cowards!" He glared at Powell. "That knight I killed? He had been sent to slit my throat, to make sure I never made it to Palanthas alive."

"Do you believe this villain?" Marckus angrily asked his comrade, though his eyes never left the swordsman.

"Perhaps I do. It's possible," Powell acknowledged in a low voice.

"Listen! It makes more sense than me sneaking in here to kill the duchess, while leaving the duke alone," Jaymes said. "Of course, you'll believe only what you want to believe . . ."

Captain Powell held up a hand. "No, I have been rethinking many of my beliefs. So has the Princess Selinda. We happen to think you may be telling the truth." He glanced at his fellow officer. "Marckus, you were the first one on the scene after the duchess was slain, were you not?"

"Aye," declared the grizzled veteran. His eyes, cold and hard, never left Jaymes's face.

"Did you see any burned fabric—any evidence of a fire around the wound? Was the cut caused by a huge sword such as the one wielded by this man?"

"No, I'd have to say the wound was caused by a knife, not a sword. There was no sign of fire. Nor were there any witnesses, though the duke claimed the Assassin fled along the top of the wall. I did think it strange that none of the guards spotted the culprit."

"Let's go have a talk with the duke," Jaymes suggested. "See what he has to say about all this."

"I won't let you near him—not while you're carrying that blade!" Marckus declared hotly.

The swordsman thought for a moment, his eyes shifting from one captain to the other. After a long pause, he sheathed the weapon then unhooked the scabbard from his belt.

"I expect this back," he said, before handing it to the surprised officers.

"I'll make no promises," Marckus said, as Powell took Giantsmiter. "But if you are telling the truth . . ."

"Wait," said Powell. Almost apologetically, he leaned forward, patted the swordsman's waist, felt the outlines of the two crossbows. "I remember you carried a little surprise under there. We better take those, too."

The two captains, carrying their own swords, flanked the disarmed Jaymes as they hurried down the hall to an ornate door. The portal was ajar, so Powell knocked, then stuck his head into the room.

"He's not here!" he said.

"I think," Marckus said, very slowly, "I might know where we can find him."

‹‹◦◉◦‹◦◉‹◦❀◦◉◦◦◉◦◦◉◦›

Dram Feldspar hopped down from the supply wagon as it rolled through the gate of Castle Caergoth. He had secured transport from the frightened teamster by standing in the road and threatening to chop the wagon's wheels off with his axe if the man refused.

Sulfie and Salty Pete were beside him, and now they jumped to the ground and rushed after him through the doors that lay in pieces just inside the hall of the keep. From the charred, broken planking, the dwarf suspected Jaymes had preceded them.

"Up here," the dwarf shouted, indicating a vast staircase rising to upper floors. "I think our boy's gonna need some help."

Axe in hand, he started up the stairs, the gnomes panting after. He reached the first landing, looked to the right and left into a pair of ornately decorated corridors. Each had crystal chandeliers, gilt-lined columns, plush red carpeting. Taking a guess, he jogged to the left down a long hallway lined with doors.

"You—hey you, dwarf!" cried a woman, coming into view down a side hallway. "Tarry a moment."

He turned in surprise. "Do I know you?" he asked the person, obviously a noblewoman, who was advancing toward him, considering he was an intruder wielding an axe (not to mention accompanied by two out-of-breath gnomes, who looked slightly mad). Her long hair was golden, her face proud, sublimely beautiful.

"No—but I've seen you before," she replied. "Here, in Caergoth, I watched you in the Gnome Ghetto—when you and the man they call the Assassin—the man you call Jaymes—escaped—with Coryn's help. You're his friend, are you not?"

"Might be." Dram glared, still suspicious. "Who in Reorx's foundry are you?"

"I'm the Princess of Palanthas," said the lady, "and I'd like to help you."

"How?"

"Well," she said, her hands on her hips, "you're looking for Jaymes and the duke, aren't you?"

"Yes," Dram admitted.

"For starters, you're in the wrong place. This is the guest wing—the residential quarters are over there."

"Is that so?" demanded the dwarf, with a confused scowl. "Why should I believe you?"

"I'm as interested in the truth as you are," said the princess. "Stop arguing. We don't have much time. Come with me."

She started along the corridor, with the gnomes shrugging their shoulders and following her at a brisk pace. Shaking his head in exasperation, Dram joined in the race.

❦

"Captain Marckus! Captain Powell!"

"Yes—Reynaud? What is it?" said Marckus.

They were escorting Jaymes toward the door of the duke's game room, when the other officer approached them at a run.

"I have a message for Captain Powell—the princess needs

you right away!" Reynaud said to Powell. "She's in the guest wing and said to tell you it's urgent! I'll take over here."

"All right. Keep an eye on the prisoner," Powell said, his thoughts immediately on the safety of his noble charge.

He rushed down the corridor and turned the corner, as Reynaud took up a flanking position behind Jaymes.

"We're on our way to the game room," said Marckus, warily eyeing Reynaud. "We're going to talk to the duke."

Another dozen steps brought them to that chamber, and Marckus reached out to open the door. He didn't see the knife in Reynaud's hand, though he felt the steel blade stab into his back.

The veteran captain turned to protest and slumped to the floor. The last thing Marckus saw before his world went black was Reynaud pushing Jaymes Markham into the game room, following the prisoner inside, and slamming the door behind him.

CHAPTER THIRTY-FIVE

LORD OF THE ROSE

These are the rooms of the duke's residence, in this wing," Selinda told Dram, gesturing to a long, high hallway paneled in dark wood. "His private apartments are down there."

The dwarf and the princess, with the gnomes hurrying along behind, trotted down the castle corridor. Dram, his axe ready, looked alertly to the left and right, still uncertain if he could trust this woman. Just as they turned into the passage, a grizzled knight of Solamnia with the epaulets of a captain lunged into their path. The dwarf instantly recognized the officer whose company had discovered the companions in the apple grove, the very knight who had arrested Jaymes Markham. The man's sword was out, and he advanced on the dwarf with a murderous glare.

"Thank the gods I found you, Princess!" cried Captain Powell, "Get away from her, you scoundrel!"

The knight closed in without waiting for a reply. Dram raised his axe and adopted a fighting crouch, ready to draw blood.

"Captain Powell—wait!" cried Selinda. The woman stepped between the two glaring combatants.

"Don't be fooled, lady!" cried the captain. "It's the same dwarf as accompanied the Assassin! They're in this together! His comrade is in the castle, already under guard—let me take him, now!"

"No! I already know that Markham is here, too!" she declared. "We're going to look for him now—and I don't believe he's an Assassin, any more than I believe you're the master of the thieves' guild!"

"What! Wait. . . ." The captain glowered, feeling uncertain. "Didn't you send for help . . . say you needed me urgently?"

"Certainly not," she replied. "I've been pacing around like a caged animal, until I finally decided I needed to do something. I encountered Dram—and we are going to see the duke together."

She frowned, suddenly. "Who told you I needed help?"

"Captain Reynaud." Powell's face darkened. He spun on his heel. "Come on!" he shouted, starting off at a run.

Dram and Selinda sprinted after, ignoring Sulfie's plaintive cries to "Wait up!" The trio raced to the end of the corridor, turning into a dark-walled hall leading to the ducal apartment.

"By Joli—no!" shouted the captain. He sprinted ahead to kneel beside a wounded, motionless man. "Marck!" he cried.

It was Captain Marckus, who lay on the floor outside the game room, bleeding profusely from a wound to his back.

Selinda also rushed to kneel and touch the man's pallid forehead. "He's alive, but barely," the princess said grimly.

Powell glanced at Selinda and Dram, who had joined them. "Either the Assassin did this, or. . . ."

"Stop blaming everything on Jaymes," said the dwarf angrily. "Can't you figure it out?"

"It's Reynaud!" Selinda said.

"Yes!" gasped Marckus. His eyes opened, glowing with a martial spark kindled by fresh outrage. "The traitor. . . ."

"Don't talk," the princess whispered. "We'll get a priest, a healer."

Dram's fingers tightened around the haft of his axe as he scrutinized the nearby door. It was banded with iron, made of stout oak timbers. Meanwhile, with Selinda's help, Powell rolled his fellow captain onto his side as gently as possible. The Palanthian tore a strip from his own shirt to stanch the bleeding.

Marckus extended an arm toward the stout door. "In there. . . ." he croaked.

"Your friend is in there too," Captain Powell said grimly, glancing at the dwarf. "If he's still alive."

Dram hurled himself against the portal but fell back and tumbled to the floor. The dwarf raised his axe to chop at it, but he was stopped by Sulfie, who stumbled up to him, gasping.

"What?" he demanded.

"Your axe . . . will take too long," she panted.

"Do you have any bright ideas?" He shook her off, spread his legs, prepared for a mighty blow.

"Pete . . . he's got a little container of the compound."

While the second gnome came staggering up from one direction, burdened by the weight of his backpack, four more knights raced into view, coming up the stairs from the great hall.

"One of you—get a cleric!" Selinda ordered. "One who knows some healing magic!" Immediately two of the knights turned and raced back down the stairs. Two knelt beside Marckus.

"Let's get him away from here, around that corner," Dram suggested. The four knights and the dwarf carried the wounded man away from the door. They set him down on a plush rug that must have cost a thousand steel in some eastern market.

The two newcomers identified themselves as Sir Rene and Captain Dayr and said they had made their way back to the castle after finding a passage up from the subterranean chambers beneath the Temple of Shinare. They shocked the others with their tale of a secret shrine located just outside the walls of Castle Caergoth.

"Temple to the Prince of Lies—here?" Selinda exclaimed in disbelief.

"Worse. It sounds as though the duke himself and perhaps one or two others have been corrupted," explained Dayr. "The priest was gloating—had us all dead to rights. Till the Assassin pulled out a little crossbow and shot him."

"Reynaud has fooled us all, serving this Prince of Lies," Powell said, his face dark with certainty.

"The army. . . " Marckus said weakly. "Reynaud betrayed the army . . . on the plains."

"Well, let's get after the bastard, then," said Dram.

They returned to the duke's room. Salty Pete knelt at the door, carefully arranging a small cask. When he extended the fuse and brought out a large, sulfir-tipped match, Dram backed away.

"First, though," the dwarf said to the lady and the knights backing away with him. "You might want to cover your ears."

⊰✧⊰✧⊰✧⊱✿⊰✧⊱✧⊱✧⊱

Coryn was choking on the gag the duke had twisted around her jaw. Jaymes was flat on his back, struck hard by a blow from Reynaud's mailed fist. His head throbbed, and he tried desperately to clear his vision, but all he could see was the foggy outline of the game room and the four people in the room.

"Shall I kill him now?" Reynaud asked his duke, standing over his prone prisoner, triumphantly clutching Giantsmiter.

"No! Not so fast! Let us satisfy his curiosity first!" gloated Crawford.

"Hurry, then," the captain snapped. "I'm eager to wet this blade with his blood!" Sir Reynaud twisted the hilt of Giantsmiter but snarled in frustration when the blade refused to flame. The captain angrily waved the blade close to the warrior's face, almost cutting him.

"Lorimar!" Jaymes gasped, trying to focus through his pain on the face of the smiling duke. "Why did you have him killed?"

The duke's answer astonished him.

"I didn't! It wasn't me!"

Coryn groaned through her gag, shaking her head in disbelief. Jaymes drew a slow, ragged breath. Reynaud, though he watched the warrior carefully, made no further attack.

Crawford continued to talk.

"Of course, I wasn't sad when he was killed. I was a little sad about his daughter—she was a tempting morsel! I would have married her in a minute. Such a loss, that was. Really, a waste, but

385

there are other wenches who know how to decorate a bedroom. The late Lady Martha wasn't bad in that respect—my next wife, I vow, will be much better!"

The duke turned to the small closet in the side of the room. Jaymes spotted a mirror on the wall in the alcove, and Crawford peered into the crystal glass when he spoke next.

"My lord? I have them both here. Should I kill them now?"

All the warrior could see was a reflection of the room in the crystal mirror. Apparently the duke was disappointed, for he leaned close and stared earnestly.

"My lord?" he repeated. "Are you there?"

Crawford turned back to his prisoners, his expression strange. "I admit, it was a good thing, for me, that Lorimar died. That made me the only Lord of the Rose!" His expression turned wistful. "Of course, I didn't obtain the green diamonds, but I could burn the Compact of Freedom! I did so right here, in this room!"

Suddenly, a stunning blast rocked the chamber. Fire and smoke poured in as the door burst, pieces smashing into the gaming table and hurling against the walls. The heaviest section of the panel tumbled sideways, and caught Reynaud in the back, knocking him down. Coryn was also thrown to the floor. The duke staggered out of his alcove, blinking, waving his hands to clear away the smoke that billowed everywhere.

Jaymes, still on his back, had been sheltered from the blast by the heavy table. He pushed himself to a sitting position. Head pounding, ears ringing, he staggered to his feet and stepped over to Reynaud. The traitorous captain was trying to rise to his hands and knees, but Jaymes gave him a swift, hard kick.

The sword Giantsmiter lay on the floor. Jaymes picked the weapon up, stabbed Reynaud, and turned his attention to the duke.

Crawford was staring fearfully at him. As Jaymes took a step toward him, the duke ducked back into his alcove, pulling the door shut. But this was no iron-enforced barrier—it was a mere panel of pine boards, and the warrior slashed it to splinters with one blow.

Jaymes followed the duke as he backed against a wall, vaguely aware of people spilling into the room behind him.

Someone, a woman's voice, shouted "Coryn!"

"My lord!" the duke was crying, banging on the mirror—which had cracked from the force of the blast. "Help me!"

Crawford met only his own crazed expression—and saw the approaching warrior. He turned as Jaymes reached him. The warrior pressed the duke against the wall, holding Giantsmiter so that the tip of his sword pricked the duke's skin above his heart.

"The green diamonds—they're why you killed Lorimar, aren't they?" he growled. "Tell me, why did you have him killed!"

"I'm telling the truth—I didn't do it!" pleaded the duke, almost sobbing.

"Who, then? Who stole the diamonds?" The sword eased a fraction, though blood stained the duke's dressing gown.

"It was Bakkard du Chagne! The Lord Regent has them—he is making a crown for his daughter! He intends to make her queen of Solamnia!"

"Bakkard du Chagne?" Jaymes's head ached profoundly. "How did he get the diamonds?"

"Because the assassins were *his* agents! He sent them! *He* ordered the death of Lorimar!"

"Why? Why did you help him?" the swordsman said. "You are still trying to help him."

"He's my lord! And I'm going to marry his daughter—the princess!" Crawford exclaimed frantically. "That's our agreement. Then I'll get to be the new king! Listen, you're a good man. I could make you my captain—my captain-general! Please, don't hurt me!"

Jaymes snorted. "You and Reynaud left good men—lots of good men—on the battlefield to die. Every one a better man than you."

"I had to get away!" croaked the duke. "I wanted to live! I still want to live! Please!"

"Too bad," replied the warrior.

The tip of Giantsmiter slipped through skin and flesh, slid between two ribs, and cut through the arteries around his heart.

Duke Crawford died very quickly.

Jaymes let him fall into the spreading pool of his own blood.

◦⊶⊙⊶⊙⊶⊙⊙◉⊙⊙⊶⊙⊶⊙⊶

When the warrior emerged from the alcove, Captain Marckus was stretched on the gaming table, and a priest of Kiri-Jolith—panting and out of breath—was administering a healing spell. The duke's miniature armies had been unceremoniously swept onto the floor.

Coryn was sitting in a chair, rubbing her wrists. Her gag and bonds had been removed by Selinda and Captain Powell.

Dram and the two gnomes rushed up the Jaymes, who had sheathed his sword. One gnome hugged each of the warrior's legs, and even the gruff dwarf looked a little relieved and happy.

"Glad to see you're all right," he growled.

"You timed it a little close," Jaymes replied, clasping his companion's hand with both of his.

"I offer my apologies," Captain Powell said, bowing stiffly to Jaymes, then to his princess. "And gratitude to you, my lady. If you had let me hang him when I wanted to, I would have made a grievous mistake, and a great injustice would have been done."

"Enough of that. We are still in the middle of a grave crisis," snapped Selinda.

"Yes," agreed Captain Dayr. "All the dukes are dead, and the three orders are in dissarray. An army of barbarians is gathered on the plains—and already has defeated the forces of Sword, Crown, and Rose."

"We need a leader who can lead us against Ankhar. Someone who has proven his worth in battle," Sir Rene said thoughtfully. "Someone who can command all the orders of the knighthood."

"Yes. It must be someone we can all serve—not just the captains, but the men in the line," said Captain Powell bluntly, staring at Jaymes challengingly. "Someone who has not been tainted by all this madness. In short, Jaymes, we need you."

"Are you all crazy?" asked the warrior, shaking his head dismissively. "Is this more of your magic?" he asked Coryn.

"No," she said, somewhat ruefully. "This is not my doing, though I can't help but agree."

Marckus waved a hand, ignoring the protests of the priest urging him to stay calm. Yet his voice was strong. "The men will follow you . . . they know you are the one who saved the army, at King's Bridge."

"You don't belong to any of the orders," Selinda said, "but in your own way you follow the Code and the Measure, and you know its power."

"Est Sularus oth Mithas?" Jaymes murmured in disbelief.

"You shall become the Lord of no Sign." Coryn looked at him frankly, her hands on her hips. Her face was smudged with smoke, her black hair was in disarray. Then, as ever, she looked very beautiful. "Just as the prophecy foretold . . ."

"Prophecy?" the warrior shot back skeptically. "That myth spread by hedge wizards and beer-pot witch-doctors! You know as well as I do what I think of that prophecy. Dara Lorimar herself though it was ridiculous when people predicted her as the Princess of the Plains. It's even more of a joke, with me as a lord!"

"The common people, even many of the knights, believe the prophecy," said the white wizard, "and they will accept you. That is what is important now. The princess and these captains, are right: You're the only one who might be able to unit and command this army, bring all three orders together to stand against Ankhar."

She glared at him as if daring him to argue. She lowered her voice. "Or would you rather Lord Regent du Chagne appoint someone else?"

He blinked, realizing that she must have heard what the duke had told him, seconds before he died. "No. I don't want that bastard to appoint anyone," he hissed.

"What?" asked Selinda, not quite certain of what she had heard.

Jaymes turned to say something to her, but Coryn grabbed his arm and gave him a sharp look.

"Later," said Coryn.

Jaymes turned to Dram, holding up his arms in frustration. The dwarf just chuckled. "Ironic, ain't it?" he asked with a wink.

The warrior's head ached worse than ever. He sat down, as Captain Dayr and Sir Rene dragged the duke's body out of the closet and dumped it unceremoniously next to Reynaud's.

Coryn rose and looked around. After a cursory inspection of the game room, she went into the duke's alcove, stepping around the pool of fresh blood. She emerged holding a long box made of shiny, dark wood.

"I recognize this chest. It was stored in Lord Lorimar's strongbox," Coryn said. "I saw him put the compact and the green diamonds in this box."

She set it on the table. It was locked, but a touch of her finger and a murmured word of magic popped it open.

"The stones are gone—but now I think I know where they are," she added, flashing a warning look to Jaymes. He nodded.

"The Compact of Freedom?" he asked.

The white wizard shook her head. "I heard the late, unlamented duke claim he burned it, and I'm sure he did—at the first opportunity. There *is* one thing. Something still left, from Lorimar's legacy."

She pulled out a white cloth. "For you, Jaymes," she said, handing the silken bundle to Selinda. "I think the princess should bestow it on you."

The Princess of Palanthas drew out the long pennant. It was a war banner, white, with several emblems in bright golden thread.

"Crown, Sword, and Rose, on one banner," Selinda said in wonder. "As in the days of the old Empire."

The princess bowed slightly and extended the banner to Jaymes, who took it with a grudging expression.

"Raise it over your head," the princess said encouragingly. "Lead the Army of Three Signs into the field against the foe."

⊱⊶⊙⊷⊶⊙⊷⊶⊙❀⊙⊶⊷⊙⊶⊷⊙⊶⊰

Bakkard du Chagne's mirror was dark. His four pawns, the lords he had raised to great heights, were dead. Lorimar had been slain at his command and the other three were destroyed by Lorimar's avenger.

Du Chagne had seen all that had transpired in the duke's game room, and he knew that his most closely held secret had been revealed to two important enemies: Jaymes and Coryn.

Action was required, but he was temporarily out of tricks. The mirror in Thelgaard was smashed, broken by the barbarian horde, and Caergoth's, cracked and damaged, was in the hands of his enemies. As to the mirror in Solanthus, the lord regent had no contact there—the silly slut of a duchess used it mainly for primping.

He was not a man given to violent outbursts, but he suddenly, impulsively, smashed his fist into the glass, shattering it and bloodying his knuckles.

⊱⊶⊙⊷⊶⊙⊷⊶⊙❀⊙⊶⊷⊙⊶⊷⊙⊶⊰

Coryn watched as the Army of Solamnia, under the Banner of Three Signs—Jaymes Markham's banner, now—marched out of Caergoth. The troops, as she had predicted, had rallied enthusiastically to a new leader hailed by their veteran captains as the Lord of No Sign. Knights had rushed from barracks and rooming houses, survivors of earlier battles had their morale lifted, and recruits had come from all quarters of the city to swell the ranks again.

Now the vast columns of the new army were leaving the city and advancing eastward along the King's Road. They were prepared to stand against the horde of Ankhar, encouraged by reports that the horde had not yet ventured south of the Garnet River. Cold winds blew from the south, and perhaps this stalemate would last through the winter, but none doubted the campaigning season would bring honor and victory to the knighthood.

The white wizard stood atop the city gatehouse tower, watching the marching soldiers accompanied by drummers, pipes, and the rousing cheers of the populace. Horses pranced, chariots rumbled, and newly built catapults rolled toward the battlefield. In the pageantry of the march, the legacy of recent defeats—and the ignominious deaths of the dukes—seemed to vanish in the wind.

Jaymes Markham cut a dashing figure at the head of the army. He wore a helm of gleaming silver, marked by a pair of curving bull's horns. The people shouted as he rode past, and he needed an escort of knights on each side to prevent them from rushing forward just in the hope of touching his boot, his leg, his horse. Coryn smiled wryly, thinking what a contrast the sight was to Jaymes the Assassin—though she had always known his destiny.

She looked over to a section of wall where Lady Selinda was smilling and waving to the army commander as he rode past. The princess, with her royal bearing, her golden hair, her supreme beauty and confidence, had grown into a leader as much as Jaymes. When the people were not cheering Jaymes, they shouted their accolades toward her. Coryn felt that uncomfortable flash of jealousy, which momentarily brought tears to her eyes.

Lady Selinda was blissfully in the dark about her father. When she learned the truth, she might yet lose her smile.

Coryn turned away, but not before she spotted Jaymes waving back at the Princess of Palanthas. The crowd also saw the eyes of the princess and the Lord of No Sign meet, and their cheers increased, soaring up from the walled city, swelling into the sky, through the heavens. Indeed, it seemed, across all of Solamnia.

Unable to watch any longer, the white wizard disappeared.

JEAN RABE

THE STONETELLERS

"Jean Rabe is adept at weaving a web of deceit and lies, mixed with adventure, magic, and mystery."
—sffworld.com on *Betrayal*

Jean Rabe returns to the DRAGONLANCE® world with a tale of slavery, rebellion, and the struggle for freedom.

VOLUME ONE
THE REBELLION

After decades of service, nature has dealt the goblins a stroke of luck. Earthquakes strike the Dark Knights' camp and mines, crippling the Knights and giving the goblins their best chance to escape. But their freedom will not be easy to win.

August 2007

VOLUME TWO
DEATH MARCH

The escaped slaves—led by the hobgoblin Direfang—embark on a journey fraught with danger as they leave Neraka to cross the ocean and enter the Qualinesti Forest, where they believe themselves free. . . .

August 2008

VOLUME THREE
GOBLIN NATION

A goblin nation rises in the old forest, building fortresses and fighting to hold onto their new homeland, while the sorcerers among them search for powerful magic cradled far beneath the trees.

August 2009

RICHARD A. KNAAK

THE OGRE TITANS

The Grand Lord Golgren has been savagely crushing
all opposition to his control of the harsh ogre lands of
Kern and Blöde, first sweeping away rival chieftains, then
rebuilding the capital in his image. For this he has had to
deal with the ogre titans, dark, sorcerous giants who have
contempt for his leadership.

VOLUME ONE
THE BLACK TALON

Among the ogres, where every ritual demands blood and every ally can
become a deadly foe, Golgren seeks whatever advantage he can obtain,
even if it means a possible alliance with the Knights of Solamnia, a
questionable pact with a mysterious wizard, and trusting an elven slave
who might wish him dead.

December 2007

VOLUME TWO
THE FIRE ROSE

With his other enemies beginning to converge on him from all sides,
Golgren, now Grand Khan of all his kind, must battle with the
Ogre Titans for mastery of a mysterious artifact capable of ultimate
transformation and power.

December 2008

VOLUME THREE
THE GARGOYLE KING

Forced from the throne he has so long coveted, Golgren makes a final
stand for control of the ogre lands against the Titans . . . against an
enemy as ancient and powerful as a god.

December 2009